BREAKING STORM

VIKKI HOLSTEIN

VULPINE
PRESS

Published by Vulpine Press in the United Kingdom in 2020

ISBN: 978-1-83919-313-2

Cover by Claire Wood

www.vulpine-press.com

For Craig.

My rock, my hero, my Superman.

ACKNOWLEDGMENTS

There are so many people to thank in this, my first published book.

To my dad, for his unending support and blind faith that I would get a book published.

To Melanie Salter, for the late-night edits, the long emails, the encouragement, and the friendship.

To Anne Mountford, for the patience, the knowledge, and encouragement.

To Andrea Delahoy, for the ego boosts when I needed them, for dropping everything to read another draft, and for putting up with my *I need to pick your brain* texts.

And to Deb Portch, for picking me up when I fall, for making me see things a different way, and for too many other things to mention.

To my editor, Libby Iriks, for her faith and encouragement on this rollercoaster ride of learning, not just on how to write a good story, but how to make it the best it can be.

To my kids (you know that you'll always be my kids, so don't roll your eyes), thank you for putting up with a slightly crazy mum and calling it normal.

To those that encouraged and supported me early on, thank you. And last but definitely not the least, to Craig. What can I say, but thank you for everything.

Dear Reader,

The fictional town of White Wattle Creek and its inhabitants have been my constant companions for the last six years. Over that time, the characters within these pages grew into people who fight for what they believe in, and for each other.

The *White Wattle Creek* series follows a group of friends who each have to face the after-effects of abuse, be it rape, emotional abuse, sexual abuse, or domestic abuse. As they discover what family and friendship truly means, they learn about self-forgiveness, trust, and love.

Although the White Wattle Creek stories deal with abuse, they don't romanticise it or go into minute detail. They simply tell of the struggles so many survivors face every day of their lives, and show that every survivor not only deserves a happy ending, but they can have that and so much more.

For the survivors reading this, I see you, I am you. For everyone else, I hope my stories set you on a path to understanding.

Thank you, and I hope you enjoy *Breaking Storm*, the first book in the *White Wattle Creek* series.

Vikki Holstein

WHITE WATTLE CREEK

BREAKING

Storm

CHAPTER ONE

Brian checked the sky, then his watch. Neither showed him what he wanted.

The clinging grey, which had dulled the sunrise an hour before, pressed down on the city and kept the temperature in the single digits.

He already ran late, even though he'd allowed fifteen minutes to make the stop on the way to work. He wouldn't need it, though. Haylee would most likely slam the door in his face, with a *go fuck yourself* shouted for good measure.

Walking the weed-edged, cracked concrete path to the house, he frowned at the missing weatherboards and cracked windows. His sister deserved better. She deserved more than the rotting steps that led to a cobwebbed porch where red-back spiders huddled under flakes of paint.

Brian shuddered when one moved, tucking itself further into the shadows, but if anything were to stop him from seeing Haylee, it wouldn't be a spider. Not when it had taken several frustrating months to find she lived only a few blocks from his house. Did she know? Had she ever thought of visiting him? Probably not, as the last time he'd spoken to his sister, she'd screamed that she never wanted to see him again.

It still sat heavy on his heart. Losing their parents had driven a deep wedge between them when they'd needed each other most.

At least, he'd needed her.

At the door, he paused and took a deep breath—and his heart dropped. Even through the closed door and windows, the distinctive sweet smoke punched the air.

1

Blocking out the automatic list of offences, he knocked instead of bashing on the door. Footsteps padded, then stopped. He resisted eyeing the peephole.

'Go away.' Muffled by the door, her voice held the same edge he remembered.

'I just want to know you're okay.'

'I'm fine, so go away.'

'Will you open the door?'

'No. Go away or I'll call the cops.'

'I am a cop, Haylee, you know that.'

'And you'll get into big trouble if I report you for stalking and harassment, so go away.'

'Just let me see you're okay, then I'll leave you alone.'

In person, anyway. She lived with a druggie dickhead, so he would never abandon her. He'd keep his distance, but now that he'd found her, he'd be keeping an eye on her.

The door cracked open an inch, but it was enough for the sight of her gaunt cheeks and bloodshot eyes to confirm his fears.

'What has he done to you?'

'Nothing, go away.'

'Haylee'—he slapped a hand against the door as she tried to close it—'just give me a minute, please.'

If he didn't get through to her, didn't get her out now, he might never get the chance again. He'd lose her to drugs or suicide, or some bastard taking his drug-fuelled anger out on her small body.

'Let me help you.'

Her chin lifted a fraction. 'You couldn't then, so why would you think you can now?'

'Haylee—'

'What are you bloody doing!' Donny strutted down the hall, his shirt stained and untucked, his jeans held to his skinny hips with an elastic strap. 'We don't talk to strangers, remember?'

2

Brian met Donny's cocky sneer with one of his own. 'I'm not a stranger.'

Donny grinned. 'You don't look like a client. Not the partying type at all, hey, Hays?'

He slapped Haylee on the butt, and Brian wanted to punch him. Just one jab, square on the nose.

'Maybe I'm not the sort of client you're used to. Show me what you've got and we can see.'

Donny hesitated and glanced at Haylee, then shifted from one foot to the other and grinned. 'If you want to see the party plan for Busy Balloons, step right in. My associate will be here any minute, we'll be happy to give you a good deal.'

Laughing, he turned to Haylee. 'You better get ready, *babe*. He'll be here soon.' With another grin at Brian, Donny sauntered back down the hallway.

'Who is *he*?'

At Haylee's silence, Brian pushed his hands through his hair. How did he get through to her?

'Just talk to me, Haylee, I can help.'

'You can't, and you don't need to.' She lifted her chin. 'I don't want your help. I don't need your help.'

'This isn't what Mum and Dad would have wanted.'

She froze at that, her features blanking so a stranger stared at him. 'Just go,' she said, and snapped the door shut.

Brian raised his hand, ready to pound on the door, but then rested his fist against the wood instead. Could he help her if she didn't want him to? If she chose to stay with a man like Donny, could he leave her here, even when every bone in his body rattled with the need to have her at home with him?

Haylee was right, though; he hadn't been able to help her before. He wanted to help her now that he had a home she could call hers again—one where she could feel safe and loved—but to bash on the door, even with cause, would prove she couldn't trust him. So, instead of breaking down the door and then Donny Sand's face, Brian turned away and headed back to his car. Next time, he'd make sure Donny wasn't home. Then maybe Haylee would let him in.

He scanned the street out of habit as he unlocked his car, then did a double take as two girls stumbled around the corner three houses down. Glancing at his watch, he relocked his car and started towards them.

'Jaiyden?'

She could have been Haylee's twin. For the last three years, they'd both hated him with a passion and refused to believe he wanted to help. He'd missed the mark with Jaiyden, and instead of helping a runaway who reminded him of his sister, he'd landed her in the middle of a sting operation. She'd lost what little faith she had in him, and he lost the chance to prove he could help her.

When Jaiyden coughed, swore and spat blood onto the footpath, the other girl grabbed her by the waist and held her up.

'We need to go to the hospital.'

'I told you no, so don't say it again.'

'But he hurt you.'

'You can either help me or leave me, Kel. I'm not going to the hospital or the police, so just leave it.'

Brian stepped in front of them and reached out when Jaiyden nearly fell to a stop.

'Jaiyden? What's happened?'

They both needed a hospital. Jaiyden's nose was swollen, and her friend's cheek had turned purple. Both had blood-smeared clothes with fresh rips, and they each stared at him with deep terror.

'Nothing.' Jaiyden steadied herself against her friend's side. 'Just taking a morning stroll.'

She bared her teeth in a smile, showing a gap where blood oozed, adding a layer of horror to her smeared makeup and dishevelled appearance.

Hands held up, he glanced at the young girl. 'Are you okay?

'I'm fine'—she rolled her left shoulder and winced—'but he hurt her.'

'I can see. And I can help.'

'No, you can fuck off.' Jaiyden turned towards the road. 'I've told you, I'm not a charity case or some fallen angel you can save.'

'But if he can help us, Jaiyden, if he can stop Spencer, maybe we should let him.'

'He's a cop, Kel. He's not here to help, he's only here to harass.'

Kel hesitated as she frowned at him over her shoulder. 'My friend just came out of the academy. He's a good guy.'

Taking a chance, he stepped closer. 'I'm a good guy too.' At least he hoped he was good enough this time. 'Tell me your friend's name. I'll call him so he can come and help.'

Kel froze, then shook her head. 'No, he wouldn't.'

'No one can help.' Jaiyden doubled over in another coughing fit and spat more blood.

'You need an ambulance.'

She laughed at him, holding her ribs while she did, then leaned against Kel. 'You're a riot, Bri.'

'I'm serious.' He pulled out his phone. 'I can call one, get you checked over, then we go from there.'

'Go from there, as in you get your buddies to arrest me, and I get my name splashed all over as a snitch and lose money 'cos no one trusts me not to give names as well as head.' She curled her lip. 'No thanks.'

'That wasn't my fault. I told you that.'

'Don't care. Don't trust cops, don't trust you.' She wrapped an arm around Kel's shoulder and turned away. 'Let's go.'

Taking most of Jaiyden's weight, Kel shuffled her friend across the road and away.

He could go after them, hassle them and prove Jaiyden right. Or he could go to work and keep tabs on Jaiyden and her new friend. He'd catch up with them in a few days—when pain and fear weren't the forces driving them to reject his help—and convince Jaiyden to tell him exactly what had happened.

He rolled his shoulders to dislodge the niggle that settled between them. Yeah, he'd catch up with them soon and make sure they both knew they could come to him. For anything.

As for Haylee? He'd keep trying to get through to her, keep trying to reach the loving, happy sister she'd been before their world had fallen apart.

CHAPTER TWO

Four years and nine months later

The blue summer sky showed no hint of it, but a storm brewed. It sizzled in the heat waves dancing a foot above the road, pulsed in the hot air blowing through the car's vents, and teased hair that should have been the colour of that morning's sunrise.

Absently, Kelsey pushed at the muddy-brown strands that needed re-colouring, lifting the damp mess off her neck for a moment before letting it drop back when it did nothing to cool her.

Flicking a glance at the rear-view mirror and the little girl who slept in the back seat, an empty juice bottle in one hand and a half-eaten sandwich in the other, it grabbed her as it often did that Pipa trusted Kelsey to protect her from what had been and what would come next. Not to mention the person she had to face now.

She ignored the jolt in her stomach and concentrated on the road as it wound down the dusty hills towards town. Seeing the sign welcoming visitors to White Wattle Creek only added to the tension throbbing at the base of her neck.

As she slowed her Hyundai, she scanned the town she hadn't seen in five years. Nothing much had changed since she'd been away. She'd expected that the struggling summer gardens in front of each weatherboard house might be greener, or that the brick school on the corner might be bigger. Even the park, seen from the road as it flattened before the bridge, still had the same Brunswick Green picnic bench, the same undercover barbeque area. Her glimpse of the main street over the river as she headed for the bridge showed the shops had stayed neat and homey, the way she supposed they did in most country towns.

How was it that everything had stayed the same in the time she'd been away, yet she'd changed so much?

Glancing in the rear-view mirror again, her fingers jerked on the steering wheel. A ute followed close behind, the driver's face shadowed by sunglasses and cap. Reminding herself to breathe, just breathe, and that a dust-coated ute wasn't the type of car she had to watch out for, she drove over the bridge, crossing the barely flowing river, and swung her Hyundai into a parking bay in front of the bakery.

Watching the traffic now, and the people in the street, tension gripped her shoulders and squeezed. She'd avoided this for years by getting jobs on farms, or fruit picking, whatever kept her out of sight and able to leave at a moment's notice. Sometimes, when he'd found them, she'd had to leave without even that.

Would he know to look here? In the little town snugged in a river bend, surrounded by hulking red gums and the wattles that gave it its name, its hills spotted with sheep and cattle grazing in paddocks that desperately needed rain?

How long would she have before he found them again?

Sweat slipped down her back making her shiver. She should keep hiding. Keep driving until they couldn't be found and her dreams no longer held her under at night. The dream, though, like the man, would always find her. Just as it had last night and all the nights before.

Maybe that was why she'd told her boss that morning it would be her last milking, and why, instead of following the salty air towards Geelong as she'd planned, she'd driven north to her hometown. Now she was here, she wasn't sure she was ready to face what came next.

Because Ethan came next.

Leaving that problem alone until she had no choice but to face it, she pushed from the car and tugged the faded and stained grey shirt that stated *I got out of bed for this?* away from her sweaty back. She hitched up the holey-kneed men's jeans that hugged her hips but gaped at the waist and decided against grabbing a change of clothes out of the small sports bag in the boot.

At least she'd been able to pack their belongings this time—which filled all two bags. Pipa's few precious toys and books always stayed in the car, tucked in her My Little Pony backpack. Op-shopping couldn't replace a favourite blanket or bear when fleeing took priority over packing.

Those days should be behind them now, but things rarely went as planned. Pipa's existence was proof of that.

As Kelsey unclipped the booster seat belt, Pipa stretched, then looked around wide-eyed.

'Are we here?'

'Yeah, Pip.' She tried a smile. 'We are.'

'We see the man?'

'Ethan,' she said, forcing the smile to stay. 'And yes, we're going to see him now.'

It seemed now was the time she had no choice but to think of him. Still, she didn't have to—and wouldn't—think of him more than necessary.

Pipa held up her hands, the juice bottle and squished sandwich stuck to her fingers. 'Yucky.'

'Yes, very.'

Scanning the street and footpath continually, Kelsey pulled a plastic bag and wipes from Pipa's backpack.

'Here.'

She held the bag out for the rubbish, then rubbed Pipa's hands, arms and face with the wipes.

'Okay, done.' Kelsey tied the bag. 'Where are your shoes?'

'Do I have to wear them?'

Bottom lip sucked in, Pipa widened her eyes and cradled her hands under her chin, looking so much like her father that Kelsey had to clamp down on the memories that tried to bubble up and overwhelm her.

Bringing another blond-haired, blue-eyed face to mind, Kelsey held her arms out. 'Okay, no shoes. But let's go before the sun fries us.'

Pipa scrambled onto the seat and launched herself into Kelsey's arms.

'Horsey ride?'

'Not today.'

The sun wasn't the only thing Kelsey wanted to avoid. Too many eyes watched as she strode to the ugly brick building with *P B & R Solicitors* scripted in silver on the glass door.

'I'm hungry.'

Pipa pointed to the bakery next door. Red hearts were scattered across the full window with messages like *Be mine* and *I love u* scribbled on them.

Kelsey had tried expressing those exact sentiments on Valentine's Day five years ago. But the only love and belonging she needed or wanted now, bounced in her arms with a mixture of excitement and fear.

'You're always hungry, Pip. We'll get something after.'

Pipa's arms tightened around Kelsey's shoulder as she stepped inside and let the door swing closed behind them.

'Will the man be angry?'

The slap of cold air made Kelsey stop and shiver, and she held Pipa closer. 'Ethan. And not at you, Pip, he won't.'

The last time she'd been here, it had been P & B Solicitors. She'd come after school, waiting in the dark and stuffy reception room for Ethan to finish for the day. When he'd walked out and smiled at her, his summer-blue eyes shining, she'd known beyond doubt that he was *the one*.

The soft green carpet and mint walls that now turned the reception area into a cool, calm space must have been his decision. Because he'd done what he'd always said he'd do—he'd added Ryder to make it P B & R Solicitors now. He'd become a part of his hometown legal group before he hit thirty. He'd even done it five years early.

Ethan had never been one to veer from the path by much. Once he made his mind up, that was it. And he'd made his mind up about her long ago. His lack of communication over the past five years said that louder than his words had that night.

And yet, in all the nights and days since, Kelsey had never stopped thinking about him.

Pipa wriggled as she scanned the room. 'Will he hurt you?'

Kelsey frowned. 'No, sweet. I told you, Ethan won't hurt me. Not like that.'

Because they both knew what *like that* meant, she hitched Pipa higher and kissed her cheek. 'Ethan's a friend.'

The word felt clunky on her tongue. He was so much more, and yet, so much less.

He'd let her be his shadow for so long that she'd forgotten what life had been like without him. She'd grown up thinking he was her other half. Had forgotten he was a separate person from her, one with his own thoughts, his own dreams.

While she might have forgotten those things and lost what she'd had with him, she knew that no matter what he thought of her, his sense of right and wrong wouldn't let him sit back and do nothing when a girl's life was on the line.

That confidence evaporated, though, when a door opened and Ethan stepped through. He looked up from the papers in his hands and recognition flared. It only took a moment for his gaze to drop and land on Pipa tucked against her hip, and for his recognition to turn to shock.

'You're back,' he said, as though she'd stepped out to grab morning tea and had just returned.

Accepting that her heart would always stutter at seeing him, at being near him, Kelsey schooled her features to hide her feelings and made her feet move to close the distance between them.

'Hello, Ethan.'

***

Thunder roared in Ethan's head so loud it drowned out Kelsey's words as she came to stand in front of him.

Images freefell through his mind, those he'd lost and grieved for the most when she'd disappeared—the pure delight of watching her ride his horses, the concentration on her face while she studied at his kitchen table, the smile she'd flashed him the last time he'd walked out to find her waiting for him.

He wanted to reach out and touch her, just to make sure he hadn't tripped over into fantasy. Instead, he stared and waited for the storm to calm enough so that he could make sense of her answers when he asked her the hundreds of questions he had.

'You said he not be angry.'

With curly blond hair—not the rich, chestnut red of her mother's—and old-soul blue eyes—not Kelsey's green—the little girl stared up at him, her thumb inching towards her mouth.

'He's not angry at you.' Kelsey tilted her chin up and met his gaze, her eyes cool, almost bored. 'He's upset with me.'

'You think I shouldn't be?'

He clenched his hands at his sides, crumpling the papers he still held, when she glanced over her shoulder to the door.

Was she thinking of leaving already? Before he'd even had a chance to get over the shock of seeing her again? He needed to know where she'd been the last five years. He needed time. Needed to regroup before he repeated history and sent her running away from him again.

'I was about to make a cup of coffee.' He stepped back into his office and gestured her in. 'You still take your tea the same?'

The formality he reserved for clients clung like a shield, but while he came to terms with the reality of having her stand in his office, he had to protect himself.

'Yes, thanks.' She glanced around the room as she walked to the chair near his desk.

He wanted to lock the door just to make sure she stayed. But she'd gone out his bedroom window the last time, and he hadn't locked the door that night. He'd done the opposite and left it open, hoping she'd take the time to see that he couldn't take her innocence, hoping she'd dress and then come and talk to him.

She'd been dealing with the grief of losing her father. Something he knew from experience turned a life upside down. He'd wanted to be there for her, to show her that life goes on no matter how bleak things might seem, except she'd stolen that opportunity from him by running away.

But how selfish was that? He was still only thinking about how he'd felt, what he'd missed, when that night, Kelsey had believed her only option was to leave the town and the people she'd known her whole life. She'd obviously moved on and left them all behind, except now she sat in his office once more, and he had no idea why.

His gaze dropped back to the girl sitting on Kelsey's knee. Though her mother didn't look at him, the child kept those big blue eyes on him, the hint of fear making him want to frown. Instead, he stepped out the door and headed for the tea room. He needed a minute, just a minute, to order his thoughts so that he could ask questions without sounding like a rambling idiot—or worse, a slighted ex. He had no right to sound like that.

The kettle boiled as he walked in and Rita reached for it. Blouse and skirt neat and tidy, greying hair in a bun high on her head, she smiled at him as he sat two more cups on the bench.

'You have an appointment?' She raised an eyebrow at the extra cup—he never had appointments on Valentine's Day. Not since Kelsey had disappeared.

'Not exactly.'

He dumped coffee and sugar in his cup, then dropped a tea bag in the other. Pouring boiling water into both mugs, he cleared his throat.

'Kelsey's back.'

'Here?' Rita glanced through the door towards his office. 'Now?'

'Yeah, here and now.'

All this time, he'd wanted to know where she was, what she'd been doing that had kept her from saying something, anything, to him. Now, seeing her and the child she'd kept secret from everyone, he couldn't help feeling a punch of jealousy when he thought about someone else taking his place in her life.

Rita touched his shoulder. 'Is she staying?'

He had no idea, only knew he wasn't letting her disappear on him again.

'Yes.'

His next words stuck in his throat, but to be able to talk, he had to get them out. 'She's got a daughter.'

'A what?' Rita's hand went to her heart. 'Whose?'

He shook his head, knowing what Rita was really asking, because, of course, he'd heard the rumours. Everyone thought that's why Kelsey had left—because she'd been pregnant with his child. But the girl wasn't his.

'I don't know.' Unclenching his fists, he picked up the mugs and started for the door. 'But I'm going to find out.'

The girl peered around Kelsey's shoulder, watching him nudge the door closed with his foot and then cross to the desk. Putting Kelsey's cup out of her daughter's reach, he leaned a hip against the desk.

'She didn't inherit your carrot top?'

The chill air held for a second, then Kelsey turned her face away. 'No.'

'How old is she?'

Her shoulders dropped with the quiet sigh. 'She's just turned four.'

He did a quick calculation. 'Three months,' he said, hating that it hurt.

But he'd rejected her, hadn't he? He'd told her to grow up, and she'd taken him literally, growing up too soon by getting pregnant three months after leaving.

Did she love whoever had stamped her daughter with his features and those eyes? Was he waiting for her somewhere? She wore no rings to show she was committed to anyone. Nothing but a thin silver bracelet on her wrist.

'Is he here, waiting?'

Her gaze shot to his, her eyes wide and fear-filled. Rising, he held a hand out as she gathered her daughter and shifted to the edge of her seat.

'Mummy?' The girl wrapped her arms around Kelsey's neck, her eyes as haunted as her mother's, and pressed her cheek to Kelsey's. 'The bad man?'

'No, he's not here.' Kelsey smoothed the girl's hair, rubbed her back. Even as she soothed, her gaze darted from the window to the door, skipping over Ethan each time.

Afraid he was losing her again, but not knowing why or how to get her back, he crouched in front of her and rested his hands lightly on her knees to connect them.

'What's going on?'

Her throat worked, and for a second he glimpsed the pain and fear tucked behind the mask she'd worn since stepping into his office. Instinct made him lift his hand to her face, just like he'd done so many times before. Her flinch stopped him cold.

'I didn't come here for this.' The slightly bored mask slipped back into place.

Now that he knew what it hid, he wouldn't let her get away with using it on him, distracting him. To give the spurt of anger time to settle, he stood and walked around the desk to his chair.

'So why did you come back after five years of silence?'

One eyebrow quirked, her head tilting a fraction before she licked her lips. She dropped her gaze and focused on her daughter. 'For her.'

Turning the child to face him, she ran a hand over the blond hair so unlike her own. 'Pipa, I want you to meet Ethan.'

He looked into those dark-blue eyes, trying to find anything of Kelsey in them. Pipa stared back, unblinking.

'Mummy?' She tilted her face towards Kelsey but kept those wary eyes on him.

'You can say hello.' Kelsey kissed the top of Pipa's head.

Hands tucked under her chin, thumb slipping towards her mouth, Pipa gave him a faint smile. 'Hello.'

'Hello, Pipa.' He tried for a friendly smile. 'It's nice to meet you.'

He met Kelsey's gaze again. 'So are we going to talk about what's going on?'

CHAPTER THREE

Brian rinsed his cup and sat it on the dish rack. He might regret skipping his usual breakfast of eggs on toast, but then again, with the day he had waiting for him, he doubted that would be the only regret.

Like an alarm set too early, the squeal from the hallway pushed any other thoughts of regret away, and Brian turned from the sink in time to see Ashley streak through the kitchen door, his sleep-spiked hair and huge grin the only things he'd escaped with from the bedroom.

Brian caught him on his second lap around the dining table. 'Whoa, there, little man! Where are your clothes?'

'Not want them.' Ashley laughed and wriggled. 'Mummy can't make me.'

'Yeah, she can, or she wouldn't be your mum.' Brian kept a grip on Ashley's wrists as he set him on the floor.

'Okay, hop on.' He wiggled his socked feet until Ashley stood on them. 'You need to get dressed, and I need to get to work.'

Ashley tipped his head back and giggled up at Brian. 'Why?'

'Because I need to get money, and you'll get cold.'

'I'n tough.' He flexed his arms as much as he could in Brian's grasp.

'Not that tough, buddy.' Brian knocked on the boy's bedroom door. 'You need to get dressed.'

'Why?'

'Are you going to look for aliens today?'

'Yes.'

'Then you need to get dressed.'

'Why?'

Brian raised an eyebrow at the kid. 'Would you want to talk to a naked alien?'

Ashley frowned, then opened his mouth and gagged.

'Exactly.'

The bedroom door opened.

'Sorry.' Haylee pushed her hair from her face with her free hand, her other holding a kicking and gurgling Rupert to her hip. 'He ran as soon as I got his pyjamas off.'

'You know it doesn't worry me, Haylee.'

'So you say.' She took one of Ashley's wrists and handed Rupert to Brian.

Brian took the open-mouthed kiss to the cheek but flicked his tie over his shoulder when Rupert tried to grab it.

'Have I acted in a way to make you think otherwise?'

Haylee didn't answer. She squatted and held a pair of undies out to Ashley. Thumb in his mouth, Ashley steadied himself with one hand on his mother's shoulder while carefully lifting one foot, then the other.

'James, find your shoes. We're going to be late for school.'

'I can take him.'

'Then you'll be late.' She held shorts out for Ashley.

'I'm an adult, Haylee. I know if I'll be late or not.'

Sitting back on her heels, she tugged a shirt over Ashley's head and helped him find the armholes. 'We haven't had breakfast yet, or the dozen runs to the toilet.'

On cue, Ashley crossed his legs.

'I'll start their breakfast.' He held his hand out. 'Come on, James, you can find your shoes, then give me and Rupert a hand.'

'Rupert can't cook, and I'm the man of the house when you aren't home.' James took Brian's hand.

'Who said that?' Brian glanced at Haylee over his shoulder. Lips pursed, she frowned at her son's back.

'Mrs Clay. She runs the canteen and said that because Mum is alone, I have to be in charge and keep everyone safe.' He lifted solemn eyes to Brian. 'How do I keep everyone safe?'

Brian pulled a chair out at the table and waited until James climbed up. 'Let me ask you this. Do you think I'm the man of the house?'

'It's your house.'

'It's *our* house.' He sat Rupert in his highchair, then turned back to James. 'Do you think I keep everyone safe?'

'Yes.'

The conviction behind that one word swamped Brian's heart with a love so insurmountable that he had to take a moment.

'I'm glad you think that, but do you remember when Rupert rolled off the couch yesterday?'

James frowned. 'Yes.'

'Did he cry?'

'Yes. But he didn't bleed or anything.'

'No, he didn't, but it still scared him and made him cry, so he didn't feel safe for a bit.'

'But he is safe. You make us safe.'

'I'm glad you feel that way, James, and I'll do everything I can to make sure you are all as safe as can be. But you know things happen, don't you?'

James dropped his gaze to the stain he traced on the table and nodded. 'Daddy made us scared.'

'I know he did.' And if Donny were still alive, Brian would make sure the bastard knew exactly what he'd put Haylee and her sons through.

'Sadly, there will always be people who make you scared, or angry, or upset. But Mrs Clay is wrong to say it's up to you to keep everyone safe. We'll all do whatever we can to look after each other, but sometimes Rupert will fall and cry. Sometimes Ashley might trip and scratch his knee. Sometimes you'll run into a door and get an egg on your head.'

He tapped the spot on James's forehead that last week had been the size of a golf ball.

'Sometimes your mum will cry, and sometimes I'll be tired and grumpy, but it's not up to you to fix it.' He cupped James's chin until the boy met his gaze. 'Do you understand?'

'I think so.' His frown returned. 'When we get another daddy, will you teach him to look after us properly?'

'I think that *if* you got another daddy, he'd already know.'

'But just in case, would you?'

How did he answer that? 'If I need to, which I really don't think I will, then yes, I will.'

James sighed, his shoulders dropping. 'Good.'

'What's good?' Haylee helped Ashley onto his seat at the table, then walked to the kettle.

'I don't have to be the man, and Uncle Brian will teach our new daddy to be nice.' James smiled. 'Can I have cornflakes, please?'

'I no want new daddy.' Ashley stood on his chair. 'No more daddy!'

'You aren't getting one.' Haylee stalked to the table and picked Ashley up. 'You've got me, and that's all you need.' She patted her son's back and glared at Brian.

'But Mrs Clay said that you need a man and we need a dad.' James glanced from his mother to Brian. 'She said we'll be apples under the tree if we don't get one.'

'Mrs Clay needs to mind her own business.' Haylee sat Ashley back in his seat. 'She needs to shut the f—'

'Fridge.' Brian raised an eyebrow at his sister. He'd been on the receiving end of her temper often, but she'd never let it show in front of the boys before.

In a bid to stop the storm of emotions circling the room from drenching them all, Brian held up a hand.

'People say things sometimes, James, when they don't know the real story. They like to talk about things that have nothing to do with them because they feel important when other people listen to them.'

'Like show and tell?'

'Yeah, kind of like that, but they show and tell other people's things.'

'Oh.' James chewed his lip a moment. 'Do I tell her to stop when she says it?'

'No.'

'Definitely no.' Haylee sat next to her eldest son. 'People are going to talk about us, James. I'm sorry about that, but I can't stop them all. Just know that you are a good person, all you boys are.' She kissed his forehead. 'I love you.'

'I love you too, Mummy.' He wrapped his arms around her neck. 'Uncle Brian says we can all look after each other.'

'He's right, we can'—she glanced at Brian—'and we will. Part of that is talking about what other people say, especially when it worries you.' She kissed each of her boys, then went back to making coffee and tea.

Like the moment of stillness before the first flash of lightning, the room quietened as the boys ate their breakfast.

When James took Ashley to find his shoes, Haylee folded her hands on the table. 'So you're going to train Donny's replacement?'

'No.' He held a hand up. 'That's not what was said.'

She stared at him.

'Mrs Clay, who I'm going to have a word with, has obviously put it in James's head that he'll get another father. He's worried the guy won't know how to look after you all. What was I supposed to do, Haylee?' He lifted both hands in question. 'Tell him that if his next dad is an arse, too bad, put up with it?'

'You could have told him that it's not a given he'll get another one, and that if by some miracle it ever happened, I wouldn't subject my boys to an arsehole again.'

'I did.' He rested his elbows on the table and rubbed his thumbs against the headache banding his forehead. 'He just wanted reassurance, Haylee. How could I not give that to him?'

'Thank you.' Though she didn't sound thankful, just hurt and tired. 'But you can reassure them all that they won't be getting another father.'

'I know it feels like that right now, Haylee, but with time—'

'I don't need time to know. I'm not interested in sharing anyone's bed. I always dreamed of having someone to love, to surprise with flowers and gifts, to share life with, but I never wanted the sex part. Being with Donny did nothing to change that.'

'I …'

'Yeah, me too.' She picked up the mug of coffee she'd hardly touched. 'And I doubt anyone else knows what to say or do about me, either. I was a freak as a kid and nothing has changed.'

'You were never a freak, Haylee.'

'Then what am I? Can you tell me? I love my boys, but I never wanted to have kids. Parenthood was for other people. So was sex. I thought it was all a big joke, like Christmas and Easter, told to gross kids out so they wouldn't do it.'

'In time—'

'No.' She slammed her cup down. 'No time, no way, no how. I don't want it, and no one is ever forcing me again.' She jerked up straight. 'I don't want to talk about it anymore. Go to work, I'm taking James to school.' She pushed from the table and hurried from the room.

Brian sat for a moment, staring at the puddles of splashed coffee on the tabletop.

Could he leave it alone? Could he just forget what she'd said?

She'd locked him out after that day nearly five years ago. He'd gone back to the run-down house, but she never came back to the door again. Never let him in.

So, the question now was, could he afford to push only to have her block him out again?

CHAPTER FOUR

Kelsey had always had a knack for pushing Ethan's buttons. The year she'd turned fourteen, she'd perfected the art and had loved facing his wrath. Over the next two years, it had become her favourite pastime. That, and imagining their lives in three years, five years, ten years. When she'd imagined those five years in the future, she never thought she'd be terrified at having to defend herself, of having his sharp mind pick every one of her words apart and find deeper meaning.

It was her own fault. She should have done this long ago. Should have swallowed the heartbreak, the humiliation, and called Ethan herself. Allowed him to tell her how disappointed he was so that she didn't have to hear it through her mother's sneered voice. Should have let him tell her he was happy that she was living her own life instead of his.

By the time she'd had the courage to ignore her mother's orders to stay away, to question the truth, they'd been running for their lives. There'd been no real lull since then. No break in the storm so she could stop, pick up a phone and call him.

She shook her head. Who was she kidding? It had always been more than that stopping her. It wasn't even the idea of having to face the guilt and shame he'd made her feel the night she left town. She hadn't wanted to hear his voice, the change in it when he'd realise it was her calling. Much as his eyes had changed when he'd noticed Pipa on her hip. Now, she had no excuses to hide behind, only stark truths that stuck in her throat.

'I'm not sure where to start.'

'The beginning?'

He stared at her as though he could keep her there by force of will. But he'd shake his head if she told him all she wanted was him, and the strength, comfort and sense of belonging he'd always given her. Until she'd ruined everything that night.

'I doubt either of us wants to go back to the start.'

'I think we both need to.'

She shrugged to cover the sick thud of her heart. 'I offered. You refused. I left.'

Ethan tilted his head and continued staring at her.

'Fine.' She cupped her hands over Pipa's ears and kissed her forehead when Pipa tipped her face up. 'I got naked, hopped in your bed and waited for you, excited to give you my virginity, and you told me to come back when I'd grown up.'

She dropped her hands to Pipa's lap and shook her head when he opened his mouth.

'No, you wanted this done, so I'll finish it. I was too young, I get that now. I know that what I felt was foolish. I get it, and I didn't come back to rehash it all or pick up where we left off, so don't worry about it.'

She sucked in a breath, her heart hammering. 'I'm here for Pipa, because she deserves more than what I had, more than I can give her at the moment.'

Pipa scrambled to her knees and hugged Kelsey's neck. 'I love you, Mummy.'

'I know, sweet.' She wrapped her arms around Pipa and held tight. 'I love you too. More than anything.'

Frowning now, Ethan opened his mouth, then closed it again.

Sick of everything, Kelsey settled Pipa back on her lap. 'Just ask, Ethan.'

'Where's Pipa's father?'

'I don't know.'

When his eyes flashed with anger, she shrugged as though it didn't matter. 'I don't want anything to do with him.'

'But you got pregnant to him.'

The slice went deep, gutting her. She wanted to scream. Wanted to cup her hands over her ears and keep screaming until she had nothing left. Instead, she breathed through the pain, glad she'd had so much practice at keeping the mask in place.

'Why are you here, Kelsey?'

She wished she knew now. She'd come for help, for support and comfort.

'We home, aren't we, Mummy?'

It's what she'd promised Pipa as they'd lain in the dark early that morning, flashes of her dream still haunting her. The promise had lulled Pipa back to sleep but had kept Kelsey awake until her alarm dragged her from the bed.

'I need to talk to Mark. I came to you first because I thought I could trust you to help.' She shifted Pipa and rose. 'I'm sorry there's nothing left between us but anger and blame. I won't bother you while we're here.'

Where she would go now, she had no idea. She'd only thought as far ahead as seeing Ethan, of asking for his help, even if he couldn't forgive her.

Before she could walk away, he leaned forward and braced his elbows on his desk. 'If you think that's all that's left between us, then you're blind. And if you think I'm letting you walk out of here without knowing what the hell is going on—'

Pipa gasped.

'Sorry.'

'I know you have questions, but right now, I don't have the energy to deal with them or you.'

He eased back in his chair and rested his hands on his stomach as he held her gaze. 'You don't want to deal with me?'

'I don't have the energy to.'

''Cos of the stupid cows.' Pipa grinned at Kelsey, melting the wall she'd started reconstructing around her heart.

'Yeah, 'cos of the stupid cows.' She kissed Pipa's nose.

'Cows?'

'Dairy cows.'

'You've been working at a dairy farm for the last five years?'

'No.' She rubbed at the headache throbbing between her eyes. 'Just the last month.'

'Where?'

'Down near Warrnambool.'

'Two hours away.' His mild words clashed with his narrowed glare.

Determined not to let fresh guilt drown her, she nodded. 'Yes.'

'You never thought to come home before? Never thought to let us know that you were alive, not dead in a ditch somewhere?'

Her vision wavered, knowing that she'd come close to that exact outcome. When she blinked the terror clear, Ethan stood in front of her, his hands on her elbows, steadying her.

She swallowed, her tongue thick in her throat. 'I told Mum where I was at the start. I asked her to give you messages. I—'

'Don't do that, Kelsey, not now.'

'Do what?'

'Lie to me.' His hands gripped her hard, then were gone as he turned away. 'You've never lied to me before, so I don't know why you are now.'

Scared her shaking legs wouldn't hold her, Kelsey sat. 'I'm not.'

'Then why did Morna tell me she never heard from you?'

The glare he aimed at her, the bunching of fists at his sides, triggered the entrenched instinct to either run far and fast or stand and fight to stay alive.

Even though she knew Ethan would never let that anger and frustration overflow into action, she angled her body, held Pipa closer and eyed the door.

Pipa scrambled up to hug Kelsey. 'Don't hurt Mummy!'

Three times, Kelsey realised. In the last ten minutes, Pipa had reacted to Kelsey's emotions three times. She couldn't help thinking that she was slowly ruining her.

'Are you afraid of me?' Ethan's hands relaxed.

'No.' She patted Pipa's back, eased her away. 'There's no need to be afraid of Ethan, okay, Pip?'

'Okay, Mummy.' But Pipa threaded her hands through Kelsey's hair and held on.

'Then you'll talk to me? Tell me what the h—' he glanced at Pipa, 'what's going on?'

Tired beyond endurance and sick to know Ethan didn't believe the most basic of truths from her, Kelsey shrugged. 'I don't know if there's any point.'

'Why not?'

She laughed, but swallowed it before it turned hysterical. 'Because you won't believe me.'

But she owed him the truth and would eventually give it to him if she stayed.

The truth, though, would most likely tear them all apart.

***

'I never expected you to leave.'

Truthfully, Ethan had never expected her to move on so quickly. He still couldn't fully comprehend it.

The girl that had lain naked in his bed, willing to give him her heart and body, had grown into a woman who held her emotions in tight check, and who was clearly keeping everything from him. The only time she opened up was when she interacted with Pipa. Now, her daughter slept, rocked against Kelsey's shoulder, and Kelsey seemed all too comfortable with the silence.

It worried him that she hadn't looked at him since sitting down two hours ago. She'd nibbled at the biscuits Pipa had tried and passed on. She'd sipped her tea, letting the conversation flow around her as, in groups of two or three, half the town dropped in to see if the rumours were true. She'd answered some questions, evading any that involved Pipa's father, and skilfully steered the conversations back to all that had happened in White Wattle Creek since she'd left.

Kelsey had grown up. Just like he'd demanded. The only thing was, he didn't recognise this Kelsey. She was no longer the determined girl who'd fallen off his pony, broken her arm and not told anyone. Or the ten-year-old who, instead of screaming and running from the stinking kangaroo carcass he'd thrown at her feet, had flown over the boulders at Bailey's Rocks, screaming that she'd hunt him down, hide spiders in his bed and stick mice in his shoes. Neither was she the sixteen-year-old who'd hopped into his bed, waiting with nothing but flushed skin and a smile. He'd been a twenty-year-old man, staring at a girl who didn't know what she offered, wishing he could take it.

He'd seen a future for them back then but had been biding his time, hoping that when she finished high school, he could tell her everything he wanted for them and their future. But, since she'd left, he'd missed the snippets of her life that had helped form the young woman who sat before him. He'd had nothing to do with the events that taught her to lie and evade, those that made her believe silence was better than talking.

How much influence had Pipa's father had on this new Kelsey?

Because ignoring the nameless man wasn't working, Ethan ran through the mental list of questions that grew with each minute Kelsey ignored him and chose the one that burned most.

'How long were you with him?'

She stared at him over the head of her sleeping daughter, lips pressed tightly together as she rocked to a rhythm only she and Pipa knew.

'You won't even give me that?'

'You wouldn't believe me.'

The memory of how he'd stood over her and called her a liar shamed him. 'I apologise for before. Getting angry wasn't the answer.'

She stared at him a moment. 'But you don't think you were wrong. You think I lied.'

'I can't understand why you would.' Propping his elbows on the table, he massaged his temples, the ache rumbling louder. 'But every time I see Morna, I ask if she's heard from you.'

'And, of course, you believe her, not me.'

'I know the two of you never got on. I know you spent as much time away from her as you could, but she's your mother. Deep down, she loves you and has been worried about you.'

'So worried she came looking for me? So worried she asked everyone to help her look?' She jutted her chin. 'Or so worried she just kept going as though nothing had happened?'

Too lost in his own grief, he'd never noticed a lack in Morna's.

'I offered to hire a private detective to find you.' He'd hired one anyway when Morna refused, but by then, Kelsey had vanished.

'She didn't need one because she knew where I was.'

'But you couldn't tell me? Or Mark? Or even Carol?'

On a sigh, she shook her head. 'No.'

'I don't understand why you couldn't. I don't understand any of this.' He let his hands drop to the table.

She closed her eyes a moment and sighed. 'No, you couldn't.'

'And you're not going to help me?'

'We aren't the same as we were.' She met his gaze. 'And I don't want to be. I came back because I can't do this alone anymore.'

'Why are you alone? Where is her father? Does he know about her?'

'Because that's how it worked out. I don't know. Yes, unfortunately.'

'You'd rather he didn't know he has a daughter?'

Would she have told him if Pipa had been his? What would she have done if things had gone her way that night? Would she be sitting there with his child on her lap, not caring if he knew or not?

'She's not a daughter to him. She's a thing. One he'd rather not have around.'

In a flash of images he didn't want to see, he understood. 'He was abusive?'

Her laugh held no humour, and in her eyes, he saw the pain she tried to smother with indifference and sarcasm.

'He hurt you?'

Silence answered him.

'Pipa?'

Kelsey's chin lifted as she glared at him. 'I never have, and never will, let him near her.'

'And that's why you're here? For help to stop him?'

'Yes.' For a moment, her mask slipped. 'I can't give Pipa what she deserves with this hanging over us. She wants a puppy, Ethan.'

Tears began trickling down her cheeks.

'She wants a home, and I want to give it to her. But how can I? How can I when he's still in the background?'

'Why were you with him, then?'

'It just happened that way.' She shook her head, scrubbed at her wet cheeks and closed up on him again. 'I came because I wanted your help before I talked to Mark. I want you to promise you'll look after Pipa if anything happens to me.'

'I'm not a lawyer, Kelsey. You know that. I do conveyancing.'

'I'm not after a lawyer. I need someone I can trust with her life.' She met his gaze. 'I thought it was you. Now I don't know.'

'You don't trust me anymore?' Losing that last part of her would carve a wound deep in his heart. 'You know I'll help in any way I can. Talk to me, tell me what's happened.'

'It's not what has happened, but what will.' She rested a cheek on the top of Pipa's head. 'I can't do anything until I know she's safe, that she'll be looked after.'

'Kelsey?' He waited until she lifted her head. 'What do you think will happen?'

'Can you promise me you'll look after her? No matter what?'

'It hurts that you think you have to ask.' He picked up his cold mug of coffee, then put it down again. 'Whatever I've done, whatever I've said, I hope you haven't spent the last five years thinking I'm a monster.'

'No.' Cheeks red, she shook her head. 'No, I haven't. I wouldn't be here if I did.'

'Then why did you wait so long to come home?'

She shook her head again, but before he could push for an answer, Pipa shifted, stretched her arms out and yawned, then blinked up at Kelsey.

'Mummy, I have to pee.'

'Okay.' Kelsey let Pipa slide off her lap. 'After that, we better find some-where to stay.' She held her hand out to Pipa and led her to the back of the building.

The last time he'd trusted Kelsey to come and talk to him, she'd disap-peared. What if she walked away this time and never came back? What if their last words were left drowning in the puddles of past hurts?

Trying to find the right words, he followed her and reached for the door handle as she did, trapping her hand under his. 'Stay with me. Like you used to.'

Kelsey didn't move. Hardly seemed to breathe.

His heart stuttered, then sank as she shook her head.

'Why not?' His hand moved with hers as she twisted the doorknob, pushing it open enough for Pipa to duck under their arms.

'I go by myself.' Pipa raced for the toilet, waited until Kelsey had pulled the door mostly closed, then started singing.

Her head bowed, forehead pressed against the door, Kelsey sighed qui-etly. 'I'll go and see Mark. I shouldn't have come here expecting you to help blindly.'

'I don't do anything blindly.'

Though maybe he had when she'd first walked in. Nothing had made sense and he'd been too quick to let his anger and frustration cloud every-thing. He might need answers for his own sake, but he needed her to trust him more.

'Finished,' Pipa sang.

Kelsey pushed the door open, forcing him to move his hand. His palm tingled with the loss of her warmth as she went to flush the toilet.

Still singing, Pipa lathered her hands to her elbows, then held them up. 'Smell.'

Kelsey bent down, sniffed. 'It's lavender.'

'Landender.' Pipa poked her tongue out.

'Don't eat it'—she pulled a face that made Pipa laugh—'it's soap.' Tugging a length of paper towel from the dispenser, she deftly cleaned up the mess Pipa had made. 'Come on, rinse off so we can get going.'

'I don't want to go.' Pipa held her arms under the tap while Kelsey scraped suds off. 'Can we get a dog?'

'We can't get a dog until we have a house.'

The sadness that threaded through her words broke Ethan's heart.

Pipa held her hands out to be dried. 'When can we get a house?'

'Not yet, Pip.' Kelsey hung up the towel and smiled softly, but Pipa pouted up at her. Sinking to her knees, Kelsey framed Pipa's face with her hands. 'I'm trying, sweet. I really am.'

'I know, Mummy.' Pipa touched Kelsey's cheek, the love between them bright enough to stab through the darkness.

It hit him in a rush of longing that he thought he'd buried under the chaos and pain. Hit the scar she'd left on his heart and made it throb.

He wanted the love and connection that family brought. He'd wanted it with Kelsey and whatever family they would have had together. Had he lost it all now? Was it time to move on from the fantasy as Kelsey had obviously done? Could he?

Kelsey stood, glanced at him and frowned. 'Are you okay?'

How did he answer that when he had no idea? 'I'm hungry.'

'Me too.' Pipa clapped her hands and ran towards him.

It felt so natural to hold his hand out, have hers slide into his grip as she skipped out into the hallway.

'We go to the bakery?'

'I was thinking the pub.' He glanced over his shoulder at Kelsey.

'I don't have time to go to lunch at the pub. I need to talk to Mark.' She smoothed her hands over her hips, then crossed her arms over her chest.

'You say you *need* to see him, but don't you *want* to see him?'

'It's complicated.'

'And you don't want to tell me?'

31

She lifted a shoulder. 'I did, but now I don't know what I can and can't tell you. I don't know what you'll choose to believe.'

Unable to shift words from his brain to his mouth, Ethan stared at her a moment. 'Since when have I *chosen* whether or not to believe you?'

'Since I walked in.' She held a hand out to Pipa. 'Come on, we need to go.'

'No!' A bead of sweat ran between his shoulder blades. 'I can call him. You'd both be more comfortable here, wouldn't you?'

Kelsey eyed him. 'What's the catch?'

'No catch. You get to stay in the cool, Pipa gets to sit with Rita and draw pictures while you talk.'

Pipa bounced on her toes and clapped. 'Please, Mummy?'

'You aren't giving me much choice.' Kelsey frowned.

'The last thing I want to do is force you, Kelsey.' Though he might have to if he wanted to keep them both safe. 'I'm trying to show you I'm here to help.'

Kelsey held her hand out to Pipa. 'Come on. We can make Mark a cup of coffee and maybe get him some biscuits.' She glanced over her shoulder at Ethan as she led Pipa to the kitchen.

He waited until he heard the kettle start to boil before he pulled out his phone. It wasn't a betrayal to warn Mark about Kelsey and Pipa, especially Pipa, as Mark would figure it out as soon as he walked in. But if Ethan could spare his friend the punch to the gut when he saw them, then he would.

It took half a dozen rings before Mark answered. 'I'm on duty, Ethan, so unless this is urgent—'

'Kelsey's home.'

'What?' In the background, the police radio chattered. 'When?'

'A couple of hours ago. I'm surprised you haven't heard.'

'I'm on my way back from Hamilton. Is she okay?'

'She's ...' How much did he say? 'She's here, and she needs to talk to you.'

'Needs to or wants to?'

'I wouldn't be asking you to come while you're on duty if it was only something she wanted.'

'Shit.'

'Yeah. How long until you can drop in?'

'I'm ten minutes away once I get back on the road.'

'We'll see you in ten, then.'

'Yeah.' His silence held a thousand questions. 'Is she okay?'

'I'm trying to make sure of that now.' His next words sat heavy in his stomach. 'And Mark?'

'Yeah?'

'She has a daughter.'

More silence followed. Ethan checked his phone, then pressed it back against his ear. 'Mark?'

'I'm on my way.'

The call ended, and Ethan pocketed his phone hoping that he'd done the right thing, that the woman listening to Pipa chat and sing in the kitchen would one day understand that he had done and would always do whatever he could for her.

CHAPTER FIVE

'Brian.'

Jewell smiled at Brian as he made his way through the fourth floor of the Melbourne West Police Complex. A year she'd greeted him with that smile from behind her desk. The one that made him want to smile back. This morning, though, it made his already heavy heart sink.

'This came for you.' Jewell pointed to the box on her desk.

'Thanks.' He reached out and took the box, tucking it to his hip, its weight sticking his feet to the floor.

Jewell's head tilted as she watched him. 'How are the boys?'

He should get to his desk and start the process of picking through the cold case he'd waited four years to get his hands on. 'They're good.'

'They didn't try to play cricket with the saucepan and eggs again?'

Brian managed a smile. 'No, though James tried sneaking an egg into his bed in the hopes of hatching it.'

'Oh.' Jewell laughed, then covered her mouth. 'Maybe you should take him to a farm so that he can see all the animals.'

'I don't know anyone in the country.' He hooked a finger in his tie and tugged. 'Besides, Haylee would never let me take them anywhere.'

'My parents have a small place about half an hour away. They'd love to have the boys visit.'

'They don't know them.' He frowned as Jewell's face reddened. 'What?'

'I've told them about you and the boys, and Haylee.' She held a hand up before he could speak. 'Nothing personal, just the stories you've told me about them and how adorable I think they must be.'

34

Unsure whether he liked Jewell talking to her parents about him, Brian rubbed the back of his neck. 'I don't think the distance matters, it's more that Haylee doesn't trust me.'

'She's living in your house. Her boys are learning what it is to have a man love them and play with them from you. If that's not a form of trust, I don't know what is.'

James's solemn face and then Haylee's annoyed one flashed in his mind. 'Haylee still won't talk to me. Won't tell me why she's so angry.'

Jewell stood and came around the desk. 'You'll figure out how to get through to her.' She squeezed his arm briefly, then stepped back. 'Have faith.'

'I don't.' Hadn't since both his parents and younger brother had been smashed between two cattle trucks, his mother's Subaru no insulation against that much metal and meat.

She smiled at him again. 'I mean, have faith in you.'

Brian shook his head and swallowed the denial.

'I do. And I think Haylee does too, or why would she have come back to you?'

It was a good question, one he'd asked himself while lying awake every night since she'd finally come home twelve months ago. But instead of answering the impossible, he turned and wove through the cubicles and desks to his own.

He couldn't worry about Haylee right now, not when the contents of the box he held and the mess on his desk involved the woman who could have been Haylee's twin in attitude and audaciousness. Both women had survived difficult childhoods and done the best they could with what they had. Both had fought tooth and nail for their independence, even though help had been at hand.

He'd been there, ready to help both of them.

Haylee had eventually come back, and though she'd accepted his help in the form of a bed to sleep in and a safe place for her boys, she wouldn't accept his emotional support or assurances that she didn't owe him anything.

The other, whose life and death existed in the box Brian set in the middle of his desk, had thrown his offers of help back at him, then disappeared.

He'd looked for her after he'd seen her that morning. Had kept looking for her until, forty-two weeks later, he'd heard that her freshly buried body had scared a couple of trail riders having a day out with their horses in the Bunyip State Park up along Black Snake Creek.

The murder case hadn't been his, but he'd looked for the baby the coroner said couldn't be more than a week old. Looked for the girl he'd seen with her that morning. Without them, he had nothing. No evidence and no identification for the girl he knew to be Jaiyden Ann Scott.

Opening the box, he took a deep breath. Imagination didn't come close to what he saw in the black-and-greyscale pictures—arms missing hands, mouth missing teeth, bones missing flesh. It turned his stomach to think what she'd gone through in her last hours.

The coroner report put most of the assault post-mortem, but she'd been beaten, tortured before she'd been strangled, then dumped naked in a shallow grave in the bush.

He dropped the first file to his desk and reached for the next, then swore when papers fell, see-sawing to the floor and under his desk. Hitching up his pants at the knees, he hunkered down, grabbed at the papers and swore when his fingers only brushed them.

'Let me.' Jewell knelt next to him.

She'd bent, reached under the desk and pulled the papers out before he could tell her not to. Even though she kept her gaze on his as she handed them to him, he grabbed them, slapped them face down on his desk, then stood, putting himself between her and the rest of the files.

'You shouldn't have seen that.'

'I didn't look.'

'Doesn't matter.' He rubbed a hand over his hair. 'Did you want something?'

She still knelt, looking up at him, her head tilted slightly.

'I can't help but think you look extra troubled today.' Like a dancer, she stood smoothly, brushed at her skirt, then clasped her hands before her.

Brian didn't want her thinking about him. He had enough to balance without worrying about hurting another person in his life.

'I'm busy.'

'You know if there's anything I can do to help, you only need to let me know.' But she didn't walk away, just stood watching him, waiting.

He didn't want this. Didn't want anything she offered. Not when he knew it would end up the same as everything else in his life—half-finished at best, neglected, hurt or broken at worst.

'There's nothing anyone can do. I need to work.' He moved to sit at his desk. Gathering the papers, he gave her a pointed look. 'There's nothing you can do, Jewell.'

When one of the papers started fluttering to the floor, she nabbed it and handed it back to him. 'Okay.'

The sigh he held in was bone deep. If she kept offering and looking at him like that, he might just cave and unload everything he carried around. Maybe then he'd be able to think without all his worries running riot. Maybe then she'd realise she picked the wrong man. His heart tightened at the thought, but he ignored it.

'Can I ask you something?' She quirked an eyebrow at his blank stare. 'How much time between those two?' She pointed to the set of mugshots he'd slapped on top of the pile.

'Two years.' Her quick frown had him nodding. 'Just a bit of a difference.'

'They look more like father and son than photos of the same man taken two years apart.'

'They do, though his father wasn't much better.' Apples under the tree, as James had said. 'Both drug dealers who loved to sample the product.'

Both murdering bastards who'd dodged paying for their crimes.

'And he's who you think murdered your Jane Doe? Spencer Bristow.'

She'd read the name upside down. Something he shouldn't be impressed by.

'He's what adds up.' He picked up the mugshots, concentrating on keeping the words from tumbling out, but something about Jewell made him nudge the line of protocol. 'Her name was mentioned with his in certain circles before she disappeared four years and nine months ago. And the girl, Kel, said Bristow's name before they bolted that last morning. His alibi is about as solid as smoke, and he's a druggie dickhead.'

Plus, his gut told him Bristow was it. 'The smirk he wore whenever he was questioned screamed of entitlement and immunity.'

'He's not smirking now.' Her frown came again. 'Must be a sad existence, for both father and son.'

'Doesn't make him any less a murderer. And his father is dead. Killed, most likely by him.' He tapped the mug shot.

'Then I hope he gets what he deserves.' She shifted, met his gaze. 'There's nothing they could get him with before?'

'They got a partial fingerprint on the tarp.'

He rifled through the files and pulled out the evidence sheet.

'Nothing they could use, though. And they found hairs that didn't belong to the victim. They didn't have enough evidence to get a DNA sample from Bristow at the time, and he refused to give a voluntary one.'

'And now?'

'Not much more.' He drummed his fingers against the paper.

'But?'

He frowned at her as ideas churned. 'I don't know yet.'

She nodded. 'I can see you need to get back to it, but I want you to know, I'm a good listener.'

He looked down at all the papers that held the shards of a life stolen.

'Work isn't the only thing that's sitting heavy on you, is it?'

'No.' How long since he'd had this? Someone to share the burdens and the triumphs of life with? 'But there's not much I can talk about at the moment.'

'Then know I'm here when you can.' She stepped closer. 'It's not wrong for you to need someone to tell you things will be okay. So I'm telling you. Things will be okay.'

'You really believe that, don't you?'

'What can I say, I'm a Sagittarius.' Her grin flashed, pushing back the gloom that settled around him.

He shook his head. 'And here I thought you were a realist.'

'I can be both, and optimistic as well.' She pointed to the notepad on his desk.

He nodded and handed her a pen. 'Maybe I can borrow some of that optimism.'

'Anytime.'

She wrote something, tore off the sheet and handed it to him. 'For when you need to remember.' She sat the pen and notepad back on his desk, then turned and walked away.

You are enough.

Brian stared at the three words Jewell had written. If they held any truth, Haylee would never have needed to run away after their parents' deaths. And Bristow would be rotting in a cell instead of having walked free for the last four years.

The guilt from the lie swamped him. When he sucked it all back in and strapped it down, the few dregs that were left sat like coals in his throat. He'd swallow them eventually. When he had Bristow in cuffs and a confession signed.

And when Haylee was free from the anger and hate that separated them.

CHAPTER SIX

Kelsey flicked the kettle on to boil for the fourth time.

Mark had arrived and chatted to Rita at her desk for a moment before he went into Ethan's office. Her ears burned with what they must be talking about. Would Mark take one look at Pipa and come to the same conclusion as Ethan?

Could she take the same silent accusations from the one she'd seen as a brother growing up? Could she risk telling Mark the truth and have him not believe her?

Stalling in the kitchen, boiling already-hot water, wouldn't get her the answers she wanted or Pipa the life she deserved, so when the kettle dinged, she poured the water.

'Are those biscuits stacked, Pip?'

'Yes.' Pipa held up the plate, the assorted biscuits forming the shape of a flower.

'Well done.' Her hand shook as she carried the coffee back to Ethan's office. 'Can you knock on Ethan's door, please?'

Pipa poked her tongue out as she balanced the plate in one hand and tapped her other fist against the door.

Coffee sloshed over the rim of the mug and burned a trail over her hand as Ethan opened the door. She could turn and go back to the kitchen, but it would only make the inevitable worse, so she followed Pipa into the room, her heart jumping as Ethan closed the door behind them.

Mark stood at the window, his arms crossed over the bulk of his police vest, his face set as he took in the length of her with a frown. He didn't come forward to hug her, or even offer his hand, and Kelsey's hope of being considered innocent until proven guilty smouldered and died.

'It's been a while, Kelsey.'

A step ahead of her, Pipa stopped, the biscuits teetering as she stepped backwards until she hit Kelsey's legs. It took everything Kelsey had not to pick Pipa up and run so that neither of them had to face another disappointment.

Before she could do anything, Mark crouched down, his body angled so that the holster on his thigh stayed out of sight.

'And you must be Pipa.'

Handing Ethan the coffee, Kelsey squatted beside Pipa.

'It's okay, Pip.' She ran a comforting hand over Pipa's head and down her back. 'You remember I told you about Mark?'

Pipa leaned against her but kept her attention on Mark. 'The peaceman?'

'The policeman, yes.' She eyed Mark. 'He's a friend, too.'

She'd been able to call both men her friend once and mean it. They'd listened to her stories, laughed with her, and told her off whenever she did something stupid.

None of that seemed to matter to them now, but it did to her. For her plans for Pipa's future. So she stood, took Pipa's hand and led her to Mark.

'Mark is a person you go to if you get scared or hurt and I'm not there.'

'Like the bad man coming?'

'Exactly.' Kelsey swallowed. 'Ethan and Mark are the people you can go to for help. Okay?'

'Okay.' Still holding Kelsey's hand, Pipa held her other one out. 'Hello, Muck.'

'Hello, Pipa.' He gently shook her hand. 'Is it okay if I talk to your mum for a bit?'

'You not make her cry?'

He glanced up at Kelsey. 'I'm not here to make her cry.'

'Okay.' Pipa turned and tugged on Kelsey's hand until she bent down. 'They look after you, too?'

The automatic *yes* stuck in her throat. It wasn't a given anymore, and she'd have to mourn that loss.

'Yes,' Ethan answered in her silence. 'We'll look after her, Pip.'

Rita knocked on the door, her smile soft as everyone turned to her.

'Pipa, I have some paper and crayons ready for you to draw some pictures if you'd like.' Rita held her hand out.

Pipa hesitated, her gaze flitting between Mark and Ethan, then up at Kelsey. 'You not come?'

'No, Pip. I need to talk to Mark. Rita will go with you. She might even draw you a flower if you ask her.' Kelsey smiled. 'Besides, you've seen my drawings.'

Pipa giggled. 'They funny.'

'They are.' Kelsey brushed the hair from Pipa's cheeks. 'You go with Rita, I won't be long, then we can get some lunch. Okay?'

'Okay.' With a last glance at Mark, Pipa skipped to Rita and took her hand. 'I draw you a picture, too, Mummy?'

'I'd love that.' Kelsey held her smile until Ethan closed the door behind Pipa and Rita.

Mark stood, then flicked a finger at her hair. 'You got skinny.'

Ignoring the accusation, she lifted her chin. 'You haven't.'

Mark tilted his head a fraction, then held out his hand. 'It's good to see you again.'

She took his hand, knowing it was too late to regret not being better prepared for the reality of coming home. If she'd stopped and considered that bringing Pipa with her would automatically trigger assumptions, she might not have come at all. Now she was here, she realised how naive she still was when it came to predicting what others would think. But she could only go forward, tell Mark and Ethan what she could, and hope it was enough to keep her out of trouble.

'So, how does this go? Do you read me my rights?'

'Read you your rights?' Mark frowned at her. 'I'm here because Ethan said you needed to talk to me.'

That was the catch. She needed to tell her story and make Mark believe her, but stop before she crossed any lines into legal territory. Only, she didn't know where those lines lay.

'And how do I know when my friend stops listening, and Constable Jones takes over?'

'What?' Mark raised his hands, then let them drop. 'What the hell is going on for you to ask me that?'

'Nothing.' She could hate that the warm giveaway blush she'd felt at her throat was rising to her cheeks but what would be the point?

Mark hooked his thumbs in his vest and waited a moment. 'Kelsey?'

It struck her, irrationally, that either man could overpower her, force her to say or do anything. To keep the fear under control she crossed to the desk and sat. Neither of them would hurt her. Growing up, they'd both made sure she could defend herself. Not that it had helped in the end.

Conscious that Mark and Ethan were waiting for an answer, she reached across the desk and chose a paperclip. She rubbed it between her fingers.

'Pipa's father is stalking us.'

'What?' Ethan stalked to the window and back again. 'Why the hell didn't you tell me that?'

'Because she's telling me.' Mark frowned at him. 'You want to stay, you sit down and shut up.' He turned back to Kelsey. 'Why is he stalking you?'

She pulled the paperclip straight, then bent it again. 'I don't know.'

'You must have some idea.'

She had plenty of ideas, but none she could voice without raising questions she didn't want to answer right now. The plan to come home, to tell all and finally have someone in her corner, had disintegrated the moment Ethan looked at Pipa and jumped to conclusions. Now, she scrambled to edit the last four years and nine months into a story they'd accept.

'He wasn't happy about Pipa being conceived.'

The paperclip snapped in her fingers. Throwing it in the bin under the desk, she reached for another one.

'As soon as we found out—' She gritted her teeth, waiting for one of them to call her out. When neither of them did, she closed her eyes to stop the tears.

'We've been on the move since the first time he made his feelings clear.' She shrugged away the memories thundering to the surface. 'Nothing has been asked of him. We've been trying to stay away from him, but he keeps finding us. I don't know how or why.'

'I need you to look at me, Kelsey.'

Mark waited until she turned to stare at him.

'What's his name?'

Lifting one shoulder, she forced her lungs to keep working. 'Spencer Bristow.'

She tossed the second paperclip, now straightened and snapped in two, into the bin. Not bothering to reach for a third, she rubbed her eyes.

'I don't know where he lives, only that he's in Melbourne.'

'What does he do?'

She should have expected the question and could save herself now by lying, but what would be the point? Mark would find out soon enough.

'He's a drug dealer.'

'Did you do drugs?'

At least that question she'd anticipated, but it still cut deep.

'No. I'd never do that.' She glanced at Ethan, then wished she hadn't when he didn't meet her gaze.

'Sell them for him?' Mark pushed.

Cold and numb, she shook her head. 'No.'

'But?'

She stared down at her hands, though Ethan's disappointment stayed in her peripheral vision.

'He asked once. The answer was no. He got'—she gritted her teeth against the memory—'angry. That's when we ...'

Did they not see? Could they not get past the fact she'd walked in with a girl on her hip and see? How could she dredge up the truth and tell them when their scepticism killed any hope she had?

'How about we try this?' Mark paused until she looked at him again. 'You don't lie to me, and I help you as much as I can.'

'And if you can't?'

Mark opened his mouth, closed it again, then frowned. 'What law have you broken, Kelsey?'

She propped her elbows on her knees and pressed the heels of her hands to her eyes. 'I don't know. I tried not to, but I just don't know.'

Ethan's scent reached her before his warmth did, and when he cradled her head to his shoulder and ran a soothing hand down her back, she leaned on him, wishing she could trust him to keep giving the comfort and faith she needed from him.

'I have just one more question for now, Kelsey.'

Not wanting to move, she nodded against Ethan's shoulder. 'What?'

'Are there any warrants for your arrest? I can look it up, but I'd rather you tell me.'

Ethan's muscles against her cheek tensed.

Unable to lean on Ethan while he waited for her answer, and gutted he needed one, she sat up and reclaimed her distance.

'I've never been arrested.'

Mark raised an eyebrow at her evasion but, keeping his word, didn't ask any more questions.

'I'll give you the weekend to sort out why you can't tell me anything but half-truths, but I need you to come and see me on Monday. I have to know what I'm dealing with, Kelsey, or I can't help you.'

She nearly laughed. Monday was a lifetime away, and waiting wouldn't change what had already been said and done. It wouldn't magically make them see the truth in front of them, and she didn't have the strength of heart to try to convince them.

But Mark expected an answer.

'If I agree, can I go? I don't like leaving Pipa for long.'

'As soon as you give me your number. Then I can contact you with a time.'

Ready for another barrage of questions, Kelsey sighed. 'I don't have a phone.'

Ethan frowned. 'Why not?'

'I can't afford one.'

Mark leaned a hip against the desk. 'What aren't you saying this time?'

Words stuck in her throat, then died when he came to squat in front of her.

'You might as well spit it out, you know I won't let it go.'

'I never missed you two ganging up on me.' She tried to smile, then huffed out a breath when he kept staring at her. 'There didn't seem to be any point. I had no one to contact.'

'You didn't think we'd want to know where you were? How you were?'

She shook her head. 'I told Mum, and I figured she'd let everyone know.'

'Your mum said she never heard from you.'

'Yeah, well, I know that now.' Her gaze on Mark, she gritted her teeth and swiped the tears before they fell. 'I was so terrified you'd hang up on me if I called. Then months passed and I didn't hear from anyone, so I figured Mum was right, that I was on my own.'

'Hey.' Mark rubbed a hand up and down her arm. 'It'll be okay. We've never stopped being here for you. Understand?'

'Even when you're so disappointed in what you think I've done?'

'I don't have enough information to be disappointed.' He wiped a tear she'd missed. 'You must have been so scared. Still are, aren't you?'

'I'm …' She pursed her lips. 'Pipa is my world. If I lose her, I don't know how I'll live. I don't know if I could.'

'You're home now, and we're going to make sure nothing happens to you or Pipa. Okay?'

'But you don't know everything.'

'I will on Monday.' He squeezed her hands. 'But from now on, Kelsey, you need me, you call me.'

He pushed to his feet. 'And to that end, get yourself a phone.'

'You can let me know what time you want to see her on Monday.' Ethan stood and walked with Mark to the door. 'I'll make sure she knows.'

'Do that.' Mark walked out, and a moment later, his voice, then Pipa's laughter came from the tea room.

Though her legs felt like water, Kelsey stood. 'I need Pipa.'

Still at the door, Ethan turned to face her. 'I'll get her, you take a moment.'

He took a deep breath. 'I know you won't stay with me, but you need somewhere you can rest and relax a bit. Let me take you and Pipa to the pub for lunch.'

'I can't afford a pub meal, let alone a room.'

'I'm asking you to lunch, so it's my shout. And as for the room'—he came to stand with her—'I was thinking you could ask Carol. I think she'd have you stay with her in a heartbeat.'

'Carol's still here?' Everything lifted. 'Really?'

'She is. And once she gets over being pissed at you for leaving, she won't want to let you out of her sight.'

Kelsey sighed as she followed him to the door. 'I guess I'll have to get used to people being pissed at me.'

'You will.' He stopped and turned to face her. 'Because people care about you, Kelsey. And that's something you'll have to get used to as well.'

He walked away, the burn of his words sinking in as she stared after him.

***

Ethan tugged at his tie as sweat trickled down his spine.

The relentless summer heat melted bits of the road, polluting the air with the acrid smell of hot tar. Coupled with the tangy scent of manure and urine trailed down Main Street by cattle and sheep trucks, the air sat heavy in his already tight lungs. Even the trees, hardened by bitter winters and sweltering summers, drooped in the prolonged dry. Dust covered everything, muting colours that wouldn't burst again until the next decent rain.

Would Kelsey be around to see it? Would she stay to see the trees turn golden and scatter their leaves? Could he convince her to?

'Can I have basketti?' Pipa clapped and jiggled on the back seat of the battered Hyundai as Kelsey buckled pink sandals onto wiggling feet.

'Spaghetti, and it depends.' She raised an eyebrow at Pipa.

The jiggling and clapping paused. Pressing clasped hands under her chin, Pipa smiled up at Ethan. 'Please, can I have basketti? Pasketti?'

Every time Pipa turned to him, his heart melted that little bit more. 'Of course you can.'

He smiled at her whoop of victory.

'Okay, Pip.' Kelsey tweaked a finger on Pipa's nose. 'Where's your other shoe?'

'I get it.' Pipa dove to rummage under the passenger seat, then wriggled back up, holding her pink sandal like a trophy.

'Ha! Well done.'

Taking the shoe, Kelsey waited for Pipa to hold out her foot, but instead of slipping the sandal on, she held Pipa's heel in one hand and traced a circle on her sole with her finger.

'Round and round the garden ...'

Pipa tugged her leg and squealed a laugh.

'Like a teddy bear ...'

Entranced, Ethan forgot the heat as mother and daughter played. His own belly jumped in anticipation when Kelsey skipped a finger up to Pipa's knee.

'One step. Two steps.'

To her hip.

'And tickle you under there.'

With both hands, she attacked Pipa's belly.

Pipa floundered in silent mirth while Kelsey tickled her everywhere.

'Why haven't you put your shoe on, Pip?' Kelsey kept tickling, skipping from Pipa's belly to her chin, under her arms, her feet, and back to her belly. 'Ethan's waiting, Pipa, and you're sitting here giggling.'

And he'd keep waiting while Kelsey played with her daughter, her smile genuine, her laughter light. He'd stand all day and night in snow and storm if Kelsey dropped her guard against him. He'd do anything to have her turn to him as easily as she'd done all those years ago. As easily as Pipa did now. He'd done something, though, that stopped her.

She'd come to him for help but had given him nothing to help her with. Other than ask him to look after Pipa. Something he'd do until his last heartbeat whether Kelsey wanted him to or not.

Did she expect him to say nothing if she took Pipa now and walked? Did she expect him to feel nothing if she left a second time?

She'd shut him out earlier, saying she couldn't trust him to believe her, but he had no idea what he'd done. She'd opened up to Mark, which still throbbed, even though she'd held most of her secrets back. Had Mark made the same mistake? Had they both said something that made her close them out?

'Okay.' Kelsey kissed Pipa's cheek, then picked up the sandal that had fallen to the floor. 'Let's get this shoe on so we can get out of the heat.'

'And have basketti.' Pipa clapped again.

'Yes, and have spaghetti.' Kelsey patted Pipa's sandalled foot, then stood and held out her hand. 'Let's go before we melt.'

When Pipa stretched her other hand towards him, Ethan took it.

They could be a family, braving the heat as they strolled down the street to the pub. Their reflection showed only a young couple, a child skipping between them, and none of the turmoil that made Kelsey glance over her shoulder every few seconds.

She slowed as they passed the newsagency.

'I have all the *Horse Deals* magazines from since you left if you'd like to look through them.' He nodded to the advertised cover stuck to the window.

She frowned. 'All of them?'

'Seemed a waste to throw them out when they hadn't been drooled over.' And they were a connection to her he couldn't toss away.

She scanned the street. 'I never drooled.'

'Came close to it, though.' He tugged Pipa's hand, who in turn, tugged at Kelsey. 'You always said you wanted to start a rescue business for neglected horses.'

She shrugged as they walked past the chemist. 'Silly dreams of a girl who thought she could fix the world.'

'Not the world.' He glanced at her. 'Just each horse's life.'

'Still a dream.' She pointed to the elaborate clock sitting high on the town hall wall. 'Has that ever been fixed?'

He wanted to push, to find a part of the old Kelsey he could connect with, something that would bridge the chasm now between them.

'A couple of times, but it never stays fixed.'

He'd find a way to fix things between them. He needed Kelsey to confide in him, to believe in him, and he needed to confide and believe in her again. They'd both damaged each other, five years ago and again today.

When she checked over her shoulder for the fourth time, Ethan turned and scanned the street.

'Is there any chance he knows you're here?'

'I don't know.' She rubbed her free hand down her face. '*I* didn't know I'd be here until three o'clock this morning.'

Worried she'd close up again if he pried, he stuck to the topic. 'Then I'd say you're safe for now, wouldn't you?'

'I've thought before I was safe and been wrong.'

Guessing what might have happened turned his stomach, so he pushed the thought aside until he could convince her to talk to him.

'What does he look like?'

'Shorter than you, blond hair, blue eyes. Skinny.' She chewed her bottom lip and shot another look over her shoulder. 'Doesn't it worry you?'

Ethan glanced around, then frowned. 'He's not here, Kelsey. And if he turns up, he's the one who needs to be worried.'

He held both hands out to Pipa in invitation. When she grinned and lifted her arms, he swung her up onto his hip.

'No. I mean them.' She nodded towards the couple in the shop over the road who stared and pointed. 'They're looking at us and wondering if I left because you got me pregnant.'

He'd heard the whispers over the years and had ignored them. Before that night, he'd believed he and Kelsey could weather anything that came their way. The numbing shock of her disappearance had lifted the moment she'd walked back into his life, but the bone-deep knowledge that they were a team, one meant to grow and evolve together, still lay shattered at his feet and ate at his confidence.

'We know the truth. That's all that matters.'

She stopped in front of the McKinley Hotel. 'Can you honestly say it doesn't bother you?'

'I can.'

He stared down at her and forgot the crushing loss of what could have been—even what should have been—when he saw she abhorred the idea of others thinking he might be Pipa's father.

'I have to say, it hurts that it bothers you so much.'

Opening the door before he broke and asked her what would be so damn bad about him being Pipa's father, he stepped into the cool of the pub.

CHAPTER SEVEN

Closing the last file, Brian put it on the appropriate pile and scribbled a note on his to-do list.

With the cold case files put in some kind of order, he at least had an idea of where to restart the investigation. Top of the list was talking to the first investigating officer. A close second was checking exactly where Bristow was these days.

He still had piles of evidence logs to dig through and had to chase up calls to other stations and units. He rubbed his eyes as he scanned the rest of his to-do list, biting hard to stop a groaning yawn from escaping.

He'd been right that skipping breakfast had been a mistake. He'd spent the last half hour trying to concentrate while his stomach growled its own heavy metal lament, which had turned from annoying to embarrassing as other detectives and officers came and went. Keyboard clacking and the murmur of one-sided conversations had become the backbeat to his hunger until the throb of his head had drowned everything out.

Lunch still didn't appeal. Swallowing food that tasted like failure was right up there with stepping on the boys' Lego. Both left him feeling stupid and sore.

Needing to do something before his head exploded, he pushed to his feet, rubbed a hand over his hair, sat down again, then stood once more. Annoyed, he shoved his phone and wallet in his pockets and strode from the room. Eating might not be top of the list, but the mess room's silence beckoned.

Detouring from wherever his itchy feet were taking him, he went to the fridge, opened it and stared at the shelves.

'Are we out of milk?' Jewell stood at the door, her head tilted to one side.

'No idea.' Brian forced his eyes to focus. 'No.'

'Are you looking for something?' Coming to stand beside him and bringing the scent of coconut with her, she peered into the fridge. 'If you're looking for the cake, Weston ate it.'

'Figures.' Distracted, he glanced at her. 'Why do you always smell like coconut?'

Her eyebrows disappeared under her fringe. 'It's coconut oil. My neighbour's wrist bothers him, so I massage it for him.'

'Nice of you.' Brian pushed the fridge door closed and busied himself with finding his cup and throwing out the empty packet of tea bags.

'He's a nice man. He lost his wife of fifty years last summer, so this time of year is hard for him.'

Brian checked the cupboards, rummaging until he found the new box of tea bags, then opened it. All so he didn't let the torrent of words flood out.

Haylee deserved her privacy. She should be able to tell him things and know he'd keep his mouth shut. But how did he wade through it all on his own and come up with solutions? How did he keep it all inside and still function?

'Brian?'

His heart throbbed in time with his head.

'Yeah, good,' he said, putting an extra teaspoon of sugar in his cup. He'd have it black, that way he didn't have to go back to the fridge, and he could walk around the other side of the table to get out.

'Are you angry at me?' Back stiff, hands clasped at her abdomen, Jewell refused to face him.

Was he?

'No.'

Angry that she made him want to confide in her, yes. Angry that the grip he had on everything slipped with each heartbeat, absolutely.

'It's not you or anything you've done.'

She turned to face him. 'Then what is it that makes you back away all the time?'

'I don't.' He took a step away, then stopped. 'I'm tired.'

He walked back to the table and sat. When his stomach grumbled, Jewell raised an eyebrow.

'Tired and hungry, I'd say.' She rummaged in the fridge, then put a plate of cheese and crackers on the table. 'Have you ever considered letting someone else share the burden?'

'Our parents died when Haylee was a teenager, so there's only me to look after her and the boys.'

Jewell's eyes clouded. 'I'm sorry.'

He lifted his cup and sipped. 'It was a long time ago.'

'Time doesn't matter when love is involved.' She sat a square of cheese on a cracker and held it out. 'So let me be sorry for the pain you still carry.'

Chest tight, he took the food. 'I keep messing up, and I don't even know how.'

'Your lives have changed drastically, rough patches should be expected.'

'It's not just rough patches, it's all the time. I try to tell her things will be okay, that the future will be better, but somehow I make her angry and then she's storming out and telling me she doesn't want to talk about it.'

Afraid he'd choke on it, he put the cracker down. 'I just don't understand what I said, what I did to make her hate me so much. And worse, I have no idea how to fix it.'

'Is it up to you to fix?' She held a hand up. 'I mean, doesn't Haylee have to work things out in her own mind and life before she can accept what you're trying to say to her? If she's still working through the things she sees as her mess-ups, then it won't be easy for her to accept that everything will be okay.'

'So, what, I do nothing while she fights her demons alone?'

'She's not alone, she has you.' Jewell reached across the table and took his cracker. 'And she knows she has you, that she can rant and cry and fall apart because you're there for her and the boys. You're her safe place, even if neither of you knows it.'

'She said she can't see herself having a future with someone.' He shook his head. 'It breaks me to think that she has so much ahead of her, but she can only see herself doing it alone.'

'Sometimes it's easier to think you don't need what's already hurt you. And sometimes, you really *don't* need it. Whatever it is, and whichever it is, she'll figure it out'—she shrugged—'and you'll support her.'

'How can you be so sure, of any of that?'

'Because people are resilient.' She topped two more crackers with cheese and held one out to him. 'My cousin is transgender, and she faced so much hate and bigotry from people who couldn't comprehend that being born with a penis didn't necessarily make you a boy.'

He took the cracker and ate it. 'But her family, you, supported her?'

'How could we not?' She handed him another cracker. 'It took a while to call her Rain automatically and to get the pronouns right, but her heart and smile never changed, she never changed, so our love never needed to change.'

'So you're saying to treat Haylee like I always have?'

'No.' She smiled at him. 'I'm saying it's going to be a rough ride while she figures out what and who she is now. Things will most likely get worse before they get better, but you'll be there for each other to the end.'

He took a deep breath and held it as her words sank in. 'It's not a one-way thing.'

'No, and relationships aren't meant to be.'

'James was upset this morning because a teacher told him he was the man of the house when I wasn't there.'

Jewell rolled her eyes. 'Poor kid. What is he? Six?'

'Five going on fifty. He's had to grow up too quickly.'

Brian topped the crackers this time and handed one to Jewell. Talking things through with her had helped order his thoughts, much like he had the files on his desk. Now the gaps in his thinking stood out.

'I told him it wasn't up to him to keep everyone safe, and that it was an impossible task as shit happens. Not that Haylee would let me swear in front of the boys.'

'She wants them to learn respect for others and have it for themselves. And you do, too, because it's not Haylee stopping you swearing in front of them, it's you.'

She smiled again, and he decided he could get used to seeing it across the table. He could get used to the conversations as well.

'So, anyway, I told him we all look after each other, but it's not up to him to fix everyone.'

'Good advice.'

He rolled his eyes at her steady gaze. 'And, yes, I can see I have to take my own advice.'

'I wish I had a lollipop to give you.'

'Positive reinforcement?'

'Why not?' She grinned. 'The way I see it, Brian, you need your sister and nephews just as much as they need you.'

He wasn't so sure Haylee would agree, but he got up and dumped his cold tea in the sink without saying so.

'You know ...'

He turned to see Jewell slide the plate of cheese and crackers into a paper mushroom bag.

'Why are you putting it in that?'

'If Weston thinks it's healthy, he won't touch it.' She put it in the fridge. 'So, what do I know?'

'What?'

'You started to say something.'

'Oh, yeah.' He rubbed the back of his neck. 'Just, thanks for listening.'

'You mean, thanks for prodding and being nosey.' But she smiled again. 'I hate seeing you so sad, Brian.'

And he hated feeling that way. Some of it had lifted the last ten minutes, and for that, he owed Jewell more than he could tell her.

'Anyway, thanks.'

'You know where I am if you need to talk again.'

He stopped on his way out the door. 'That sounds like you know something more.'

She lifted her hands and shoulders. 'Maybe, but it's not my place to say. If Haylee talks to you and you have questions you don't want to ask her, I'm here. Until then, just be with your family and try not to worry so much.' She walked past him but stopped and put her hand on his arm. 'It will all work out.'

Unsure he trusted his luck as far as that went, he returned to his desk, tidied up and looked over his to-do list.

His relationship with Haylee wasn't the only thing playing on his mind. He sat down, booted up his computer and started tracing the last months of Jaiyden Scott's life, searching for any intersections she had with Spencer Bristow or any of his crew.

He'd find the last known whereabouts of Bristow as well, and see what he'd been up to lately. A man who could murder his own father, then a new mother, wouldn't stop at that. There would be other bodies with Bristow's fingerprints on them, Brian was sure of it.

He sat straight. There had been a fingerprint and hair. He still didn't have enough to get a warrant for Bristow to give DNA, but there had to be a way to use what he had. Then, when he found Bristow, he'd snap handcuffs on him and slap him with every charge owed.

Bristow had been slipping and bribing his way out of those handcuffs since he'd been old enough to run from the police. His father had bribed and killed to keep his son out of jail and had been murdered as a thank you.

Brian frowned, scratched a big fat star on his to do list and wrote *apples under the tree*. It would be a kind of justice, wouldn't it, if he could find a way for Henry Bristow to help put his son away for life?

Jewell kept telling him to have faith, and in a way, he did—in the process of putting together a case, of his ability to get the work done. But when it came to getting true justice for the victims, for Haylee and the boys, and for making things right in his life? That, he couldn't trust. Not yet, not while every other word had Haylee scowling at him or ignoring him.

So, he'd stick with the process, get the work done for the victims, and hope that one day he'd find the right words for Haylee.

CHAPTER EIGHT

Kelsey pushed the pub door open and stepped inside. The lunch crowd chatted around the dozen tables in the bistro and along the curved counter.

Ethan stood at the bar talking to a woman with bright pink hair. Pipa, still on his hip, nodded and gave a shy smile when the woman spoke to her.

Kelsey sighed. The whole day had been a ping-pong match of *your turn to be hurt*, and she didn't know how to forfeit the game. Unsure what to do with her hands now they didn't hold Pipa, she shoved them in her pockets and crossed to Ethan.

When the woman looked up, Kelsey stopped. 'Carol?'

'Kelsey? How …?' Carol blinked, then pushing through the bar flap, she walked towards Kelsey.

Kelsey waited. Whatever Carol was about to do—punch her or give her a mouthful—she'd deserve it. She'd run when she should have trusted her friends would help. She'd hidden when she should have come forward, and she'd lied when she should have shouted the truth.

Instead, she'd hurt the people she loved. And so, she braced for the blast she deserved and stumbled when Carol took the last few steps at a run and threw her arms around Kelsey's neck.

She held Carol tight as memories of laughter and shared birthdays swirled around them. They'd made wishes and shed tears together since kindergarten and raged at each other's broken hearts through school. Countless times they'd gone out to ride under a full moon, along trails through the bush. They'd been sisters in deed if not in blood and had stood hip to hip against the wrongs of their tiny world.

'I missed you so much.'

'You left.' Carol shuddered. 'You left and didn't come back. You didn't call, you didn't ...'

She pulled back but kept a grip on Kelsey's arms. 'Why did you do that?'

'I'm sorry.' It wasn't enough. Nothing would be. 'I wanted to, I just ...' She shook her head.

'Mummy?' Pipa wriggled in Ethan's arms.

'It's okay, Pip. You're okay there.' Kelsey wiped her palms over wet cheeks and smiled when Carol did the same. 'I am sorry. I should have known you all didn't hate me.'

'Where did you get an idea like that?' Carol stepped back. 'Ah, your mum. I asked her where you'd gone when you didn't turn up for school. She said you'd nicked off and wouldn't come back.'

Carol lifted a shoulder as Ethan and Pipa joined them. 'I didn't believe her, but then you *didn't* come back, and I didn't know how to find you.'

'Like when the boss went away and we not know where he went?' Pipa leaned towards Kelsey, her arms open.

'Kind of.' Kelsey took her from Ethan.

Pipa turned to Carol. 'He not tell us, and Mummy had to get the cows and milk and clean 'cos she not know where he was or if he was going to be back to do stuff.'

'Wow.' Carol blinked at Pipa. 'Your mum used to do that, too.'

'Go so she not have to milk cows?' Pipa frowned and shook her head. 'Uh-uh, she always milkeded them. Even when they were pains and she swored at them.'

Carol threw her head back and laughed. 'Oh man, she does take after you!'

Kelsey let the usual leap of fear come and go. She'd have to tell them soon and could only hope they didn't see Pipa differently. And if they did? Well, she'd left everyone behind once before, and if it meant Pipa stayed happy and safe, she'd do it again.

'Anyway, we're here because Ethan thinks you won't mind us staying with you for a day or two, just until I can sort something else out.'

'Of course.' Carol gave her a one-armed hug. 'I've just got a puppy, but he won't bother you. Much.' She waved a hand before Kelsey could open her mouth. 'Okay, so he howled half of last night, but tonight will be better.'

'A puppy?' Pipa bounced on Kelsey's hip. 'Please, Mummy?'

'You love puppies?' Carol grinned at Pipa. 'Done, then, and you can keep him occupied.'

She turned back to Kelsey. 'Just one thing. If you decide to take off again'—she cocked a pierced eyebrow—'tell me this time. I bet I can give you more reasons to stay than go.'

'I will. Thanks.' Kelsey knew she deserved the reminder. Still, it stung.

'I knock off at four, so just drop in then.'

Carol walked to the bar, scribbled on the order pad, ripped off the sheet and came back.

'I figure you remember the layout of the town?' She gave the handwritten address to Kelsey. 'And hey'—she threw her arms around Kelsey's neck again—'I missed you, too.'

Carol turned, then, and went back to serving behind the bar.

'I've already ordered your favourite.' Ethan gestured to an intimately small table, then pulled a chair out for her and one for Pipa. 'It shouldn't be long.'

'My favourite?'

'Roast pork and veggies.' He frowned as he helped Pipa onto her seat. 'You still like that?'

'I do, yes, thanks.' She clasped her hands together on the tabletop.

He sat opposite her. 'You don't sound sure about it. If you'd rather something else, I can change it.'

'No, it's not that.' Might as well just say it. 'I haven't had it since I left.'

'Why not?' He rested his forearms on the table, his knuckles brushing hers.

Staring at that one point of contact, Kelsey shrugged. 'I couldn't afford it when I had more than one mouth to feed.'

'You do know if you'd come home at any point, I would have helped you, don't you?'

'It's never been that simple.'

'Then tell me.'

She moved her hands away from his and sat back in her chair. 'Not here, not now.'

Unrolling the napkin from her cutlery, she handed it to Pipa, who began folding it to join her own.

Ethan shifted forward. 'What else happened? Because this is about more than what went on between us that night.'

Heat crawled up her throat. 'Not here. Not now.'

She'd never talked about how lost she'd felt when she'd been grieving her father. He'd loved her. He'd had faith in her and believed in her. She'd never told anyone about how she'd turned to her mother. Or of the sting of the slap she'd received, or the words her mother had hissed.

He died of shame. He died because of you.

She'd run to Ethan's that night, seeking the warmth and love she'd been so sure he felt for her, but instead, she'd set a nightmare in motion. And that was only one of the reasons she couldn't talk to him about it now.

She swallowed the guilt lodged in her throat. 'I didn't mean to hurt you before. I only meant that you have a reputation, and I thought you'd be worried about it.'

His shoulders sagged as he stared at her.

'I don't give a sh—' He pursed his lips and glanced at Pipa. 'I don't care what the gossips say. Even if they knew the truth, they'd still gossip. I care about you and what you think, what you won't tell me and why.'

'I can't. Not yet.'

The gossips would talk for days, weeks if she had a panic attack in the middle of the pub. They'd stretch and bend her story, tie it in knots until any truth became buried so deep it wouldn't matter.

So she wouldn't be telling him during lunch at the pub.

But even in another place at a different time, there were some things she could never tell him.

***

Ethan ate quietly as Kelsey and Pipa chatted about playing with Carol's puppy, Carol's pink hair, all the pictures on the pub wall that showed the town flooding over the years, and anything else Pipa's imagination conjured. Like the time Pipa's yellow boots floated away down the river. Or the time Kelsey had bundled Pipa up and carried her through a storm—something Pipa obviously looked back on as an adventure, not a trauma. All things he'd missed experiencing with her, with them, and now wanted.

Even stories about packing and moving—which they must have done a lot—were told with a giggle from Pipa, and he wondered if Kelsey could see that she'd given her child an unquestionable faith that she was loved, wanted and needed.

He began to understand what else Kelsey wanted for Pipa—a home, stability, a place to grow up and create shared memories with family and friends. Things most kids took for granted because most parents had them to give.

'Your dad would've loved her.' He nodded at Pipa.

'He would have.' But her eyes clouded.

'He'd be proud of you, too.'

She shook her head at that. 'Not according to Mum.'

'No.' He toyed with his half-eaten meal. 'Which is one reason you spent most of your time at my place.'

It humbled him. She'd chosen him and his home as her safe place. And she'd chosen to come to him for help.

'She convinced you not to come home.' It wasn't a question now.

At Kelsey's slow nod, he struggled with the notion of a mother abandoning her daughter when she was needed the most. His own mother had

63

shown him every day that she cherished him, and even though he'd buried her seven years ago, her warmth and love still surrounded him.

Finishing the food on his plate, he set his knife and fork across it, then pushed it aside. Kelsey had seen his place as a refuge once, and he wanted her to see it that way again. Until she could see it as more. See it as her home.

He'd hurt her, though, by rushing, pushing for answers to questions he didn't know how to ask. So, he'd step back, come at it from another angle. Because he wasn't giving up.

'You know, Pipa, I can cook a mean spaghetti bolognaise.'

Frowning, Pipa looked from Ethan to her mostly eaten meal and then at Kelsey. 'How does he know it's mean?'

'He means he cooks yummy spaghetti.'

'Oh. Mummy cooks mean basketti too.'

'I remember.' Ethan nodded, catching Kelsey's quick frown. 'So, I was thinking, you could come to my house over the weekend. I could cook and you could see my horses.'

He nodded at Kelsey. 'You can look at those magazines.'

'Horsies?' Pipa clapped her hands, sending pasta through the air to land on his plate. 'I love horsies! Please, Mummy?' She turned, clasping those hands under her chin.

He'd cornered Kelsey now, was making her choose between keeping her distance from him and making Pipa sad, or sacrificing her personal space and making Pipa ecstatic.

They'd gone from sharing everything to this, and it gutted him.

Kelsey reached over and began cleaning Pipa's hands and face. 'When would suit you?'

He shouldn't have been surprised that she chose to make Pipa happy. The old Kelsey had always stood up for the underdog, picked the runt of the litter, took the neglected and abused and showed them love and compassion.

'I have fire running training on Sunday, so tomorrow would be better.'

Playing it cool, he glanced towards the stage tucked in the corner of the room as Carol carried two chairs onto it and set them side by side.

'If you come in the morning, Pipa can help me feed the animals.'

It was a low move, using Pipa to get Kelsey to his place so that she could see, feel, remember what it was like, but desperation had him grabbing at whatever advantage he could.

A look passed between mother and daughter, one that had Pipa grinning and bouncing in her seat.

Covering his relief with a smile, he pointed to the stage where Carol settled into one of the chairs, propped one foot on the other, then spoke into the mic.

'This song is for my new friend, Pipa.'

Carol settled the guitar on her knee and waved at a grinning Pipa before her eyes flicked in Kelsey's direction. Her face dropped slightly, her smile sticking as she glanced at Ethan and tipped her chin up in warning.

The hairs on the back of his neck stood up, his muscles coiling ready, but he turned slowly.

Kelsey had gone white—not even a dash of colour in her cheeks. When she angled her body towards the door, Ethan stood and strode around the table to sit next to her.

When she spoke, her lips barely moved. 'He's found us before without it being announced to the world where we are.'

'But he's not here, Kelsey, remember that.'

He took her hand, shock hitching up to panic as she stayed eerily still, her face set, her chest jerking with each breath.

He shuffled his seat closer and leaned in. 'Pipa is safe, no one here will let him near her or you. You're home now. Safe.'

Her hand clamped on his, making him wince. Tremors ran through her, into him. He'd felt them before, when the rumble and flash of a thunderstorm lashed his house. He'd distracted her, then, with stories of the clouds playing smash-ups to make the thunder.

This fear of hers, this deep terror of being discovered, of having to pick up and run, couldn't be so glibly distracted. So he gave her the comfort she'd often preferred when she'd wanted solace. His warmth and his strength.

Riveted to Carol singing her song, Pipa stayed oblivious. It didn't take much of a leap to understand it was the only reason Kelsey let him hold her, comfort her. But eventually, her breathing slowed and the grip she had on his hand eased.

By the time Carol had finished singing and Pipa had clapped long and loud, Kelsey had control again. Letting his hand go, she shifted, dislodged his arm and nudged him away.

Pipa turned and grinned. 'Can I sing, Mummy?'

'I don't know, Pip. Not yet.' Kelsey's smile held for a second.

Carol stopped beside Pipa's seat and grinned down at her. 'How was that?'

'It was so good.' Pipa reached out and touched the guitar, plucked a string. Eyeing Kelsey, she snatched her hand back.

'Maybe you can come in and sing with me when we do karaoke.' Carol glanced at Kelsey. 'Like your mum used to.'

'Mummy sings in the car, and the shower, and when the cows are naughty so she doesn't swear at them. She sings when I'm naughty, and when I can't sleep. Maybe you can sing with us, Mummy.'

'Wow.' Carol shook her head. 'She gets going, doesn't she?'

But Kelsey only nodded, her jaw clenched.

Ethan took a chance and ran his hand down Kelsey's hair, then leaned over and kissed her temple. 'I'll be back in a minute.'

He followed Carol to the bar.

She rang up his total, took his card and swiped it. 'I've decided I'm throwing a party for Kelsey. Starts about six.'

'She's not going to like it.'

'Maybe not, but there's a lot of people who'll want to see her and catch up.'

She handed him his card and receipt.

'Besides, everyone else will be happy to do the talking, she just needs to sit there, smile and enjoy the food.' Carol flashed a smile of her own. 'So you'll be there?'

He shrugged. 'Why not?'

Carol laughed and winked at him. 'Sure, why not.'

He'd take the laughter, the whispers that flew from one end of town to the other. He'd take Kelsey's detachment, her insistence on keeping her secrets. He'd give her the room, the assurance, the shoulder when she needed it.

Maybe then she would see she could trust him and tell him the truth. Then he'd find a way to convince her to stay with him.

He just hoped she didn't disappear before he had his chance.

CHAPTER NINE

Brian sat in his car, holding his securely locked briefcase to his chest as he stared at the house that had slowly become a home.

He had Haylee to thank for that. Bit by bit, she'd transformed the minimalist place where he'd slept and eaten into a place of comfort and colour that both soothed his jaded soul and encouraged the boys to play and explore.

He'd taken charge of the tiny front garden after the first druggie bastard caught Haylee planting snapdragons. She'd jumped at every sound outside for weeks after.

The snapdragons had died in the first heatwave of the summer, as had most of the other flowers he'd neglected. It wouldn't do, leaving all those dead spots, when Haylee and the boys filled the rest of his life with the chaotically controlled moments he'd come to love.

As soon as the season broke and the ground turned to the dirt it was supposed to be instead of concrete, he'd sit down with the boys and plan a garden both functional and fun. One he could take pride in and hopefully give Haylee something to smile about when she walked past.

For now though he needed to get inside before Haylee panicked about a car sitting in the driveway.

Even as he opened his car door, a little face appeared between the lace curtains of the lounge room window. Ashley poked his tongue out and crossed his eyes, then shoved his fingers up his nose. Haylee's face appeared above him, her eyes wide as she scanned the street. Spotting his car, she frowned and tugged Ashley from the window.

Brian could never pick what mood she would be in or what word or action would set her off. It made him feel like the worst brother in the world that he had no idea what he was dealing with, how to make it better, or how to prove to her that she wasn't just taking up space in his home.

Giggles broke out as soon as he opened the front door, and they got louder as he stepped inside, the scent of roast beef making his stomach growl.

Sliding the file into the drawer of the desk that sat beside the door, he flicked the latch so exploring fingers couldn't get hold of what eyes and minds so young should never have to see or comprehend. Hell, he wished he hadn't seen and didn't know half of what he had and did.

The giggling turned to whispers as James and Ashley tried to creep up behind him.

Brian headed into the kitchen where Haylee crouched in front of the oven and checked the roast. Face reddened, she glanced at him a moment before her gaze slid behind him, and he took courage in the slight twist of her lips.

'Are the boys home from work yet?' he said, loosening his tie.

'Rah!'

Arms gripped his thighs and held tight as he pretended to stumble in shock.

'Where did you come from?' He bent and grabbed James around the waist, lifting him up and flipping him to hold him upside down. 'And where has your head gone?'

Ashley let go of Brian's legs and fell to the floor, laughing at his brother dangling upside down. James grabbed hold of Brian's belt, laughing breathlessly, and tried to beg for Brian to stop.

Showing mercy, Brian lowered him to the floor, laying him next to his brother, and tickled them both until they couldn't breathe.

'Why haven't you grown yet? And where has your beard gone?'

'I not have beard.' Ashley wriggled.

Brian frowned at him, pushing a finger against his smooth, chubby cheek. 'I could have sworn you had a beard this morning.'

'Uh-uh.'

Mischief danced in Ashley's eyes, and Brian couldn't help the kick to his heart. A month ago, those eyes would have held terror.

'You better not have used my razor to shave it off.'

In his highchair, Rupert clapped and gurgled out encouragement.

Not wanting him to miss out, Brian grabbed him from his seat, laid him next to his brothers and tickled them all until none could draw breath to squeal.

'You're putting them to bed after this.' Haylee pointed a spatula at her two eldest sons. 'Wash hands and faces, then up to the table.'

As James and Ashley ran from the room, Brian scooped Rupert up and sat him back in his highchair, then went to the fridge, snagged a bottle of iced tea and held it up to offer Haylee one.

'No thanks,' she shook her head and glanced at Rupert. 'I'll be up all night as it is.'

'I can stay up with him this time. You need some sleep.'

She levelled him with a glare. 'I'm his mother. I'm supposed to be sleep-deprived.'

'I'm your brother, their uncle. I'm supposed to help.'

'You have enough to think about without taking on my problems.'

Turning back to the stove, she began dumping roast beef, roasted spuds and carrots, and steamed veggies on each plate.

Brian stepped towards the dining table that separated them. 'Your problems *are* my problems.'

'That's just it, isn't it?' Haylee whirled to face him, fists clenched around tongs and a serving spoon. 'You never complain about having to save your stupid sister from druggies, from her mistakes, her life. You don't complain about the mess the boys make. All the questions they ask. The time they take up.'

She pursed her lips until her chin steadied. 'You shouldn't have to be a surrogate father or make promises to James like you did this morning.'

She hung her head, her shoulders shaking.

'God, Haylee.' Brian stepped around the table and pulled her against his chest. 'They might not be my sons, but they're mine, they're part of this family. And I'll do anything and everything I can to wipe away the stain Donny left on them.'

Keeping her body stiff, her hands at her sides, fingers still clenched around the utensils, she rested only her cheek against his shoulder.

His chest hurting from holding his breath, Brian stroked a hand over her hair and let it rest against her back.

'You're part of this family, Haylee. You're mine as much as they are, and there's no way I could love you any more than I already do.'

Her shoulders slumped against his chest and the spoon and tongs clattered to the floor. 'I'm so tired.'

'I know.'

Footsteps beating a path from the bathroom to the kitchen had her pushing away from him. He said nothing as she wiped her cheeks with her palm, then scooped the utensils from the floor and dropped them in the sink.

'You know I'd never ask you to leave, don't you?'

'I know, okay.' She sat the boys' plates a little too hard on the table.

Holding his tongue, he sat and pulled the chair out beside him as James and Ashley ran through the doorway.

'Walking please, boys.' Haylee frowned at them.

Perfectly synchronised, they both stopped and dipped their heads. 'Sorry, Mummy.'

'Okay.' She pointed to their plates. 'Up you hop. No talking with mouths full, no flicking food, no kicking under the table.'

James and Ashley glanced at each other, the opposite sides of their mouths lifting so that they smiled as one.

'And no jokes,' Haylee said, her back still to them.

'Mum would have been proud of you.'

'Ya think?' Haylee lifted an eyebrow as she sat between Rupert and Ashley. 'I think she'd be heartbroken.'

'I think you're wrong.' He leaned over and helped James cut his meat.

'I *know* you're wrong.' She turned her attention to Ashley, helping him separate his peas from his corn and cut his meat.

Brian left it as they ate. The boys made sure they swallowed before talking about what they might do on the weekend. Nothing of Donny showed as they laughed and played while sticking to their mother's rules. Nothing of Donny's selfishness or malice lived in their constant inclusion of their baby brother. Donny might have given them his seed, but Haylee had grown them, nurtured them, and made sure they fell as far away from their father as possible.

Unlike Bristow, who'd been encouraged to be just like his father, and his father before him. Would he have turned out differently if he'd been shown kindness and empathy?

It was an impossible question to answer. Besides, only the facts mattered, because only they were real. And the facts were that Bristow came from a long line of thieves, murderers and drug dealers. Henry Bristow had left enough blood and grief behind to fill a whole evidence room.

Fork halfway to his mouth, Brian froze. Could that be it? Could that be one of the puzzle pieces? His skin prickled as he rolled it around in his head. They couldn't get a DNA sample from Spencer Bristow without a warrant, but if he could get a related match with Bristow senior, then he had another chink in the chain of evidence.

'You okay?' Haylee reached out and touched his still raised hand.

'Yeah.' He finished the movement and chewed. 'Just working some things out.'

'Like?'

'Work stuff.' He met her frown with one of his own. 'And that the boys have the best chance at life because they have you.'

Her eyebrows shot up.

He shook his head before she could argue. 'I've seen some kids come in for doing horrific things, and yet, they had the nicest parents who loved them and wanted the best for them. And I've seen kids whose parents care more about money or drugs, or whatever, but they find the strength to pull themselves out of that cycle.'

He tipped his head at James and Ashley as they kept Rupert entertained. 'They had a shitty start with a man who didn't care about them, but you pulled them out of it, and they love you, more than anything. They have a mother who protects them, loves them and teaches them the value of life.'

'They'll remember him.'

'They will.' He nodded. 'But they'll remember you, too.'

He let her silence be. He'd told a truth and she needed to find a way to accept it. Once she did, she might be ready to accept the rest—that he loved her and the boys more than he could say. They were family, and there was nothing more important to him than that.

CHAPTER TEN

By the time the tenth carload of people arrived at Carol's house, Kelsey was ready to walk. The hugs and laughter each person brought into the backyard reminded her of what she'd left behind five years ago—and what she could have again if things were different. But the questions, so innocently asked, made her fear that if she answered them, she'd have to take Pipa and run again. How many times could she dodge the truth before someone looked closer and figured it out?

'She's a cutie, isn't she?' Zoe tipped her bottle of Great Northern beer towards Pipa.

Out of all Kelsey's old school friends, Zoe had been the least annoyed, the least curious about why she'd left and how she'd come back with a daughter.

Their circle had been tight growing up. Kelsey and Carol had dared, cajoled and begged Zoe and her twin Lilli to join them on some of their moonlit rides. They'd spent weekends camping in the bush with no adults to stop them screaming and laughing, dreaming of bigger, better things. But it seemed none of them had achieved those wild dreams of adventure and love, excitement and passion.

Before it had all fallen apart for Kelsey, she'd shared moments with Ethan when her heart gave a thud that flooded love through her so completely that no other reality existed for her except the two of them together forever. Even now, when he glanced at her from across the yard, that thud resonated through her.

Her new reality, though, consisted of keeping Pipa safe and alive with no room for anything else. Especially not naive dreams that had been dead for five years.

Pipa, who sprawled on the grass in the fading light, the puppy wriggling in the ecstasy of having someone to play with, had dreams of her own now. Though, right at that moment, no one would guess the young girl with twigs stuck in her hair, her knees stained green and brown, her face red with effort and joy, wanted to be a people helper when she grew big like her mummy. She wanted to make sad people happy. Wanted to stop bad people hurting others. She wanted to give love to those who didn't have anyone to love them.

Guilt jabbed pinprick holes in Kelsey's heart because Pipa already did those things. Even when she winced at a shouted laugh or edged towards Kelsey when someone came over to dig for gossip, Pipa never failed to charm and make people smile. For once, she was truly happy. Content. A normal girl. Something she hadn't had the chance to be up until now. The truth slapped Kelsey hard.

Pipa had been brought up in secrecy and isolation, as much to protect as to defend. Though she'd never complained, thrown tantrums or demanded what other kids had, Kelsey knew Pipa suffered, wanted. How could she not when rolling around with a puppy was the epitome of being a kid?

Instead, Pipa had learned to hide, to stay in the dark even when the bad man yelled and screamed. She'd known to stay quiet when he broke furniture and bones. She'd known to stay hidden when he'd tried forcing Kelsey to scream for the girl he wanted dead.

'Hey.' Zoe nudged an elbow into Kelsey's arm. 'Where'd you go?'

'Nowhere.'

Not to the cabin with the loft. Not to the musty couch where she'd experienced so much pain.

She couldn't afford to go there tonight. Not when more people laughed their way into Carol's backyard, setting up camp chairs and coolers. Not when conversations turned gazes to her and Pipa every few seconds. So she forced the memory away, burying it under those she needed to access for everyone who wanted to play *remember when*.

And then, standing before her, no longer gangly but rather lean and lanky, Jex eyed her as though he didn't believe she sat before him.

'I was worried I'd get here and you'd be gone again.'

'I'm not going anywhere.' She stood slowly, not sure what she expected, and *oofed* out a breath when he pulled her to his chest and wrapped his arms around her.

'We didn't know where you'd gone … if you were okay.'

Rubbing his back, she let Jex hold on. 'Yeah, I've been told that.'

'You're staying?' He eased back, but kept his hands on her shoulders.

'I am.' For now, at least, she thought.

At the tug on her shirt, she glanced down, then moved in the circle of Jex's arms to pick Pipa up. 'Pipa, this is another friend, Jex.'

Pipa ran a finger over the stubbled beard covering Jex's jaw and giggled when he pretended to bite her finger. 'Hello, Jex.'

'Hello, Pipa.' He let them go, stroking a thumb down Kelsey's cheek as he did. 'A lot of people missed you.'

'I'm beginning to realise that.' She glanced over at Ethan.

'And worried about you.' He tilted his head and followed her gaze to Ethan. 'Him especially.'

She didn't trust herself to answer that, so she set Pipa back on her feet to play with the waiting puppy.

Jex snagged a camp chair someone had vacated and dragged it a few feet to sit next to Zoe. 'You're not going to say we shouldn't have worried?'

Kelsey couldn't lie, so she shrugged. 'I looked after myself and survived.'

Jex leaned forward and propped his elbows on his knees. 'We know you'll stand and fight for the people you care about. We've all got stories we can tell. Everyone remembers how fierce you were when those idiots cornered Lilli in school to see if they could make her cry, and how viciously you called out homophobes when they came after me. And I'm guessing for her'—he nodded towards Pipa—'you'd be triply ruthless.'

'Yeah.' Zoe held up her beer in salute to another group walking up the driveway. 'You saved me from those same boys when they thought I was Lilli.

Even Carol, who takes shit from no one, could name a dozen times you stuck up for her at school.'

'We all did.' Kelsey shifted in her seat. 'I can name plenty of times you all stood up for me.'

'But that's it.' Jex helped Pipa crawl up onto his knee but gently pushed the puppy down when it tried to follow. 'You didn't stick up for yourself. So we worried about you. A lot.'

'Mummy fought the bad man.' Absently, Pipa touched Jex's chin. 'Even when he said bad words and yelleded.'

'Did she?' Zoe raised an eyebrow.

Jex cleared his throat. 'Who else do you know here, Pipa?'

'Ethan.' She clapped her hands and nearly crawled over Jex's shoulder to look for him, then pointed. 'Over there!'

'How about we go say hello?' He stood and squeezed Kelsey's shoulder as he walked past her.

Zoe blew out a breath and ran a hand through her hair. 'There's more to that, isn't there?'

Kelsey could only nod.

'The bad man is her dad?'

'Yes.' She swallowed and hoped she could keep breathing through the tightening of her chest. 'He's stalking us.'

Narrowing her eyes, Zoe scanned the crowd. 'If you're scared he's going to come and take her, you have to know, none of us would let him, whoever the bastard is.'

'Not scared, terrified. And not just take her …'

She swallowed, memories bubbling to the surface, popping with flashes of suppressed screams, pain, the horror of the things he'd done as he tried to force her to tell him where Pipa hid. The memory of having his fingers on her, in her, pinched at her lungs and tightened her chest to strangling point. But there were too many people, too many eyes, too many whispers—she couldn't let it take the last of her control.

Before she could get Ethan's name from her mind to her lips, he strode through the crowded backyard and crouched before her. His frown worried, he reached up to frame her face with his hands.

Jerking back, Kelsey shook her head. If he touched her, she'd break, fall apart. Because she knew, in that moment, if she fell, he'd catch her. And then how could she walk away?

'It's okay, Mummy.' Pipa gripped Kelsey's hand in hers and pressed it to her cheek.

'Here, Pipa.' Ethan tugged the puppy down from climbing on his lap. 'Can you take Snow inside for me?'

'Okay.' Pipa took the puppy by the collar but kept her gaze on Kelsey.

'I'm okay, Pip.' Kelsey tried to smile. It hurt—her face, her heart, her soul—but she held it until Pipa led the bouncing puppy through the back door.

'What happened?' Elbows on his thighs, hands between his knees, Ethan stared up at her.

She could only shake her head, the vice squeezing her chest too tight to talk.

'Something did. You were fine talking to Jex, then you started talking to Zoe again. Did she say something?'

'Hey!' Zoe punched his shoulder. 'I didn't do anything.'

'Well, something happened.' He glared at Zoe over his shoulder.

'Well, it wasn't me.' But she frowned.

'Stop.' Kelsey held up a shaking hand. 'Just stop.'

But her tears didn't. They trickled, then ran, falling in big drops from her chin to her hands clutched in her lap.

Afraid she'd fly apart if she moved, she kept her gaze on Ethan. This time, she didn't flinch when his hand cupped her cheek, or hesitate when he stood and pulled her to her feet. She followed as he led her into the house and down the hallway to the lounge room. When he sat on the couch and pulled her against him, wrapping his arms around her and tucking her into the long-forgotten pocket of refuge, Kelsey breathed him in and let his warmth soak into her bones. She pretended, just for a moment, that she'd never offered herself to him that night, that she hadn't disappointed him, that he hadn't crushed her.

'Mummy?'

Ethan loosened his arms as soon as Kelsey moved. Leaning forward, she picked Pipa up, swung her onto Ethan's lap and enfolded her into the circle of their arms.

More tears fell when Pipa sighed, snuggled in and rested her head on Ethan's chest.

'The bad man not here?'

Only in her head.

'No, sweet. He's not. He won't be.'

'But you scared?'

'Sometimes.' Kelsey traced a finger along Pipa's cheek. Cocooned in their own security blanket of Ethan's warmth and scent, her words came easier. 'He won't get anywhere near you, though, ever. You know that, don't you?'

Pipa nodded, her hand lifting to Kelsey's chin. 'I won't let him hurt you, Mummy.'

'Oh, Pip.' Kelsey closed her eyes a moment. 'You won't have to worry about him anymore, okay?'

'Why not?'

'Because,' Ethan's voice rumbled around them, '*I* won't let him hurt either of you. Neither will Mark, or Rita, or Carol, Zoe, or Jex.'

He moved so that he could look down at them, and he held Kelsey's gaze. 'You have people to help you now, to stand beside you in this.'

'I know.'

He stared at her a moment longer, waiting, but she had nothing to say besides that single simplicity.

Outside, someone put music on. It competed with the laughter, the shrieks, the fun everyone else was having.

Pipa cupped her hands around her mouth. 'We have to go back outside?'

Kelsey wanted to say no, but Carol had thrown the party for her at short notice. Maybe she could find somewhere quiet for Pipa.

'There you are.' Carol rushed into the room, went through to the kitchen and came back with three bowls, stacked one on top of the other. 'We're about to fire up the barbie.'

'We're going to take Pipa to the lookout.' Ethan shifted away from Kelsey, then stood and took Pipa with him.

'But …' Carol frowned at Kelsey, then gave a slow nod. 'Okay. Fine. I'll try to save some food for you.'

Carol turned and walked down the hallway and the sound of the back door slapping followed a second later.

'I should stay.' Kelsey rubbed a fist against her chest, the tightness building again.

'They're panic attacks you're having, aren't they?'

She nodded. 'I thought I was dying the first time.'

'When did they start?'

She had to swallow. 'Six months ago.'

'How often do they happen?'

'Often enough that I know I'll live through the next one.' She tried to smile.

Ethan ignored it. 'And if you stay here, you'll have another one?'

'Honestly, I don't know.' It was no use trying to dodge the topic. 'They've been coming hard and fast the last twenty-four hours.'

'Do you know why?'

She laughed, then sobered. 'Staying in one place too long puts me on edge, but so does moving somewhere new.'

'This isn't somewhere new, though, is it?'

'The place isn't, but aren't we all new to each other again?'

He didn't answer, just stared at her, then slowly leaned in and brushed his lips across her brow.

Before she could comprehend what that meant, he turned and headed for the front door with Pipa on his hip like she'd always been there.

High up on the bank of an ancient river, Henty Lookout gazed down on the town where orange streetlights were organised in neat blocks. Further out, the lights from farmhouses dotted the hills and valleys. Ethan's place, had it been visible through the bush and blue gum plantations, would be a lone light to the south.

He hadn't bothered to leave a light on for five years, though. Hope that Kelsey would come home had never tipped over into believing she would actually knock on his door. Having her in his house, in his space again tomorrow would be a great start, but he wanted her and Pipa there permanently. But asking her would be …

He lifted his gaze to the first star waking in the darkening sky. Well, it would be like asking a crush out on a date, but so much more was at stake.

Palms sweating, heart thudding an unsteady beat, he waited as Kelsey stood beside him. She held Pipa's hand as the girl stood balancing on the low metal barrier surrounding the lookout.

'I forgot how pretty it is up here.'

He dipped his attention to the town below, saw cars cruising the streets, heard dogs barking, the bass of someone's radio.

'You should have come back. Better yet, you shouldn't have left.'

Before she could open her mouth and shoot something back, he crouched down and took out his phone. 'There's a geocache around here somewhere, Pipa. Would you like to find it?'

He scrolled through his photos for the one he'd taken of the film canister he'd found a few weeks ago. It would be wonderful if it still held the little pewter horse he'd put inside. Either way, Pipa would get a kick out of finding the geocache and swapping something for whatever was inside.

'This is what you need to find. It's around here, but you have to stay this side of the barrier, okay?'

'Okay.' She leaned against him as she studied the photo. 'Okay.'

With a nod, she wandered over to the lookout marker and checked behind the stubbly grass poking out of the dirt.

'What are you doing?' Jaw set, Kelsey kept her narrowed gaze on Pipa. 'Why are you doing it?'

'I'm giving Pipa something to do while you talk to me. And I'm doing it so I can understand.'

'Why?' She turned to him, the anger of moments before draining to leave weary resignation behind.

'Because you've never been one to give in, give up. I know you won't when it comes to Pipa, but with us? With things that used to matter to you? You let go too easily.'

He closed the gap between them, and she proved him right by pulling back.

'Don't. Don't back away from me. Please.'

'I'm not doing this now.'

'Then when?'

'I found it!' Pipa ran to them, the canister held high, the grin on her face bright in the last reaches of the sunset.

Kelsey crouched down and hummed over Pipa's find.

Ethan's spike of frustration lost its momentum as Kelsey helped Pipa pry the lid off the canister. Pipa's reverent *oh* when she tipped the horse out onto Kelsey's hand smoothed warm pleasure over the last rough edges.

'Do I keep it?' Eyes wide and shining under the streetlight, Pipa stared up at him.

'If you have something to swap it for.' If she didn't, he'd find something in his car.

'My baselet?' Pipa touched the thin chain on Kelsey's wrist.

'No!' Kelsey snatched her hand away and cradled it against her chest.

Pipa's face dropped, her hands reaching for her mother, and Kelsey opened her arms and drew her daughter in.

'I'm sorry, Pip. I'm sorry. But it's your mum's. It's all I have left of her to give you.'

Pipa's mum?

Stunned, Ethan opened his mouth, but no words would form. He replayed the morning's events over in his head. Kelsey hadn't introduced Pipa as her daughter. Had shut down when he'd jumped to the logical conclusion that she was.

'You're not her mother.'

'I love you, Mummy.' Pipa pressed a hand to Kelsey's cheek. 'You keep my baselet.'

'Kelsey.' He squatted down beside them.

She threw him a glare, then turned back to Pipa. 'It's yours, Pip. It's up to you what you do with it.'

'You my mummy.' Pipa touched the bracelet, then opened Kelsey's hand to stroke the tiny horse.

The struggle played over Kelsey's face, then she held her wrist out to Pipa. 'Here, you take it and swap it.'

Tongue poking out, Pipa unclipped the bracelet, then gently dropped it into the canister. Kelsey snapped the lid back on.

'Go put it back.' She waited until Pipa skipped away before she pushed to her feet.

Ethan followed and turned her to face him. 'Kelsey.'

'Not now.'

She held out her hand as Pipa ran back and climbed on the low barrier. 'Do you want me to tell you the story my dad told me about White Wattle Creek, Pip?'

'Your daddy telled you stories, too? Like you tell me?'

Wobbling as she turned to grin at Kelsey, Pipa grabbed Ethan's offered hand.

'He did, and this is one of my favourites.'

Kelsey lifted her face to the darkening sky for a moment, then focused on Pipa.

'Years ago, there was a man call Wal Arton. He worked on a sheep station not far from town, but back then, there were no cars, the roads were all dirt tracks, and the town only had a few houses. The people that lived here built a fenced yard around a big wattle tree that everyone called the white wattle, because its leaves and trunk turned silver through the seasons.'

'Pretty.' Pipa stared up at Kelsey, riveted.

They'd been kids, restless on a hot night when Kelsey's father had brought her up to the lookout, away from the boiling temper of her mother, and had let Ethan tag along for the ride. He and Kelsey had stood on the barrier as Pipa did, trying to push each other off, even as they clung to each other to stay on. That night, he'd told them the story Kelsey now told Pipa.

'They used the fenced-off yard as a meeting place, or a holding place if someone found a stray horse or cow. Or, if they caught a bad person, they'd tie him up to the tree and wait for the police.'

'Like Muck?'

'Yes, like Mark, except they rode horses and took days to get here.'

'Wow.'

'So, one day, Wal had an argument with his boss.'

'Like you did this morning?'

'Kind of.' Kelsey smiled. 'But Wal's boss was mean and grumpy.'

She'd captured Pipa's imagination, taking them both away from the now and into the story. It made Ethan want to reach out and touch her just to make sure they still had a connection.

'But instead of packing his things and leaving, Wal saddled his horse, took the boss's dog, let all the sheep out of the home paddock and disappeared. The boss was very angry'—she mocked a frown at Pipa and pursed her lips—'and sent his best men out to find Wal. The boss wanted his dog back and to make Wal round up all the sheep he'd let out. But when they found him, Wal refused to go back and said the dog had run away.'

She glanced at Ethan, as though daring him to correct her version of local history. She didn't have to warn him, though, not when there was a chance Pipa would cry as Kelsey had all those years ago at the true version— that Wal had convinced the men he'd shot the dog so that it didn't give away his hiding place. Even though her tears wouldn't last long, Ethan couldn't stand to see Pipa's eyes fill with that same shocked horror.

'So, they took Wal to the white wattle yard, down by the creek.' She gestured to the streets below. 'They tied him up under the tree to wait for the police to come. But that night, as he sat watching his horse eat its hay, his hands and legs tied with rope, he heard a dog whining.'

Eyes wide, Pipa gasped. 'His dog not run away?'

'No, he loved the dog, even though it wasn't his, and he'd told the men it had run away so they wouldn't take it back to the boss. But the dog loved Wal too and came back to rescue him. The men who'd captured Wal recognised the dog, and while they tried to catch it, a good friend of Wal's untied him, helped him to his horse, and they galloped off into the night, the dog giving a last bark in the opposite direction before disappearing.'

'Did the dog find Wal again?'

'He did.' Kelsey smiled as she brushed a hand over Pipa's hair. 'It's said that Wal and his friend took the horse and dog to Bailey's Rocks, not far from here, and that's where they all lived, hiding from the boss and the police.'

She lifted Pipa to her hip and kissed her cheek.

'Wow.' Pipa played with Kelsey's hair while a frown crunched her eyebrows. 'He loved the dog like you love me.'

'Yes.' Kelsey nodded. 'You grew in Jaiyden's tummy, and she gave birth to you and loved you from the first moment. But you're mine, and you always will be.' She tapped Pipa's nose. 'Even when you're old and have kids of your own, I'll still love and protect you.'

'When I old, I protect you.' Pipa kissed Kelsey's cheek.

Her face pale now, Kelsey closed her eyes and rested her forehead against Pipa's.

Worried that Kelsey would hold everything until she fell, Ethan opened his arms to Pipa. His heart sighed when she held hers out, letting him lift her to his chest and hold her close. If he could offer the same comfort to Kelsey and have her accept, his world would right itself.

'I've never kept Jaiyden a secret.' She spoke to him but kept her distance. 'When Pipa started talking, it was safer for her to call me Mummy. Besides, she deserves to know she belongs, that she's loved.'

Hands curled under her chin, her head resting on Ethan's shoulder, Pipa yawned. 'Mummy loves me.'

'I do.' Moving closer, Kelsey kissed Pipa's temple, then ran her thumb down the girl's nose.

Ethan moved slowly, deliberately, so that Kelsey would have no doubt of his intentions. He put his arm around her shoulders and, when she didn't protest, pulled her close so that he held them both against his chest.

He wanted them like this always. No, better than this. He wanted no secrets between them. No strained silence. No distance. None of which could happen until Kelsey talked to him. And that would only happen when she realised she could trust and rely on him.

So he had to ask before she built up her defences again.

'Come home with me.'

He held his breath as she stiffened in his arms.

CHAPTER ELEVEN

Come home with me.

Like a firework shot from her heart, hope blew, sparkled bright, then fizzled to nothing before Kelsey could grab hold. Saying yes would mean peace for her and Pipa, would give them a place to rest without worry and fear. She could soak in Ethan's strength, bask in the memories of a time when her hopes and dreams had still been within reach. She knew now that they'd been untouchable, unreachable, but they had been there, at her fingertips.

Did the joy and exhilaration of those memories outweigh the lost hopes and dreams that could drown her? Did Pipa's safety and happiness outweigh anything she would feel, good or bad, on returning to the place she'd always thought would be her home?

Of course the answer was yes. Always had been and always would be.

Stepping back, she kept her gaze on Pipa. 'It can never be like it was.'

'Why not?' The edge to his voice confused her.

'Because.' She shrugged into the silence. 'I can't do this again.'

'Do what, exactly?'

'This.' She stepped back and wrapped her arms over her chest so she didn't reach out. For him, or Pipa. 'I don't want to make the same mistake twice.'

'And living with me would be a mistake?'

Her gaze flew to his before she could stop it. 'There will be no *living with*. We're staying for a short while, that's all.'

She held up a hand before he could turn his glare into words. 'I want Pipa safe. I want her to sleep in a bed of her own, to wake up without the fear of having to run again.'

Taking a breath to calm herself, she rested her hand on Pipa's back. 'I want all that for her, and I'll do whatever I can to give it to her, so we'll come home with you for the short term, but there will need to be rules.'

Ethan stared at her, then, pressing the key, walked towards his car, its lights blinking bright as it unlocked. 'Do you want them written up, or can they just be verbal?'

Still in his arms, Pipa leaned to look at Kelsey over his shoulder. 'We have to go back to the party?'

'For a little bit.' Kelsey leaned close to kiss Pipa's cheek and hoped she wasn't making the biggest mistake of her life. 'Then we're going to stay with Ethan.'

'We see his horsies and puppy?'

'Max isn't a puppy anymore, but yes, we can see them.'

'You can help me with the animals tomorrow.' Ethan buckled Pipa into her seat.

'We sleep first?' She yawned and stretched her arms over her head, her eyes already half-closed.

'You can sleep, Pip. We'll be here.' Ethan kissed her forehead, then stepped back for Kelsey to do the same.

He closed the car door, then leaned against it. 'So, what are these rules?'

'We stay in the spare room.'

'That will have to be a rule for tomorrow night. The spare bed isn't ready, and you and Pip need sleep. I'll take the couch tonight.'

'Which means we take your bed?' The one she'd snuggled down in, naked, so excited she hadn't had room for nerves.

'Yes.' He held her gaze.

Her nerves came now, but arguing would only make a bad situation worse.

'I don't want you to undermine my parenting. What I say goes as far as Pipa is concerned.'

'Do you honestly think I would?' He straightened and stepped towards her.

Kelsey stepped back and held up a hand before she could stop herself. 'No, I don't think you'd hurt me or deliberately undermine me, but I've done this alone up until now, and any outside influence I've endured has been bad.'

'You mean Spencer Bristow?'

'Yes.'

But Spencer Bristow hadn't just hurt her, he'd nearly destroyed her. Then, without even knowing it, he'd tipped her world on its axis and left her empty and broken. He'd torn the last hope of a future with Ethan, or anyone, to shreds.

Determined not to get stuck in her memories, she opened the passenger door and hoisted herself up into the seat, but as she leaned out to pull the door closed, Ethan reached out and held it open, then stepped to where she sat.

Watching her, he lifted his hand and traced his fingers over her cheek. 'What is it you won't tell me?'

Hoping his words and actions meant he understood and forgave her, she sifted through everything she still kept secret.

'I don't know where Jaiyden is. She has to be somewhere, hiding like we are. Defending Pipa by staying away.' Tumbling out now, the words wouldn't stop. 'I don't know how she'll find us. I've tried to stay invisible, to not leave a trail. He's found us, but Jaiyden never has.'

She gripped Ethan's shirt. 'I've looked for her, in every face, in every bus window, on every street, but she's never there. I look, but she's not there.'

Because she's most likely dead.

But those words wouldn't come, only echoed in her head as the darkness wobbled outside their bubble of light.

'She asked me to look after Pipa, and I'm trying, but there's so much I've stuffed up, so much Pipa has seen that she shouldn't have. There's so much she's missed out on, and I …'

Ethan's arms came around her and held her as she fought to breathe, to stay connected. He held her as she shook and through her tears.

'Just breathe for now.' He stroked her hair, her back. 'We'll figure the rest out. For now, just keep breathing.'

Tipping her head back with one hand, he held her against him with the other and stared at her, his eyes dark in the starlight.

For a moment, Kelsey held her breath. What would it be like if he lowered his mouth and kissed her? Or if she tipped hers up to meet his. Eyes half-closed, brain still oxygen-deprived, she closed the gap and brushed her lips against his.

'No. Not like this.' Ethan stepped back, closing the door firmly before crossing to the driver's side and getting in. He kept his gaze out the windscreen as he made the tight turn around the lookout marker.

Heat rushed from Kelsey's toes to her hair. She'd kissed Ethan. She'd kissed him, and he'd pulled back, said no. Mortified, she clenched her hands at her sides.

At least now, she knew his touches, his words, were nothing more than that—words and touches from a friend who knew she was in trouble, nothing more.

Once again, she'd read everything wrong, only this time, she couldn't disappear into the night.

***

Ethan took them back to the party. Though Pipa fought sleep, she rested her head on his shoulder and closed her eyes when he lifted her from his ute.

He would have taken them straight home, but Kelsey had to get her car and they both needed time to regroup. At least this time he'd be able to talk to her about what had happened, and why—again—he couldn't take what she'd offered. Accepting, as much as he dreamed of doing it, would have been the biggest mistake he could make. But he'd made too many already, jumping to conclusions and pushing when he should have waited. The few times she'd reached out to him for comfort or support, he'd given it without thinking or taking the time to appreciate that she still sought his guidance. He'd bullied her to make too many decisions, ones she would have made in her own time, but if he continued, he'd only push her further away.

Instead, he needed to step back, as hard as it would be, and wait for her to open up to him. Once she trusted him with the secrets that haunted her, he'd show her there could be more between them. But until she sought him out, he would give her the space she needed.

'You're back.' Carol greeted them as they walked up the driveway and handed Ethan a stack of plastic cups.

'Yeah.' The scent of barbequed onion and charred meat made his stomach growl. 'How many people were you expecting?'

'Not this many.' She gave them each a paper plate. 'But the people I invited brought others.' She shrugged.

'Any excuse for a party, I guess.' Kelsey scanned the crowd, her eyes travelling over the people who stood or sat in smaller groups around the backyard.

Carol frowned. 'A lot of people were worried about you. Don't forget that.' She pointed to a food-laden trestle table set up near the barbeque. 'Help yourselves.'

'Carol?' Kelsey put a hand on her friend's shoulder. 'I'm sorry I hurt you and that I'm not handling all this'—she waved a hand to encompass the crowd—'very well.'

'I don't know what's happened in the last five years, Kel, and I hope one day you can tell me, but I know it hasn't been good. I can see it in the way you're always looking over your shoulder, always on edge, always second-guessing everyone's motives.'

Carol slid an arm around Kelsey's waist. 'I'm glad you're home again, and I guess I went overboard trying to show you that we missed you and want you to stay.'

Kelsey smiled. 'You wouldn't be Carol if you didn't go overboard.'

'Hey, I've matured past the jump first, think later stage. I'm on the straight and narrow now.'

'Really?' Kelsey laughed, and Ethan could have kissed Carol. He'd definitely hug her later.

'Yes.' Carol swatted Kelsey's arm. 'You just wait and see, I'm not the same Carol you left behind.'

'I don't think any of us are the same.'

She scanned the crowd, this time with an introspection that made Ethan ache for her. It was obvious she'd missed growing up with her friends and the sense of belonging it gave to have those shared stories and experiences.

'I guess you're right.' Carol looked at him, then, and rested a hand on Pipa's back. 'Do you want to put her in my bed?'

'No.' He shook his head. 'She's not heavy.' He'd hold her until his arms dropped off if it gave Kelsey even a small measure of security.

'Well, we're going to mingle.' Carol took Kelsey's arm. 'As soon as we get something to eat.'

Kelsey walked away with a single glance back.

'Is she okay?' Jex handed him a can of Great Northern.

'She will be.'

Though Kelsey hadn't asked for Pipa's parentage to be kept secret, it wasn't his place to repeat what he'd learned. She'd tell people about Pipa if and when she was ready. Until then, he'd keep Pipa and Kelsey's secrets close to his heart.

'You can tell me to mind my own business,' Jex turned so his back was to the yard, 'but is she yours?' He nodded to Pipa.

'She's not.'

And there was no faceless man to hate for giving Kelsey what he hadn't, only one who needed to pay for making Pipa and Kelsey afraid to live their lives as they should. He might not be able to wipe the past for them, but he'd make sure they looked to the future with more than the next hiding place in mind.

'She knows we're all here for her?'

'She will.' He raised his beer in a salute to Jex. 'And once she does, things will get a lot easier.'

'They're bad, aren't they? More than either of you are saying?'

He trusted Jex, trusted that he wouldn't add to the gossip already rushing around town. Still, it wasn't his place to tell him everything.

'If you see anyone out of place, or hear of anyone asking about her or Pipa, call Mark first, me second.'

Jex searched the backyard. 'Someone is looking for them?'

'That's one way of putting it.'

He'd locked eyes on Kelsey as soon as she'd stepped outside again and, ignoring the notion that he stalked her as well, didn't let her out of his sight.

His arms burned as he chatted and laughed with friends, but his heart lightened each time Kelsey searched the crowd for him, her frown shifting to relief each time their gazes met. His arms might scream and cramp, but as long as Kelsey trusted him to hold Pipa and keep her safe, he would.

When she made her way over to him and smiled as she took Pipa from his arms, he resisted the urge to touch her.

'I'm glad you're reconnecting with old friends.'

'I'm not used to talking so much.' She swayed gently, the way parents do. 'I've been hiding and avoiding things like this for four and a half years.'

'You don't need to anymore.'

'As far as I know, he's still out there.' She lifted her face to the clear, starry sky. 'I have to lie to everyone to protect her, and in lying to everyone, I can't really reconnect.'

She shifted her gaze to his. 'What will my friends think when the truth comes out?'

'The ones who matter will understand.' He'd make sure they did, or that they at least kept their opinions to themselves.

'I know that look.' She raised an eyebrow at him. 'You can't make people understand if they don't want to know the truth. There's always someone who'd rather spread juicy gossip.'

'So ignore them and know that those who care about you will be here, no matter what has happened or will happen.'

She shook her head. 'That's easy to say when you don't know all that's happened.'

'Then tell me.' He made the mistake of reaching for her.

She stepped out of reach. 'Not when I don't know if you'll hold me up or let me down.'

'If this is about the kiss, we can talk about it.'

'It's that, and it's what you believed about me before we went to the lookout, what you still believe.' She pressed her lips together. 'I can't trust you yet. I don't know if I ever will, not with all of it, and I need to deal with that.'

'You came to me today, Kelsey.'

'I did, and in my head, it went a lot differently.' She rubbed Pipa's back. 'I was right about one thing, though.'

Hesitant, because nothing positive could put that sadness in her eyes, he swallowed. 'What were you right about?'

'There's only one reason to be here, and that's Pipa. She's all that matters now.'

He could argue and opened his mouth to start, but she shook her head. 'It's all it can be. All I want it to be. I can't keep rehashing the past with the hope of there being a friendship between us. It's just not going to work.'

'You don't think we can be friends?'

'Not like we used to be, no.' Then she turned and threaded through the groups dotted around the yard.

Someone waylaid her before she reached the house, so she sat on the offered seat, her back to him, and answered questions that made her alter the truth in order to protect the young girl she'd claimed as her own.

Without Pipa's weight, his arms were as empty as the hope he'd held, however briefly, that they were forging a new relationship. One that would give them a future full of love, trust, hope and family.

CHAPTER TWELVE

Dodging the floorboard that moaned like a disturbed ghost, Brian made his way down the dark hallway to the lounge room.

He'd tried to sleep, but knowing that Haylee hadn't gone to her room, Rupert's sleeping pattern still backwards, Brian couldn't lie in his soft bed, the fan overhead moving the air over his body, while she sat up looking after a very wide awake baby.

At least, he'd keep telling himself that was the reason for his insomnia. But between cursing his inability to make phone calls and get answers over the weekend and running through his conversation with Jewell, picking it all apart and hoping he got to talk to her like that again, he wasn't getting any sleep. Haylee needed some, though, so instead of tossing and turning in his bed, he'd talk her into going to hers while he entertained Rupert.

Soft light from the kitchen spread to where Haylee lay on the floor, head on a pillow, hand on her son's tiny leg as he wriggled happily in his bouncinette.

Brian didn't move for minutes, just stood and watched his sister sleep. It wasn't something she'd done much of since moving in with him a year ago, five months pregnant and still grieving.

He couldn't fathom why she'd grieved Donny, why she'd shed tears over the man who'd left bruises on her skin and in his son's hearts and minds. Brian couldn't do anything about Donny now, but he could make sure that Bristow and others like him didn't continue to get away with the vile things they did to people.

And if he kept on that train of thought, he'd upset Rupert before he had a chance to prove to Haylee the baby would be safe and happy with him. Sitting on the couch, he let out a quiet breath and turned his mind to Jewell.

A year he'd wasted in trying to keep her at a distance, no more than a work colleague. She'd offered calmness and hope, and until today, he'd refused both. Did it mean more that he'd bent now, on the day he'd reopened Jaiyden's murder case? Or was it just that today he'd felt the cracks more? Either way, she'd offered and he'd taken.

He'd have to tell Haylee. Lying to her even by omission would cause a strain they didn't need.

'What are you thinking?' Haylee didn't move as she stared up at him.

Looking down, he realised he sat hunched over, hands fisted against his knees, scowl clenching his jaw. Not ready to confess just yet, he forced himself to relax, then leaned over and plucked Rupert from his bouncinette.

'His hair still amazes me.' Cradling the baby close, he breathed in the scent of innocence and talcum powder.

'Meaning?' Haylee sat up, knees hugged to her chest.

'You're dark-haired, like me and Dad, so James takes after you. Donny was blond, so Ashley takes after him. But this little guy,' he turned Rupert to face him, 'where the hell did the red hair come from?'

'Are you trying to ask if Donny is the dad?' One eyebrow rose while her lips thinned.

'I'm not asking anything like that, Haylee. Stop reading shit into everything I say.'

Rupert's grin disappeared. A beat later, he sucked his bottom lip into his mouth. Brian bounced the baby on his knee, cooing babble to him until the grin returned.

'You were always good with Jamie when we were younger.'

'I was fifteen, a live-in babysitter.'

He'd resented it at the time. His friends roamed the streets until well after dark, sneaking smokes and drinks from their parents. They'd been cool while he'd sat and watched his four-year-old brother trying to scribble on the walls.

'No, they trusted you with him.' Her gaze fixed on Rupert.

'You were ten, Haylee. They didn't let me anywhere near you when I was that young.'

'I miss them.'

Three words that could never capture the depth of the feeling.

'I know.' Kissing Rupert's head, Brian took a deep breath. 'I have a confession.'

'So now we get to the heart of it.' She gave him a small smile. 'You've been lighter but distracted since you came home.'

'I talked to Jewell today.'

'Jewell?'

'She's an unsworn at work. A civilian,' he added at her blank look.

'There's more to this, isn't there?'

'I honestly don't know. Maybe?' He shook his head. 'I talked to her about you.'

Haylee stilled. 'Me?'

He'd started, so he'd finish and hope he made the right call. 'She's put up with me ignoring her for the last year, but today, I just needed someone to talk to.'

'Okay.' Haylee held up a hand. 'One, you've been ignoring a woman for a year? One who's obviously interested in you? And two, why haven't you been talking to anyone?'

'One, yes, and weirdly, yes, I guess.' Though he frowned. 'And two, because I don't need everyone knowing our business. And it wasn't to complain about you, it was to sort out my thoughts and fears. Jewell listened and gave her brand of advice.'

He frowned again. Jewell knew more than she said, and he didn't like not knowing what she kept to herself.

Haylee picked at a stain on her shirt. 'What advice did she give?'

'To talk to you, and to trust that we'll get through anything because we've got each other.' Trusting himself, he wasn't ready to do yet.

'She sounds like a smart cookie.'

'She is.' More than she'd shown, more than he probably deserved, too. 'She said that sometimes we don't want what has already hurt us, and sometimes we don't actually need it.'

The stain took all Haylee's concentration. 'What did she mean?'

'You really don't know?'

'I don't.' She smoothed down her shirt, then gripped her hands over her knees. 'I'm not ready yet.'

'Ready for what? A relationship? No one expects you to be.'

'No, I'm not ready to face why I don't want a relationship, why I may never want to be with someone.' She frowned. 'Or at least why no one will ever want to be with me.'

Brian shifted Rupert on his knee. 'Haylee, if this is because of Donny …'

'It is, but it's mostly not. It's me, Brian. It's something in me that …' She sucked in a breath. 'I'm not ready. The boys are my priority. Getting them through the next day is all that matters.'

'I hope you know that no matter what it is, you can talk to me.' He picked up the remote and flicked on the TV. 'I hope you also know that you're my priority. Getting you through each day so that you can be there for your boys is all that matters.'

She lifted her gaze to his. 'And who gets you through the day?'

'Honestly?' He leaned forward. 'You. Knowing I come home to a house warmed by the activity of three energetic boys and their mother who loves them.'

She stared at him, tears shimmering in her eyes. Then she blinked, swallowed, and they were gone.

Beyond tired, he flicked through the channels, not confident he'd find anything worth watching at two a.m.

'Get some sleep, Haylee. I can watch Rupert.'

She let her legs relax enough to cross them in front of her as she eyed him, obviously expecting a catch.

'You can trust me, okay?' He met her gaze and waited. Hoped.

'I know I can.' She bit her lip, then sighed. 'Don't let him watch naked women.'

She stood up, bent close and kissed Rupert's red hair. When she moved fractionally and kissed Brian's forehead, he nearly dropped the baby.

Without another word or a backwards glance, she left him sitting there, mouth open, heart hammering. Looking down at Rupert, his mouth opened in a shocked *O* as well, Brian shook his head slowly.

'You saw that too, hey, little man?'

Standing Rupert on his knee again, hands supporting the jiggling baby, Brian smiled. 'Maybe we're getting somewhere after all.'

Rupert babbled and dribbled.

Nodding, Brian wiped the baby's chin. 'Yeah, I know, don't get my hopes up yet.'

Determined not to think too hard about anything, he sat Rupert on his knee, facing the television. 'Let's see what crap is on offer at two a.m.'

CHAPTER THIRTEEN

Exhausted from hours of listening to everyone's stories about the last five years—and from censoring her own—Kelsey escaped inside.

She'd always known Ethan enjoyed social gatherings, and it seemed that hadn't changed. He'd made his way around to everyone, talking and laughing, always only a few steps away from her. Whether he'd meant to or not, he'd given her a safety net of sorts. One that had helped her relax.

Now, on her own in the relative quiet of the empty house, she paced the lounge room, absently patting Pipa's back. She'd been right to tell Ethan they couldn't have a friendship like they'd had before. They couldn't go back to the people they were, and she couldn't trust as freely as she once had.

Besides, she had enough to worry about without constantly reading more into Ethan's actions. She kept telling everyone she'd come home for Pipa, so now she'd make sure Pipa was her only focus.

Outside, someone turned up the music volume, causing her skulking headache to explode into a steady hammer strike. Sinking onto the couch, cradling Pipa against her shoulder, she let her head fall back and closed her eyes. Tomorrow, she'd come up with a plan. One that would keep her on track for giving Pipa the future she imagined. And one that didn't rely on getting the help she'd come home seeking.

As she made mental lists and drifted on the edge of sleep, the music and voices from outside throbbed up the hallway, rising and falling like breath.

And then she stood in a desert where people danced around bonfires that reached the sky, and thick smoke, like a bruise against the clouds, rippled with lightning. She panicked. Where was Pipa?

Terror pushed her through the crowd of people as they talked and laughed, pointing their fingers at the trail of bloody footprints she left.

At the edge of the group, a flock of woolly sheep stopped her, their fangs dripping with blood and poison. Behind them, tall yellow cactus plants grew lambs in fat pods. They wriggled and kicked until the pods burst, splatting them to the ground where they bleated for their mothers.

As one was about to tear its way into the world, Spencer appeared, the rusted knife in his hand slashing out and slicing the pod open. The lamb hit the ground and lay still.

'They're mine.' Spencer grinned wide. 'They're all mine, so I can kill them if I want.' He sliced another pod, again depositing a dead lamb to the dust.

The sheep sank their fangs into her legs as she ran through them to get to Spencer. He vanished as she reached him, his laugh lingering as she tried to pick the rest of the lamb pods before he returned.

Too late, another lamb fell lifeless to the ground, a grinning Spencer standing over it.

'Help me!' She called to where Ethan stood off to the side, his hands punching a steady beat against a primitive drum that echoed like thunder.

'It's not for me to do.' He nodded to a lamb budding on one of the plants, then at Spencer lifting the knife. 'Hurry, or they'll all die.'

Her scream welling from deep within her, she flung herself at Spencer, knocking him to the ground. Then he was on top of her, the musty couch below.

The lambs screamed as she did, the sheep trampling her body as Spencer did. Lights exploded and the sheep caught fire, their fleece flashing red and blue with the flames. The lambs fell silent, then, their tears puddling silver on the ground beneath them.

Spencer stood over her, his face alternating blue and red. 'Now I kill them all.'

Turning, he pulled a dozen knives from his pockets and ran for the lambs dropping to the ground, their tiny bodies wriggling and wet.

Her own body heavy, Kelsey stood, though she had nothing but her hands as weapons. Clenching her fists, she glanced at Ethan again.

'It's for you to stop him.' He shrugged and pointed to Spencer. 'Better hurry.'

As she charged, the beat of the drums was silenced, and Spencer, grinning like the Cheshire cat, faded away.

When the lambs began to yell, demanding the music be started again, Kelsey wrenched her eyes open to the red and blue flashing through the window. It dropped her heart even as her pulse spiked.

They needed to run, to go before Spencer returned and tried to kill Pipa as he had the lambs.

Voices came down the hallway, all jumbled and raised, all male. Holding Pipa close, she forced her feet to move. If she could reach the door, she could disappear into the night and keep Pipa hidden.

All that mattered was keeping Pipa safe and out of Spencer's reach.

'Kelsey?' A hand gripped her shoulder.

Swallowing the scream, she pivoted, yanking free, then headed for the door again. Even as she reached it, reached for it, a hand shot out and pressed against it, trapping her.

'Kelsey, look at me.'

And see his grinning face? Hear the threat in his voice when he demanded the spawn he wanted to kill? No! She'd run far and fast until he gave up looking for them. She'd run forever if she had to. So she spun, the hallway a new escape, and choked on a sob when she saw it blocked with people, all standing and staring at her.

She glanced down at Pipa, still asleep against her breast. Was this the moment she lost? Was this the moment Pipa lost a second mother in her short life? And where was Ethan? He'd promised to look after Pipa. Where was he now that she needed him?

'Where is he?'

'Who?'

She jerked around, not trusting her eyes. 'Ethan?'

'I'm here.' He held his hands out. 'You're safe.'

'He was here.' She glanced around the room, Spencer's laughter still ringing in her ears. 'He was killing the lambs.'

'Look at me, Kelsey.'

Taking a deep breath, the dream still too raw to relax, she shifted Pipa to her shoulder, then met Ethan's gaze.

'It was a dream, I know.' She licked her lips, the taste of that musty couch a memory she couldn't easily forget.

'He's not here.'

'I know.' But she stepped back when Ethan reached for her. 'I know he's not, but the threat of him finding us is still real.'

Mark stood close by and tipped his head at the crowd gathered behind him in the hallway. 'Give me ten minutes to deal with this. Then we'll sit down and talk.'

Kelsey nodded, the red and blue lights flickering around the room making sense as the adrenaline that had fuelled her attempted flight fizzled away and left her shaking. If she hadn't been holding Pipa, she'd sink to the floor and give in to the need to cry and never stop.

'Come and sit down.' Ethan guided her to the couch. 'I'll make you a cup of tea.'

'I don't know if I can drink one.'

'You can try.' He stood a moment. 'You were running again.'

Closing her eyes, the lambs from her dream bright against her lids, she shook her head. 'I've run so many times that when I get scared, whether it's the middle of the night or day, it's now an instinct to head to the nearest door.'

His chest stilled. 'And now?'

She frowned as she met his gaze. 'You're worried I'll disappear while you're in the kitchen?'

'Yes.'

She shook her head again. 'I'm not going to run away, Ethan. Not when I know Pipa is best protected here.'

'And you?' He stepped closer and crouched down in front of her. 'Do you see you're better protected here?'

'You still want to look out for me?'

'Why wouldn't I?'

'So many reasons.' She stared at his chest. 'Pipa isn't mine. Not by birth, anyway.'

'And you think that makes a difference?'

She met his gaze and wished, even though it was hopeless, that she could lean in, have him enfold her and Pipa, and be one with him. Wishes, though, were for the young, and she was no longer the girl who dreamed of sharing a home and family with Ethan. All she wished for and dreamed of now was a semblance of peace for herself and a future for Pipa.

She shrugged. 'It never has for me.'

'It doesn't for me, either.' He pushed to his feet. 'I hope one day your go-to response will be to run to me, not away.'

'I did that once.' She kept her gaze on his shoes. 'I ran to you when I had nowhere else to turn, when I was alone and hurt and scared.' She looked at him, then. 'I don't have the strength to put that trust in you right now. Not when I need it to face the next few days.'

'I hope you can see the difference between now and then, Kelsey. And I hope one day you'll understand that I would have helped you with anything that night. But I couldn't give what you asked.'

'I do.' Except the wound he'd left, the shame she'd carried since then, clouded any path that led towards leaving the past behind and starting fresh. 'The past can't be changed, though. I can only focus on what's happening now, and that's keeping Pipa safe.'

Ethan nodded, his face set. 'Then that's what we'll focus on.'

He left her, the clatter of cups and a kettle boiling coming from the kitchen seconds later.

Kelsey sat in silence, counting the strobing flashes of red and blue through the window until they stopped. The room eerily still and quiet now, she held her breath until Mark let himself in the front door. He kept the silence as he walked to an armchair and sat, his head falling back against the head rest as he closed his eyes.

'You're tired.'

He opened one eye and managed to glare at her. 'I wonder why that would be.'

'I've only been home a day.'

'Exactly.' He sat forward as Ethan brought three mugs in and handed him one. 'And I need to know you aren't going to go bolting again any time soon. Especially when leaving now will only put you and Pipa in more danger.'

'You've found Spencer?' Kelsey gritted her teeth against the need to hide.

'Not yet, which worries me.' He sipped his drink. 'How long since you last saw him?'

'I ... it was ...' She rubbed her forehead. The time for evasion had run out, but she hadn't had the chance to fortify herself against the fallout she knew was coming.

'Can I sit with you?' Ethan waited until she nodded, then sat next to her on the couch, his warmth thawing some of the ice settling in her bones.

'Six months.' She kept her gaze on the mug Ethan sat on the coffee table for her. 'I still don't know how he found us. I was so careful. But he did. He ...'

She sat straighter when Ethan rested his hand on her back. Just a small comfort, but one she didn't deserve. Not from him, anyway.

'He wants me to hand her over.' She met Mark's frown. 'He thinks he can make me just hand her over.' Still unable to comprehend that, she shook her head. 'There's no way I would. Ever. No matter what he does.'

And he'd already done a lot. She had the scars to prove it, though some only *she* could see, feel.

Outside, a car idled past. A truck rumbled down the main street and a dog barked, inviting others to join in and start a chorus.

Carol broke the heavy silence when she walked into the room and sat on Kelsey's other side. 'Everyone's gone home. The clean-up tomorrow is going to suck.' Then she cleared her throat, tapped fingers on her knee. 'Do you want me to go?'

'No.' Kelsey grabbed Carol's hand and held tight. 'Stay, please.'

Mark shifted, drawing her attention. 'I know it's hard, but I need you to tell me as much as you can.'

'I know.' Still, she hesitated.

Beside her, Ethan sat his mug on the floor, then held his arms out for Pipa. 'Why don't you start with Jaiyden?'

'Jaiyden?' Mark pulled a pen and notebook from his vest. 'Jaiyden who?'

She kissed Pipa's forehead before moving her into Ethan's arms, then lifted her chin, took a deep breath and nodded. 'Jaiyden Scott. She's Pipa's mother.'

For a moment, Mark sat and stared.

'I didn't steal her.' She frowned at him. 'Jaiyden wanted to name me guardian as soon as Pipa was born.'

Mark wrote in some sort of shorthand. 'Wanted to?'

That was the sticking point. 'Yes, she told the midwife and the midwife said she'd make note of her wishes, but also that I was too young to be Pipa's guardian because guardians have to be eighteen.'

'They do.' He tipped his head. 'And you were eighteen three years ago.'

'I was.' She shrugged and gripped her mug harder, staring at the milky liquid. 'And I was alone and terrified and desperate enough to call my mother.'

'And?' His voice quiet, Ethan rocked Pipa.

'She said I'd done my dash, that no one cared, and if I came back, you'd all let me know exactly what you thought of me.'

'And you believed her?' Carol's hand went lax in hers.

'At the time, yes.' She shoulder-bumped Carol. 'We'd fallen away from each other those last couple of weeks. You were going through things with your parents.'

Mark huffed and Kelsey shot him a glare. 'And you were off at the academy, so don't you act all high and mighty.'

She sobered again. 'Mum didn't just shun me after Dad died. She took every chance she could to blame me, to make me feel so worthless that I just wanted to leave and never come back.'

She turned to Ethan. 'So, I ran to you. Then, when I dragged myself home heartbroken and ashamed, she told me I deserved it, that my father had known what a slut I was and had died of shame because of it.'

Carol linked their fingers again and squeezed. 'He died of a ruptured aneurysm.'

Kelsey smiled sadly at her friend. 'To her, it was the same thing.'

'I might not have been there then, Kelsey, but I am now, and I have the means to help.' Mark lifted his notebook. 'I just need you to answer a few questions so that I know what I'm up against.'

A few? She almost laughed. 'Okay.'

'You'll answer them?'

'I'll answer everything I can.'

Closing the notebook, Mark picked up his mug, drained it and set it down again. 'I'll make this easier, Kelsey. I'm not interviewing you. I haven't cautioned you. And as I've said, I'm not going to arrest you for telling me the truth.'

'No, but you won't be happy.' Before anyone could ask, she pushed the words out. 'Jaiyden was a prostitute.'

'You think we'd jump to the conclusion you were too?' Mark's voice stayed even, but his eyes hardened. 'You should know us better than that.'

'I thought I did. I thought I could come back here and everything would be all right.' She met Ethan's gaze again. 'I knew you'd be angry, even ready to kick me out, and deep down, I knew I couldn't blame you if you did. But I never thought you'd look at me and see a person who could just fall into bed with someone else. That I could keep a child's existence secret from its father out of spite, or lie to you about my mother.'

'I keep thinking,' Ethan began, 'that if I went back to that night, reacted differently, then you'd have stayed, and we wouldn't be here now. You wouldn't have had to deal with everything that's happened the last five years.'

'No.' She gripped his sleeve. 'I could never think about changing anything. If I did, Pipa wouldn't be mine. Most likely, she would never have been born.' And that, she didn't even want to imagine.

So she took a moment, then faced Mark. 'I found work at a racing stable near Caulfield a week after I arrived in Melbourne. It was only a five-minute walk from the track to where I was staying with a bunch of other stablehands, and I passed Jaiyden nearly every morning. After the first week, we started saying hello, had quick chats about the weather, how stupid some people were. Just stuff.'

She shrugged off the memory and prepared for the next. 'Nearly three months after that first hello, I missed her at the corner where we usually met. I cursed myself for not getting her number or address so that I could contact her, and then I heard her scream. Even at five thirty in the morning, people were around, going to work, coming home. Dealing. No one stopped, or even looked.'

'You did.' Ethan rocked Pipa.

It struck Kelsey that Pipa still slept, held by Ethan, his warmth and protection a soft blanket around her.

'I did.' She swallowed the heat in her throat. 'A man was attacking her. He'd dragged her into an alleyway, but no one cared. He beat and raped her, and no one did anything.'

Staring at the carpet, she could see it all again. 'When I tried to stop him, he threw me across the alley like I was nothing.'

Ethan, Mark and Carol each growled their favourite expletive.

'I wasn't hurt.' She looked at each of them in turn, then held Ethan's gaze. 'I was scared shitless, but not hurt.' Not compared to the other times at least. 'I threw bricks at him, rubbish, anything I could find, because I was terrified he was going to kill her.'

The sickening sound of flesh being pummelled, of Jaiyden's weakening pleas had never left her subconscious.

'When he finally stopped beating her, he told us he'd kill us if we said anything. And I believed him.'

Needing the connection, she reached out and gently ran her hand over Pipa's back. Before she could pull away, Ethan grabbed her hand and held it tight.

Weak enough to give into the need for his touch, his support, she shifted and leaned her shoulder against his. 'I don't know what drug Spencer was on that day, or the others, but it made him almost inhuman.'

'Ice,' Mark said. 'What I've found so far says he was a big dealer just over five years ago. Things started to go south around the time you dealt with him.'

'Why?'

'Sampling his own goods too often, I would think.'

Glad Mark hadn't laughed her off, Kelsey took a deep breath and let it out slowly. 'Do you know why he wants Pipa so badly?'

'No.' Standing, he tucked his notebook and pen away. 'I can take a guess and say the drugs fucked him up, and whatever reason he has is totally valid to no one but him.'

'I just don't understand it.'

'You don't have to.' In two steps, he crouched in front of her and frowned. 'I have one more question for tonight.'

She knew what it would be. 'Where's Jaiyden?'

Mark nodded.

'I thought that would have been your first.'

'Probably should have been, but I needed to know some background.'

'So you knew you wouldn't have to arrest me for kidnapping?' She tried to smile.

The fury still hardened his eyes, but when his fingers touched her face, they were gentle. 'So I knew what motivated you to keep a child in your care, instead of handing her over to the police, child services or her parents.'

'He would have found her.'

'Maybe.'

'No,' she shook her head, 'he would have. I stayed with Jaiyden after that day. She had no one to look after her. When she found out she was pregnant, she said she wanted a better life for her and her baby. Then Spencer turned up about a month later and went at her again when she still refused to sell his drugs.'

Kelsey had shielded Jaiyden with her own body, taking the kicks and punches, praying the baby wouldn't be hurt.

'When she told him she was pregnant, he went so still. He said if she didn't get rid of it, he would. Told her she was his, and she'd do whatever, whoever, he wanted. Told me I was his, too.'

Oily slick nausea slid through her stomach. 'We ran that day and tried to stay hidden. But he'd find us, and we had to run from him three more times before Pipa was even born.' She met Mark's hard stare. 'So, no, not maybe. If I'd handed Pipa over, whoever she ended up with wouldn't have been able to protect her like we did. Like I have.'

'Why not?'

'Because I love her as much as Jaiyden did.'

'So where is Jaiyden?'

'I don't know.'

Dead, her heart and head said.

'She got scared when we were leaving the hospital. She told me to take Pipa and go, to hide, that she'd find us. She wanted him to see her, that she had no baby. Then she'd come back.' Unable to stop the tremors that ran through her body, she curled in on herself. 'She'll come back. She'll find us and come back.'

'Okay, okay.' Mark took the tissues Carol held out and pressed them into Kelsey's free hand. 'That's enough for now.'

'Is it?' Fisting the tissues, she wished she could throw something and have the satisfaction of seeing it shatter the way her heart had done. 'It should have been me to go. Jaiyden should be raising Pipa.'

'No.' Sitting forward, Ethan handed Pipa to a surprised Mark. 'You can sit there and tell me you weren't hurt when some bastard throws you across an alley. You can talk about beatings and rape, leaving out everything else that must have happened at that bastard's hands. But you do not get to talk about swapping places with a woman who disappeared four years ago and expect me not to react.'

Kelsey stared. 'I …'

'*I* need to know you're safe. So does Pipa. You might not care about you, but everyone in this room does.'

Stopping to suck in a deep breath, his jaw jumping, Ethan raised their joined hands.

'I've promised to look after Pipa, though you didn't need to ask. And I could never *not* look after you. So let me do it. Just let me do it for a bit, okay?'

Shifting her gaze from Ethan's to Pipa cradled against Mark's bulky police vest, she shook her head and closed her eyes as tears ran down her cheeks.

'Okay.'

***

Though the sun barely peeked over the trees shading the east of his house, sweat already slipped down Ethan's back. But not all of it could be blamed on the early morning heat. He'd been up since dawn and, while waiting for Mark, had filled the two hours since with cleaning stables, fixing the dripping tap in the garden and cleaning up the tack room to make sure no creepy-crawlies hid where Pipa could find them.

The distant whine of an engine clearly in need of a service had him flicking a glance at the stable clock. Mark was early, but as Ethan had filled time by sweeping the breezeway floor, he didn't mind.

He'd also cleaned Kelsey's old riding gear and sat it out on the rack near the tack room. During the last few years, whenever he'd taken her saddle and boots out to oil them, he remembered the tracks she'd convinced him to ride with her because she thought they'd be fun. Mostly, they'd turned out to be riddled with mud or had ended in a tangle of gorse, so they'd had to spend half the day doubling back.

He regretted ever telling her to shut up so he could hear the wind chatter through the leaves. Knowing it was too late to take back the times he'd told her she laughed too loud, talked too much or annoyed him, he started for the house.

Today, he hoped he could convince her to use the saddle and boots. Maybe then he could begin to show her they could get back to the times where he could make her laugh or squeal and run with just a look.

Tugging his shirt up, he wiped it across his face as he rounded the house in time to see Mark hoist himself out of her car. On another day, he'd have smiled or come up with a sarcastic jibe.

Mark's frown stopped him even trying. 'This thing drives like a tank.'

'Sounds like one too.'

'She deserves better.' He fisted the key a moment, then tossed it at Ethan.

His hand snapped out, caught the flash of silver aimed at his head, then he frowned at Mark. 'I know.'

For a moment, they stayed silent and stared at each other. Ethan planted his feet, slid his hands into his pockets. 'What aren't you telling me?'

'She needs to talk to someone.'

'I know.'

'Then why aren't you doing something about it?'

'I'm not going to push her and have her disappear again. She'll talk to me when she's ready.' He just hoped *he'd* be ready.

'When she does, I know who to contact.' Mark glanced over his shoulder as another car slowed for the turn into Ethan's driveway.

'What else is going on?'

Mark dug the toe of his boot in the dirt. 'I've been there for you since we were kids, Ethan, but right now, I'm so pissed at you, at her, at the whole goddamn thing that I can't think straight.'

Instead of taking the chance to let off some steam with an argument, Ethan tipped his face to the sky. 'We've been there for *each other*, and to tell you the truth'—he looked back at Mark—'I'm just as pissed as you are, if not more.'

'I lost the brat I considered my sister. You lost the girl you figured was your future.' Mark walked towards the waiting car, where Jex was waving from behind the wheel. 'You have a chance to get that part of your life back, but she'll always see me differently now, will always act differently, and that cuts deep.'

Without waiting for a reply, Mark ducked into the car, settled his sunglasses on his nose and nodded to Jex.

Ethan stayed where he was while Jex did a five-point turn in the tree-lined driveway, then kicked up dust on his way out.

Mark was partly right—Kelsey would be different around him now, but they'd all be a bit awkward for a while, wouldn't they? They'd all changed the way they looked at each other since Kelsey's disappearance and would probably change more before they settled into a new way of life now that Kelsey was home. All he could hope was that it drew them all together again.

No. He shook his head—he wouldn't leave it to hope, or luck. He'd do everything he could to make sure he came out of this with Kelsey by his side.

With thoughts focused on how he'd begin, he strode back to the house, then checked himself when the front door opened a crack and Pipa peeked out.

'Morning.' Ethan walked slowly towards her.

'Good morning, Ethan.' She squinted up at him in the bright morning light. 'Mummy still asleep.'

'She's very tired.' He held out his hand. 'Would you like to help me do chores? Then we can have breakfast.'

Still in the shorts and shirt from last night, her feet bare, Pipa held his hand, jumped down the front step and smiled up at him. 'I'm hungry. I like your house.'

He couldn't deny the quick silent *yes*. 'You're always hungry. And wait until you meet the chooks and horses.'

'Do you have a dog?'

'I do. Max. He's old and grumpy.'

'I love dogs.'

'I know.' He smiled down at her and some of the bubbling disquiet eased when Pipa grinned back. 'Have you fed chickens before?'

'I feeded them at Mummy's work. They lay eggs. I like eggs.' She skipped beside him, making chicken noises.

'I guess you know how cows sound as well.'

'They go moo. And they fart.' She covered her mouth and chuckled. 'One pooped on Mummy's head and it was yucky, but Mummy said the poo was nice and warm, and she tried to chase me 'cos I laughed at her, but I too fast and she not catch me.'

'Your mum has chased me a few times, too.'

'With cow poo on her head?'

Ethan laughed. 'No, but with a mouse in her hands and thunder in her heart.'

'Thunder is in the sky. It's clouds playing smash-ups.'

He froze, one hand on the gate of the chicken pen and looked down at Pipa. 'Did your mum tell you that?'

'Uh-huh.' Pipa nodded. 'She said you told her, and you be right, so I not be scared.'

'I'm glad.' For things he couldn't even say.

'Let's feed the chickens and see if they have any eggs we can cook for breakfast.'

'I make Mummy bekfast sometimes.'

'Do you?'

'Yes, I cook her toast.'

His heart melted. 'I bet she loves it.'

Pipa grinned and his heart rolled over. Kelsey might think no one could or would look after and love Pipa like she did, but she was wrong. He'd do anything, be anything, sacrifice everything, to keep Pipa grinning up at him. He'd do it all for her—and for Kelsey.

As they fed the chooks, let Max off his chain and picked some flowers that had so far survived the summer, Ethan tried to concentrate on Pipa's excited questions.

Only once or twice did he find himself thinking about Kelsey sleeping soundly in his bed and wondering what he could do to ensure his future consisted of more of the same.

CHAPTER FOURTEEN

Saturday

Brian adjusted the shade mesh guarding the boys from the sun as they splashed in the shallow pool. His backyard wasn't big, but it fit a clam shell sandpit, a barbeque, some chairs and the inflatable pool. Enough for the boys to have fun, squealing while they pelted each other with water and toys—or sand and toys, depending on which battlefield they sat in.

This morning, though, Haylee sat with them and kept them under control, bouncing Rupert on her knee as he giggled at his brothers. It was different to how things had been last weekend when Brian had watched them for five minutes while Haylee ducked inside to change Rupert's nappy. They'd all frozen when the back door had slammed open and Haylee stepped back outside. Brian, in jeans and socks, had been standing ankle-deep in water with James tucked upside down under one arm. Ashley had been lying on his back in the water, legs trying to deflect Brian's hands from grabbing him as well.

'They splashed me,' Brian had said by way of explanation.

Haylee had rolled her eyes, muttering something about raising four boys, then ignored him while he tried to get the boys back every time she wasn't looking. He'd gone inside that night soaked and exhausted, wondering how the hell Haylee did it, day in, day out, with three of them.

Four, really. He bit back a smile, turning in time to see James freeze, water leaking through his fingers before he could launch it at Brian's back. Now Brian let the smile show, though it was more a baring of teeth.

James tried to copy, looking more like a slobbery puppy, then choked on a squeal as Brian stepped into the pool, this time in shorts and bare feet. Gritting his teeth, he lowered himself into the four inches of water, though he wasn't sure he liked the feeling of his testicles floating inside his suddenly too loose shorts.

Maybe he should put more water in the pool. Or change his shorts.

'Cold?' Haylee watched him, a not-quite smile on her lips.

'It's—' He cleared his throat, deepened his voice. 'It's fine.'

The boys grinned at each other, then began skidding back and forth in the water, making it slosh from one side of the pool to the other.

Brian glared at them, but their grins grew bigger. Rupert giggled.

Brian slid his hand below the water, made a loose fist, then clenched it, water squirting to smack James in the chest.

Haylee flicked him a look, then stood up, letting the water drain down her legs before stepping from the pool and taking Rupert with her.

Then it was on.

James jumped up and plastered his thin, wet body against Brian's chest while Ashley did the same to his back. Sandwiched between them, water dribbling down his spine to the small of his back, he tried to pull Ashley over his shoulder. Skin slippery, Ashley dodged, his giggles high-pitched, almost frantic, as he dashed away, only to come back and launch himself at Brian again. Catching Ashley to his chest, Brian pulled James into a bear hug, tickling them both as much as he could with hands full of slippery skin and wriggling bodies.

A powerful stream of water hit Brian between the shoulder blades, smacking the breath from his lungs. James and Ashley stilled in his arms when the water flowed over his shoulders and spilled onto them.

As one, they turned and looked at Haylee as she stood glaring at them, an empty bucket hanging from one hand, her other arm secured around Rupert as she balanced him on her hip.

'You know,' Brian let the boys go and stood slowly, 'one day, Rupert will be too big for you to hide behind.'

'One day,' she agreed, jutting her chin. 'For now, though, he and I are a team. Besides, one of us has to be the grown-up.'

'We were just having fun.'

'Yes, well, I've seen what your *fun* can turn into.' She set the bucket down, then nodded to the barbeque where a plate of fruit and a bowl of cold chicken and salad sat waiting for hungry mouths.

'Snacks!' James jumped out of the pool and headed for the food.

'Wash your hands.' Haylee caught Ashley and turned him towards the house before he followed his brother. 'Now,' she said to James, who reached out for a piece of chicken.

'They're already washed.' He held up his still-wet hands.

'In water your bum has been in.' Haylee raised her eyebrows.

James shrugged. 'I have undies on.'

Brian hid a smile. 'They *are* boys.'

'I know, and boys can get into as much trouble as they want because they have a penis.'

Ashley covered his mouth, the giggle slipping between his fingers.

Brian straightened and looked down at Haylee. 'You think I've got away with things because I'm a boy, and you haven't because you're a girl?'

'It's how it goes.' She turned away from him, prodding Ashley towards the house and throwing a frown over her shoulder at James.

Brian stayed where he was. Haylee wouldn't say more in front of the boys, anyway, and fighting now would only undo the small wins he'd had lately.

At least Haylee seemed more relaxed around him now. She'd been angry as she'd struggled through puberty and young adulthood, with him trying to be mother, father *and* brother. He'd failed on all fronts despite joining the police force at eighteen so that he'd have a steady job and an income to look after her. He'd kept her clothed and fed and got her through school.

Then, she'd seemed to hit a wall. No job he'd suggested piqued her interest. No amount of begging got her out of her room except when she emerged at night dressed only in black and went out with black eyes, black lips, black fingernails. If she'd been trying to steal something, she would have succeeded in not being seen. Too late, he'd realised his sweet sister had fallen in with the wrong crowd, and worse, she'd found the wrong guy to hook up with.

When money they couldn't spare had started disappearing, he'd given her an ultimatum—and lost her. It had taken him just three years to fuck things up so badly that he'd had to sell their childhood home and keep tabs on Haylee through work, losing everything that had ever mattered.

When Haylee had knocked on his door, her belly swollen with Rupert, arms hugging James and Ashley, terrified, to her hips, Brian had nearly closed the door and reopened it just to be sure he wasn't hallucinating. Instead, he'd opened it wide, had brought them in and fed them while Haylee struggled to get through each day. Slowly, they'd gotten used to him, and no longer jumped every time he took a step towards them.

'You okay?' Haylee touched his arm, her fingers light against the bunched muscle.

'It's never had anything to do with you being a girl.' He stared down at her. 'It's about you being my baby sister, and me failing you.'

'You failing me?' She laughed without humour. 'Because *you're* the one who lost the plot when our parents died. Brian, I rejected everything you ever did for me, stormed out without a word, got pregnant to a drugged loser, stayed with him because it was easier, then landed on your doorstep because anywhere else I went would have seen us dead in a week. You haven't said *I told you so* once, haven't pointed the finger or laid a guilt trip on me. Nothing.'

She shook her head. 'Yeah, *you* failed *me* big time.'

'I haven't been a saint either, Haylee.'

'Yeah, well, I still win.'

'Do you want to?'

She dropped her chin to her chest. 'I don't know. I'm just so confuzzled.'

Brian couldn't help laughing. 'James or Ashley?'

'James. He can't get confused right.' She kept her gaze on the ground.

119

It burned his heart and lungs, shortened his breath. 'What do you want me to do, Haylee?'

'Tell me I'm an awful person, that I've stuffed everything up, that you're ashamed of me. That you were right.'

'Okay.' He glanced to where Ashley and James sat on the grass, Rupert on his stomach between them, watching as they ate the cold meat and flicked lettuce at each other.

'I'm right, Haylee, always have been. I'm right to be ashamed about the woman before me having so little self-worth. That the only thing you have stuffed up is a few moments in your life.' He raised his hands slowly and rested them lightly on her shoulders.

'I'm right in saying you are an awful person if you think that raising those three boys the way you have hasn't been enough.'

Shifting his hand to put a finger under her chin, he tilted her face up, forcing her to look at him. Wiping the tears from her cheek, he swallowed. 'You are a great mother, Haylee. The best sister anyone could ask for. And Mum *would* be proud of you, no matter what you think. Because I know *I'm* damn proud of you.'

Haylee hiccupped, then fell against him, her arms winding tight around his neck. Brian held her close, her ribs shuddering as she tried to hold everything back.

'Let it go.' He stroked her spine, cupped her head as she finally gave in, let out the soul-wrenching sobs she'd been holding back for six months. Hell, probably for thirteen years since their mother, father and seven-year-old brother had been killed.

'Mummy?' James tugged at Haylee's shirt.

Brian let her go, expecting her to step back and put a leash on her emotions. Instead, she picked James up, hugged him and kissed his cheek, all with tears streaming down her face.

'I love you, James.'

Taking him to where his brothers watched them, she sat down, pulled Ashley onto her lap and picked up Rupert. 'And I love you, Ashley. And you, Rupert.'

She kissed each of their cheeks, then looked up at Brian. 'And I love you, too.' Reaching out, she pulled him down beside her, leaned over and kissed his cheek.

'I love you too.' He kissed her forehead, then grabbed James around the waist, threw him over his shoulder and tickled him. Ashley laughed at his brother's legs kicking in the air.

It gave Brian hope when Haylee grabbed her middle son and tickled him until he was a blubbering mess on her lap. They'd turned a corner, and though they still had a long way to go and secrets that needed telling, he could be content that she'd opened the door wider and let him step through.

So they'd take the weekend to play, talk and strengthen the bonds they'd started to forge. Monday would come soon enough, and when it did, he'd work on bringing a shitstorm down on Bristow.

CHAPTER FIFTEEN

A squeal woke Kelsey from murky sleep.

The bedroom door stood open and Pipa's voice carried down the short hallway. A deeper rumble followed, and instinct had Kelsey sitting up, ready to run, gather, go.

Before panic took over, she stopped and heard Pipa laugh. Judging from the direction the voices were coming from and the clanging sound of metal against metal, Kelsey assumed Pipa helped Ethan in the kitchen.

Kelsey could march out there and demand Ethan keep his distance, lay down some new rules. But, how could she ruin the growing relationship between Ethan and Pipa when he was giving her exactly what she needed. Things Kelsey had tried so hard to give her, but had failed in so many ways.

Sitting and regretting everything she'd done wrong—or remembering last night—would only darken her already black mood, so she swung her legs over the side of the bed. She'd try not to think about it being Ethan's bed, either. She couldn't let the memories of last time smother her.

Instead, the steady beat against her temple alerted her to the checklist of pains and aches throughout her body. Trying to run her fingers through her hair, she winced when matted knots caught and tugged her scalp, and as she rubbed her eyes, sleep gritted against her knuckles.

A shower would help. Maybe once she felt half-human, she'd be able to walk out and see Pipa and Ethan playing happy families without wanting to break down again. Or scream.

As the shower filled the ensuite bathroom with steam and scalded her skin, she washed tangles from her hair and sweaty grime from her body. It helped lift the fog of fatigue from her mind.

Ethan, as always, was right. To be back here was to be safe. She'd always imagined that feeling happy and at home would come with it, but if Pipa felt all three, Kelsey could live with just feeling safe.

They'd have to get a place of their own soon. And as much as it would break her heart to see him every day, it would have to be close to Ethan so that Pipa could grow up knowing a good man watched out for her.

Shutting off the shower, she pulled her hair over her shoulder, but as she squeezed the water out, she realised that if she kept lying to herself, it would only make things harder. She didn't want to feel just safe or at home or happy. She wanted to feel it all at once.

And she wanted Ethan.

But the mirror showed her exactly why she could never have him. The scars that marked each encounter with Spencer reminded her of those that didn't show, the ones that only she knew existed. They would throw up a barrier between them because she had no way to prove that the innocence she'd offered and kept for him had been stolen against her will. If she told him and he hesitated in believing her, even for just a breath, it would kill any hope she had left that there could be anything, even friendship, between them.

As much as she kept saying she hadn't come back for it, her mind kept turning back to it—the possibility of a relationship with Ethan. But what happened last night didn't matter. Nothing *would* happen because he didn't want her.

Expecting pain to flash and burn, she frowned at her reflection when only a vast emptiness settled cold in her heart. Turning away from the mirror, she grabbed a towel and blanked her mind of anything other than the next step—dry hair, arms, body, legs.

Done, she opened the door and stopped. Her clothes lay in a sweaty, dusty heap on the floor where she'd dropped them last night. Their bags still sat in the boot of her car, and her car was still at Carol's.

Clutching the towel to her breasts, she eyed the door. Walking out virtually naked would only prove to Ethan that she had an ulterior motive for being here. Besides, she couldn't afford to let him see how kissing him made her want to do it again.

There had to be something wrong with her, didn't there? Something dark in her that made her keep wanting him, even after he'd rejected her twice.

Blowing out a sharp breath, she glared at his dresser. She'd borrowed shirts from Ethan countless times before, but this time she hesitated before pulling a t-shirt from his drawer. She slipped it over her head, then pulled out a pair of boxers from another drawer.

Heat rushed to her cheeks. Between the towel and his clothes, she had no real choice. So she pulled the boxers on and tugged at them in an attempt to make them cover more.

Running a hand through still-damp hair, she marched out the door but slowed as she walked down the hallway, past the two bedrooms Ethan's parents had hoped to fill but hadn't been able to. One had been turned into a study when Ethan was a boy. The other, his old room, she'd often used once he'd moved into the master bedroom.

It had been the perfect place for her to escape punishment for whatever sin she'd committed in her mother's eyes, or to dream of the time when this house would be as much hers as Ethan's. Or how they'd fill the rooms with love, laughter, babies and everything Kelsey had missed out on with her own mother.

Moving past the memories before they took hold and woke the pain, she stopped at the glass sliding doors flanked by floor-to-ceiling windows. The view out over the patio and into the garden hadn't changed. Things had grown, of course. Like the wisteria covering the metal arch. A month before Kelsey had left, she'd helped Ethan paint the arch, then they'd planted the foot-high climber. The day had ended with both of them wearing a layer of Brunswick Green and a sense of achievement that even her mother's wrath hadn't been able to dull.

Kelsey noticed that Ethan had kept her flower garden, had weeded it and filled it with the riot of colour he'd grimaced at when she'd first planted it. Did he know what that meant to her? Could he know that one gesture, conscious or not, pulled at her heart the most?

Rubbing her arms, she turned for the lounge room and stopped again. The hallway opened up into the open-plan living and dining area she'd always loved. A welcoming space with an open fireplace set between two huge windows, its grey stone chimney regal against the red brick of the house that had always felt like home.

On the mantle sat photos of Ethan and his parents, trophies and statues of horses. All the things that were as much a part of the house as the foundations. A huge framed picture of Ethan's father, sitting astride his horse while mustering in the high country, Ethan looking so much like him now, hung on the expanse of the chimney. A scattering of smaller pictures hung around it, telling the story of the Ryder family growing from two young singles into a brilliantly happy couple and then a family of three.

Without a photo wall featuring her own family, Kelsey had loved studying the pictures of Ethan growing up. She'd known him for most of his life, but the pictures added to his story. They showed the love of his parents, for their son and each other, and made the tears aching in her throat want to break free.

Sitting among all that love and those memories was a photo in a handmade frame that Kelsey thought Ethan would have thrown out five years ago. Three burnt fingers and a singed fringe had been her payment for decorating the small wooden frame. At twelve years old, she hadn't stopped to think of a better way to burn the pattern into the wood. She'd just borrowed her dad's pliers, a nail, and a candle from her mother. Heating the nail in the flame every few seconds had taken time and concentration. The swirls and dots she'd thought would be easy had been frustrating and stilted. Even so, she'd been proud of her unique gift for Ethan's birthday. Now, seeing her young, innocent face grinning back at her in the childish frame made her want to grab it and hide it away or burn it.

How had she been so oblivious, so blinded by her own feelings to not see the truth?

'Mummy, we made bekfast. Come sit. Ethan says Max is old and grumpy, but he loves me. Look.' Pipa grabbed Max's collar and dragged him out from where he'd sprawled under the dining table. 'Max, sit.'

Max sat but glared at Kelsey.

'Max, down.'

Max flopped, rolled on his side and went back to sleep.

'He loves you all right.'

Before Pipa could pull Max up for another demonstration, Kelsey squatted down and opened her arms. The ache in her head and stomach eased when Pipa ran up, wrapped her arms around Kelsey's neck and held tight.

A spatula in one hand, frying pan in the other, Ethan glanced at them as he dished omelette onto the plates set on the table. 'Sleep well?'

'Yes, thanks.' Better than she had in five years. Heat rose up her throat to spill into her cheeks. Dreaming of him, she'd keep to herself. One more secret to hold wouldn't matter when others were deeper, darker.

'I did too.' Pipa rocked them both. 'Ethan's bed is soft and snuggly. And it has good dreams. Did you have good dreams? You didn't wake up when I did, so I found Ethan and we fed the chooks and let Max off and he peed on the flower I was going to pick, so we picked the other ones 'cos you don't want dog pee smell while you're eating, do you, Mummy?'

'No, you don't.' Rubbing Pipa's back while holding Ethan's gaze, she swallowed. 'You need to take a breath when you talk, sweet, or you'll pass out.'

'Ethan said that too.' Pipa gave one last squeeze, then stepped back and grabbed Kelsey's hand. 'We made mucky eggs from Ethan's chooks. I broked the eggs and stirred them, but Ethan cooked them 'cos he's bigger.'

'Mucky eggs?' She helped Pipa onto her chair, then sat next to her.

Ethan sat a plate stacked high with toast in the middle of the table and took the seat opposite Kelsey. 'Pipa doesn't think my eggs look much like omelettes.'

'They look mucky.' Pipa picked up her fork, loaded it with egg and managed to get most of it into her mouth.

While the food kept Pipa quiet for a while, Kelsey chanced a glance at Ethan. He concentrated on his food with a single-mindedness that left no room for anything other than the most basic of acknowledgements.

With her appetite gone, she pushed the eggs around her plate.

'You don't like them?' Ethan moved his empty plate to the side and reached for another piece of toast.

She lifted her fork and saluted him. 'They're mucky, what's not to like?'

But as she ate, all she tasted was sorrow and heartache.

***

Ethan kept his mind on his plate for as long as he could, but the sight of Kelsey—barefoot with one of his shirts hanging to the tops of her thighs and his boxers only just clinging to her hips—commanded his attention.

Keeping his hands busy with toast he didn't want, he glanced at her. 'I miss your hair.'

She frowned, a forkful of eggs halfway to her mouth. Finishing the move, she chewed slowly, the pattern on her plate apparently fascinating.

'I like Mummy's hair when it's orange.' Pipa reached out and played with the still-damp ends that curled over her shoulder to her waist.

Ethan wished he could do the same.

Pushing her plate in front of Pipa, Kelsey rubbed her hands on her thighs. 'The red stands out too much.'

'Is that a problem now?'

Her hesitation was a knife to his heart. 'I guess not.'

'Don't guess.' The resolve to keep his distance nearly crumbled, so he slid Pipa's empty plate over, stacked it on top of his and rose. 'Have anything planned for today?'

'Horsies!' Pipa clapped, sending the egg on her fork across the table and onto the floor.

Max opened an eye. The dog would wait obediently, and most likely flood the floor with his drool, so Ethan pointed. 'Clean it up, boy.'

Struggling, Max sat up and eyed Pipa, still in her seat and grinning at him.

'Clean it up, Max.' She scooped another forkful.

'No, Pip.' Kelsey tapped the plate. 'Either you eat it, or you give your plate to Ethan.'

'But Max is hungry.' Pipa pouted but sat back in her chair and put the egg in her mouth.

'I'm betting he's already had his breakfast.' Kelsey tilted her head when Pipa said nothing.

Fascinated, Ethan stood, holding forgotten plates, and drank in Kelsey in full mother mode.

'Has he had his breakfast, Pip?'

'He could have more.'

'So, he *has* had his breakfast.'

Pipa's pout turned stubborn. 'But he could be hungry.'

'Dogs aren't like kids. They don't need to eat every five minutes.' Reaching out, she tucked a curl behind Pipa's ear. 'If you feed a dog too much, they get sick. You don't want to make Max sick, do you?'

'No.' Pipa glanced at Max staring up at her, then at Kelsey. 'Would he die?'

'If you feed him the wrong thing, he could.' She shifted in her seat and turned Pipa to face her. 'Will you promise me to do your best to look after Max?' She held up a finger before Pipa could speak. 'That means helping Ethan feed him, making sure he has water, making sure he doesn't eat things unless he's told, and cleaning up after him.'

'And pat him and brush him?'

'That too. But you have to have me or Ethan with you, okay?'

'Okay, Mummy.' Her gaze slid to Max again.

The drooling had started.

'When we get a puppy, I can look after it, too.'

Absently sitting the plates on the breakfast bar, Ethan grabbed some paper towel. 'You can learn with Max so that you know how to look after a puppy.'

'I do it.' Pipa put her hand out for the paper towel as Ethan went to squat down next to Max.

He glanced at Kelsey. At her nod, he handed Pipa the paper. Standing with his hand on the back of Kelsey's chair, his knuckles brushing her shoulder blade, they watched Pipa wipe the puddle off the floor, then dab at Max's muzzle.

'Why he leaking?'

Smothering the laugh, Ethan cleared his throat. 'He's drooling.'

'I can drool.' She opened her mouth.

'No.' Kelsey put her hand over it before Pipa could show them. 'No drooling in the house.' Removing her hand, she wiped a stray speck of egg from Pipa's chin. 'How about we get cleaned up, get dressed, then we can have a look at the horses.'

'We lookeded at them. Ethan said I can ride if you let me. Will you let me? I be good. I won't scream or run or fall off.' She clasped her hands under her chin.

Ethan didn't know how Kelsey held up against the onslaught. Practise, most likely.

It hit him hard and fast. The need, the *right* to practise being a good father. He wanted it with Pipa and Kelsey, and any babies they would have together. He imagined spreading his hands over her belly, feeling life move inside it. Then he imagined sliding his hands over her skin, his mouth following.

'Ethan?' Kelsey stood, putting herself between him and Pipa. 'If you don't want to, just say so.'

'Want to what?' He'd missed something while his brain had been in fantasy mode.

Something hardened in Kelsey's glare.

'Sorry, I wasn't listening. I was thinking about something else.'

The hard edge left her eyes, and for a moment, everything showed. The pain, the helplessness, the shame.

'Yeah, I can figure where it went.' She turned away and lifted Pipa. 'We'll get out of your way.'

He grabbed her arm, held it even when they both stilled. 'Am I hurting you?'

'My arm, no.'

'Are you scared of me, Pipa?'

Those dark blue eyes met her mother's.

'You can tell the truth, Pip.'

Focusing on his hand, then his face, Pipa shook her head. 'No. I not scared. But you hurt Mummy.'

'I'm not hurting her.'

'She cries when her heart hurts.' She touched a hand to Kelsey's cheek. 'You make her cry.'

He eased his grip but didn't let go. 'I don't want to hurt you, or your heart.'

'I don't think we can help it.' One side of her mouth lifted, but her eyes stayed sad. 'I keep making the same mistakes, but I won't anymore.'

'The only mistake has been in the timing.' He ran his hand up her arm, then back down to her wrist, but before he could catch her hand, she moved away.

'It always will be.' Leaning over so that Pipa could collect the plates from the bench, she walked to the sink. 'I need to see my mother.'

'I can come with you.'

'I'd rather go alone.' She glanced at Pipa.

Understanding, he nodded. 'Then I'd love it if Pipa could stay here, help me with the horses.' And at least he knew Kelsey would come back.

'I don't know how long I'll be.'

'Take as much time as you need.'

She smiled without humour. 'I won't need much.'

Then, she looked down at herself and frowned. 'I forgot. I need to get my car. Our clothes are in the boot.'

'Mark dropped it off. I can grab your bags if you tell me which have the clothes.' At her blank stare, he frowned. 'Kelsey?'

'They both have clothes.'

'Then I'll bring both in.' He slid the key from his pocket. 'Anything else you need?'

Kelsey shook her head, her cheeks flaming.

'What is it?' He wanted to touch her again, wanted to hold her. Instead, he started for the front door, but stopped with his hand on the knob as he looked back at her.

'Nothing.' She walked to the table to gather the rest of the dishes, Pipa at her side, ready to help.

Stepping out into the heat, he pulled the door closed and jogged over to her car. Before he grabbed anything from the boot, he wound her window down to let the stifling heat out.

Opening the boot, he stared. Two gym bags. That's all she had? All she owned? Clothes in just two gym bags. Neither of them weighed a great deal, either. Slinging one over his shoulder, he slammed the boot closed.

The kitchen stood clean and empty when he got back, the dining table wiped down and the chairs pushed in. For five years, he'd walked into a quiet, soulless house, no longer the home it had been whenever she'd stayed with him before. She'd filled it with life and heat but had taken that with her when she'd left. He could feel the beginnings of it again now, the lightness in the air, the edge of something more.

Pipa's giggle from the bathroom arrowed straight to his heart. He walked past, peeking in to see Pipa dancing in the bathtub while Kelsey tried to wipe as much skin as she could with a soapy face washer.

He deliberately dropped their bags on his bed, then went back down the hall and knocked on the bathroom door.

Pipa grinned at him. 'I like your bath, Ethan.'

Kelsey kept her back to him as she rinsed the face washer under the tap.

'I'm glad.' He grinned back.

131

Pipa lifted a sudsy arm to her poked-out tongue.

'Don't eat the soap, Pip.' Kelsey grabbed Pipa's arm and wiped it clean. 'Ask Ethan if you can borrow a towel.'

'Can I please borrow a towel, Ethan?'

'Sure you can.' He stepped into the bathroom, chose a purple towel from the cupboard and handed it to Pipa. 'There you go.'

'Thank you, Ethan.'

'You're welcome, Pip.'

Lifting an eyebrow at him, Kelsey began drying Pipa. 'You got the bags okay?'

This was the Kelsey he wanted to see. The one who viewed sarcasm as a second language, and who would give as good as she got.

'I managed.'

Wrapping Pipa in the towel, Kelsey lifted her out of the tub. 'We'll get changed then.' She walked past him and turned for the bedrooms.

When she stopped at the spare room, he held a hand up. 'They're in my room.'

Kelsey turned slowly towards him. 'What?'

'I put them in my room.'

'We aren't staying in your room again.'

'Where we sleep?' Snuggled in the towel, Pipa looked from Ethan to Kelsey. 'We sleep in the car?'

'Not this time, Pip.' Frowning, Kelsey headed further up the hallway to his room. 'Ethan has a spare room we can use.'

Spare for now, at least. He'd work on changing that once Kelsey stopped seeing him as the enemy.

'Can Max sleep with me?' She reached for the dog over Kelsey's shoulder, her fingers wiggling as though she could touch him when he followed them into Ethan's room.

'He snores.' Kelsey dumped Pipa on the bed.

Giggling, Pipa stood up and bounced. 'Like me?' She imitated a loud snorting snore.

Ethan covered the laugh with a cough.

'Worse.' Kelsey spared him a glare as she rummaged through one of the bags, pulled out pink shorts and threw them to Pipa. 'Stop bouncing on the bed, Pip.'

'Why?'

'Because you'll bounce all the good dreams out of it.' She held up two shirts, one red with the Cookie Monster *nom-nomming* on the front, the other blue with a rainbow pony. 'Which one?'

'Rainbow pony.' She glanced at Kelsey. 'Please.'

'Okay, get dressed.' She gave the shirt and a pair of undies to Pipa, then looked from Ethan to the door with a raised brow as she pulled some clothes from the other bag.

He ignored Kelsey's silent request for him to leave the room. If he couldn't have them both safe and comfortable in his bed, he could at least let Kelsey have it. He'd happily sleep on the couch until she trusted him again.

'You'll be able to see the stables from your room, too, Pip.' He pointed at the view from his window. 'Better than you can from here.'

'I have Max and the horsies, Mummy.' Pipa bounced once. 'I be a big girl now. I sleep on my own.'

It took him a moment to realise what he'd forced Kelsey to lose. That closeness she'd shared with Pipa for four years had been yanked out from under her. Because she wouldn't protest Pipa's independence, wouldn't stifle her newfound confidence in herself and her surroundings. No matter how much it hurt to let Pipa grow up, Kelsey would do it.

'I'm so proud of you.' She bent and kissed Pipa's cheek. 'You can put your bag in there as soon as you're dressed.'

He hadn't thought it would be possible, but Ethan loved her more in that moment.

To stop himself from telling her and pushing her further away, he turned for the door. 'I'll be out at the stables.'

'Before you go, Ethan.' Kelsey handed Pipa her bag and waited until Max had followed her from the room before turning on him. 'That was underhanded and mean. You don't get to make those decisions.'

'Pipa made the decision, but yes, I'd hoped for this outcome. I'm sorry. I didn't appreciate the full consequences until now.'

'So just what were you hoping for then? That I'd fall into bed with you?'

He shoved a hand through his hair. 'That you'd be comfortable and safe in my bed, whether I was in it with you or not.'

Her shoulders sagged as she stared at him. 'There was a better way to do it, but it's done now. Pipa is happy and that's all that matters.' She turned her back to him and picked up her shirt. 'I need to get changed and go.'

Pipa's happiness, though, wasn't all that mattered to him. Whether she liked it or not, Kelsey's life, future and happiness mattered as well. They'd talk about it soon. Once she said whatever she needed to say to Morna, they'd say what needed to be said to each other.

And he wouldn't stop talking until she believed him.

CHAPTER SIXTEEN

With the boys asleep on the couch tangled together like puppies and Haylee in her room taking a nap with Rupert, Brian was left alone watching muted re-runs of *M*A*S*H*.

The house felt settled, quiet. He'd come to treasure these moments; though others shared his space, he could still let his mind sort through what came next at work, in his life.

Jewell stood in line behind Bristow. Tired of pushing thoughts of her away, he let them play, but stopped before she settled in. Jaiyden took her place, staring at him as blood ran from her nose, the bruise on her cheek purpling as he watched. When she turned and walked away, he followed. Standing over the shallow grave, her body wrapped in a tarp, her hands missing, he clenched his fists.

'Find my baby.' Jaiyden stood beside him, staring at her corpse.

'I'm trying.'

'Try harder.' She stepped into the grave, lay down, and covered herself with earth and grass.

Waking with a jolt, Brian ran a hand down his face. Easing off the couch, he made sure not to wake the two whirlwinds still curled together.

In the kitchen, he filled the kettle, flipped the switch and stood staring absently at it while it made noises about having to boil.

Fingers itchy, he grabbed a pink felt-tipped marker and a crumpled piece of paper that had escaped the boys' scribbles. Writing Jaiyden's name on the top left of the page, he filled in the dates he knew from memory—when he'd run into Jaiyden that last morning, when she'd had the baby forty weeks later, and when she'd been found two weeks after that.

He wrote Bristow's name on the right and filled in the flimsy alibi he'd given about selling balloons for Valentine's week, and the dates, times and places he'd been caught selling drugs or dishing out his brand of punishment to those that crossed him.

Frustrated, Brian drew a tree and scribbled pink apples beneath it. He named them Spencer Bristow, Push—his right-hand man—and Henry Bristow. He labelled the branches with *Jaiyden, Kel, baby*. Again, he added Jaiyden's information. Under the other two names, he could only put question marks. He frowned at them, crossed them out, and wrote a description of Kel, and that the baby would now be four years old. It didn't help his case, but at least it was something.

Haylee walked in and yawned. 'Kettle's boiled.'

She went to the kettle and pulled two cups from the cupboard. Heaping sugar in one, she poured steaming water in both, dunked the tea bag in hers twice and let the other one steep. Taking the milk from the fridge, she glanced at the piece of paper he'd flipped over, then stopped and frowned.

'Bristow? As in Spencer?'

Of course, the pink marker showed through the back. About to roll his eyes, he stopped.

'Wait, what? What do you know about him?'

Clutching the milk carton to her chest, she stared at him. 'Bristow is bad.'

'I know.' He stood and raised a hand to comfort her but stopped when she flinched. 'Haylee?'

'I know him, okay. Donny did deals with him. He's …' She licked her lips, then bit the bottom one. 'He's bad. Crazy. He's not someone I want to think about right now.'

She sloshed milk in their cups, sat the carton on the bench and bowed her head. 'He gave Donny the drugs that killed him.'

'Hales.'

'Don't. I know you think I grieved him, and part of me did. I have the boys because of Donny and I can never regret that.' She lifted her chin and met his gaze. 'But I can regret and be ashamed that I've often thanked Spencer in my prayers. Because of him, the boys have a chance at a normal, happy life. James will never forget. He was old enough to have it impact him. But I know that what you've done with him, for him, will mould the man he'll become. The men they'll all become because they have you to look up to.'

Humbled, touched, Brian opened his arms and sighed when she walked into them.

'No one would hold those prayers against you.' He kissed the top of her head. 'And the boys have you to look up to, always have. You're the reason they'll come out of this with hearts full of love, minds full of wonder.'

'I guess they're pretty lucky kids to have us both then.'

'One day, Haylee, you'll find someone—'

'No.' She stepped back, ran her palms over her cheeks. 'It's not for me. I've got the boys and you. That's enough.'

Grabbing her drink, she headed for the door. Stopped. 'Would it help if I wrote down the times I knew where he was? Who he was with?'

'Donny?' He frowned.

'No.' Haylee rolled her eyes. 'Spencer.'

'Oh.' He shook his head. 'Not if it's going to upset you.'

'It runs around in my head whether I want it to or not.' She shrugged. 'Maybe getting it out will purge some of it.'

'Okay.' He waited until she'd turned away. 'You're one of the bravest people I know, Haylee. Even if you weren't my sister, I'd still love and admire that about you.'

Her step faltered when she walked away, leaving him in the quiet before the storm that the boys would surely bring when they woke.

Sitting at the table, he flipped the paper over, picked up his pink marker and filled in the date for when Donny had died twelve months ago. Knowing Spencer had given Donny the drugs that had killed him wasn't quite a puzzle piece, but it was something he hadn't had before. All he needed was a few more pieces and his picture would grow into something he could use to wrap Spencer in.

CHAPTER SEVENTEEN

Trying to slow her heart rate by taking deep breaths, Kelsey turned off the main road into her mother's driveway.

Before her father had died, Kelsey had enjoyed the short walk from the high school to the last house on the edge of town. Young magpies would sit awkwardly on the dried grass, their squawks at odds with the melodic yodel of their parents, while crimson rosellas would flit between the gum trees and wattles. And once she'd made her way down their gravel driveway and through the gate into their front yard, there'd been the spicy scent of the mustard plant running wild in the forgotten rockery. The lavender.

It had been home, even if it hadn't been sweet.

The place had changed over the years. The lawn was trim and green, the wild and colourful flowers had been replaced with a rigid-edged garden close to the house. The plants were neat. Ordinary.

Even the house looked stiff, the once sunny weatherboards she'd helped her father paint replaced with stark white cladding. The happy blue trim now dark red.

Worried her mother had moved without telling her, Kelsey parked in front of the garage, its updated facade now matching the house.

This was where her father existed now, in the space he'd called his for the first sixteen years of Kelsey's life. His memory lived in all the tools he'd held and used, the things he'd created and worked on. Her mother owned all those pieces of her father now that he was gone, leaving Kelsey with nothing but the memories she struggled to hold onto.

Opening the door of her car, she stood and stared, searching the open garage for her old bike, the bits of horse gear she'd stored among her father's things, or anything from her childhood. If she went in there, would she feel her father's energy? Could she find an item of his to slip into her pocket so she'd have something, anything, to cherish?

'What do you want?' Arms crossed, chin jutted, her mother stood at the open front door.

Visitors always went to the front door, family to the back. So, she was a visitor now, and an unwelcome one.

'I haven't seen you in five years, so I thought we should talk.'

Her mother scowled, digging deep lines either side of her mouth. It could easily have been ten years that had passed judging by the grey saturating her hair.

'I have nothing to say to you.'

'Nothing?' Kelsey did, though. 'Not even that you lied to me and everyone else?'

'No.' Glancing at her watch, Morna tapped a foot.

'Just, no?' Kelsey clenched her hands at her side. 'Do you even care that people asked about me? You knew I wanted to stay in touch with them, but you lied and told them I'd never called, never left messages and phone numbers for them.'

'Ethan would have looked for you, found you and brought you home. I didn't want you here.'

Even being prepared for the answer didn't stop the quick bite of grief. 'Have I ever meant anything to you?'

Morna lifted an eyebrow. 'Trouble. It's all you've ever been. All you ever will be.'

'You loved Dad, didn't you?' Kelsey pointed to his things in the garage. 'Aren't I at least a connection to him for you, like you are for me?'

'I loved him beyond reason, beyond life, and he loved me. Then you came along and split his time and heart.' Morna glared at Kelsey. 'I lost half of my husband to you, then I lost him completely, and you sat there, crying like you weren't the reason he'd died.'

'I wasn't the reason.' Not that it mattered now. Her mother clearly hadn't changed, and Kelsey had to bury the hope that she ever would.

'No'—Morna curled her lip—'just like you aren't the reason your daughter will grow up fatherless.'

'She'll grow up knowing she's loved.' Cold even as the heat shimmering off the car sent sweat down her back, Kelsey held still. 'And I told you that he's not around because he wants to hurt her.'

'Well, he told me you stole his daughter and won't let him see her. You always were a selfish brat, and now you're teaching your daughter the same.'

'*He* told you? Pipa's father?' Kelsey shook her head, trying to clear it. 'You've talked to him?'

Morna sniffed again.

'Why? Why would you talk to him? When did you talk to him? How …?'

'He contacted me, looking for you.' She crossed her arms over her chest. 'He explained that you and some other girl stole his daughter. I told him I'd only heard from you once, that first week after you left.'

'You gave him my number and address?'

'He asked for them.'

'So did Ethan, Mark and Carol!' She fisted hands in her hair until her scalp stung. 'Why would you tell him things you wouldn't tell the others?'

Morna glanced over her shoulder at the neatly clad house. 'He was grateful.'

'He paid you to tell him where I was?' Not even the nausea could squeeze past the rage choking her.

Morna merely shrugged. 'I figured someone owed me for everything you'd stolen from me.'

'How many times did you tell him where to find me?'

'You only called me three times.'

'When I left, when Pipa was born'—easing down to sit sideways in the driver's seat, she stared blindly at her feet—'and six months ago when I told you I wanted to come home.'

Because of Morna's greed, Jaiyden had missed Pipa's first steps, her first words, her first smile. Because of Morna's hatred, Kelsey still dreamed of that musty couch, of the bruises Spencer had left in and on her body. He'd stolen what she'd always thought she'd give to Ethan, he'd destroyed every semblance of peace and safety Kelsey had, and replaced them with fear and mistrust.

Forcing herself to look at her mother, Kelsey suppressed a shiver. 'I could tell you that I hate you, that I hope you rot in hell, but that would put me at your level.'

Needing to look Morna in the eye, Kelsey pushed out of the car, satisfied that her mother had to look up at her.

'You tried to break me down while I was growing up, but you didn't bet on me figuring out how to live without your love and support.'

Kelsey nodded to the shed. 'I had Dad, and no matter how much you thought that was wrong, it wasn't. Besides, I was lucky enough to have Ethan, Mark and Carol. They were my family. And now I have Pipa. She'll know from me what you never will, what you'll never deserve. Love, affection and respect.'

Though she wanted to shout and rage, she lifted her shoulders and took a calming breath. 'You lost those things when you could have so easily had them. And you're the one who has to live with that, because I'm done wanting, needing and wishing for anything from you.'

She turned for the shed. 'I'm taking something of Dad's to keep.'

'You touch anything and I'll have you charged with theft.' Morna nodded, her smile sharp. 'Then where would your precious Pipa be?'

Her mother's words stopped her cold. 'You really hate me this much?'

'It's not about hate. It's about my husband leaving everything here to me, not you.'

'He left me things. I know he did.'

Her mother's smile slipped. 'Who told you?'

'He did.' He'd shown her the box of letters and birthday cards he'd kept that she'd made him growing up. His treasured album of stamps.

'He lied.'

'No, that's one thing he never did. But you have.' Kelsey got in the car. 'I'm not the desperate daughter trying her hardest to make her mother love her anymore, so I'll grant you your wish and never visit you again.

'But know this,' she closed the door and stared at the things of her father's she'd never see or touch again, 'I won't hide who you are from other people anymore. I won't be party to your lies and deceit. If you keep spreading rumours about me, I'll counter them with the truth, no matter how it paints you.'

Heart hammering, Kelsey started the car while Morna stared, her mouth open and face slack. Instead of warming her, reconnecting with her mother had Kelsey shaking, her bones icy, her heart blank.

Instinct took over on the drive back to Ethan's. Muscle memory that had never gone rusty took her the ten kilometres out of town, had her turning down the dirt road that led to his property. But it left her when she stopped next to his ute.

She sat in the idling car, sweat drenching her clothes as she waited for tears of rage and loss to come. Lifting her hands, just to make sure they still existed, she stared at fingers that trembled. Anger could explode, spill and burn. Fear could propel, pummel the heart and lungs until they burst.

But she felt nothing …

And nothing was terrifying.

So she sat. With nothing flowing through her.

***

Ethan stepped over Max as he walked a circle.

'Good, keep your chin up. Snotty knows where he's going. You don't need to watch him.'

Seated on the horse, Pipa lifted her chin and gripped the loose reins tight. 'Can Mummy ride when she gets back?'

He hoped she would. He'd missed seeing her ride, the confidence coming off her in waves, her joy obvious.

'We'll ask her when she gets here.'

Which should be soon. She'd just turned into his driveway—her car might be small, but it sounded like a Harley when it slowed down. He'd have to have a look and see what was going on with it.

'Okay, turn him towards me. Good.' He smiled as Snotty single-stepped his way to Ethan. 'Now, ask him to stop.'

The horse stopped before Pipa lifted the reins.

'Well done.' He patted Snotty's thick neck and smiled up at Pipa.

Her bright eyes and huge grin tugged on his heart and made him pause. What would he do if they left? If Kelsey could never forgive him? Could never see their future as he could? Could he imagine a future where Pipa's smile wasn't his to cajole out? Where he couldn't hear Kelsey's car and think, *yes, she's home*?

'I go get Mummy!' Pipa held her arms out, her helmet cracking against his forehead as he lifted her down from the horse.

Wanting to give Kelsey some time, he held Pipa's hand. 'How about we unsaddle Snotty for now? Your mum would probably like a cool drink before she comes out to see how well you ride him.'

And Kelsey hadn't turned the car off yet.

'Put your helmet away.'

He steered Pipa in the direction of the tack room while he led Snotty into the stables and slipped the bridle and saddle from him. Sitting them outside the stable, he slid the door closed and gave Snotty's muzzle a quick pat as the pony stuck his head out and nickered to his stable buddy. The chestnut poked her head out of her stall and watched Ethan as he walked past her towards the back of the house.

Kelsey's car was still running when Pipa joined him.

'She must have the air conditioner going,' he mused.

'The stupid air ditioner doesn't work 'cos the man lied and said it did but it wouldn't cool a ice block in a freezer.' She grinned up at him again. 'Mummy said so.'

'Did she?' He stomped his boots on the mat outside the patio door, wanting to feel the tug of a grin instead of panic when Pipa copied him. 'Can you do me a favour?'

'Yes.' Pipa clapped her hands and bounced on the spot.

'Can you water the plants for me?' The place would probably be flooded by the time he got back, but he didn't care. Not when the car still idled out the front.

'Yes.' Pipa spun a circle. 'How?'

'Take this.' He grabbed the hose and turned the tap on, letting the water trickle out. 'Just hold it near the bottom of each plant for a bit, then do the next one.'

'I water them. Max can help me.'

'Great idea.' He pointed at the dog. 'Stay with Pipa.'

Giving Ethan a look, Max sat, then flopped to his side. Groaned.

Leaving Pipa, Ethan bolted through the lounge room, ran out the front to Kelsey's car and yanked open the door, staggering at the heat that spilled out.

'Bloody hell, Kelsey! Are you trying to kill yourself?'

She didn't answer, just stared out the windscreen while sweat ran down her face and soaked her clothes.

Fear bit hard. Turning off the ignition, he dragged Kelsey from the car and shook her shoulders when she stared through him.

'You aren't doing this again.' He slammed the door closed and turned her for the house. 'Walk.'

She wobbled, so he steadied her with an arm around her waist until he got her to the front door and inside the house. Glancing through the window at Pipa holding the hose over her head, then Max's, he steered Kelsey up the hallway, toed his boots off and left them where they fell.

In his bedroom, he let go of Kelsey long enough to strip down to his boxers, and then he removed Kelsey's clothes, too, so that she stood in her bra and undies. In the bathroom, he set the shower to breath-hitchingly cool and then dragged her under with him.

It took thirty seconds before she blinked, shivered, then raised a hand to push the hair from her face.

When she lifted her gaze to his, her blank stare turned to confusion. 'What ...?'

'Later.' He snapped the water off. 'Don't look if you don't want to see. I don't have time to be a prude.'

He let his soaking boxers fall, grabbed a towel and swiped it over his body. Snatching up his jeans, he pulled them on, then turned to Kelsey and threw the towel to her. Pulling on his shirt, he walked out of the room.

He had to before he grabbed hold of her and didn't let go.

Before he raged about the scars on her body that hadn't been there when she'd left.

Before he broke and begged her to let him in.

***

The shivering had nothing to do with the cold shower.

Kelsey hugged the towel to her chest, though modesty had nothing to do with the move. It was purely defence, and so she waited in silence until Ethan had stalked from the room, taking the cloud of anger and frustration with him.

Closing her eyes, she left the ensuite and didn't open them until her knees hit his bed. She turned and let them fold, sitting on the edge of the mattress. Goosebumps puckered her skin as water trickled from her hair down her back.

Did she have the energy to dry it? Did she have the energy to keep ignoring the questions that thumped her heart? Did she deserve the seething hate, the deliberate emotional attacks her mother had raised her on? Did she deserve the guilt that clung even though she claimed the woman meant nothing to her anymore?

How did she get through this now that she had none of the support she'd always thought she'd have? Her father had loved her, and she could still feel it, but Ethan? She made him angry without even trying.

146

On her own, then. She'd deal with this as she'd dealt with everything during the last five years—one day at a time and with Pipa's wellbeing in mind. They'd survived that way Pipa's whole life. They'd survive the rest the same way.

'Kelsey?'

Forcing her chin up, she opened her eyes and faced Ethan.

'I talked to Mum,' she said.

'No shit.'

Still sitting with the towel bunched against her chest as her only defence against nakedness, she nodded to the bed beside her. 'Pipa's okay?'

He frowned at her as he sat two feet away. 'She's reading to Max in the lounge room.'

'Okay.' Hooking her hair over her shoulder, she squeezed water onto the towel. 'It's hard to know exactly where to start.' A spurt of anger returned, giving her the words. '*She* told him.'

'Who told who?'

'My mother told Spencer.' She turned and hooked a knee up on the bed. 'He contacted her at the start. I don't know how. We thought we'd been careful not to give him any information.' She stared at Ethan's hands clenched on his thighs. 'He found Mum, though. Visited her. Paid her to tell him where I was. The three times I caved and rang her because I had nowhere else to turn, she kept it from you because you would have brought me home again, but told him instead.'

Frowning at Ethan, Kelsey shook her head slowly. 'We had to run because I rang her when I first moved and left phone numbers and an address. Jaiyden has missed seeing Pipa grow because I rang Mum from the hospital.' She couldn't hold it back this time. 'He beat and raped me because I rang her six months ago and told her I wanted to come home.'

The room held its breath. Seconds ticked by as Ethan sat in icy silence.

Well, if he didn't care enough to react, then neither would she. 'I don't know if it's better or worse that she's kept everything of Dad's but nothing of mine,' she said, a detached calm making it easier to talk. 'She's changed the house, memorialised everything that was his and eliminated me. She's hated me all this time because Dad dared love me.'

It choked her a moment. Swallowing it back, she stood and made sure her legs would hold, then one-handed, her other still holding the towel, she pulled her bag over and rummaged for clothes.

Cold, she pulled out jeans and a shirt, clamped the towel under each arm, then wriggled damp legs into the jeans. 'I always knew she hated me, but to have her admit it guts me.'

Ethan stared at her, his jaw so tight she was sure his teeth would shatter. Slipping the shirt over her head, she tugged it down and let the towel drop. 'I know you're mad at me. I can't blame you. I *don't* blame you.' She tried a smile but stopped when her throat clogged with emotion. 'We'll be out of your hair as soon as I find somewhere to stay.'

Leaving him silent, simmering, seething, she walked down the hallway but stopped to watch Pipa run her finger across the page of a magazine, the story she made up for Max one of ponies and puppies.

Preparing to break Pipa's heart, her own ticking down to self-destruct, she took a breath and opened her mouth.

'Don't.' With a hand on her shoulder, Ethan turned her to face him. 'You don't drop all that on me, then prepare to walk away.'

'You didn't say anything.'

'Didn't say how I'd like to see Morna rot for what she's done to you, both as a child and now? Didn't say how I'd like to pull Bristow apart, piece by piece, make him beg for mercy, then laugh as I twist a knife in his chest? But I wouldn't kill him. I wouldn't give him that. I'd keep him alive. Mark would help me. For this, he'd help me.'

He shoved a hand through his hair, paced two steps away and then back again. 'I won't stand back while you gather up what I've come to love, to want, and watch you walk away. I didn't get a chance to stop you last time. You jumped out my window and took my right to sit you down and explain how, as much as I wanted you, as thin as my control was getting where you were concerned, I could never take what you offered that night.' He shoved

148

both hands through his hair. 'God! Do you have any idea how you nearly killed me by doing that?'

Not trusting herself, she stared at him.

'Hard to talk when it's all bubbling inside, isn't it?'

He had her there. Still, she tried. 'You can't do anything to him.'

He glanced at Pipa over her shoulder and leaned in close. 'Why the hell not?'

Meeting him toe to toe, nearly nose to nose, she bared her teeth. 'Because then he'd have stolen you from me, too.'

The air shifted between them. If he stepped back from her now it would shatter what hold she had left on her emotions. So she stepped back, putting distance between them.

'I need to think, to sort through this without arguing with you.' Or wanting his arms around her, tight, to stop everything from flying apart.

He stood a moment, staring at her, then walked past her and scooped Pipa up off the floor. 'Put your boots on.'

He tossed Pipa over his shoulder, but Kelsey knew he spoke to her.

'Mummy.' Pipa wiggled fingers in a wave as they moved past. 'Come with us.'

They disappeared through the door and out onto the patio, but she didn't bother calling to ask where they were going. She knew Ethan took Pipa to the stables.

Max sat at her feet, sneezed, then stared up at her.

'Yeah, I know, get my boots.'

Unsure where to go from there after spilling one of her most terrifying secrets, she walked back to the bedroom, found her boots next to the bed and pulled them on.

She wouldn't think about that now. Wouldn't worry herself sick wondering what would happen next.

Pressing a hand to her stomach, she headed through the patio doors and down the path that led to the stables.

She wouldn't worry about the rest of the story yet, either.

***

'Meet Dusty.' Ethan held out the lead rope.

The chestnut would grow into a big, stocky pony once it was fed and muscled up—and once its fear didn't eat all its energy.

The pony stood braced, one ear directed to where Kelsey stood, her hands at her sides, the other pointed to the stable door and freedom.

If Kelsey had horse's ears, Ethan guessed they'd be a mirror of the pony's. The thought made him pause. He'd never imagined Kelsey would question herself or her ability with a horse. She never had before. She'd always jumped in, jumped on if she thought the time was right. Because as far as horses went, she *had* always been spot on.

As for their relationship, she'd been spot on there, too. Ethan had loved her for a long time, but he'd been falling *in* love with her, with the Kelsey he could see maturing and growing. He'd thought he had time, back then, to talk to her, to plan. She'd been quicker than him, though, and had made the first move before he'd been ready. But she wouldn't make that move again. He'd seen that when they'd been nose to nose.

So, he'd find the right time, the right way. Starting with what he knew she needed.

'She's been taught to lead and that's about it.' He took two steps to stand in front of Kelsey, the pony following his every move with big brown eyes that said *stay away, just stay away.*

'She's having trouble trusting me after her last owner belted her with a whip every time she did something wrong.'

'She didn't do it wrong, he did.' Kelsey took the rope, her focus now on the pony. 'How old is she?'

'Three.'

'How long have you had her?'

'Two weeks.'

'Why do you want me to work her?' She glanced at him.

'Because you'll understand her. You always did understand them when they came to me like this. You were always better with the rescues than anyone I know.' He couldn't help pushing a dried curl of slowly reddening hair behind her ear. 'I'm sorry.'

'For what?'

'For not being there. For what happened. For not handling it well earlier and making you think whatever it is you thought.' Resting his palm against her cheek, he brushed the tears away with his thumb. 'We'll talk about it when you're ready. Just know, right now, I'm here for you. Always have been. Always will be.'

Leaning forward, he kissed her cheek, her forehead, then, very gently, her lips.

Turning before she had the chance to say anything, he walked to where Pipa bounced from foot to foot, the grin on her face becoming his favourite thing to see.

Even as he saddled Snotty, talked to Pipa and answered her stream of questions, he listened to Kelsey murmur to the pony before she started leading it to the round yard behind the stables.

Following her, he took his first easy breath since Kelsey had walked back into his life. She had no trouble picking up the old rhythm he'd desperately missed. Her voice was gentle, her body guiding the pony to answer the questions she asked.

Standing while Pipa played with the end of the reins he held and chatted to herself, the horse and the clouds, he watched Kelsey pick up the frayed threads of trust and start to weave them back together. He envied the pony her undivided attention, the flow of communication, her smile when the pony understood and answered what she asked.

'Mummy and the pony is dancing.' Pipa twirled in a circle under Snotty's nose, then reached up and stroked his soft muzzle.

'They are. She is.' And he loved it. Loved her.

'Let's see if Snotty remembers what he's supposed to do.' Otherwise, he'd start to think about Bristow again.

He'd battled the urge to break and smash things when she'd slipped that bit of information in with the rest. Just dropped it in there like an afterthought. But it had taken guts to say those words. He wanted to kill the bastard, rip his arms from their sockets, cut his balls off with a rusty knife, splatter his blood, beat him to a pulp, revive him, then do it all again, and again.

'Ethan?' Kelsey's hand on his arm pulled him back from the red haze of fantasy. 'Don't go there, it doesn't help.'

Staring down at her, knowing she was right but unable to stop, only able to imagine what she'd endured, he reached out and enfolded her in his arms.

If she'd struggled or stiffened, he'd have let her go, no matter what it cost him. But her arms circled his waist and held on.

'Hugs.' Pipa held up her arms.

Still holding Kelsey close, Ethan bent and scooped Pipa into the hug. They'd done this before. Entwined bodies and heat. The other times, though, Kelsey had been battling fear. Now, fully aware and engaged, she wrapped her arms around him and snuggled her head against his chest as Pipa did.

For the first time in five years, his heart relaxed. For the first time in five years, he believed they could do this, be this. She might not believe it yet, not fully, but she'd let part of the wall crumble. The one she'd built to keep him out.

Now he had to find a way to make sure she didn't have a reason to build it up again. Treating her like he used to—when she'd been fearless, ferocious, exhaustive in her need to learn, to grow, to experience whatever she could— would be a start. So caught up in what she'd taken from him, he'd forgotten what she'd given him before she'd left. Love, laughter and frustration, exactly when he'd needed it. It had hurt to keep his distance from her, to hold her away when he just wanted to drown in her.

He'd make sure she got used to being with him like that again. He'd give her reasons to be fearless with him. She was already ferocious when it came to Pipa, but he wanted her to fire up, speak her mind, tell him he was being an arse and kick his butt when he needed it. He wanted her to be confident in herself and in them. To hold his hand in public without worrying about what others thought. He wanted her to accept his touch, his kiss, without holding back.

It was time to start changing that, to get them back to where they had been, but not like before. Not as friends dancing around their feelings, waiting for the right time, because that time was now, and he wanted everyone to know.

'Will you and Pipa come to fire running training with me tomorrow?'

'When is it?' She leaned as much as she supported, took as much as she gave.

'Four o'clock.'

'Okay.'

It was a start. Being around the dozen or so people who would be there, most of whom Kelsey had grown up with, would give him a chance to show her he didn't care who saw them together or knew how he felt. He didn't care about anything they had to say. All that mattered was how she felt, what she said, and what she still didn't say.

'I missed you.'

She lifted her head and frowned. 'I missed you too.'

So, there was still more she had to tell him.

'Pipa wants to show you what Snotty can do.'

Kissing Pipa's cheek, then Kelsey's forehead, he set Pipa on her feet. 'Better get your helmet.' He turned to Kelsey when Pipa skipped off to the tack room. 'You'll tell me the rest?'

Nodding, Kelsey stared after Pipa. 'Thank you.'

'For what?'

She shifted her feet, took a breath, then faced him. 'For showing Pipa what it's like to have a decent man in her life.'

'And you?'

'I'm not decent anything.' She went to turn away.

He put a hand on her shoulder to stop her. 'I want to show you what it's like to have a decent man in your life.'

She half-smiled. 'You always have.'

Humbled, he smiled back, and when he kissed her, he lingered. 'One day, you'll understand exactly what you've always meant to me. What you always will.'

'But I've done things.'

He gave in, ran his hand over her hair. 'Some have been done to you. Just like that pony, it wasn't your fault.'

'I could have fought him, could have screamed.'

'Why didn't you?' Though he'd already guessed.

'She was sleeping in the loft.' Kelsey licked her lips as Pipa skipped out, two helmets swinging by their straps, and grinned at them. 'I couldn't let her hear that, see that. She saw the aftermath and that was bad enough.'

'You saved her.' So many times, she'd saved the girl who wasn't hers.

Kelsey shook her head. 'She remembers the bad man. She knows I was hurt.'

'She knows you love her beyond measure. She knows her birth mother loved her. She knows that no matter what's going on or how you feel, you'll be there for her, to protect her, to make sure she's happy and healthy.' He shook his head before she could counter his argument. 'You're too quick to be hard on yourself. Trust me on this, I can see it. Anyone looking at the two of you can see it.'

'And if everyone thinks I lied to them?'

'Do you think they will? Do you really think they'll turn their back on her because she doesn't have your blood in her veins?'

Crouching to clip Pipa's helmet on, she took the second one and stared at it a moment.

'Ride Snotty with me, Mummy.'

Kelsey raised an eyebrow at Pipa.

Hands clutched under her chin, Pipa bounced. 'Please.'

'The saddle is big enough for both of you.' Ethan took Kelsey's helmet, sat it on her head and buckled it. 'Show your daughter what it's really like to ride a horse.'

He waited and saw the answer in her eyes before she took the reins, checked the girth, then swung up onto the horse. Wriggling back as far as she could, she held her arms out for Pipa.

'Thanks,' she said as he settled Pipa in front of her.

'You're welcome.' Not wanting to miss the opportunity, Ethan slid his phone from his pocket and brought up the camera.

Reins in one hand, the other settled against Pipa's stomach, Kelsey nodded. 'Come on, Snot.'

'Come on, Snot.' Pipa giggled, tipping her face up to grin at Kelsey.

Ethan snapped the shot, then pressed record when Kelsey nudged Snotty into an easy canter around the yard. Forgot to keep the camera on them when he couldn't keep his mind, his eyes off her.

CHAPTER EIGHTEEN

'And that's the story of the Muscle Fairy.' Brian tucked the sheet under Ashley's chin.

The boy could barely keep his eyes open as he grinned, then yawned. 'Another one?'

'Nope.' Brian kissed him on the forehead, then did the same to James. 'Night, boys.'

'Do you have a sparkly hammer?' James leaned up on one elbow as Brian walked to their bedroom door.

'No.' He raised an eyebrow until both boys lay down and closed their eyes.

'What about a pink tutu?' Ashley asked between giggles, no doubt imagining his uncle in work boots, shorts, singlet and a pink tutu, just like the Muscle Fairy.

'It's in my closet.' Brian flicked the light off. 'You can wear it tomorrow.'

Both boys burst out laughing.

The fact that Brian *did* have a pink tutu hanging in his wardrobe would surprise the boys in the morning.

Walking into the lounge room, he paused. Haylee sat on the couch, her back stiff, her hands clasped in her lap.

'Rupert in bed?' Brian came and sat in the lounge chair.

Haylee jerked a nod.

So, it was time. But now that it *was*, he wasn't sure he could sit and listen to Haylee's words. Just as he was about to stand and pace, she cleared her throat.

'James is Donny's, no question,' she said. 'He was the only one I'd been with at that time.'

Gut dropping to his toes, Brian wanted to bury his face in his hands. He'd been afraid of this for so long. Even before Haylee had come home scared of his slightest movements and shutting down whenever he showed anger. Crying herself to sleep most nights.

'Despite what you might think, Donny was my first. I didn't love him. I wasn't interested in sex, but everyone expected us to be doing it, so I let him.'

Brian clapped his hands over his ears, making them ring. 'I didn't need to know that.' He screwed up his nose.

'Don't be such a baby.' She frowned at him, a flash of anger momentarily hiding her pain. Then it was back, clouding her eyes until they shimmered with tears. 'Donny owed Spencer money.' She closed her mouth with a snap, her gaze dropping to her tightly clenched fingers. 'He owed a lot of people money, or drugs.'

Brian did drop his face to his hands then. Breathing became a luxury he couldn't afford. Not when his heart couldn't beat out the required rhythm.

'I was still young enough, *innocent* enough that I was worth at least a portion of what he owed.'

How had he not seen this? How had he not put two and two together earlier?

Raising his head, he met Haylee's wet gaze. 'I want to kill him.'

'Get in line.' Jaw clenched, Haylee stared at him. 'Donny would pretend afterwards he was too stoned to stop them, that he hadn't meant for it to happen, that they were just supposed to have a bit of fun.'

Because focusing on what the bastard had done to his sister would feed the urge to demolish something, like the city, like every drug-fucked bastard who thought they could do anything to anyone because they wanted to, he pushed up, paced to the kitchen door and back again. He kept moving until the red haze of bloodlust simmered down to a deep thirst for Donny's body to meet with a fast-moving truck. Or his fists. Losing his job would nearly have been worth it had the bastard still been alive.

Nearly. He stopped, sucked in air and met Haylee's gaze. She'd be left alone again and disappointed in him if he threw away his job, his future on someone she deemed not worthy.

Lucky the bastard's already dead, then.

'The one who gave me James also gave me chlamydia.' She held a hand up as if to stop a typhoon of raged curses from erupting. 'He was eight weeks prem and so tiny.' She cupped her hands, cradled. 'When I got pregnant with Rupert, I was terrified it would happen again, that I'd lose him. So I told Donny it stopped now.' She shrugged. 'And it did.'

'Just like that?'

'Well, no.' She flexed her fingers. 'I told him I'd cut off his balls in his sleep. Even demonstrated it one night when he said some friends were coming over the next day.'

A laugh broke out of his mouth, startling him. 'Sorry.'

'Don't be.' Her lips lifted, but she didn't smile. 'I got treatment. Made sure the boys were okay. Then Donny died, and I thought, great, I don't have to worry about that part anymore.'

'So you came here, to me.'

'I did.' She nodded. 'I could have found a shelter. But I couldn't go anywhere else. I knew you wouldn't turn me away or snub the boys, even though part of me wanted you to.'

'Why?'

'Because I deserved it, didn't I?' She frowned at him. 'There has to be consequences.'

Squatting in front of her, he took the hands she'd clasped tight again. 'You're only punishing yourself, Hales. The boys deserve a mum who's happy. You deserve to be happy. Don't cheat yourself out of that.'

'I don't want this to be how you see me now. I don't want it to change how you treat me.' She stared at him. 'Or how you see the boys.'

'It won't.' He loved all three boys more than life, would give up everything he had for them, even his last breath, his last drop of blood. Ashley and Rupert having different druggie scumbag fathers didn't matter. Haylee was their mother.

To prove it, Brian stood and walked quietly to the boys' room. Haylee's soft footfalls followed him.

Hand on the doorknob, Brian glanced at her. 'No matter what, I would never hurt them, you know that.'

Haylee nodded, arms wrapped around her waist as she watched him crack open the door and walk into the room.

James slept as he usually did, face planted in the pillow, knees tucked up under his body as though he played head-down, thumbs-up. Brian didn't have to question that the life in that bed was his blood, his soul.

His to protect.

Teach.

Love.

Turning to where Ashley slept with his hand fisted at his chin, thumb slipping from his relaxed mouth, Brian felt the same emotions fill his chest. He could never turn away from the boy or show him less love and affection than his older brother. Ashley was as much Haylee's son as James, and as much Brian's nephew as well.

Squatting next to the bed, Brian gently smoothed the hair back from Ashley's forehead. 'Sleep well, little man. I'll always be here for you.'

Kissing his nephew's cheek, he pushed to his feet and turned to find tears streaming down Haylee's cheeks as she watched him.

He lifted a hand to her cheek as he passed. Letting himself into her room, he crossed to the cot where Rupert, half-asleep, grinned up at him. Brian leaned down, picked the baby up and crooned. Rupert snuggled in and closed his eyes as Brian rocked him to sleep. Slowly, gently, he settled Rupert back in his cot and ran a hand over that red fluff of hair.

Turning, he opened his arms and sighed when Haylee didn't hesitate, just stepped into his embrace, her arms tight around his waist, face pressed to his chest.

'I'd be lost without you all. I could never love any of you less.'

His words seemed to crack something in Haylee. Hanging tightly to him, her whole body shook as she cried against his chest.

'Come on.' Hugging her to him, he walked her back to the lounge room and sat next to her on the couch while she emptied all her pent-up fear and pain onto his shirt.

He watched the first ten minutes of *Contact* without taking in any of the movie as he absorbed the slowing shudders of Haylee's body, the hiccupped sobs she tried to swallow as she began to pull herself together.

Just as Elly and Palmer got naked, Haylee sat up, wiped her cheeks with her palms and sucked in a shaky breath.

'Don't even think about saying sorry.' Not that he cared, but knowing she'd be self-conscious about puffy red eyes, Brian didn't look at her, just watched Elly make her quick escape when the questions got too hard.

'I wasn't going to.' Haylee leaned over and kissed his cheek. 'Want a cuppa?'

'Thanks.'

He didn't follow her to the kitchen, although he wanted to. Instead, he formed his side of the debate, predicting hers, and had what he thought was an airtight argument by the time she walked back in, a steaming mug in each slightly shaking hand. Passing him one, she stood staring at hers. She held up a hand when he opened his mouth to speak.

'I know what you're going to say, and I know reporting it is the right thing to do. That I'll be protected, that I can't keep looking over my shoulder for the rest of my life.'

Setting her cup down, she perched on the edge of the couch. 'I know all that. And I *will* report it. But I'm not stupid enough to think anything will come of it, or that I won't have to look over my shoulder anyway.'

'I won't let anything happen to you, or the boys.' He set his cup down before he cracked it.

Needing to see something other than the shadow of stark memories in her eyes, he cleared his throat. 'Do you mind the boys wearing a pink tutu?'

She blinked at him, then shook her head as if to clear it. 'They don't have a tutu.'

'I know, but I do.'

160

Haylee stared at him, the shadows giving way to curiosity. 'Is there something you want to tell me?'

'No.' He picked up his cup and took a sip. 'I bought it last year for the Royal Children's Hospital fundraiser.'

'Oh.'

'Would you mind if I did? Have something to tell you, I mean.'

She tilted her head as she frowned at him. 'No.'

'But?'

'I'd have questions, I guess.'

'Like?'

'Do you have a little black dress I could borrow?' She smiled, and that one quirk of her lips made everything worthwhile.

'It's red,' he said, loving hearing the laugh that bubbled in his sister's throat.

They both sobered and looked at each other.

'You're not alone in this Haylee, you know that don't you?'

'Yeah.' But her gaze strayed to the hallway where her sons slept.

CHAPTER NINETEEN

'Hoped you'd be here.' Carol dropped a camp chair next to Kelsey's and flopped into it. 'Figured I'd bring Snow anyway, but he'll be happier rolling around with Pipa.'

'Pipa's just as happy to roll around with him.'

Carol tipped her sunglasses down and looked Kelsey over. 'How are you?'

As it wasn't the polite enquiry Kelsey had received half a dozen times already, she shrugged. 'Honestly, I don't know.'

'You'll tell me everything?' She shrugged, then, and pushed her glasses back up. 'You don't have to, of course.'

'I'm still getting used to talking about it.'

In silence, they watched Ethan, Zoe and two others run to the tanker trailer, grab hoses and branches, then race to stand and aim the flow of water at the targets.

There hadn't been any hesitation between Kelsey and Carol when they'd been younger. Anything and everything had been discussed, dissected, dreamed. Glancing at Carol, catching a glimpse of the hurt half-hidden by sunglasses, Kelsey leaned towards her friend. 'I went to see Mum yesterday.'

'How'd that go?'

Where did she start? 'She got rid of everything that was mine. That garden we planted?'

Carol nodded. 'The fairy garden we made so we could catch some?'

'Yeah. Gone. Not just pulled up but gone. Made into a parking space.'

'Wow.'

'She's the reason he found us a few times.'

'The Spencer dude?'

Kelsey shivered. 'Yeah, him.'

'I don't know what to say.' Again, Carol ran a hand down Kelsey's arm, then squeezed her wrist. 'You know that if he turns up here, there's at least a dozen of us he'd have to try and get through before he got to you or Pipa.'

'I do.' She did now, and she believed it. They'd all stand for her and Pipa. 'Thanks.'

'Besides,' Carol dropped the sunglasses back in place, 'I'd be pissed if you took off for another five years.'

'I won't.' This time, when she looked at Ethan, she knew she couldn't run again, no matter what happened. Pipa loved him, and Kelsey could never break her young heart like that. Or Ethan's.

Her own heart gave a stutter when Ethan smiled at her. It swelled when he blew her a kiss and missed the yelled *GO!* that started his run. Behind when he was usually first to the trailer, Ethan fumbled the branch, only had it half on the hose before the water came through. The soaking rainbow haloed him for a moment and made Kelsey's heart, head and soul sigh in unison.

Hoots of laughter echoed across the paddocks. Black Angus cows lifted their heads and chewed as they stared at the noisy humans. A kookaburra, finding them all humorous, joined in. Then someone started the slow clap. None of it mattered when Ethan began to stalk towards her, the glint in his eye making her heart jump.

She could run. Had done it so many times before when he'd worn that look. She'd probably get a few metres before he caught her. But she stood and waited until he stopped in front of her. He slipped his arms around her waist, pulled her against his wet shirt, then dipped his head to kiss one corner of her mouth, then the other.

Everything fell away when his mouth settled firmly on hers. His lips nudged, encouraged, until hers moved with his. It took no effort to lift her arms, wrap them around his neck and press herself closer. He tasted of sunshine and a hint of sweat. All Ethan.

She wanted more, so much more. Of him, of them. She wanted to tell him she loved him. That in him she could see a future full of love and hope. Full of the dreams she'd kept tucked away, but that now flew around her head and heart.

His hands pressed her closer until she felt his heart drum against hers. Then he shifted, his mouth asking, urging. And she let go, gave him everything she had and everything she didn't dare voice.

His groan vibrated through her.

Someone coughed.

Ethan gentled the kiss, nibbled the corner of her mouth, then pressed his cheek to hers. 'I forgot we had an audience.' His lips touched her ear, her jaw, her mouth. 'But somehow I don't care.'

It took her a moment to catch her breath, for the words echoing in her head to find a voice. 'You keep kissing me.'

He hesitated, his lips light on hers. 'You don't like it?'

Of course she did. More than she'd imagined she would. But ...

'You didn't want me kissing you two nights ago.'

He eased back to stare down at her, the frown darkening his eyes. 'You'd just had a panic attack. I wasn't going to let you kiss me only to have you back off and turn it around on me.'

'You think I'd regret kissing you? That I'd blame you?' The sigh in her heart turned to a scream as it freefell through the void.

'You've stepped back from me every time I've tried to get close to you, Kelsey.' As though proving his point, his arms stopped her doing just that. 'You've had reason to, and no reason to trust me. I'm giving you one now.'

His hands slid up her body to frame her face, his thumbs sweeping over her cheeks. When he lowered his head and hesitated, Kelsey held her breath, then lifted her mouth to his.

A fraction of the pressure delivered a kiss that made Kelsey's knees weak. Eyes still closed when he lifted his head, she waited for her world to stop spinning. Opening her eyes, she blinked, hoped that all of what she felt didn't show.

Serious now, his gaze searched hers. 'I love you, Kelsey. I've always loved you. I just couldn't do anything until now.'

She opened her mouth but couldn't force the words out. Shaking her head to try and shuffle order into the chaos, she watched his face close up and knew his heart took the same bruising fall hers had.

Hurting for him, for them, the lost time, she lifted a hand to his cheek. 'I don't want to do this anymore.'

'Then don't.' Ethan held up his hands and stepped away. 'I can't force you to believe me. I can wait, but it hurts when I know and can see and taste how you feel about me.'

'Let me finish what I was going to say.' She grabbed him by the shirt and pulled him so his body bumped hers. She stared up at him as he glared down at her. 'I don't want to fight this anymore. I don't want to push you away. I don't want to keep telling myself it's all in the past.'

He was, always would be, her memories, her now, her dreams. 'Every time I look at you, I see my past, my present, our future.' She touched his face. 'Pipa loves you, just like I knew she would. I knew she'd tether me to you. I knew that and came anyway because as much as I kept telling myself that I didn't, I *did* come back here for this, for you. Because I love you. I've never stopped.'

Wrapping himself around her, he pressed his lips to her ear. 'Promise me you won't leave again. No matter what.'

'There are still things—'

'No.' He gripped her shoulders. 'No evasions, no buts. I'm asking you to stay with me not just for now or because you have to.'

The future she'd always dreamed of burst around her so big it nearly swallowed her whole. Could she trust herself to accept it? Could she risk losing it if she hesitated? Her answer froze on her tongue when the police car pulled up and Mark got out.

'I need a word with you both,' he said, stopping beside Ethan.

A quick scan showed Pipa still played with the puppy, but Kelsey's nerves jumped. 'What's wrong?'

'I need you to promise me you won't disappear.'

165

She couldn't help the reflexive turn towards Pipa or curb her movement even as Ethan reached for her.

Mark's gaze dropped to their joined hands. 'Ethan called me about Morna. I went to see her this morning.'

It was worse, she realised, when you had everything you wanted, but then someone else tipped the balance at will. 'She's told him, hasn't she? He knows.'

'She denies any involvement. I'll be talking to her again later today.' His gaze flicked back to Ethan's. 'I suggest you both stay away from her for now.'

'I don't want to be anywhere near her.' Stepping back until she felt Ethan's warmth, she looked over to where Pipa still played with Snow while Carol watched over them.

Mark followed her gaze, then rubbed his forehead. 'Look, I don't know much yet. I've got an idea, but until I know more, just take it easy. There's no use panicking. Mistakes are made that way.' He held out the personal police card on which he'd already written her name and *Monday 9 a.m.* underlined three times. 'Anything happens, and I mean anything, you call me.'

She took the card as dread pooled in her stomach. It made it official, real, to tell a police officer, didn't it? It limited the time she had to believe that everything would be okay.

Mark tapped a finger to the card. 'You'll be there?'

Kelsey could only nod.

Mark looked at Ethan. 'I'll need your statement too.'

Ethan nodded. 'I figured.'

Kelsey rubbed at the headache now throbbing at her temple. 'So, what happens now?'

'I'm not on call tonight,' said Mark, shrugging, 'so I was thinking of bringing the dogs and camping in the swamp paddock.'

'The swamp paddock that's right near the road, and the two dogs that will bark if a car goes past?' Kelsey angled her body so she could frown from Ethan to Mark.

'Are you going to get mad at us for cramming five years' worth of worry and care into a few days?'

'I'm living this. Treating me like a child only hurts me.'

'We're living this now too. Look at me, Kelsey.' He nodded when she glared at him. 'You're still keeping things from us. I can see it.' He shook his head when she opened her mouth. 'I'm not playing tit for tat, but just as you're holding things back to protect yourself, we're doing it to protect you.'

Faced with his honest concern, the tiredness that bruised his eyes, she slumped her shoulders. 'I've lived with too many lies and evasions, I don't want to anymore.'

'Then we'll start now.' He squeezed her shoulder. 'I don't know where Bristow is, but I'm not taking any chances that he's already looking for you again, or that Morna hasn't contacted him.'

'I'd say he'd have to be stupid to come here looking for you,' Ethan put in, 'but stupidity seems to be his default setting.'

'That's it, though.' Kelsey rubbed her arms, though the sun fried them. 'He's not stupid. He's manic, and he's dangerous.'

'Then help me stop him.' Mark tapped the card she still held. 'Tell Ethan what you have to tonight, then tell me everything tomorrow. In the meantime, let us look after you and Pipa.'

She quirked an eyebrow at him. 'I'll let you *help* look after me and Pipa, but there's no way I'm stepping back and not doing the job myself.'

'Fair enough.' He nodded, then smiled and tugged her hair. 'Good to have you back, little red.'

***

Tucking the sheet over Pipa's shoulder, Ethan straightened. At his feet, Max huffed a sigh, lay down and closed his eyes.

Kelsey stepped over the dog to lean down and kiss Pipa's cheek. 'Good night, sweet.'

Eyes closed, Pipa burrowed down into the bed. 'Night, Mummy. Love you.'

'I love you too.' Running her hand over Pipa's hair, she kissed her forehead. 'I'll be on the couch if you need me.'

Ethan wanted to correct her, to tell her his bed was where she belonged. Instead, he took her hand and led her down the hallway to the lounge room.

She'd been quiet since they'd left the barbeque after training. Pipa had chatted until she'd fallen asleep five minutes down the road. She'd yawned through her bath, argued that she wasn't tired but had agreed to go to bed because Max needed to go to sleep. Through it all, Kelsey had smiled, frowned, reasoned and acted like the competent mother he'd come to admire. Underneath her facade, though, he could see shadows lurking.

'Would you like a cup of tea before you tell me whatever it is you think I'll react badly to?'

'It's not just that.' She followed him to the kitchen and stood in the doorway as he made tea and coffee. 'I haven't talked about it before. I don't know how to start. And ...'

'And?'

'I need you to let me get it out, let me say it all before you say anything.'

He handed her the cup of tea. 'I'd be stupid to promise not to say anything, but I can promise to listen.'

She raised the cup to her lips, blew off the steam, lowered it again, then took a deep breath. 'I got sick, after ...'

'After he raped you?' He wouldn't force her to say it, but not using the word would only compound the misplaced shame and guilt he knew she held onto. So, he'd say it for her, even though her flinch made him want to throw his coffee cup across the room and let it smash against the wall.

Kelsey's gaze dropped to his hands. Forcing himself to relax the death grip on his cup, he raised it in a gesture for her to keep going.

'I thought I was sick from shock, or from stress.' She pressed a hand to her stomach, started that barely there rocking.

'No.' He dropped his mug in the sink, the coffee bitter in his mouth. 'Don't you go there. Stay with me. Stay here.' He took her cup, let it crack against his, then gripped her shoulders. 'Kelsey?'

'I'm here.' She curled cold fingers around his wrists. 'Can we sit down?'

Leading her to the couch, he sat, pulled her close and wrapped his arm around her shoulders until she rested her cheek against his chest. 'He raped you.' Her involuntary shiver made him pull her closer. 'You were sick.' He kept his voice level, though everything inside him wanted to break free and wreak havoc until nothing of Bristow existed.

'I was sick.' She picked up the thread and wove it. 'I was terrified to go to the doctor in case it was something bad.'

'They didn't test you when you reported it?'

Silence clashed in his ears.

'You didn't report it.'

'I couldn't.' She shifted, then sighed when he wouldn't let her go. 'I was too terrified that he'd find us again. That someone would figure out Pipa wasn't mine and take her from me. I still am.'

'You said Jaiyden named you Pipa's legal guardian, and you're old enough now?'

'She did and I am, but I have no proof. They could still take her, couldn't they?'

'The midwife would have written it down. There'd be documentation of it.' His brain working now, he kissed the top of her head. 'And even if they question your ability to look after her, they'd only have to see you in action to know she belongs with you.'

'And if they don't?'

'It's no use borrowing worry.' He kissed her forehead. 'So, what did you do if you didn't go to the doctor?'

'Researched what it could be.' Her pause had his heart thudding heavy.

'And?' Guessing at this point would only hurt them both. If he took a leap and guessed wrong, it could destroy what had finally started between them.

'I did a process of elimination.' She shrugged, though he knew she wanted to bolt. 'First, I decided to take a pregnancy test.'

He gave her until the count of thirty. 'And?'

'Took me a week to work up to taking it, before I realised I was making things worse. If he'd given me something, I risked exposing Pipa, or worse, getting so sick I couldn't look after her.'

The kick of his heart drummed in his throat, his head. 'And?'

'It came up positive.' She shook her head. 'I didn't know how to feel. Part of me was relieved it wasn't a disease. But the other part, the bigger part, wasn't.' She spread her fingers before her, then clenched them. 'I didn't want part of him growing inside me.'

'I'd say that's normal.'

She shook her head and kept her gaze on her hands. 'It doesn't excuse it.'

'What?'

'That I was selfish. For two weeks, I cried whenever Pipa was asleep. During the day, I worked as hard as I could so I didn't have to think. Then one day Pipa asked if she could have a brother or sister. It was like a punch in the stomach. How could I blame this tiny thing for what its father had done?'

She looked at him then, guilt and fear clouding her eyes. 'Pipa would never have been born if Jaiyden had felt that way.'

Her tears ran, and his heart broke for her.

'Two days later I started bleeding.' She shook her head, her misery a blanket she held close. 'They never tell you that miscarrying can take hours of pain. No one tells you how terrifying and soul-destroying it is.'

'Let me hold you.' He shifted, relieved when she moved with him and rested her head on his shoulder, her hand on his chest.

Another yawn ended in a hiccup. 'I got tested for everything a couple of months ago. I don't know how, but he gave me nothing else.'

But he'd taken so much. Something Ethan ached to balance out, one way or another. Unsure if he could speak without his rage surfacing, he let the silence stretch.

'I needed you to know now, so you could change your mind before …' Her shoulder shrugged under his arm. 'Anyway, I'll check on Pipa.' She pushed away from him.

He let her get up and take a step away. 'Do you think I'd blame you for something you had no choice in?'

Standing with her back to him, she lifted one hand, then let it fall to her side again.

'Do you think'—he rose slowly to stand behind her—'that I would blame you? That I wouldn't want you because you reacted in a way most people would, then accepted what a lot couldn't?'

'What if I made it happen?' She stayed where she was, her body shaking. 'What if I got what I deserved?'

'No.' Spinning her to face him, he clamped his hands on her shoulders and waited until she lifted her gaze to his. 'Are you telling me that you're taking responsibility for the workings of nature, of the universe, and that you believe you caused yourself to miscarry?'

Her mouth opened, then closed again.

'Let me ask you this, then. Has it ever worked like that with anything else in your life?' At her blank stare, he pushed on. 'Have you ever won in the show ring by wishing for it? Ever had something fall in your lap simply because you wanted it?'

Obviously sensing a trap but not seeing it, she frowned. 'No.'

'Why not?'

She chewed on an answer, then lifted one shoulder. 'Because I had to work for it.'

'So why think you have the power to make something like this happen?'

While she thought about that, he ran a hand over her hair and kissed her forehead. 'What I want to work for is us. I want us to be together. You, me, Pipa, and whatever we create between us.' She jerked in his grip. 'We're being honest with each other, aren't we?'

At Kelsey's slow nod, he loosened his grip and rubbed the muscles that bunched tight under his hands. 'All of this matters because it's happened and it's part of who you are now. But'—he cupped the back of her neck and rubbed—'I'm not going to let you think it will be a barrier between us, what we are, what we can have. Like a family.' He took a deep breath. 'Do you want a family with me?'

171

'I started planning a family with you when I was fourteen.'

'And now?'

'Now, I've added Pipa to the picture of us.' She lifted a hand to rest it on his cheek. 'Because I love you. And I want everything with you.'

CHAPTER TWENTY

She couldn't mistake the look in his eyes for anything other than what it was.

Triumph.

It both thrilled and terrified her. Trying to push the terror back, she pulled up a smile. 'You know I'll still annoy you.'

'I look forward to it.' He dipped his head and took her mouth in a soft, slow kiss.

Questions parachuted their way into her mind. What if she fumbled the kiss? What if he touched her and she froze? What if he wanted more and she couldn't do it?

'Hey.' He lifted her chin until their gazes locked. 'Don't go there.'

Filling her lungs, then letting the air out slowly, she nodded. 'It's easier not to when you're here.'

He pursed his lips. 'We don't have to get into it now, but counselling is another option.'

The jolt in her heart had her shaking her head. 'I don't know if I can.'

He took her hand before she could escape and held it in the warmth of his. 'I'll be there for you and do as much as I can to help you, but you need to talk to someone who knows what to do, what to tell you.'

'I haven't told anyone else. I don't know if I can.'

'We can talk about it later.' He raised their joined hands to rub his thumb along her cheek. 'You're exhausted.'

'I am.' And she couldn't help glancing at the couch. Sleeping alone, without his warmth, his strength scared her more than the thought of sleeping with him and freezing up if he touched her.

All that flew out of her mind when a fist pounded on the door.

'It'll be Mark.' Ethan held her hand a moment longer and squeezed it before letting it go.

She stayed where she was, close to the hallway, to Pipa, as Ethan opened the door a crack, then wider, the light spilling out to wash over Mark.

'I've got Billie and Mac down in the swamp paddock. You'll hear them,' Mark said, glancing at Kelsey. 'I'll be down there too.'

'I hope you get some sleep.' She rubbed her forehead, her eyes refusing to focus.

'I think we all need some.' Ethan motioned Mark back outside. 'I'll be back in a minute,' he said over his shoulder.

'Night, Kelsey.' Mark lifted a hand to wave.

Kelsey returned it. 'Goodnight, Mark.'

She left them to whatever talk they needed to have, most likely about protecting her and Pipa—not that she didn't like it, but did they have to be so secretive? She walked down the hallway, stopped at Pipa's door and peeked in.

Tucked up, face relaxed in sleep, she hadn't stirred. Max was sprawled on the foot of the bed, snoring. Kelsey didn't have the heart to move him. Pulling the door almost closed, she pressed her forehead against the doorjamb.

'If you're worried—'

Ethan stopped when she whirled to face him. Her heart thumped louder than Max's snoring.

Putting a hand to her chest to make sure her heart stayed inside, she bit her lip. 'Sorry.'

'Don't be. I didn't mean to scare you.' Hands in his pockets, he tipped his head slightly. 'I want you to feel safe here.'

'I do, I'm just not used to other people being around.'

They stared at each other a moment.

174

'I'm not worried.' She knew what he'd been about to say. That she didn't have to worry about him pushing her, asking for things she didn't know if she could give yet.

He held his hand out. She put hers in his and followed him to his room. Glancing at the door to the ensuite, she chewed the inside of her lip. 'I'm not a prude.'

Ethan stopped in the act of pulling his shirt over his head and looked at her. 'No.' He finished tugging off his shirt, balled it up and shot it past her so it landed near the door. 'I was ...'

'Angry?'

He unbuttoned and unzipped his jeans, then pushed them down and stood with his boxers hanging low on his hips.

'What's more than terrified?'

Frowning, Kelsey tore her gaze from the exposed skin that made her hands tingle.

'You came home, sat in that furnace of a car, wouldn't talk to me, and I had no idea what was wrong. I didn't know if you'd been hurt, if the heat had fried your brain, if you were suffering from a panic attack ...' He pushed a hand through his hair. 'When you finally came back to me, I wanted to ...'

He turned away and sat on the edge of the bed.

Legs shaky, Kelsey stepped away from the door and went to sit next to him. 'I'm sorry.'

'I don't want you to be sorry, Kelsey.'

'What do you want me to be?'

'Mine.'

He offered her everything, she realised. All those hopes and dreams she'd packed away and carried with her everywhere they'd moved. He offered, not only because it was what he wanted, but because he knew she wanted it too. No fear or hesitation leapt up in her. Instead, she felt a welling of love, joy and rightness. She was his, had been all this time, and would be forever.

'I am. Forever and always.' She rested her head on his shoulder. 'And you're mine.'

His arms slipped around her and pulled her onto his lap. Cradled, warm and safe, she sighed, relaxed against him and closed her eyes. Drifted.

Ethan rubbed her back. 'Get undressed so we can hop into bed.'

She merely lifted her arms and his chuckle vibrated against her.

'Stand up.' He gripped her hips, helping her stand, and pulled her shirt over her head.

Feeling tired and groggy didn't stop her from worrying about her scars and what Ethan would think of them. When his lips pressed against the one on her shoulder, she squeezed her eyes closed to will her tears away. If she started crying now, she wouldn't be able to stop. Not when her defences were so low.

His knuckles brushed against her stomach as he undid her jeans. When he crouched in front of her, she held onto his shoulders. He squeezed her left calf, and she smiled at the cue used on the horses so they'd lift a leg. Obliging, she shifted her weight and gripped his shoulders tighter.

Once he'd freed her legs, he stood. She let her hands drift over his shoulders and his chest to his ribs.

For a moment, he stared down at her, his hands on her hips. 'You need sleep. Let me hold you.'

'Okay.'

He moved away and folded back the bedsheet, then held out his hand.

Swallowing, she focused on him and only him, took his hand and let him steady her as she crawled onto the bed.

He slid in next to her and pulled her down beside him. With his chest pressed against her back, one arm around her waist and the other under her cheek, he tangled their legs and pressed a kiss to her shoulder. 'Okay?'

'Yes.' Inadequate as the word was, it was all she could say. How did she put into words the way his warmth cocooned her, thawing all those places she thought forever frozen? How did she tell him his strength at her back, his arm around her, made her feel safer than she ever had? How did she tell him nothing had ever felt as good, as right, as his skin against hers?

'Will you sleep?'

She wiggled, trying to get closer even though their bodies were as close as they could be, and froze when his erection pulsed against her.

'You know that just because it's there, doesn't mean it gets used, don't you?'

She did. She knew. Ethan would never do anything unless she wanted him to. But that one pocket in her mind that strained with memories and nightmares tried to break free and take over.

'Kelsey?'

'I know.' The words rushed out, taking her breath with them. She tried to gulp in more air. Tried so hard not to go back to the time when her face was shoved into that musty couch, her back exposed to that cold room.

The pain.

'Here, see if this is better.' Ethan rolled her towards him, pulled her up onto his chest and wrapped his arms around her shaking shoulders.

She rested her cheek against his heart, counted the rushed beats and tried to slow hers to match. As his slowed, so did hers.

His snore surprised her. When it continued but dipped and rose, she propped her elbows on his chest, lifted her head and frowned. 'You're humming?'

'It works on the horses when they're worried.'

'You're not angry?'

'At you? No.'

She nodded, understanding but not wanting to think about it. 'I'm—'

'Say sorry, and I will be.' He pillowed his hands behind his head and raised an eyebrow at her.

'Okay.' She traced the hair smattering his chest. 'You made me feel safe, holding me like that.'

'It's all I want to do.'

She cocked an eyebrow at him and smiled when he rolled his eyes.

'You know what I mean.'

'I do.' Serious again, she leaned down and kissed his chin. 'I have nothing else to go on other than … I've never come close to being near anyone but you.'

He frowned. 'You never fooled around with *anyone* before?'

Glad the gloom hid the burn that rode up her chest to her cheeks, she shook her head. 'I only ever wanted to be with you.'

'Well …'

Ethan speechless was a treat. One that made her smile, kiss his cheek, his jaw and settle on his mouth.

On a groan, he cupped her head with one hand to fit their mouths better. Still, he didn't rush, didn't push. Didn't ask for more than she gave.

And he'd wanted to hold her. Just hold her. He would do that now if she pulled back or asked him to stop. There'd never be a point of no return with him. Never a moment when *no* wouldn't stop him. With him, she'd never feel the need to say it.

Even now, as their heartbeats galloped together, as his muscles bunched and flexed, his hands stayed gentle on her face, her shoulders.

As much as he wanted her, she knew he held himself in check to let her get used to him like this, to them being together.

For now, her fear stayed tucked away, tamed. Feeling courageous, she freed the hand she'd fisted against his chest, drifted it down his body and traced a fingertip over his boxers and along his length. His gasp, then her name groaned, encouraged her.

Following her instincts, Kelsey straddled him, deliberately pressing against his erection. His mouth found hers, setting free discarded dreams that burst heat over her skin and settled in her blood. It swamped her, set her heart beating fast against his and made her ache for more of him. She rocked her hips to a rhythm that invited his soul to dance with hers.

'You need to sleep.' But he kissed her again. Long and deep, his lips pulling at her heart.

'Are you trying to convince me, or you?' Her voice as unsteady as her arms and legs, she held on as they stared at each other.

'Both.' He nipped at her neck. 'You do need sleep, though.'

'I need you.'

He stilled.

Her heart raced in the silence. Had she gone too far, asked too much this time? Should she stop? Move?

About to gather her defences around her once more, she froze when he reached up and traced her jaw with a shaking finger. 'The moment you want to stop, tell me. If I do anything you don't like, tell me.'

Confusion warred with the ache he'd woken within her. Unsure how to get them back to the place where words weren't needed, she stared at his chest. 'People in movies don't talk this much during sex.'

He shook his head and frowned. 'Movies are make-believe. This is real, and I want you to talk to me. Tell me what you like, what you don't. And,' he sat up and held her close, his hips slowly thrust against her, 'we aren't having sex. I've waited a long time for you. Nothing but making love with you will do for me.'

Kelsey opened her mouth and closed it again. Maybe they did need some words. 'I've waited a long time too.'

With his eyes on hers, he skimmed his hands up her back to her shoulders, then down to her bra. 'Can I?'

With a nod, she licked her lips and shivered as he slid the straps down her arms. He cupped her elbows, urging her to stand, and slid her underwear down her legs. When he squeezed her calf again, she laughed. It turned to a choked groan when his breath tickled her belly, his tongue wet against her skin.

She pushed away the niggling memory of the pain that came next, concentrating instead on the rush she felt as his hands kneaded her muscles and his lips traced over her skin. When he pulled her back onto his lap, his teeth grazing her neck, his fingers tickling the side of her breasts, she sucked in a breath.

'Don't you need to take yours off?'

'Soon.'

'Soon?'

'There's too much I want to do first.'

'First?' Still anticipating the imminent pain, her brain struggled to make sense of it all. 'What do you mean?'

'This.'

He rested his hand high on her thigh, and she flinched before she could stop it.

'This isn't just getting naked and getting it done, Kelsey. It never will be.' His thumb moved in slow circles, edging closer to where she instinctively knew she wanted him to touch.

'There'll be times when you want it quick and primal. Times when you want it long and sweaty.' He pressed warm lips to her neck, where the blush flowed out to cover her whole body.

'But for this time,' he continued, his thumb resting against her, 'it will be a discovery. For both of us.'

'I don't know what else there is to discover.'

'Let me show you.' His thumb pressed against her before she could reply.

She sucked in a breath and let it out on a moan that would have embarrassed her if she'd been coherent enough.

'You've never done this?' His lips lingered on her shoulder, his fingers picking up the automatic rhythm of her hips.

She couldn't talk, couldn't think with all the sensations zapping through her body. Galloping track work, flying over jumps, flinging her arms wide while the horse beneath her dashed through the bush didn't come close to the rush Ethan's hands, mouth and body gave her.

Wanting to touch, to give, she lifted shaking hands to his shoulders, dug her fingers in as something in her belly gathered. It snagged her breath, dripped his name from her tongue, then exploded, rocketing her up higher than she'd ever been.

The moment of panic, the sensation of falling, stopped as soon as Ethan's arms closed around her, holding her so their heartbeats drummed as one.

'How …?' Lifting her head from his shoulder took an effort, but she needed to see his face. 'How can I do that to you?'

His smile was slow, sexy. 'Any way you want.'

'Any way?' Bold now, she traced a finger down his chest to his boxers and quirked an eyebrow at his groan.

'Maybe you should take these off.' She snapped the elastic against his skin.

He moved quickly, pushing her onto the bed and kicking the boxers off as he leaned over and dragged a drawer open. He held her gaze and sheathed himself with the condom.

She cleared her throat. 'Next time, I do that.'

'Absolutely.' Nestling himself between her thighs, he paused. 'This okay?'

'Better than.' She reached up, pulling his face to hers, and kissed him with everything that welled up inside her. He wouldn't hurt her. Wouldn't scare her. Would always look after her. And she would do the same for him.

When he pressed against her, easing himself in, she closed her eyes and let the tears fall.

'Kelsey?' He kissed her cheeks, holding his body still.

'No. Don't stop. I don't ever want this to stop.'

She moved against him, then with him, showed him with the rhythm of their joined bodies that what they did, what they were together, was everything good, everything right.

And when he groaned her name, she held him tightly until they both fell asleep.

***

The first streaks of sunlight squeezed between the curtains as the cockatoos made their morning flight overhead to the river. Magpies warbled, their songs dotted with the higher chirps of sparrows, the caw of a crow.

Awake and energised, Ethan eased out of bed. Humbled when Kelsey reached out to him in sleep, he caught her hand and kissed it, holding it until she relaxed again.

Scooping up his jeans, he hopped down the hallway as he tugged them on, remembering as he did that he had another house guest. Stopping before he reached Pipa's door, he buttoned and zipped.

If she still slept, he didn't want to wake her, so he pressed one finger against the door and peeked around it.

Max stretched out beside Pipa, his paw on the magazine she'd spread out before him. Pipa spoke in rapid-fire sentences, so Ethan could only catch a few words of what she said, but it was enough to know that she entertained Max with a story of a puppy who snored.

Pushing the door open fully, he stepped in. 'Good morning, Pipa.'

A growl locked in his lungs when she jumped, squealed and clapped a hand over her mouth.

Max sat up and growled. When he saw it was Ethan, he hung his head and wagged his tail.

'It's okay, Max. You're a good boy.'

Ethan came into the room and sat on the edge of the bed. Dealing with Kelsey's fear had been heart-wrenching but dealing with Pipa's was soul-destroying.

'I'm sorry, Pip. I should have knocked first.'

'It's okay.' So much like Kelsey, Pipa chewed her bottom lip. 'Mummy still asleep?'

'She is.' He thought of Kelsey, naked in his bed. 'Do you want to see her?'

Pipa shook her head but turned it into a nod, her big blue eyes meeting his. 'Max snorded. Mummy doesn't snore.'

'No, she doesn't.' He reached out and brushed his fingers over her hair as he'd seen Kelsey do so often. 'Did you sleep okay without your mum here?'

Pipa frowned. 'Max snorded, but he kept the bad man away.'

Ethan's heart broke. 'None of us will let the bad man anywhere near you, Pip. Mark and his dogs are outside, Max is here, your mum and I are just down the hall.' He rested a finger under her chin. 'You have Rita, Carol and Snow, Jex, Zoe, and so many other people who will protect you. None of us will let him near you.'

'You look after Mummy, too?'

'Yes.' He nodded. 'Forever.'

He had just enough time to shift his weight so that she didn't knock him off the bed when she launched herself at him and hugged him around the neck, holding on tight.

'Hey.' With no choice but to hold onto her and rub her back, he rocked her. 'It's okay, honey. You're okay.'

Hoping he was right, he stood, Max jumping off the bed to follow as Ethan headed to his bedroom. Flicking back the sheet, he bent and lowered Pipa onto the bed next to Kelsey. When Pipa's hands captured his cheeks, he stilled.

She stared at him. 'I love you.'

Kissing her forehead, he closed his eyes a moment. 'I love you too, Pip.'

Her smile as she snuggled up to Kelsey lit a fire in his heart. Like Kelsey, he'd fight tooth and nail to keep her safe, just like he would fight to keep them both right here, where they belonged.

Leaving them to sleep, he paused in the doorway where Max sprawled and gave him a scratch. 'You look after them.'

In the kitchen, he put the kettle on, broke some eggs into a bowl and started making mucky eggs. By the time Mark knocked and let himself in, Ethan had downed two cups of coffee and three pieces of toast while making a mountain of food for everyone.

Mark sat at the table, hands behind his head, legs stretched out before him. 'Other than a mob of 'roos, a couple of foxes and three deer, nothing tried to get onto your property last night.'

The dark smudges under Mark's eyes coupled with the beginnings of a beard had Ethan frowning. They were all tired, and none of them would get much sleep until Bristow had been stopped.

'I didn't think I'd heard the dogs.' He sat a mug of coffee at Mark's elbow.

Mark grunted and sipped his drink.

Ethan dished up four pieces of toast and a good chunk of the eggs and slid the plate in front of Mark. He served himself and saluted with his first forkful. 'I'm thinking, once this is all over, we can take a camping trip to Bailey's Rocks.'

'Sounds like a plan.' Mark shovelled eggs and toast into his mouth.

'So,' he said, glancing towards the hallway, 'Kelsey still asleep?'

'Yes.' Ethan couldn't help the grin, but remembering what Kelsey had told him last night, he sobered. 'Don't let her evade today.'

Frowning, Mark set his knife and fork down and picked up his coffee. 'Evade? Or avoid?'

'Both.'

'Avoid what?'

Ethan hated going behind her back. Although he didn't mention anything she'd told him in confidence, he didn't like the ball that lodged in his gut. But the secrets she'd kept had nearly destroyed her, destroyed them. He couldn't let her keep them now. Not when he feared they'd fester and eventually eat a hole in the confidence and love she'd only just begun to trust.

'Don't let her avoid telling you everything.'

Mark gave a nod. 'I'll make sure she doesn't.'

Max lumbered in and, after sniffing the air and giving Ethan a glare, flopped on the floor next to Mark.

'Morning, Max.' Mark prodded the dog with his toe, rubbing the offered belly when Max wriggled onto his back.

Pipa came around the corner and stopped.

'Pipa, you remember Mark?' Ethan held out his hand.

Stopping to pat Max, Pipa eyed Mark, then nodded. 'Hello, Muck.'

'Morning, Pip.' The smile that tugged at Mark's mouth eased some of the shadows under his eyes.

'Max snores,' she said, leaving the dog to climb up on Ethan's lap.

'Mucky eggs!' She grinned up at Ethan.

How could he resist? Handing her his fork, he settled her more comfortably on his lap. She dug in, getting most of the first forkful in her mouth, then tipped her head back to look at him.

'Do you snore?'

184

'No.' Ethan slanted a look across the table. 'But Mark does.'

'Mark does what?' Kelsey walked in, her damp hair edging its way back to its fiery copper, and Ethan's heart did a slow roll, settled back into place, and his world righted.

***

Kelsey met Ethan's gaze and didn't care that the flush started low and rose to her face. He'd held her all night, his chest to her back, his hand possessive on her breast, his breath on her neck. He'd cocooned her in warmth and safety, love and peace.

Still surrounded with that love and safety, she walked to him while Pipa grinned at them both.

'Snore!' Pipa giggled as Kelsey kissed Ethan hard and fast, then dropped a soft one on Pipa's upturned face.

'Mark snores, does he?' Kelsey smiled at him across the table, feeling a sharp tug of guilt when she noticed the smudges of fatigue under his eyes.

He stared at her. 'I need you to be totally honest with me today.'

She jerked back. Sitting at the table beside Ethan, she wondered exactly what had been said before she'd come out. 'I was going to be.'

'You were? And now?'

She lifted her chin and crossed her arms over her chest. The flush that crept up her neck and cheeks now had nothing to do with warmth and peace.

'You might have to arrest me for smacking an officer if you keep up that high-and-mighty tone.'

'Is that all I'll be arresting you for?'

It wasn't Ethan's fault. He'd taken her away from it all for the night and made her forget that everything could, and most likely would, fall apart. But she still had to pay the price for her actions. Now, reality snapped her back and sucked her in, ready to spit her out again.

'I guess you'll be telling me soon enough.'

'Mummy?' Pipa started scrabbling off Ethan's lap.

'No, Pip. Stay there.' She dug up a smile. 'I'm fine.'

Pipa frowned at Mark. 'Mummy stopped the bad man from hurting me. You not make her cry.'

Mark stood before Kelsey could and walked around the table until he squatted between her and Pipa. Putting a hand on each of theirs, he squeezed Kelsey's but kept his gaze on Pipa.

'I don't want to make her cry. I know she'd do anything to protect you, so I'll do all I can to protect her. Okay?'

Pipa frowned at him, then at Kelsey. 'We don't have to go?'

'No.' Kelsey shook her head, realising that she hadn't even contemplated running this time. 'We're not going anywhere.'

Beside her, Ethan let out a breath.

Kelsey held hers, because despite last night, they still had a long way to go before either of them trusted without hesitation. Knowing it punctured the confidence Ethan had given her.

'Nine a.m., Kelsey.' Mark stood, grabbing his keys and phone from the table. 'Don't make me wonder if you're coming.'

'I said I'll be there.' Feeling the sharp sting from knowing he lacked faith in her, she frowned at him. 'But I'll need to bring Pipa with me.'

Ethan rested a hand on her shoulder. 'I've taken leave for a week, so Pipa can come with me to the park while we wait for you.'

Was he worried she'd skip town? Is that why he wanted to keep Pipa with him?

Unsure of how much she should lean, or how much Ethan trusted her, Kelsey shook her head but couldn't look at either of them. 'You didn't need to do that.'

'I did it because I wanted to be here for you.' Ethan's hand squeezed. 'Don't shut me out now, Kelsey. Please.'

'I'm not.'

She wasn't shutting him out if she acted with self-preservation in mind, right?

'But when you still don't trust me not to pick up and run, especially now …' She gritted her teeth, determined to get her words out without crying. 'It cuts. Deep.'

Conscious of Pipa watching them all and listening, Kelsey shook her head again. 'It's not the right time for this discussion.'

'I think it is.' Mark held his hand out to Pipa. 'How about we take Max out to say hi to the pups?'

'You have puppies?' Pipa scrambled off Ethan's lap.

It would be useless to argue, so Kelsey said nothing as Pipa took Mark's hand.

'As for the other thing,' Mark said as he grabbed his cap from the couch, plopped it on Pipa's head and glanced at Kelsey, 'he's not coming into my town without me knowing. And he's definitely not getting anywhere near either of you.'

Pipa skipped to the door with him and gave Kelsey and Ethan a wave before she disappeared outside.

Ethan turned her seat so that she faced him. He put his hand on the back of her neck and stared at her with all his anguish and grief so naked she couldn't look away.

'I don't believe you'd pick up and run, but I can't help the terror that clutches my chest when that choice is there for you. I can't help thinking about the day after you jumped out my window, when I couldn't find you anywhere. I had to wait five years for you to come back, Kelsey. I can't go through that again.'

'I'm sorry.' She'd never contemplated how distraught he would be to lose her.

Ignoring the protesting creak of the chair, she sat on his lap and cradled his head to her shoulder. 'Running again, leaving you isn't a choice for me now, Ethan. It hasn't even entered my head.'

He lifted his, found her mouth with his lips and branded hers.

Threading her hand through his hair, she held him away and looked into his eyes. 'Do you believe me? That this is where I am, where I will always be? With you?'

The sigh that vibrated from his body to hers was one of deep release.

He kissed one cheek. 'Yes.'

And the other. 'Yes.'

Then he took her mouth in a kiss that broke the storm inside her, and she poured everything she was, everything she had into that one touch of their lips.

'You're mine,' she said. 'And I'm yours. Always.'

CHAPTER TWENTY-ONE

Running on adrenaline, Brian shot off emails, requested information and played phone tag with at least three people. He fought the craving for a cup of tea—he'd skipped that morning ritual to get out the door and to work quicker—and promised himself one as soon as he finished the request for Henry Bristow's records.

It kept him busy, nearly busy enough to forget Haylee's silence that morning. He hadn't tried small talk, wanting to avoid slipping up and asking if she'd made an appointment yet. She would, of course. She'd come in, slice herself open and let all her secrets ooze. Then he'd dig through everything to find the puzzle pieces he needed to put Bristow away.

He could have saved her some torment and questioned her last night, but he needed to make it official. Giving Bristow's legal team any sort of crack to hammer at injustice wasn't going to happen.

So, instead of getting under Haylee's feet and on her nerves, he'd left early. He'd missed the boys' laughter and mischief, that early jolt that woke his soul better than any energy drink ever could.

Signing and sending an email, he checked his incomings. With nothing that could let him move forward with any of his cases, he pushed away from the desk before he snapped. He'd get his cup of tea and see if any of the cheese and crackers were left. Anything to keep his hands moving and his mind off Haylee.

The quiet of the mess room set his teeth on edge. At least the kettle rumbled as it boiled, providing a backbeat to the headache drumming at his temples.

Scrubbing his mug under the tap, he gritted his teeth. He needed people to get back to him. He needed answers. He needed people to do their bloody jobs so he could do his. He'd asked questions, and someone had the answers. They just needed to give them to him. Was it that hard?

Jewell reached past him to turn off the tap. 'You have a visitor.'

His shoulders snapped straight. 'Haylee?'

'Yes. She's waiting downstairs.'

Tension clamped his muscles. Was she making a personal call, or ... 'She asked for me?'

'She wanted a message passed on to you.' Jewell held up a sticky note.

Can I see you before I make my statement, please?

'I'm not being nosey. I'm asking because I like Haylee, and you.' Jewell paused. 'Is she okay?'

He didn't know the answer to that.

'She will be.'

Now that the wound had opened, it would start to heal, wouldn't it? He'd be there for her, give her whatever she needed, even if it was only time or space. No matter what she thought, she'd survived everything because of her strength of character and her heart. She loved her boys and would do anything for them. So how could she not be okay eventually?

'Was there something else?'

Jewell didn't answer as she watched him sit his cup upside down on the sink. He turned for the door.

'Maybe you should take a moment?'

He frowned at her over his shoulder. 'Why?'

Nodding at his wet hands, untidy shirt and scowl, Jewell lifted an eyebrow.

He strode back, grabbed a paper towel, wiped his hands, straightened his clothes and adjusted his tie. Holding his arms wide, he tilted his head at her.

'Better.' She crossed her arms and leaned against the bench. 'I know you need someone to be angry at right now, and I'd rather it be at me than you go down and scowl at Haylee, but this is the only free pass you get.'

The air whooshed out of his lungs, making his shoulders sag. 'I'm sorry.'

'Like I said, I understand.' Two steps and she was in front of him and taking his hands in hers. 'I'm kinda glad you're comfortable enough with me to use me like that, but if you want a punching bag, I'm not your girl.'

'I would never do that.' He tugged at his hands, stopping when she didn't let go. 'I could never physically or verbally use you, or anyone, as a punching bag. Even the term sickens me.'

'Because you stand up for the innocent, the good, and try to put the bad away.'

'Damn right.'

She stood before him, not looking the least bit scared or angry.

Considering her, he frowned. 'What was that?'

'My brother is a psychologist. I've picked up a few things.'

She grinned at him, bounced on her toes to look over his shoulder, then kissed him so quick, he didn't have time to react.

'You looked like you needed it.'

'You're nothing like I thought you were.'

'You're pretty much like I thought you were. But then, I've watched you a lot over the past year. I doubt you thought of me unless I was in front of you.'

He shook his head and found he could smile. 'I thought of you.'

'And now you need to think of your sister.' She let his hands go and stepped back. 'At least you don't look like you want to stomp on someone now.'

She grabbed two bottles of water from the fridge. 'I told them we wouldn't be long.'

'We?'

'She has Rupert with her, and as young as he is, I don't think she'll want him around those sorts of vibes.' She handed him a bottle, tugged him out of

191

the mess room and towards the elevators. 'And as great an uncle as you are, if you get called away, you can't take him with you.'

'You'll look after him?'

'If Haylee trusts me to.' She glanced up at him. 'And I guess if you trust me too.'

'I do.' And wasn't that something.

They waited in silence for an elevator. When a door opened, he let Jewell step in before him. Alone with her in the small space, Brian closed his eyes and rested his head against the cold metal wall. 'So, what car does your brother drive?'

'An FJ. A black one. He keeps telling Dad he'll paint yellow stripes on it.'

'A Tigers fan?'

He stood straight and gazed down at her. This woman, whom he'd ignored during the past year, kept surprising him with her heart and mind. She understood he needed a moment of diversion and gave it. What did he have to give in return?

'He is, and Dad is a diehard Pies man.'

'Footy season must be tense in your family.'

'It used to be,' she said, her lips twitching, 'until Mum laid down some rules.'

'Oh?'

She grinned as the lift stopped and she stepped out before him. 'Let's just say that she always manages to get the unfinished jobs around the house done before the semi-finals. This year she had her long-awaited herb garden and vegetable patch dug and planted. Next season she plans on finishing it all off with a pond.'

'I don't doubt she'll get what she wants.'

'We Taylor women usually do.'

She cleared her throat as they approached the front desk where Haylee was signing the attendance book and Rupert was kicking his legs and babbling to anyone who'd listen.

Haylee glanced up as Rupert reached chubby arms to Brian. 'If I'd told you exactly when I was coming in, I would've freaked out too much knowing you'd wait for me.'

'You don't have to explain.'

Conscious of everyone around them, he lifted Rupert to his chest and kept his gaze on his sister's pale face. 'I figured it might be today seeing as Ashley has the morning at school with James.' He passed her the bottle of water. 'You know I'm with you through whatever comes, right?'

She licked her lips, then lifted her worried gaze to his.

'I do.' Her smile edged towards being true. 'I'm still stuck on why, but I know you are.' She stepped forward and kissed Rupert's cheek, then Brian's. 'And it's time you know it goes both ways. I'm here for you, too.'

Before he could find his voice, she turned away and followed an officer through the safety barriers and into a room where she'd purge herself of all the pain others had inflicted on her.

'Her boys have a terrific family unit to draw on.' Jewell wiped a tissue across Rupert's chin, catching a thread of dribble before it tethered to Brian's shirt. 'Whatever start they might have had, they're surrounded by love and support now.'

'It's what they deserve.'

'It is.' Jewell glanced around, leaning back to look outside the full-length glass windows to the chairs and tables arranged in the shade of the building. 'Do you have time for a break?'

But at that moment, Brian couldn't think past the fact that his sister was alone in her misery. He'd said he would be there for her, through anything, but in this, he had to leave her alone.

'She'll be okay, Brian.' Jewell pressed a hand to his back, nudging him forward. 'She knows you're out here and will be here when she's finished. She knows her baby is being looked after by the person she loves and trusts the most.'

He stayed silent as she led him outside, chose a table to sit at and pointed him to a chair.

'I'll be back in a minute.'

She left him, but he watched her as she waited in line. She smiled and chatted with the cashier and stopped to talk to someone else waiting in line. A compliment about shoes, by the way the other woman lifted a foot and beamed. Making someone's moment with a few words was a gift Jewell used as often as she could, and he wondered who did that for her. Not him. Not in all the time he'd known her had he done anything, said anything to truly light her up as she did others.

He looked down at Rupert, who was clearly teething, and replaced the baby's fist with his own finger, letting Rupert lock onto the right spot and gnaw.

'What do I do?'

'With what?' Jewell sat two paper cups on the table, both well out of Rupert's reach, even when he stretched right back and strained against Brian's hold.

'I didn't forget you.' She held out a third cup. Empty.

Rupert babbled his thanks, then rapped the cup against Brian's chest and babbled some more.

'I think you just made his day.'

'I figured he'd want one as well.' Jewell smiled, then laughed when the cup caught Brian on the chin. 'Sorry.'

'Don't be.' One hand holding Rupert close, he reached for his cup but gave it up as a bad idea when Rupert wriggled.

'Here.' Jewell held her hands out. 'Mine's too hot to drink yet.'

With a new audience, Rupert went into a serious monologue, the cup acting as an elaboration for certain points. All through it, Jewell *ooed* and *aahed*, gasped in mock shock, laughed.

'You make it easier,' Brian said, knowing he'd caught her off guard when she blinked at him.

'I've been out of sorts all morning.' He laughed at himself. 'I've been out of sorts for a long time. But you've made it easier.'

'Well, as far as you're concerned, I do have an ulterior motive.'

He smiled. 'I'd like to talk about that some more, in private.' He quirked an eyebrow, feeling happy when she giggled.

'I've noticed you do things and say things to lift people without ever expecting anything in return.'

She shrugged. 'I have four brothers.'

'I don't think so.' He picked up his cup and sipped.

'Like this,' he said, pointing at his cup, 'I've never told you how I like my tea, but you know. You know because you care. You care because it's who you are.'

'Like I said, ulterior motive.'

'And if you had no ulterior motive, you'd still be out here, getting me a drink, playing with Rupert because you know we need the distraction. You would have still made the cashier smile, would have still complimented that lady on her shoes.'

'You make me sound like something special.'

'Because I think you are.' He shook his head. 'I know you are.'

'You want to know what I think?'

He tilted his head, not sure he was going to like it, but nodded anyway.

'I think you know in your gut that this is it, that whatever Haylee says in there today is going to change the direction of the case, but you're afraid to trust it, trust yourself, so you put it on me. At least then you'll have some-one else to blame if it all goes wrong.'

Heat erupted, a savage burn under the skin. Words, both chilled and cutting, locked in his throat. Because she was right. To a point.

'I wouldn't blame you. I'd find a way to make you angry at me and then blame that on you. And yes, I do know, in here'—he fisted a hand to his stomach—'and here'—he moved it to his heart—'that things are about to change. I don't know how, or even if it has more to do with Haylee than the case, but I know.'

'And you don't trust it?'

He struggled with the truth, but looking at Jewell, he couldn't lie. To her, or to himself anymore.

'I didn't. For a long time, I couldn't. I never saw my parents' accident coming. I never thought Haylee would leave home before she was sixteen and shack up with a drug addict. I never imagined her boys would freeze with terror if I moved too quickly.'

He had to take a breath. Had to squash the need to fist his hands and shake them at the world.

'I never believed Jaiyden would die the way she did.'

Jewell reached across the table and waited until he unclenched one hand and put it in hers.

'I think you did.' She held his hand tighter. 'And that's what scares you. You did in some way know, but you ignored it. And who wouldn't?' She tugged until he stopped trying to pull away. 'Who would want to believe that bad things are about to happen? Especially if you have no way to stop them.'

'You slice me open.' He could feel it. Everything he was, everything he thought he should be leaked out into a puddle at his feet.

'Hurting you is the last thing I want to do.' She let go of his hand and moved into the chair next to him. 'I only want you to see what I see.'

'And what's that?'

'A man who would do anything, be anything to protect those he loves. Even those he has no connection to. You help people every day. You deal with the worst of them most of the time, but you still help people. It's who you are, but it takes a toll on you.' She traced a finger over his brow, smoothing out his scowl. 'I think you knew this would happen if you let me in.'

'Is that goodbye?'

His heart burned, but he'd take it, swallow it down like the bitter pill of wisdom it was. Because he had known. He'd stayed away because he'd known she would see him, really see him, and expose what he'd tried so hard to hide.

'No.' She leaned in and rested her head on his shoulder. 'Unless you want it to be.'

'No.'

'But you still don't trust it, or us.'

Could he? With so much at stake, could he reach down and take hold of what he knew to be right and true, and free it?

'I want to.'

'Then that's a start.' Kissing his cheek before she straightened, she bounced Rupert on her knee.

'I think you picked up more from your brother than you're letting on.'

Her smile was quick and full. 'I dabbled a little too.'

'Dabbled?' It was easy to lift his arm and drape it over her shoulder.

'Okay, so it was a dare. A bet, really.' She shrugged. 'Mica said he was the smartest out of all of us, so I enrolled in the same uni course as him.'

'And?' Intrigued, he watched the blush creep into her cheeks.

'I finished third in the class.'

'And Mica?'

She grinned then. 'Fourth.'

They sat in silence as Rupert chewed his fist. There hadn't been many moments of easy silence in his life, especially not with a woman he could see himself spending more time with.

Letting his fingers massage her nape, he breathed her in. 'It's been a roller-coaster ride sitting out here with you, but you still somehow make it right.'

'You would have brooded otherwise. Besides, if we're going to do this,' she waggled a finger between them, 'then you're better off knowing what you're getting into. I'm not going to hide who I am, then show you the real me once I've snared you. It's not fair on either of us.'

'I like who you are.' He touched a finger under her chin and tipped her face to his. 'Thank you for distracting me, and for being you.'

And as good and as tough and enlightening as the break had been, what was to come needed his full attention, because Jewell had been right, his gut said that change was coming, something was about to happen.

She'd been right about the other times as well. Listening to that tremble in his belly was only part of the equation, though, for how did he solve the equation when his instincts never differentiated between good and bad, only that there would be *something*?

Things had to swing in his favour. If he didn't get the answers he needed, he'd find a way to get them. Maybe then the torment Haylee hugged across her chest as she walked towards him would lessen.

Words clogged in his throat as Jewell handed Rupert over and pressed her cheek to Haylee's. He'd ask her one day what she'd said to Haylee in that moment. They were words that made Haylee hug Rupert close and nuzzle his copper hair as she took a deep breath in before letting it out again. For that alone, he owed Jewell more than she'd ever know.

'Will you walk me to my car?' Haylee held her hand out to him.

'Of course.' He took hers and squeezed lightly to still its slight tremor. 'I don't want to say the wrong thing, but I need to say I'm proud of you.'

'I couldn't have done this without you.' She squeezed his hand back. 'And I'm proud of you, too.'

'I don't feel like I've had much to be proud of since Mum and Dad died.' He frowned down at her. 'Maybe we both have more to be proud of than we thought.'

'Maybe.' She nodded to Jewell, then walked with him to the car park. 'I think I'll take the boys out for some ice-cream.'

'Do me a favour?' They stopped at her car. 'Bring me home an ice-cream?'

Her smile lifted his heart. 'I can do that, and the boys would enjoy some time at the corner park while we wait for you to get home.'

'I'll swing past and give them a push on the swings.' He dropped a kiss on Rupert's head, then opened the door for her. 'I can push you, too, if you want.'

'Like you used to? No thanks.' But she smiled. 'I don't think my stomach could handle the heights now.'

Her smile meant more than pushing his point, so he grinned at her. 'I'll see you, and my ice-cream, later.'

He waited as she got in the car and drove away. Waited a moment longer as the pulse of traffic moved through the city. They'd passed a milestone, one that had sat heavy between them for years. They had more to pass yet, but his gut, for once, told him they'd be okay.

CHAPTER TWENTY-TWO

Kelsey purged her heart of Spencer's attacks while Mark took down her guilt and shame in some sort of police shorthand. He sat beside her at the desk, his police vest bulking up an already broad chest, his eyes hard. His voice, though professional, held a hint of the friend she'd grown up with, the brother she'd adopted as her own. Her friend Mark had walked from Ethan's house two hours before, and Mark the cop now sat beside her.

'You've gotten better at the intimidation thing.'

The cup of tea Ethan had made her earlier and the mouthful of omelette she'd eaten somersaulted in her stomach. Eyeing the bin, just in case, she balled a handful of ripped, sodden tissues.

'You've gotten better at avoiding.' Mark tilted his head, tapping the pen on his notebook. 'I told you before we started that I'm not interviewing you. You're giving a statement.' He softened a fraction. 'You've done the hardest part already. I just need a few gaps filled in.'

Kelsey shifted in her seat. Her eyes and throat ached. Her heart rippled. What if he didn't believe her? What if he did?

She swallowed, took a breath and reached for another tissue. 'Like what?'

'Like the time between the first assault and finding out Jaiyden was pregnant.'

Wrapping the new tissue around the others to hold them all together, she fisted her hand around them. 'After we left the alley, she took me to the building she stayed in. It was trash. A heap of girls squatted there. Took guys there.' She stared at the wall behind him. 'Three weeks later, I came back from work to find her throwing up. We both knew what it meant. I got her a pregnancy test to be sure.'

'Did she go to a doctor?'

Kelsey scoffed. 'Next time use a condom, he says. Didn't even bother to ask questions.'

It still made her mad.

'He looked at Jaiyden and made an assumption, then wondered why Jaiyden called him a dickhead.' Kelsey shrugged. 'We figured we'd just keep doing what we were doing. Jaiyden wouldn't even think of aborting. Wouldn't talk to me for a day when I told her she had a choice.'

'She worked while she was pregnant?'

'Not in the way you're asking. I was working as a stablehand for a while, but when he kept finding us and we had to start moving around, we got seasonal work. Both of us. Picking fruit, rousing, a few milking jobs. She liked working outside. Out of the two of us, she was the morning person. Funnily enough, she was happiest when she was mucking around in the mud.'

Kelsey half-smiled, the ache in her heart making her tremble.

'One question.' Mark tilted his head. 'Why do you keep saying was?'

Tears sprang before she could stop them. 'I haven't seen her since Pipa was a week old.'

'She just left you to look after her baby?'

'No, not voluntarily.' Kelsey wished she could say yes, that Jaiyden had walked out on her newborn daughter and left Kelsey to raise her.

'I need you to be straight with me, Kelsey. I can't work with hints and allusions. I need you to spell it out, everything.'

'I don't know what happened, not for sure.' She strangled the ball of tissues. 'But I think he took Jaiyden that day. He took her and I never saw her again.'

His face too passive, Mark leaned forward. 'Tell me exactly what you mean, Kelsey.'

She swallowed a hiccup. 'I think he killed her.'

For a moment, Mark didn't move, just stared until Kelsey squirmed.

'You never thought to mention this first? Never thought to tell me on Friday that you suspect the mother of the child you claimed as yours has been murdered? By the very man you're now running from?'

Growing up, she'd often been the cause of Mark's anger, but the crackle of rage that whirled around him now chilled her. 'I never claimed her as mine. You all assumed.'

He angled his head slightly.

'I couldn't, okay!' She swiped at her tears, angry that they made her look and feel weak. 'I could hardly even think about it without breaking. And,' she jabbed a finger at him, 'would you have believed me?'

His jaw clenched a moment. 'I've told you from the start, I'm here to help. If you don't believe it, or me, at least respect that beyond me caring about you, it's my job, my duty, so trust that.' He stared at her, then shook his head. 'I need to know everything, Kelsey. No evasions now. No secrets.'

Shame was a hot, quick flare. Clenching her hands on her lap, Kelsey stared at the table. 'What else is there?'

'I need Pipa's birth date, where she was born, the doctor's name, the name of the midwife who Jaiyden spoke to about making you Pipa's legal guardian, if you remember it. I can try to chase it up so you've got proof.' Taking her hand in his, he squeezed it lightly. 'So far, you haven't broken any laws.'

She winced at that. 'We used false names sometimes.'

'For what purpose?'

'Just when we stayed at caravan parks.' She lifted a shoulder. 'Just in case.'

'Did you sign papers under a false name?'

She took a moment to make sure. 'No. We always paid cash when we stayed somewhere. Jaiyden used her own name on Pipa's birth certificate and didn't name anyone as the father.'

'So far, so good.' He tilted his head. 'Is there anything else you're worried about?'

'Will I be charged with kidnapping?'

He hesitated. 'Child services may want to get involved.'

Panic slammed her back and took her breath. 'And if they do? They can't take her from me! They can't—'

'Kelsey.' He pulled her to her feet, gripped her arms and gave them a quick shake. 'Look at me.'

She tried, but his head blurred, tripled. 'Can't breathe.'

'You can. Look at me.' He snapped the words out. 'Exhale first.'

She tried but quickly inhaled half a lungful of air. She tried again and kept going until she could suck air in through her nose and blow it out through pursed lips.

Lifting her hands to show she was okay, she eased onto the chair again. 'I'm the only mother she knows, the only love and safety she has,' she said. 'They can't take her from me. I won't let them.'

'Can't you see that Ethan and I are just as invested in her happiness and safety as you? Don't you know that we've agonised over the both of you since you came home?'

'It's not the same for you.' She waved a hand between them. 'Once Spencer is no longer stalking us, you can forget about it.'

'Fuck that, Kelsey!' He paced away and back again. 'Things like this, no one ever forgets.' He shoved a hand through his hair. 'I need to make some phone calls so that we know what the next step is.' He scowled at her. 'And you need to get your head around the fact that we're involved, that beyond this'—he jabbed a finger at the police creed hanging on the wall beside her— '*I'm* involved just as much as you are now.'

A trio of dings from the front desk had Mark stalking to the door and yanking it open, though he paused a moment.

'Ethan's isn't the only world you turned upside down when you left.' Mark looked at her over his shoulder. 'Just think about that next time you want to take a shot at me or withhold something that could let me help you.'

Without waiting for an answer or an apology, he marched from the room.

Pipa's giggle and then Ethan's voice came from the foyer. She quashed the need to walk into Ethan's arms when Mark led them to where she sat.

'What's wrong?' Ethan reached for her as Pipa did.

'I need to pee, Mummy.'

She shook her head at Ethan, took Pipa in her arms and without looking at Mark made her escape. She needed a minute. Just a minute to get herself under control, to deal with the fact that although Mark hadn't told her he thought Jaiyden was dead, he hadn't told her he thought she was alive, either.

Pipa sang on the toilet, her young voice innocent and carefree. It clenched her heart. How did she explain that Jaiyden might never come back to them? How did she tell Pipa without falling apart that she'd never get to know the mother who'd loved her?

***

'What's going on?' Ethan stared at the door Kelsey had closed quietly behind her and Pipa.

'I can't discuss it with you without Kelsey's permission.' But Mark's worried frown stayed on the door as well.

'If something's happened, I need to know.' Something had put that stoop in her shoulders, that emotional void in her eyes.

'She had a panic attack.' Mark sat at his desk and started typing as though it was nothing.

'You really won't talk to me about it?' Ethan shoved a hand through his hair.

'That's how it goes.' Mark shot a hand up when Ethan stepped forward. 'You want me to break her trust, my oath as a policeman, my workplace rules of confidentiality, just because you want to know? She'll be out in a few minutes, and if she says it's okay, we can all talk about it, but until then, you need to sit your arse down and wait.'

Ethan sat and tapped his foot, listening to the clock ticking on the wall a form of torture.

'You believe I'm right about Jaiyden,' Kelsey said from the doorway, Pipa holding her hand as she studied Mark. 'You didn't want to tell me, but you believe me.'

'I'm sorry.' Mark gestured to the seat between him and Ethan.

She frowned at it, then shifted her gaze to Ethan's. 'You'll stay?'

It swelled his chest and closed some of the distance that had settled between them. 'Absolutely.'

Too pale, too quiet, she stared at nothing. Even when he pressed his knee and thigh against hers, she didn't lean into him or even look at him, and the distance between them trebled.

'I have a favour to ask you, Pipa.' Mark opened a drawer, pulled out a manila folder with a cartoon police officer on the front and held it out to her.

'Can you colour this and write your name here?' He tapped the police badge on the picture. 'Then you can be a special police person.'

Pipa clutched her hands to her chest and tipped her head back to look up at Kelsey. 'Can I, Mummy?'

'I think you'd make a great special police person.' Her lips moved to form a smile, but it carried no emotion.

'You can work over here.' Mark put the folder and some pencils on the floor.

Pipa didn't hesitate. She hopped down from Kelsey's lap and sprawled on her belly on the carpet.

After a moment of watching Pipa start to write her name carefully, Mark turned back to them. 'I need to make some phone calls to homicide and CIU.' He met Kelsey's gaze. 'They'll want to talk to you.'

'CIU?'

'The criminal investigation unit. Two detectives will be travelling from Warrnambool, so it will take a few hours to organise and get them here.'

'What do we do in the meantime?' Ethan put his arm around Kelsey's shoulders and tried to rub some energy into the stillness that gripped her.

'I'd suggest you get some rest, something to eat.' Mark frowned at Pipa. 'I suggest you find somewhere else for her to stay, too.'

'She'll be with me,' Ethan said. That's what Kelsey needed from him the most—for him to look after her precious girl.

'Good.' Mark stood, then squatted down beside Pipa. 'Special Officer Pipa, nice work.' He smoothed a hand over her head. 'When your mum comes back later, I'll have this signed and ready for you, okay?'

In answer, Pipa jumped up and threw her arms around Mark's neck, and although he smiled, the burden he carried dulled it. Ethan had bigger worries, though, like how to help the one who sat beside him, too quiet as the world around her moved on.

'We'll head home, then.' He rose and held out his hand to Pipa.

Mark stood and helped Kelsey to her feet. 'I'll let you know what's going to happen as soon as I can.'

When Kelsey only nodded, Ethan met Mark's gaze over her head. Yeah, something else was wrong. He didn't know what, and neither did Mark judging by the frown he gave.

With Kelsey's silence surrounding them, Mark led them back through to the front desk and got Kelsey to sign out.

Before Ethan stepped through the front door, he faced Mark. 'You've made a bad situation bearable, so thanks.'

Mark sighed. 'I think we're all just doing the best we can.'

'We are. And I'm going to do more.'

Mark nodded. 'Good.' He glanced over his shoulder as the phone rang. 'I'll make those phone calls.'

He closed the door between the foyer and office and left Ethan staring after him.

Pipa didn't let him stand and brood for long. 'What we do more?'

'Have fun, laugh, play.' He tweaked her nose. 'All the good things.'

'I like fun. Mummy bakes cake and we eat it with no plates.' She giggled and covered her mouth. 'But we not tell anyone.'

'Your secret is safe with me.' And it gave him an idea.

She bounced in his arms and sang to herself as they walked to the car. 'We go home?'

'We are.' He kissed her nose, then helped her into her seat.

All the while, Kelsey kept quiet. She stared out the window as they passed through town, where a few stray Valentine's Day hearts still clung to shop windows, then past the childhood home she barely glanced at.

As they continued out of town, the gums along the side of the road strobed sunlight and shadow, the crows hopped and dodged traffic as they pecked at roadkill, and all the while, Ethan tried to think of something to say.

He slowed at the dirt road. From here, he had three kilometres to get her to talk. Otherwise, when they got home, he'd lose her to acres of land, or she would find chores to do so she didn't have to talk.

'So, this summer has been a scorcher so far.'

He caught her sideways glance.

'Autumn will be tough if we don't get some rain soon.'

'There's a storm coming.'

He ducked his head to look at the sky through the windscreen. 'You've never been wrong predicting them before.'

'No.'

'You need to tell me what you're thinking.' He slowed to avoid a pair of blue-tongue lizards sunbaking in the middle of the road. 'I can't fix things if I don't know what's wrong.'

'That's it.' She lifted her hands. 'You don't need to fix it.'

'I don't understand.'

She took a deep breath. 'I can defend myself. Have done a few times now.'

'No one says you can't or haven't.' He glanced in the rear-view mirror, glad to see Pipa preoccupied with the shadows pulsing over her legs.

'You and Mark made sure I could when I turned fourteen.'

'We did.' He had an idea where she was heading, but he'd let her get there in her own time and her own way. She'd had too much taken from her, had lost too much control for him to take more.

'You all keep saying to let you help, that you'll get between him and me.'

'Yes.'

If she asked him to step back, he'd have something to say. No matter what she wanted, he wouldn't leave her alone when he knew she needed him. If she hated him for it, too bad.

'I don't want to face off with him. I don't want to be anywhere near him ever again, but if it comes to it, if they get him when we're in Melbourne, I don't want you shielding me. I won't let him see what he's done to me by hiding behind you.'

She pushed the hair from her face. 'Having you beside me, knowing you're there for me is more than enough to get me through anything life throws at me now.'

'Well.' All the fight rushed out of him, leaving his shoulders slumped, his heart oddly light. Holding out a hand, he waited until she linked her fingers with his. 'I still think I have a reason and a right to five minutes alone with him.'

'You and Mark both, I think.'

'I'd fight Mark to go first.'

'Why not?' She waved her free hand in the air. 'The two of you always used to make up reasons to roll around and show off.'

'Show off?'

She glanced at him. 'You weren't?'

Lifting her hand to kiss her knuckles, he grinned. 'Maybe.'

'I like it when you do that.'

'What, show off?'

She laughed and he nearly ran off the road. Pulling over, he framed her face with his hands and kissed her. 'I like it when you do that.'

'It's getting easier.'

He kissed her again and grinned against her mouth when Pipa giggled.

'Why you kiss Mummy?'

'Because I love your mum.'

Kelsey pulled back and stared at him wide-eyed, but Ethan only grinned. 'You'll get used to it.'

Her hands cuffed his wrists. 'I don't want to.' She touched her lips to his, then his cheek. 'I don't want to get used to the rush it gives me, the way it makes me shiver inside.'

'You'll get used to it, but I'll make sure you never lose the rush.'

To show her, he sucked her bottom lip into his mouth, bit down lightly and swallowed her gasp. And, for a moment at least, he'd taken that stark worry from her mind.

CHAPTER TWENTY-THREE

Brian sat at his desk, typing notes on another case, though Jaiyden's face floated in a corner of his mind. He'd done as much as he could for her and now had to wait the allotted time before he got the information he needed to move the investigation forward.

He'd review Haylee's statement first, and he braced himself for the ding that would indicate an incoming email. The DNA request would take longer, but by the time it came through, he'd have everything else ready.

He closed his eyes. Haylee had asked him not to see her differently, and he'd told her he wouldn't, but God, how could he not? How could he read her statement as a brother and ignore the pure rage that he knew would crash through him? How could he read it as a detective and not want to render his own justice? How did he look at her and not imagine the violence the typed words only hinted at?

The same way she looks at her boys and loves them.

So, he'd find a way to harness the cyclone that threatened to rip him apart. He'd do his job and help bring what peace he could to Haylee.

And Jaiyden.

When the ping came, he finished the sentence he typed, hit save, then toggled to his email. After the second read-through, when he could look at the information without seeing Haylee in the words, he started to jot down notes. Times. Days. Names.

He spotted the passage that had clutched his gut the first time he'd read it. Now, he took his time, evaluated each word and what it meant.

Donny wanted to take extra in the lead up to Valentine's Day. He figured he could make back what he already owed Spencer, maybe a little more. He got angry when Spencer sent someone else. They argued. Donny wasn't going to let Spencer double dip. If he gave the new guy a free shot with me, Spencer would still want a turn when he got back. Donny wanted to know where Spencer was. The guy said Donny would find out if he didn't stop whining.

A week later Spencer came for the rest of the money that Donny owed. He was ... weird. Almost happy. Didn't stop him beating me while he raped me. He kept saying things were going to change, that he'd buried his demons and life was going to get better.

Now, Brian opened Jaiyden's file and compared Haylee's words with Bristow's informal questioning.

Fuck off, I didn't kill nobody. Week before Fuck Day is busy. I supply a lot of parties.

With drugs?

I'm in the balloon business, you know that. Blowing them all up, delivering them. I don't go anywhere, do anything except business that week. So fucked if I could've killed anyone, let alone traipse up into the bush and bury them.

Brian remembered the smirk Bristow had worn the whole time. They'd both known the truth. Unfortunately, they'd also both known that Brian had no proof.

He had something now at least.

Still, he finished taking notes, reading over both Bristow's and Haylee's files again. He was hunkered down on his dozenth pass when a shadow fell over his desk. Blinking, he had to crack his neck left, then right before he could straighten. It was worth the shooting pain when Jewell smiled down at him.

'I'm on lunch break.' She glanced at the papers surrounding him, then shook her head before he could speak. 'I know you haven't eaten and that you don't want to leave this, so I can grab something for you while I'm out.'

He sat back and clasped his hands behind his head, nearly groaning as his back stretched out. 'You know, I'll happily take you up on that offer.'

She pressed her lips together and stepped closer. 'Are you okay?'

Was he? 'Ask me in about a week.'

'I will.' She smiled. 'Do you have any preference for lunch?'

'At this point, I wouldn't have a clue.'

'How about I surprise you, then?'

'You do, constantly.'

Again, she'd found him in a bad spot and pulled him out long enough for him to gulp in some fresh air so that he felt ready to dive in once more. When he took that breath and reviewed everything, his to-do list became a find-out list.

Haylee's statement mentioned talk of a Harley chick and a whore. Jaiyden and her friend Kel fit the description, but searching for a first or last name of Harley, or Kelly with all its variants, gave him nothing.

Frustrated, he automatically reached for a pen when the phone on his desk rang. 'Detective Senior Constable Rowland, homicide.'

His computer dinged. Toggling to the screen, he frowned, sat straighter.

'Senior Constable Jones, White Wattle Creek. I've just seen your active whereabouts on one Jaiyden Scott.'

Brian had put the flag on her name in the Law Enforcement Assistance Program database last week.

'Yeah,' he said, scribbling down the constable's name as blood rushed in his ears, 'I just got the LEAP flagging from that. What have you got for me?'

'I'm taking a statement from a Kelsey Anne Davidson. Says she knew a Jaiyden Scott, and that Scott went missing four years ago. She suspects a Spencer Bristow to be involved.'

Brian closed his eyes. 'And the baby? The coroner said she'd recently given birth.'

'Pipa Jade Scott. Alive and well.'

'You've seen her?'

'I have. Look, can I speak freely?'

'Go for it.' He preferred it to the formal jargon that got them nowhere.

'I've known Kelsey for most of my life and all of hers. She's been through hell the last five years protecting Jaiyden and then Pipa from Bristow. She's scared, exhausted and hanging onto the hope that Scott is still alive.'

'She's not.' And he hated what he had to do next. 'I'm going to need her to ID the body.'

The muffled *shit* would have made him smile under other circumstances.

'I'm going to make a few phone calls and get back to you.' Already flipping through his mental files for what he needed, he scribbled a few notes. 'Is she a flight risk?'

'No. She knows what she's up against, and she knows here is the best place for her.'

'Good. I'll be in touch.'

'Cheers.'

Hanging up the phone, Brian eased out a breath, took in another one. He didn't need his gut to tell him this was the huge hole he'd been trying to fill with the other pieces he'd found. His blood sang and his feet itched with the need to get up, to go and finish what he'd feared he never would.

'You look like you just won the lottery.' Jewell stood with a bakery bag in one hand, a bottle of water in the other and a knowing smile on her lips. 'You got some good news?'

'I did.'

He'd never have made the connection between the Harley chick and Kelsey Davidson. She was the huge puzzle piece he'd needed to move forward.

'You kept telling me to have faith.' And wasn't that humbling. 'Thank you.'

'You're welcome.' She held the bag and water out to him. 'I can see you're energised but take a moment and refuel. You don't want to burn yourself out.'

'No, I don't.' Not when he had time at the park and ice-cream to look forward to. And not when a possible future with Jewell stood before him.

'I'm sorry I tried so hard to ignore you for a year.'

Her smile bloomed. 'You had to try that hard?'

'I did.' She deserved the truth. 'Honestly, I figured you were too good for me to mess with.'

'That's sweet.' She stepped closer. 'But I think I should be the one to decide if the man I'm interested in is good enough or not.'

She pointed to the food. 'Refuel.' Then she walked away.

He'd started a storm there. One he looked forward to exploring. First, though, he pulled the salad roll from the bakery bag, flipped his notebook to a new page and started a list of questions he had for Kelsey Davidson. Phone calls and paperwork would come next. Then, finally, he'd have an official identification for Jaiyden Scott and the hammer strike he needed that would break the case open and see Bristow officially questioned.

Looking forward to that event, he ate, drank the water and worked until everything lined up ready for him to call Jones back and get Kelsey Davidson to Melbourne.

CHAPTER TWENTY-FOUR

Kelsey sipped the water Mark gave her. It rasped against her throat, then chilled her stomach. As long as it stayed there this time, she'd be happy.

'You did great.' He sat across the desk from her, eyes tired.

'I don't feel great.'

Falling off a horse at full gallop had hurt less than telling the detectives of Spencer's abuse over the last five years. They'd dug everything out of her and left her empty. Empty, yet full of rage and dread.

'So, what happens now?'

'I'll finish up, knock off, change, then take you home.'

Home. It soothed some of her anger. She had home and spending time with Pipa and Ethan to look forward to, instead of feeling alone and trying to find the next safe place to hide. She now had what she'd believed she'd lost and would never get back.

'I meant as far as all this goes.' She waved a hand around the interview room. 'What happens now?'

'We wait to hear back from detectives in Melbourne and Warrnambool, but I doubt it will be before tomorrow now.' He looked at his watch. 'Although it is only three thirty. Still, I'd say that tomorrow we'll know more about what comes next.'

He ran a hand through his hair. 'For now, you sit tight. I'll finish up my running sheet, then I'll take you home.'

'I'm sure if I called Ethan, he'd come and pick me up.'

'Why, when I'm heading out that way anyway?' He pushed to his feet. 'I won't be long.'

It was clear he hid something, but as it burned some of the fatigue from his eyes, she didn't ask. If he, Ethan and Pipa planned something, then she'd let them whisper over the phone and chuckle behind her back.

They could all do with experiencing something normal, especially if it was mixed in with a bit of fun and excitement after everything that had happened. And if it taught Pipa that not every bad situation meant they had to run and hide, then Kelsey would suffer a million of their secrets.

Crossing her arms on the table, she rested her head on them, closed her eyes and let the background noise of the station radio filter through her mind. She'd have to start sorting out her own future soon. Whatever waited around the corner, she needed to sit down with Ethan and talk about what came next in their relationship.

The possibility that Spencer would find them still sat heavy on her chest, and now, despite everyone reminding her she had plenty of people to stand up for her, she also had more people to worry about. Spencer would hurt anyone close to her if he thought it meant he could get to Pipa. Both Ethan and Mark would roll their eyes and tell her off if they knew she was worrying about them, but how could she not? She'd had hands-on experience of what Spencer could and would do.

The light knock on the door jolted her upright.

'Sorry, I figured you'd jump no matter what I did.' Mark walked in holding two steaming mugs and sat next to her at the table. 'How are you feeling?'

'Scared.' She shrugged at his raised eyebrow. 'I figure I'm past dodging questions.'

'Good.' He raised his cup in a salute, then took a sip. 'So, what's scaring you the most?'

'That I don't know what's going to happen next or how long I'll need to keep looking over my shoulder.'

'You know you have all of us, for that and everything else.'

'I do.' She warmed her hands on the mug. 'But that scares me too. What if he comes after you or Ethan? What if he finds out Carol is my best friend and attacks her?'

Instead of rolling his eyes, Mark nodded. 'I've thought of all of that, and you know what I realised?'

'You're a cop?'

He shook his head and half-smiled. 'No, Miss Smart-arse. The difference is, none of us are scared and alone. We all have the benefit of close relationships, security and knowing help is only a phone call away.'

'You're still mad I never called.' She nearly rested her head on his shoulder, but he still wore his uniform and vest.

'I'm angry that you thought you couldn't. I'm angry your mother kept that information from us deliberately.' He tapped his fingers on the table. 'I guess I'm hurt we'd all fallen away from each other so much that you thought you couldn't contact any of us.'

'Everyone had their own lives. And'—because they were being honest—'I was too ashamed. I'd stuffed up with Ethan, big time. He hurt me, but I'd overstepped. I could say I was young, grieving for my father and desperate, but the truth is, I wanted Ethan. I wanted what his parents had had, what your parents do.'

'He nearly quit.' Mark turned his head and met her gaze. 'I'm not trying to make you feel guilty, but I think you need to know what it was like for him when you left. He had no way of knowing if you were even still alive … and it nearly tipped him over the edge.'

'I'm beginning to understand that.'

It was something else they needed to sit down and talk about. Not a rehashing of the past or a blame game, but a clearing of the air and honesty about how they'd felt when everything had happened.

'And I know I shouldn't have believed Mum when she told me no one cared that I'd left, but at the time it made me more determined to make something of my life, so I could come back and show you all how well I'd done on my own.'

She lifted one shoulder. 'Then things happened and all of a sudden I was hiding with a baby. After that, keeping Pipa alive and with me was my only priority.'

'If you had come home, we would have helped.'

She nodded. 'I know that now. But if I'd come home earlier, they'd have taken Pipa from me.' She pressed a fist to the pain in her heart. 'I don't think I'd have been able to deal with that. No matter what any of you could give me, losing her would break something in me that no one could ever fix.'

'You're not going to lose her. It'll be reported that you have custody of Jaiyden Scott's daughter. It has to be. But she's loved, looked after and thriving. There's no way they'll take her from you.'

Her skin prickled. 'You have to report it?'

'I do, so do CIU. And, I haven't done it yet, but I want to contact SOCA for you as well.'

'I don't understand.'

This time, he turned in his seat to face her. 'It's the unit for sexual offences and child abuse. You've told us about the rape, but it needs to be properly reported, Kelsey.'

'I've just finished telling the detectives everything, and now I have to tell another stranger so they can decide if I'm telling the truth?'

'No.' He took her cup, sat it on the table and took her hands in his. 'They determine if they have enough evidence for Bristow to be tried by the criminal courts.'

'And if they don't?'

'Then you take him to court civilly.'

'I don't know if I want to.'

'You don't have to decide now.' He squeezed her hands. 'But I would like to, with your go-ahead, start the ball rolling with SOCA. At the very least, you need counselling, Kelsey. And Pipa, too.'

'I'd like Pipa to speak to someone.' She nodded. 'I just don't know if I need to.'

'You do.'

He cocked his head when the station phone rang. Getting up, he checked his watch. 'Ten minutes and I would have been out of here.' He nodded to her mug. 'Finish that, and we should be ready to go in ten.'

She sipped her drink as Mark's muffled tone punctuated the mumbled chatter on the radio. Did she need counselling? Could she go over everything again, have her emotions and actions picked apart and analysed? Could she not when it meant it would help her deal with whatever second-hand damage Spencer had done to Pipa? Being as honest with herself as she had been with Mark, she had to answer yes, she could and would sit through anything to help Pipa. And if it helped her enough that she stopped smelling that musty couch and reliving the pain and humiliation and feeling ashamed, then maybe it would be worth it.

She'd think about it later and talk to Ethan. He'd agree with Mark, of course. Not that she could blame him. If she were in his position, she'd push for him to get help, too. She rubbed her forehead and cursed under her breath.

'Kelsey?' Mark stood at the door, his face once more the blank mask he'd worn the first day she'd come home.

She stood. 'What's wrong? Is it Pipa? Ethan?' He blocked her only exit. She could tackle him. Might even get past him if she surprised him.

'They're fine.' He held his hands out. 'Pipa is safe.'

The panic welled. 'But?'

'I have some other news.' He stayed where he was and held her gaze. 'About Jaiyden.'

Kelsey sat. 'She's dead.'

'I talked to a detective earlier. He's working on a cold case and has a Jane Doe that needs identifying. I'm sorry.' He came to sit next to her again. 'He's confident his Jane Doe is Jaiyden Scott.'

She pressed her lips together and gritted her teeth that wanted to chatter. The sliver of hope she'd held for four years cracked. Shards of it lodged in her lungs so every breath hurt.

'What do I do? How do I tell Pipa?'

'We don't know for certain it's her.'

'I do.' She shook her head. 'No, I won't say anything to Pipa until I know for certain, but I know.' She closed her eyes. 'I think I've known since she walked from the hospital that day.'

'Again, I'm sorry, but I've been asked to see if you'll go to Melbourne to identify her.'

She hadn't thought that far ahead. 'Jaiyden had no one else to look after her or help her. No one to look at her and name her.' She hugged herself. 'Pipa and I are all she had, all she has, so yes, I'll go and see her.' And she'd say goodbye and that she was sorry.

'Okay. I need to make some more phone calls to finalise transport and times.' He checked his watch. 'Will you be okay here for a bit longer?'

Sucking it all back in, she lifted her gaze to his. 'I'm not going anywhere, Mark.'

'I don't doubt that, but this is a blow and I want to know if you'll be okay.'

'I'm ...' She rubbed shaking hands over her face. 'I'll be okay.'

She waited until he turned away. 'I missed you, Mark.'

'I missed you too, little red.'

She sat in the echo of his words while flashes of Jaiyden ran through her mind. They'd found time to laugh while Pipa had grown in Jaiyden's womb. They'd shared times of joy between the running and terror. They'd made memories to look back on, only now Kelsey would be the only one to recall them. She'd keep telling Pipa stories about the woman who'd carried her for forty weeks and how, after fifteen hours of labour, had nearly skipped down the hospital hallway with her baby snugged to her chest.

Pipa had grown with the story of Jaiyden singing to her that first night and every night during the first week of her life. She'd grow with the stories Kelsey told her of how Jaiyden had loved her from the first moment and all through the morning sickness and mood swings. Pipa would never question that she had been, and always would be, loved.

Jaiyden's death would leave its mark on them all and a hole in their lives that could never be filled, but they'd survive, and together with Ethan and all the people Pipa could now add to her family, they'd make new memories to keep and stories to hand down. They'd live their lives in a way that would make Jaiyden proud, and wherever she watched from, Kelsey would make sure Jaiyden knew she'd never be forgotten.

'Kelsey?' Mark stood at the door once more, his uniform replaced with jeans and a shirt. He hadn't changed out of cop mode, though, and Kelsey sat straighter.

'What?'

'I need you to listen to me, okay? I need you to stay calm until I've finished.'

'Pipa?' She stood, her heart hammering.

'She's fine. She's at home with Ethan.' He came in and put his hands on her shoulders. 'Someone made a report to child services.'

'A report?' She frowned. 'You already said that would happen.'

'No, a member of the public. They reported that Pipa is malnourished and has been mistreated.' He waited a beat. 'Because Pipa's guardianship is in question, the department wants to investigate it further.'

'But she's well looked after. I've done everything I can to keep her happy and safe.' Everything Pipa had missed out on clawed at Kelsey. 'What do I do?'

'I've told them as much as they needed to know. They're happy that you've found accommodation and are looking at settling here.'

'But?'

'But whoever reported it was very convincing.' He squeezed her shoulders. 'They're going to get in touch and make an appointment to see you and Pipa on Thursday.'

'They can't take her.' She steadied her jaw. Falling apart would only prove she wasn't fit to be Pipa's mother. 'What do I need to do?'

'Kelsey, you're already doing everything.'

'No. I'm not. I've been running to survive. I want to live life now. I want Pipa to have confidence that this is what our lives will be now. Ethan has given us a home, and I intend to do my share there, but that's not going to be enough, is it? They're going to look at me, at what I'm doing, not what I'm being given by others.'

'Ethan will factor into it, but yes, it'll be on you to prove you can feed her, clothe her and support her both physically and emotionally. They'll look at whether she functions within the range for her age, which we all know she does.'

'I need to figure things out.' She patted his arm. 'I can't let them take her because they think someone with a job, a phone and plenty of money would look after her better.'

'That's not how it works, Kelsey.'

'I can't take that risk.' She'd lost Jaiyden; she wouldn't lose Pipa. Not when it was in her hands to stop it. 'Can we go home now?'

***

'It's smelling good, Pip.' Ethan opened the wall oven a crack. On his hip, Pipa leaned forward to peer at the chocolate cake.

'We eat with no plates?'

'Definitely.' He closed the oven and set Pipa on her feet. 'But I think we can make the table pretty.'

'With flowers?'

'We didn't buy any.' He held his smile in as Pipa's eyes went wide.

'We buy balloons and plates and stuff!'

'We did.' He pointed at the shopping bag on the kitchen bench. 'How about we start with the tablecloth.'

He handed Pipa the bag and pointed at Max to sit where he was. 'It's nothing for you, boy.'

'We get Max something next time so he not miss out?' Pipa held up the hot pink plastic tablecloth.

'We can do that.' He took the packet and opened it for her. 'You know, Pip, your mum used to bake chocolate cake nearly every time she came here. The last time, she rode her horse from town to here, just to cook a cake and eat it while she did her homework.'

Kelsey had actually been escaping another argument with Morna.

'Was it yummy?' Pipa struggled to put the thin sheet on the table, but when he stepped forward to help, she said, 'No, I do it.'

'We didn't get to eat it.' He shoved his hands in his pockets as Pipa pushed and pulled at the plastic. 'She burned it and set off the smoke alarms.'

'Mummy burns the sausages, but I like the crunch.' She bared her teeth. 'Done!'

The tablecloth hung crooked, the corners falling along the edges, and it was too far up one end, but Ethan smiled. 'Good job. What next?'

'Balloons!' She clapped and ran back to the bag.

'I not have big air.' She handed him the packet of balloons. 'But when I bigger, I blow them huge.' She held her arms wide and puffed out her cheeks. 'Mummy says when I big, I can be anything, except a unicorn 'cos I already a person.'

'What do you want to be?' He sat on the floor and readied himself for the taste of balloon rubber.

'I be a helper.' She stood next to him and leaned on his shoulder as he blew up the first balloon. 'I make people who be sad, happy again.'

How could he not love her?

'I think you already do that, Pipa.' He shifted and put his arm around her. 'You have a beautiful heart.'

'Mummy says that too.'

'She's right. And she's right when she says you can be anything.'

'I can dance with horses like Mummy?'

'Definitely.' He handed her the inflated balloon. 'If you watch your mum and me and listen when we teach you things, you'll be dancing with the horses in no time.'

He'd talk to Kelsey about getting a pony for Pipa. One that Pipa could learn to ride on and they could then pass down to the next child. Because he wanted more kids with Kelsey. He wanted to give Pipa the siblings she'd asked for. He wanted to fill their house with as much love and laughter as it could hold. And he wanted Pipa to be as much his as she was Kelsey's.

Max huffed a bark from where he'd sprawled out near the front door.

Pipa stopped playing with the balloon and eyed the door. 'Is that Mummy?'

Ethan could curse Spencer for putting that instant fear in her, but thinking like that would only make him angry when they all needed the brightness and happiness he strived for.

'We'll check.' He pushed to his feet and held out his hand. Pipa took it and walked with him to the window.

Outside, Mark's green XR6 pulled up beside Kelsey's Hyundai.

'It's Mark and your mum.'

Ethan frowned as Kelsey stepped from the car and walked stiffly beside Mark towards the house. Pipa had already turned for the door and Ethan let her tug him along.

'Mummy need a hug,' Pipa said, trying to reach the handle.

She needed more than that, but he opened the door and let Pipa run out. She launched herself, wrapped her arms around Kelsey's neck and gave her a loud smacking kiss on the cheek.

Kelsey smiled and kissed Pipa's forehead. 'Is that chocolate cake I smell?'

He'd forgotten the cake. While Pipa filled Kelsey in on the shopping and decorating they'd done, he went to the kitchen and turned off the oven. He stayed a moment to calm the spike of his heart rate.

Over the last few days, Kelsey had gained confidence in her steps and conviction in her tone. Now, her words—though inflected with cheer and wonder—fell lifeless in the room meant to pulse bright with anticipation. More than fatigue and the horror of retelling her story had put that stark pain in her eyes. And yet, she hadn't come to him, as Pipa had gone to her, to reconnect and anchor herself.

So, he went to her.

She sat on the floor with Pipa on her lap, her attention on the balloon they kept in the air. When he squatted down beside her, she spared him a glance. He wanted to touch her, just a fingertip to the tension at the corner of her mouth, but she'd thrown those barriers up between them again.

'What happened?'

'I can't yet.' She flicked the balloon and sent Pipa rushing after it before it escaped under the dining table. 'There's too much to condense down to words.'

'I don't want you to shut me out.'

She met his gaze. 'I'm not. I just need to work things out.'

'We can't do it together?'

'It's on me. It's mine to figure out.'

'Do you trust me?' He held out a not so steady hand and felt the urge to pull her to him when she took it. Instead, he helped her to her feet.

'How many times did I come home to find you playing with a horse?'

'Too many to count.' She let him lead her to the patio door.

'We see the horsies?' Pipa followed, then ran back to Mark and grabbed his hand. 'We see the horsies.'

'I don't know if I should stay.'

Kelsey frowned. 'Could you? Please?'

The burn started in Ethan's chest and spread with each step towards the stables. He couldn't help her yet, but putting her with the filly would. She'd find her centre and maybe the words that locked her away. Shoulders stiff, hand shaking in his, she stayed silent as he led her to Dusty's stall.

Though Pipa stayed close, she took Mark to say hello to Snotty.

'I ride Snotty.' She lifted her arms for Mark to pick her up. 'Mummy make him go fast and she hold me so I don't fall off and it was fun.' She giggled when Snotty blew a breath over her face. 'And Ethan teach me how to ride and dance with the horsies like Mummy one day.'

'Your mum will know what we went through watching her ride, then.' But Mark frowned at Kelsey standing like a statue.

Ethan lifted the halter from its hook and held it out to her. 'This always worked when it got too much with your mum. So, do what you love, what you know you can do. Do what will help shift whatever it is that's eating at you, then we can move forward.'

She stared at the halter, then him. 'This isn't for you to fix.'

'I don't know that I've ever fixed anything where you're concerned. You've always looked after yourself.'

She shook her head. 'Yeah, but I always knew I had you as a safety net.'

'You still do.' He met Mark's frown with one of his own, hoping to find an answer there. When he didn't, he questioned Kelsey. 'What is it you've given up on?'

'It might not be my choice.' She took the halter and turned away from him.

What was that supposed to mean? He waited until she'd led the filly to the round yard and for Pipa to settle on an upturned bucket in the shade, then he stood shoulder to shoulder with Mark.

'Can you tell me anything?'

'She's asked me to.'

Ethan shoved his hands in his pockets. 'How bad is it?'

'Depends.' Mark rubbed the back of his neck. 'One I think she knew, the other blindsided her.'

He glanced at Pipa, and although she grinned at Kelsey, he wouldn't risk upsetting her. 'They found her?'

'Yeah.' Mark nodded, then turned his back to Pipa and Kelsey. 'She's been asked to go to Melbourne to identify a body believed to be Jaiyden's.'

Ethan dug a toe in the dirt. 'When?'

'Tomorrow. I did some fast talking and organised to take you all.'

'That's …' He shook his head. 'Thanks.'

'I understand now what Kelsey says about her being the best one to look after Pipa. I don't trust anyone else to look out for all of you.'

'I get that too.' He squared his shoulders and filled his lungs with the scent of eucalyptus and dust. 'So, what is it that's made her lose all hope?'

'Someone made a report to child services about Kelsey mistreating Pipa.'

Ethan did a double take. 'What? Why? How?' He sucked in a breath. 'Who?'

'I can't say anything about it, other than they want to interview Kelsey and Pipa later in the week.'

'They won't separate them. Not once they see them together.' He paced away and back again. 'She's not giving up.'

He glanced at her over his shoulder. She flowed now, her steps smooth, her voice an encouraging croon as the filly circled and turned around her.

'Oh God, she's not giving up,' he said again, the truth icing his veins. 'She's desperate and scrambling for ideas to guarantee they stay together.' He turned back to Mark. 'And she's convincing herself she has to do it alone.'

Mark frowned. 'Why?'

'I don't know, but I'm going to find out.'

'While you're doing that, find a way to get her to agree to counselling. I've made an e-referral for her.' Mark's gaze stayed on Kelsey. 'It takes a day or so to go through, and she'll probably need that to process everything anyway, but it'll be there for when she's ready.'

Ethan let his shoulders drop. 'Thanks.'

'We're all here for each other.' Mark shrugged. 'It'll only be a matter of time until she fully understands that.'

'I hope you're right.' Ethan shoved his hands in his pockets. 'Because something has to give soon, and I don't want it to be her.'

CHAPTER TWENTY-FIVE

'See, it is fun.'

Brian gently pushed Haylee and Rupert on the swing, sending Rupert into fits of laughter that made Haylee chuckle. Playing in the sand beside them, James and Ashley joined in so that the playground came alive with their joined mirth. Brian slipped his phone from his pocket and recorded the scene. The boys would get a kick out of watching it later.

'They're going to need a bath,' Haylee said, nodding towards Ashley and James, their legs, hands and faces splotched with sand.

'They aren't the only ones.' He wiggled his fingers at Rupert and was rewarded with another chuckle. 'I think the heat claimed more ice-cream than we ate.'

'I remember when we used to race to see who could eat theirs the fastest and you always got a brain freeze.' She smiled. 'It was about the only thing I could beat you at.'

'That and cartwheels.' He grinned at her. 'And dress-ups, of course.'

'True.' She rested a cheek on Rupert's hair. 'I haven't been able to think much about those times. It reminds me of just how far I am from that innocent girl, with all her hopes and dreams.'

'Not that far.'

He sat on the swing next to her but soon gave up trying to find a comfortable amount of butt overhang on the skinny plastic seat.

'Maybe you won't be able to decorate the moon with glitter and lipstick, but you've done a damn good job of turning our house into a home with character and life. And on a budget, too.'

She shrugged. 'I didn't have much choice, budget-wise.'

'Don't do that. It pisses me off.'

Both boys stopped and stared at him.

'Sorry,' he said to them. 'But it does.'

He swivelled his swing to face Haylee. 'You have a passion and a gift, one you've no doubt worked at despite the limitations you had. You love finding things that have been used and discarded, giving them a second life. And there's people out there who'd pay you to do that for them.'

'I don't have any qualifications.'

'That's just an excuse.'

She turned her head to glare at him. 'I have the boys to look after.'

'They have me as well. Look,' he reached out and swung her to face him, 'nearly everything can be done online these days, but honestly, you don't need someone to tell you this is what you're good at, that it's what you love doing.'

'I don't even know where to start, Bri. Or how.'

'Then let's go home and find out.'

She shook her head, then rolled her eyes when he lifted an eyebrow.

'Fine.'

He grinned. 'See, that girl is still in there, Hales. You just need to trust her'—he touched her cheek—'and forgive her.'

He swore under his breath and pulled a tissue from his pocket as the tears streamed down Haylee's cheeks. He held it out to her.

'I didn't mean to make you cry.'

She wiped them away and sniffed. 'It's just ... How can she ever forgive me?'

'For what?'

'Everything. Just everything.'

'Do you expect the boys to blame their younger selves for what's happened so far in their lives?'

'They're just babies.'

He stood, held out a hand and waited until she'd let him pull her to her feet. 'You weren't much more than that when Mum and Dad died. And I didn't do a very good a job at raising you.'

'You did everything you could.'

'Which was nowhere near enough. If I could go back, I'd do things differently. I'd be your big brother instead of trying to be everyone.'

'We can't go back. And if we did, I wouldn't have the boys.' She kissed Rupert's pursed lips. 'I might not like how I got them, but they're mine and I love them.'

'Can we talk about that?' He held up a hand. 'Not that, but about the fact you never had a boyfriend until Donny.'

'He wasn't my boyfriend.' She stared past him, her frown sad. 'He was just a guy in our group. But then everyone else either overdosed or was arrested and other people assumed we were together. I guess Donny did, too.' She licked her lips. 'I don't know what's wrong with me, but I've never wanted to have sex.'

'Oh God!' He covered his ears.

'Don't be such a baby.' She swatted his arm. 'You wanted to talk about this.'

'I did.' He dropped his hands to his sides. 'And there's nothing wrong with you, Haylee.'

'How do you know?'

'Because I did some research.' Thanks to Jewell. 'And you're not alone in not wanting …' He waved a hand in the air. 'You know.'

When she laughed, he ran a hand over his hair. 'I'm glad you find it amusing.'

'I find you amusing. Big, tough Brian can't say the word sex.'

'I can say it, just not when it involves my sister.' But she smiled at him, so he'd take the humiliation. 'How about we go home so we can talk about this and your future as an upcycling decorator.'

'Upcycled decor.' She nodded. 'I like that.'

'Good.' He started walking backwards towards the cars and called out to the boys. 'Come on, you two. Let's go home, get cleaned up and start working out your futures.'

'I be a dinodoor finder.' Ashley held up his toy dinosaur.

'I want to be a knight.' James handed his dinosaur to Ashley. 'They get to ride horses and help people.'

'You should go into the mounted branch,' he said, ruffling James's hair.

'The what?' James squinted up at Brian.

'The mounted police branch. You get to ride a horse and be a police officer.'

James reached out and put his hand in Brian's. 'I can help people, like you do?'

'Something like that.' He held his other hand out to Ashley. 'And I think you'd make a great dinosaur finder.'

'I hatch one.' Ashley grinned.

'I'm sure you'll try.'

As Brian helped Haylee strap the boys into their seats, he smiled. They'd hit the point where the future didn't seem like a scary black hole. And, as he drove home, he realised his own future was a wonder of possibilities.

He pulled up in front of the house and let Haylee park her car in the garage. A pinch in his gut and a niggle along his spine made him frown. When he pulled up behind Haylee, he shifted his shoulders, but the sensation didn't go away. He checked his mirrors for anyone loitering, then stepped from his car and scanned the street.

'Brian?' Haylee walked towards him.

'Go inside.' He glared at a car driving past and locked its number plate in his memory.

'Spencer knows, doesn't he? That I made a statement.' She hugged Rupert to her chest. 'He knows and he's going to do something.'

'Take the boys inside.'

He pulled out his phone. Maybe getting the local uniforms to drive past a few times would be enough to dissuade any of Spencer's contacts from doing anything.

'Brian?' The pitch of Haylee's voice had him turning, running. Haylee pointed a shaking finger to the slightly ajar door. 'I'm sorry.'

'It's not your fault.' He led them to the car and handed Haylee his phone. 'Call the police.'

He glanced down at the two boys huddled against their mother's legs. 'It'll be okay.'

They'd come too far to let Bristow, Donny, or anyone, take their home or their new-found hope from them, so he'd tell them it would be okay until his throat bled.

Crouching down, he put a hand on each boy's shoulder. 'I know you're scared. So am I.'

'You are?' James stared at him wide-eyed. 'But you're grown.'

'Grown-ups still get scared. It's how we know what matters and what we should or shouldn't be doing.' He tugged at the thumb Ashley sucked on. 'Being scared isn't a bad thing. It's okay to feel it, but I don't want you to feel it all the time because I want you to know we're a team, a family who all look after each other. Okay?'

They both nodded, but fury burned through his veins when he thought about the nightmares they'd have now. He stood before his rage showed on his face and made them afraid of him, too.

'I need to go in and see.' He held a hand up before Haylee could voice the terror that jerked her head up. 'They're not in there now. I need to see what's been done.'

'Then so do I.' She stepped towards the door with him.

'No, Haylee. I don't want you seeing it.'

'Because I'm a girl and can't handle it?' Anger burned the fear from her eyes. 'If you look, so do I. This is my life, Brian, my choice, my demons that need to be faced so they don't chase me for the rest of my life.'

'The boys—'

'Need the same.' She lifted her chin. 'I'd rather them not see it, but they know something's happened. They always heard the bashing and crashing at Donny's, but it was like there was a ghost, hiding, waiting to jump out and scare them.' She took a deep breath. 'You say it'll be okay. So let us see the damage and then we'll help make it right and okay again.'

Arguing only wasted time, so he held his hand up. 'Let me make sure it's empty first.'

She pursed her lips. 'If you try and hide anything from me …'

'I won't.'

As much as he wanted to shield them from the food spread over the kitchen floor and the stabbed furniture, it would destroy the growing trust between them. Still, he paused in the boys' room. Their toys and clothes had been dumped on the floor, their mattresses upturned and stripped. But the words scrawled on the wall in Vegemite were what jerked his heart.

DIE DEMON SPAWN.

The groan behind him had him spinning to the door, his hand automatically going to his empty shoulder holster. 'Bloody hell, Haylee!'

She stood staring at the wall, Rupert on one hip, Ashley on the other and James clinging to her leg. 'You took too long.'

'I was assessing.'

'Yeah, me too.' She met his gaze. 'The police said they'd call when they were coming.'

He nodded. A cold berg wouldn't be top of the list. He could wish it was, but that wouldn't change anything.

'We'll stay at a hotel tonight.'

'Can I pack anything?'

'No.' He went to squat in front of James. 'You want a hug?'

James nodded, then slipped his arms around Brian's neck. Lifting him, Brian hugged him to his chest. 'It'll be okay.'

Haylee looked at the wall again, then turned and walked away. Donny, Bristow and the others had stripped her of everything once, he wouldn't let them do it again. So, with James snuggled against his chest, he followed

Haylee out to the cars. They'd go to a hotel tonight, and he'd find a way to show them all that the futures they'd been considering were still possible.

CHAPTER TWENTY-SIX

Though the sun barely slipped over the horizon, magpies warbled and crows cried their throaty caws, either cursing or calling the breeze that tickled the bedroom curtain.

With Ethan curled against her, his legs tangled with hers as he snored softly, Kelsey lifted a hand to a thin line of light drifting over them. She shivered as the energy of the edging storm stood the hairs up along her arm. But it was the storm whipping up a frenzy in her mind and heart that threatened to fragment her, and no matter how hard she pushed against the cyclone it created, she couldn't stop the deluge of guilt and fear that rained down on her.

Ethan's arm slid around her middle and pulled her back to his chest. His lips pressed to her shoulder; his teeth nibbled at her neck.

'Morning.' Voice heavy with sleep, he hummed in his throat. 'You taste good.'

'I'm glad.'

He propped himself on one elbow, rolled her to her back and frowned down at her. 'How long have you been lying awake worrying?'

'Not long.' She shrugged when he just kept staring at her. 'About an hour.'

'Why didn't you wake me?'

'It's no use both of us being tired.'

'What else is it?' He ran a thumb across her cheek. 'There's something you're not telling me and it's pulling us apart.'

'There's stuff I need to work out and do.'

'Like?' He slid his legs over hers, preventing her from getting up. 'You came to me with secrets and I fumbled the way I handled it, but we've moved past that, haven't we?'

'It's not a secret.' She fisted a hand on her chest. 'You know I need to prove to child services that I'm good enough for Pipa.'

He tilted his head. 'You've done an incredible job raising her. No one can say different. You came back when you had no idea if you'd be welcomed or run out of town, and that's more courageous than anything I've ever done.' He ran his hand down her arm and linked their fingers together. 'You came back because you knew Pipa would grow here. And look at her now, sleeping in her own room, making friends and learning that there are people who will look after her. You're teaching her that.'

'But I have to do more. I have to find work and enrol her in kindergarten. I have to prove to strangers that I'm the best person for her to grow up with.'

He frowned down at her. 'We. We have to do all that. Why do you think you have to do this alone?'

'Because they're looking at me, judging me, and I need to prove that I can do it without you.'

'Bullshit.' He said it softly, but it resonated through Kelsey's chest.

'Reverse our situations. Do you let me scramble on my own, make myself sick with worry and slowly shut you out?'

She pressed her lips together.

'Yeah,' he nodded, 'that's what I thought.'

He lowered his forehead to hers and she closed her eyes against the tears. 'We're in this together, aren't we?'

'Yes.'

'Then don't shut me out, please? Talk to me, tell me what you're thinking, what you're lying awake worrying about.'

Raising her hands to his face, she cupped his cheeks. 'What if I can't do it? What if they say I'm not good enough and take her?'

'We won't let them. And how could they say that? Mark told them the report was wrong. We'll all attest to what a good mother you are. And so will

Pipa. All they'll have to do is see the two of you together.' He kissed her. 'As for a job and money, you know you don't have to worry about that.'

'I'm not going to sponge off you, Ethan. I need to work, to do something. And Pipa needs to have chores and learn the value of achieving something, too.'

'See? You're always thinking of Pipa and what benefits her. Though we will talk about the sponging comment later.' He pressed his lips to her cheek. 'As for work, I've been giving an idea some thought.'

'I've had a few different jobs, mostly farm work, but I was thinking of seeing if there's anything going at FoodWorks or the bakery.' She shrugged. 'Anything for now that will show I'm a responsible adult.'

'Or you could start your own business.'

'Huh?' The idea made her heart jump. 'How could I start a business?'

'Easy. You already have the skill and the passion, and if you play your cards right, you already have the facilities.'

'I don't understand.'

'You do, you're just too scared to contemplate it yet, but you should.' He stroked her hair. 'You've dreamed about doing equine rehab work since you first rode a pony. Why not do it now and prove to Pipa that you're right.'

She stared up at him, holding her breath. 'About what?'

'That she can be and do anything she wants. That where she came from doesn't matter, only where she's willing to go. And that if she wants something bad enough, she can make it happen if she puts her mind and heart to it because that's what you do, what you've always done.'

'How do you reach into me and pull out everything I am?'

'Because I love you. I see you. Always have. Always will.'

This time, she kissed him, giving him everything he'd given her, but she had to stop when her throat closed up.

He held her close, his hands soothing on her skin. 'Tell me what else is wrong?'

Words tripped, stuck, so she swallowed hard. 'I don't know if I can get through today.'

'Baby, you will.' He leaned back and looked down at her. 'You know you will because you can't not.'

'If it's her, if it's not ... I just ...' Tears started falling. Terrified they wouldn't stop, she held her breath until the swell subsided. 'I just wish I didn't have to think for five minutes. About any of it.'

'I can help with that if you want.' His hands stayed soft, soothing as he waited.

She lifted her arms, wrapping them around his neck, offered her lips to his and tried not to let guilt creep in as Ethan slowly lit her body from inside out. By the time he'd pushed her to her peak for the third time and slipped inside her, she thought of nothing but him—how he made her feel, how she could draw a groan or a gasp from him if she moved a certain way, if she nipped at his neck. She forgot everything while she flew with him but gathered it all back as she lay in the quiet aftermath.

'Shower with me.' He pulled her with him to sit up on the bed. 'Then it's only Pipa we have to get ready.'

'Okay.'

In the shower, Ethan washed her hair, conditioning it until he could run his fingers through without them catching, then soaped the rest of her with his sandalwood body wash. Almost too gently, he kissed her as the water slicked the soap from her skin.

'My turn.' She picked up the body wash, but he reached for it.

'You don't have to.'

'I know.' Stopping to wipe the water from her eyes, she looked up at him. 'What is this, Ethan?'

'I'm just saying that you don't have to.'

'And I wouldn't if I didn't want to.' She shook her head. 'This isn't a one-way thing.'

But she had just used sex as an escape. Her guilt doubled, and so she handed him the bottle. 'Sorry.'

She stepped from the shower.

'Kelsey, wait.'

She grabbed two towels as he turned off the taps, the absence of splashing water leaving silence echoing off the tiles. Handing him one, she held hers to her chest.

'You can finish your shower. I'll get breakfast started.'

'I'll cook breakfast with you. Just give me a minute.' He rubbed the towel quickly over his body and followed her into the bedroom.

Was he worried about leaving her alone now? Did he think she'd do something?

'You believe I'll get through this?'

'Of course.' He stood a foot away, his hands clenched at his sides. 'You'd never leave Pipa, no matter what happened.'

So they'd jumped one hurdle only to come up against another. Not that she could blame him for thinking Pipa was her only motivation. She'd told him enough times she'd do anything for her. Still, it cut that he didn't see, didn't know that he was as much an anchor for her as Pipa. And what did it say about their relationship that he was prepared to be there for her, to soothe her with his body, his hands, his mouth, but he didn't expect her to feel or do the same for him?

'I'd never leave you, either,' she said, but they both heard the silent *again*. And didn't that say it all.

'I'll start getting Pipa ready.' Pulling on jeans and a shirt, she rubbed her hair dry.

Ethan said nothing as he dressed. Just touched her shoulder as he walked past her on his way to the kitchen.

By the time she got Pipa up and dressed, the ball of nausea in her stomach churned and gurgled to its own disco mix. Pipa kept up a steady stream of chatter, to Kelsey, to Max and when they got to the kitchen, to Ethan.

'You need to eat, Pip.' Ethan tapped her plate. 'We've got a big drive today, remember?'

Grinning, Pipa scooped cereal into her mouth, leaving a splash of milk on her chin as she chewed. 'Can Max come?'

Kelsey frowned. 'Don't talk with your mouth full. And you know Max can't come. He'd get sick in the car.'

'Oh.' She chewed some more, then swallowed. 'Can we get him a present for staying home and being a good boy?'

Kelsey relaxed her shoulders. Pipa had done nothing to warrant Kelsey's short temper but try to make the two adults in her life smile.

'I'm sure we can find something for him.'

Finishing the cup of tea Ethan had made her, she tried to ignore the dread settling in her belly. Ethan was right. She'd handle the day, but she'd do it without using him as a crutch either physically or emotionally. If they really were a team, then he deserved more than that from her.

With her mind settled, if not eased, she concentrated on gathering the breakfast dishes and wiping the table. When a car pulled up in the driveway, though, the kitchen and dining room were clean, but her hands still shook.

Pipa clapped. 'Is Muck here? We go for a drive now?'

'He is and we do, so grab your bag, Pip, and go to the toilet.' Kelsey started for the door, but it opened before she got there.

Mark stepped in, closed the door behind him and leaned against it. He nodded to Ethan, then turned to Kelsey. 'Morning.'

He still looked tired.

'Morning. Have you had breakfast?'

'I grabbed something from the bakery.'

He studied Kelsey a moment longer, then broke into a grin as Pipa ran into the room, her bag slung over one shoulder. She threw her arms wide and took a running jump at him.

'Muck!'

As though he'd expected it, Mark caught her against his chest.

'Morning, Pip.' He ruffled her hair. 'Are you ready to go?'

'Yes.' She wriggled and grinned. 'Ethan says we take your car because Mummy's car is a pile of sit.'

'Whoa, there.' Mark put a finger against Pipa's lips and sent Kelsey a raised eyebrow smirk. 'Special police people don't say those kinds of words.'

He pulled a laminated card from his pocket and held it out to Pipa. 'Do you promise to be honest, caring and not to swear?'

'I pomise.' She curled her hands under her chin, her grin wide.

Mark gave her the card and Pipa's eyes lit up. Throwing her arms around Mark's neck, she smacked a kiss on his cheek.

'Thank you, Muck.'

Overcome, Kelsey looked at Ethan, feeling a kick of worry when he didn't smile back. Turning her attention to Pipa, she wiped the spot of milk from her chin.

'Did you go to the toilet?'

'I don't need to go.'

'Yeah, you say that now,' she couldn't help her clipped tone, 'then five minutes down the road, you'll be busting.'

'No, I won't.' But she'd already started squirming.

Mark patted Pipa's back and set her on the floor. 'How about you go to the toilet while I talk to Ethan and your mum.'

Glancing at the adults over her shoulder, Pipa ran from the room.

'I better go and supervise.' Ignoring the glances from both men and trying hard to contain everything flying out of control around her, Kelsey followed Pipa.

Pipa had only beaten Kelsey to the bathroom by seconds, but she already giggled at the bubbles dripping from her hands onto the tiled floor.

'Come on, Pip, you know not to do that.' Kelsey pried the soap away, threw it in the sink and snapped a towel off the rail.

'I'm sorry, Mummy.' Soapy hands at her side, Pipa hung her head. 'I love bubbles.'

Kelsey sank to her knees. She'd taken her anger and pain out on the one person who didn't deserve it.

'I know, Pip. I'm sorry.' She held her arms open, and when Pipa stepped in, she hugged her, stroked a soothing hand down her back and kissed her hair. 'I'm sorry I snapped at you. How about tomorrow I run you a bath with lots of bubbles?'

'Higher bubbles?' Pipa grinned.

'Higher bubbles up to here.' She tapped Pipa's chin.

'Can Max have a higher bubbles bath, too?'

'I don't think Max would enjoy it.'

'Oh.' She played with Kelsey's hair. 'Can he have a bath another time?'

'Maybe. You'll have to ask Ethan.'

'I think we can find time on the weekend,' Ethan said from the doorway. 'Mark wants to know if he can have a piece of cake.' He held his hand out to Pipa. 'I said you had to make sure he doesn't take one that's too big.'

Sensing something, Pipa hesitated, her arm slipping around Kelsey's shoulder.

'Off you go.' Kelsey kissed her cheek and stood. 'We'll be out in a minute.'

Pipa walked to Ethan and, taking his hand, she tugged until he squatted down. 'Don't hurt Mummy, please.'

'I don't mean to.' He glanced at Kelsey. 'But I'll try harder not to.' He cupped Pipa's cheek, his hand huge but gentle against her small face. 'We'll be out in a minute.'

After Pipa left, Ethan stayed where he was, propped his elbows on his knees and ran his hands through his hair. 'I don't know what happened this morning.'

It was no use dancing around it.

'I took what you offered without giving back. You gave it without thinking I'd do the same for you. It wasn't right, on either part.'

'Wasn't right? How is loving someone, giving them the five minutes they wanted and needed, wrong?' He shook his head, lifted his hands and then let them drop. 'How is what we did for each other wrong?'

'That's just it, though. We didn't do anything for each other. You gave me what I needed but wouldn't let me give you what you needed.' She fisted her hands in her hair, the words getting jumbled on the way from her head to her tongue.

'I need you to know that I can face today on my own, that I need to do what I have to in order to keep Pipa without relying on what you give us.' She hurt him without meaning to, but she needed him to understand. 'But I want you with me today, Ethan. I want us to be together for everything that's good and bad in our lives.'

A flash of anger lit his eyes when he opened them. 'You just don't need me.'

A tap on the door made her jerk, but Ethan stood and opened the door.

'We need to get going.' Mark looked from Ethan to Kelsey and frowned. 'Everything okay?'

'Fine.' Talking about it now would only make things worse, so Kelsey hung the towel on the rack, then started for the door.

'Kelsey.' Ethan reached for her.

'We need to get this done.' She sidestepped him, slipped past Mark and found Pipa licking crumbs off the plate Mark must have had his cake on.

'We go now?'

'We do.' She held her hand out to Pipa. 'Have you got everything?'

'Yes.' She held her bag up.

'Let's go.' Mark walked in, scooped Pipa up and took her outside before Kelsey could protest.

'I need to say something.' Ethan stood behind her. 'This morning wasn't wrong. It wasn't one-sided by any means. You were right there with me.'

She turned to face him but kept her mouth shut when he lifted a hand.

'I wanted to give you that time in the shower,' he said, 'to show you that I cherish you. That it's not only in bed that I can make you feel like that.'

'I already know that.'

'Good.' He tilted his head. 'That makes the next bit easier.'

He stepped up to her. 'I'm here for you because I know you're there for me, too. You think you didn't give back to me this morning? Do you have any idea how it makes me feel to be the one who can take you away from it all for five minutes? Do you have any idea how it feels to be the one you open up to? And,' he leaned closer, 'do you have any idea how it feels to know you're there for me as well, for all those things and more?'

'Yes.' She lifted her chin, staring him down.

'But you still stand by not needing me today.' He rocked back on his heels and shoved his hands in his pockets.

While the hurt hung over him like a cloud, Kelsey knew she wouldn't be able to explain in a way to make him understand. Afraid that if she reached for him, he'd turn away, she mirrored his stance.

'I do want you with me today, Ethan. I can't imagine there being a day when I don't want you with me.'

'I don't understand the difference.'

'I know.' It was up to her to be brave and try to mend the gap she'd created, so she leaned in, rose up on her toes and kissed him lightly. 'As long as you know that I love you.'

She waited, nodding to herself when he stayed silent. 'We better get going.'

'Kelsey?'

She stopped with her hand on the doorknob.

'There's no scenario where I turn away from you.'

Not trusting her voice, she nodded again.

'I didn't mean to make today harder.'

'Today will suck, no matter what.'

'It will.' He rubbed his hands up her arms to her shoulders. 'And I'll be here for it, however you want me.'

If she leaned on him now, would she be able to stand on her own afterwards? She'd done it until now, hadn't she? But was it really a case of all or nothing? Stand on her own or give it all up to him?

No, it wasn't. She could lean on him, as he would on her, and she could still face what was to come because she knew he would be there when she needed him.

'I just want you with me.'

'Then let's get this done.' He reached past her, opened the door and ushered her out into the morning heat.

CHAPTER TWENTY-SEVEN

Brian ignored the comings and goings around the office. Whatever energy he had left after last night went towards tackling the mountain of emails, phone calls and forms, most of which went into the file he now added Haylee's and Kelsey's statements to.

If all went well, he'd have his search warrant in an hour or so, ready for when Kelsey gave him a positive ID on Jaiyden. He rubbed the back of his neck. He'd ask her to volunteer Pipa for a DNA swab, too, and though he'd rather not, he'd subpoena her for it if he had to.

Checking his list and the time, he gathered what he needed for the meeting with his boss. Before he could stand, his personal phone buzzed in his pocket. He pulled it out, surprised when it showed a text from Mark Jones.

Taking longer than I thought with a four-year-old. Jones.

Brian had experienced the difference between allotted time and actual time spent when dealing with kids, so he'd booked the viewing time an hour later. That Jones let him know impressed him, so he typed back.

Apptmt @ coroner's @ 12 noon, so no rush.

His phone dinged ten seconds later.

Should be there well before then. Jones.

Pocketing his phone, he walked to the sergeant's office, knocked on the open door and entered when Steve, typing rapid-fire, held a finger up and pointed to the seat in front of his desk.

As Brian sat, Steve hit a key triumphantly, then swivelled in his seat. 'Rowly, I heard about your house. Haylee and the boys okay?'

'They will be.'

'You know there are services you can access, in case any of you need to talk?'

'I do, but we've got it covered for now, thanks.'

'As long as you know.' He nodded towards the folder Brian held. 'What else do you have for me?'

Brian passed the file over. 'It would be great if you could get the ball rolling on the warrant application. I'm hoping to have everything ready to go as soon as I have positive ID on the body.'

Steve flipped through the file. 'This was his last known whereabouts six months ago?'

'Yes, and a few of his people have been seen coming and going over the past few weeks.'

'Okay, I'll get it done.' He closed the file, rested his elbows on the desk and steepled his fingers. 'You're going to need more than just an ID for the coroner.'

'I know. I'm going to push for DNA from the girl.'

'And that will make sure she is actually his daughter.'

'Yeah. I don't have any doubts in that regard, though.'

'Get it done, anyway.'

'I've got a few of hours before they get here, so I'll keep going on some other stuff.'

'Good. And Rowly,' Steve reached for the phone on his desk as it rang, 'let me know how it goes.'

Taking it as the dismissal it was, Brian rose and walked back to his desk. He loosened his tie and flipped open the top button of his shirt. If he could, he'd use one of the three hours he had until Kelsey arrived to find somewhere dark and quiet to catch up on some sleep.

'I just heard about the break in.' Jewell stopped beside his desk, her gaze critical as she searched his face. 'You didn't sleep last night.'

'We spent most of the night planning the clean-up and redecorating. The boys didn't fall asleep until after three a.m.' He clenched his teeth against a yawn. 'Then Rupert was wide awake, so Haylee and I took turns snoozing.'

She clasped her hands in front of her. 'And what sort of redecorating ideas did the boys come up with?'

He shook his head and found a smile. 'James wants a castle theme and Ashley wants dinosaurs.'

'So nothing drastic.' She tilted her head.

'Haylee has plans to incorporate both their ideas in their bedroom.' He shoved his hands in his pockets and leaned a hip against his desk. 'They trashed it, smashed their toys, painted the walls with Vegemite. Who does that?'

He closed his mouth and shook his head. 'Sorry.'

'I'd say you're entitled to your anger and your fear.' She held up a hand when he sucked in a breath. 'It was meant to target Haylee?'

'Who told you that?'

'No one. I don't put much stock in anything I don't hear from the source, so I'm asking you.'

'Yeah, it was aimed at her.'

'Or made to look like it was?'

He took a moment, staring hard at Jewell as possibilities surfaced, and had to stop the spew of hot words that bubbled up from his belly. 'She'd already made a statement. It wasn't aimed at her. She'd already done what she needed, so it wasn't to stop her.'

'I wouldn't think so.'

He shook his head and held her gaze. 'It was aimed at me. They struck at her and the boys to get to me.'

'To distract you, yes, that's how I see it.'

He lifted an eyebrow at her. 'Ever thought you might be sitting behind the wrong desk?'

She scrunched up her nose. 'No. I can't stomach what some people can do to others. Besides, I like my job. I like helping investigations go smoother.'

'You do that well, and thank you.'

Her cheeks reddened. 'Anyway, you're busy. I just wanted to say I'm here if you need anything.'

'It's going to be a long day, but if you're free after work, I wouldn't mind five minutes to sit with you and talk.'

Her smile bloomed. 'I'd love that.'

'Good.' Able to take a deep breath and let it out, he smiled at her. 'Thanks.'

This time she laughed. 'Let me know if you need anything else.'

'I will.' He moved around his desk and sat. 'And Jewell?'

She stopped and looked back over her shoulder. 'Yes?'

'I'd like you to meet Haylee and the boys. If that's something you want to do.'

She turned and stared at him for a moment. 'I'd love to.'

The next step wasn't so easy. 'Then, maybe one day, we can all go out and see your parents.'

Eyes bright, she nodded once. 'I'd be delighted to introduce you to my parents.'

'Good. Good.' Could he be any more awkward? 'Good.'

With a laugh, Jewell stepped back to his desk and picked up a pen. 'May I?'

When he nodded, she peeled a sticky note from his depleted stack and scribbled something down.

'For when your tongue unties.' She handed the pen and note back, then turned and walked away.

Twice, he read the number she'd written after her name, committing it to memory, then folded the sticky note and slipped it in his pocket. It was time to talk to Haylee about his growing feelings for Jewell and all their futures. He had his own ideas about the house, the boys and what he'd like to give Haylee. Would the future he'd envisioned stand now that the home they'd built together sat bruised and empty? Until he talked to Haylee, all the questions that buzzed in his mind would have to wait.

Waking his computer, ready to dive into emails and forms again, he glanced at the clock. He had about two and a half hours before Mark Jones arrived with Kelsey Davidson.

Things would get hectic then. He'd move fast on the DNA request because Bristow had people watching, and if any of them saw Kelsey at either the Coroner's Court or the police complex, things wouldn't just be hectic, they'd be deadly.

CHAPTER TWENTY-EIGHT

Vance Joy played low on the car's speakers while the air conditioner tried to fool Ethan into thinking that it wasn't already thirty-two degrees outside and that the ultraviolet rays cutting through the windscreen wouldn't fry exposed flesh in seconds. He'd learned to work in the heat when he had to, but today it pushed him into irritable restlessness during the long car trip.

Already he'd spent two hours battling with the hurt of needing Kelsey when she didn't need him, then another hour wrestling with the idea that she could want him without needing him. Of course, when he'd finally worked it out, the car had been too quiet to talk to her.

Through his silence, she'd sat in the back seat with Pipa, playing a version of I-spy that would have had him laughing any other time, having thumb wars and reading a tattered copy of *The Monster at the End of This Book*.

Now, Ballarat loomed and time threatened to run out before Kelsey had to identify her friend. Something she'd convinced herself she had to do alone.

'You taking Dyson Drive?' It would skirt them around the sprawl of the city, cut them through to the freeway, but he needed some air and time with Kelsey.

Mark shrugged. 'We've got a bit more time than I thought.' He glanced at Ethan. 'Something you want?'

'There's a playground at Victoria Park.'

'Want me to push you on the swing?'

His smile locked in his chest. 'Last time you did that I nearly broke my nose.'

'Just because I dare you to jump, doesn't mean you have to do it.'

'I like swings.' Pipa clapped. 'Can we go on the swings, Mummy?' A beat of silence followed. 'Please?'

'If we stop.'

'Playground it is.' Mark glanced in the rear-view mirror, his frown deepening.

Though Ethan couldn't see her, the dull note to Kelsey's words worried him. If she thought he would, or could, stand back while she faced one of the hardest moments of her life, then she underestimated what a relationship meant to him. Or what she meant to him.

As Mark negotiated the outskirts of Ballarat, Pipa spied something beginning with *E*.

By the time they pulled up at the park, Kelsey had run through the usual answers of apple, window, unicorn, Ethan, Mark, pony, horse, and guessed all the things beginning with *E* that Ethan would have.

'I give up.' Kelsey unclipped Pipa from her seat. 'What do you spy beginning with *E*?'

'Everything!' Pipa threw her arms wide, laughing.

'She's got you there.' Mark twisted in his seat to hold his hand up for Pipa to high five. 'Well done, grasshopper.'

'That was a good one, Pip.' Kelsey opened her door. 'Come on, toilet before play.'

They walked away, Pipa obviously taking Mark's comment to heart and pretending to hop like a grasshopper though she looked more like a gangly frog, and Kelsey pulled a hair tie from her pocket and bundled her hair into a looped ponytail.

'What's going on?' Mark punched him in the shoulder as he sat, staring after her. 'You aren't fighting, but you aren't talking to each other, either.'

Ethan closed his eyes and let his head tip back against the headrest. 'She told me she doesn't need me, that she can do this alone.'

'She asked you not to come?'

'No. She said she wants me here, just doesn't need me.'

'If you believe that, you're stupid.'

Ethan rolled his head to look at him. 'Gee, thanks for the words of wisdom.'

'You want wisdom, then how about this. You've both survived the last five years without each other. You would have done better together, I've got no doubt about that. But you each got through it. So, yeah, she'd get through today without you, but you'll both get through it a hell of a lot better together.'

Mark's fingers drummed on the steering wheel, his frown aimed at nothing. 'Besides, I'd be pretty damn happy if someone thought they didn't need me to hold them up but wanted me to anyway.'

Ethan took a moment to run that through his head, to see what he'd missed when Kelsey had said it, and admitted his bruised feelings had got in the way this morning.

'Thanks,' he said and pushed from the car.

The walk to the toilets gave him time to berate himself. When Kelsey and Pipa emerged, the sun caught their hair, blond and red, so opposite but so perfect together.

Pipa grinned, took that running jump he'd never take for granted, and threw herself into his arms. He breathed her in, what he wanted for her and what he wanted to be for her cementing in his heart.

Glad when Mark stepped from the car, because he'd nearly blurted it out, Ethan set Pipa back on her feet. 'How about you check out the playground?'

Kelsey stood silently beside him while Pipa ran to Mark, bounced from foot to foot as he locked the car, then held his hand out to her.

'Can you push me on the swing, please?'

'Absolutely.' Mark grinned down at Pipa. 'As long as you push me, too.'

At Pipa's belly laugh, Kelsey took a deep breath.

Ethan rubbed the tension gathering at his nape. 'I owe you an apology.' Standing shoulder to shoulder with her, he turned his head to look at her. 'I probably owe you more than that, but I haven't figured it out yet.'

'You don't. I didn't say it right this morning. I hurt you, and I'm sorry for that.'

'I think we hurt each other.' He moved to stand in front of her. 'I thought you were stepping away from me, but I know you want me here.'

'I want you everywhere.' She rolled her eyes at his grin. 'I needed to know that I could stand on my own, that leaning on you didn't make me dependent.'

'And now?'

'I've realised it's not one or the other. I can lean on you and still be strong, still face the things I have to. I could do this today without you if I had to, but I'm glad I don't. I'm glad you're with me.'

'I'm glad I'm the one you want with you.'

Because he needed to, he reached out and ran his fingers through her ponytail. 'I love that your hair is nearly yours again.'

When he leaned in, she met him, kissed him exactly as he'd wanted to kiss her. Long and deep, as if they stopped time.

'Come on, you two, don't make me find a hose.' Mark slapped Ethan's shoulder and gripped harder when Ethan ignored it.

At least Kelsey smiled when he stared down at her. The blush crept up her throat, so he kissed her there as well.

'Any time you need a place to escape for a few moments, I'm here. It doesn't mean you can't handle things. It means you're strong enough to accept help when you need it.'

'And to give help when it's needed.'

'Kelsey,' he framed her face with his hands, 'that's never been in question. Ever.'

Mark started towards the car with Pipa in tow. 'How about we get this done, so we can get home and have a couple of beers.'

Kelsey took Ethan's hand, squeezing it as they followed. 'Keep your beer. I think I'll settle for a cup of tea and watching the storm come in.'

Mark glanced west as Pipa climbed into the car. 'You think one's coming?'

Kelsey nodded.

Ethan opened her door. 'I'd bet on it, then.'

She slid in and smiled up at him even though worry and heartbreak still filled her eyes. When he leaned down and kissed her softly, Pipa giggled and Mark sighed.

Once they hit the freeway, the hills and bends siphoning them closer to the urban sprawl of outer Melbourne, Pipa's chatter turned to quiet snores. In the silence, Mark hit a button on the stereo so that Kip Moore sang of kissing lipstick and lost loves.

'As much as it kills me to say,' Kelsey said, making Ethan jump, 'I want it to be Jaiyden. I want to know what happened. I want to be able to say goodbye to her.' She choked on the words, but then her voice strengthened. 'I want to help put him away, for her, for me and for anyone else he's hurt.'

'You will.' Ethan shifted in his seat so he could see her. 'You will because it's what you've been working towards for nearly five years. You will because you have the resources and the security to do it.'

She nodded, jutting her chin forward. 'And I have the support of people who love and care about me.'

He smiled at her. 'Yeah, you do.'

'About bloody time you understood that.' Mark glanced at her over his shoulder. 'Now don't forget it.'

'I won't.' She reached forward and squeezed both their shoulders. 'Whatever happens today, we're all here for each other.'

As Mark swore under his breath at the congested traffic heading towards the West Gate Bridge, Ethan turned to face the front. He'd be there when Kelsey said her last goodbye to Jaiyden. He'd be there, too, when she played her part in putting Spencer where he belonged. He'd be there, as she'd be for him, because they were together, a team. Today and always.

***

Kelsey unclipped her seatbelt. Mark already had Pipa out of the car and on his hip. He stood in the heat while he waited, pointing out the building they'd be going to and promising he'd bring her back to Melbourne one day to visit the zoo and the Eureka Skydeck.

During the trip, dread had sat heavy on Kelsey's chest. Now they'd arrived, it glued her to the seat. She'd said she could do it, that she could stand on her own to identify Jaiyden, but when her empty stomach threatened to revolt and her legs shook so much that she couldn't move, it seemed impossible.

Her door opened and Ethan squatted down beside the car. He rested a hand on her thigh as he looked up at her. 'What do you need?'

'Honestly? I don't know.'

Turning her head to look at the building, she deliberately slowed her breathing. 'I'm losing Jaiyden today, and I could lose Pipa tomorrow.' She met his gaze. 'I never took her to the zoo or a circus or a show. We've never been to the movies or even a big shopping centre.'

'Do you think that makes a difference?'

'Yes.' Her vision blurred, so she knuckled the tears away. 'She's missed out on so much and they're going to see that.' She put her hand on his, relief a wave when he twined their fingers.

'And now I have to face Jaiyden and not only say goodbye but sorry, because I haven't given Pipa the life she envisioned for her.'

'Do you know what I think?'

He stood and pulled her to her feet. 'I think that loving a child so much, teaching them the value of doing and being good, raising them to love and be loved despite the tragedies they're too young to know they've suffered, means more than a visit to the zoo or the movies.' He cupped a palm against her cheek and kissed the other. 'You're raising a smart, loving and courageous girl.'

To steady herself, Kelsey slipped her arms around his waist. 'She's all those things, and more, but so was Jaiyden.'

'And so are you.' He pressed his thumb under her chin until she lifted her gaze to his. 'She's a curious, sharp and well-mannered kid because you've encouraged her to be. Acknowledge your part in the daughter you've raised, Kelsey. Be proud, because I know I am.'

'And if they take her anyway?'

'We'll do everything we can to make sure they don't.'

'I've thought about that a lot this morning and about what you've said.' She frowned at the building. 'When this is done, can I talk to you about it all? About what I want to do as far as work and Pipa go?'

He smiled. 'I'd love that. Now,' he pressed his lips to her forehead, 'are you ready to get out of this heat?'

Would she ever be ready to walk into the building that held what remained of Jaiyden?

'I'm ready to put her to rest and to help put Spencer away for what he's done.'

'We're here for you.' Mark flanked her, Pipa still on his hip, as they walked towards the building. 'You don't need to worry about anything but what you need to do in there. Okay?'

Her smile came easier. 'I know, and thank you.'

She trusted Mark to look after Pipa while she did what she had to because he'd do anything to keep her safe. Even as they walked into the foyer of the Coroner's Court, Kelsey could see that he scanned faces and doorways while Pipa chatted to him.

Kelsey's dread crept back in as the clerk at the counter took their names before leading them down the hallway to a private room.

'Detective Rowland is waiting for you.' He pointed to the door and left.

Kelsey clenched her hands at her sides, then reached out and opened the door. The room, big enough to hold a grieving family, its walls a soft, pale green, held a large table and a smattering of chairs.

The man sitting at the table looked up and stood when they entered.

'Thank you for coming.' He held his hand out to Kelsey.

She shook it, studying him as he did her. 'Jaiyden only ever called you Brian. I never knew your whole name.'

'And I only knew you as Kel. It made it impossible to find you.'

He shook Mark's and then Ethan's hand. When they'd all sat, Mark and Ethan flanking her again, Brian clasped his hands on the table and leaned forward. 'And I did try to find you and Jaiyden after that morning.'

'You did?' It lifted some of her anxiety, enough that she could let that long-ago morning play over again without the layer of horror.

'She talked about you,' Kelsey told him. 'I think you should know that she didn't blame you, and it's not why she refused your help that morning.'

Brian sat back in his seat and blew out a breath. 'Well. Thank you, that means a lot.'

Kelsey rubbed a shaking fist to her chest as she followed his gaze to Pipa sitting on Mark's lap. 'This is Pipa. Jaiyden's daughter.'

'I gathered.' He shifted his attention again and held Kelsey's gaze. 'You've raised her?'

'I have.'

'On your own?'

'Yes'—she glanced at Ethan—'until now.'

'Mummy loves me.' Pipa reached for Kelsey's hand. 'I have my own room, and Max loves me, and Ethan, and Muck.'

'We do.' Kelsey traced a finger down Pipa's nose. If she hesitated now, if she let everything crush down on her, she might never move again. So she smiled at Pipa.

'Can you do me a favour?'

'Yes.' Pipa bounced on Mark's knee. 'What?'

'Can you find me a bottle of water, please?'

Pipa tipped her head back to look at Mark. 'We find water for Mummy?'

'Sure we can.' He winked at her.

'You'll stay in the building?' Brian sat a briefcase on the table and looked at Mark. 'My house was vandalised yesterday, so I'm being extra cautious today.'

Mark frowned but nodded. 'Sure, we'll go for a walk down the hall and see if we can find a vending machine to eat our money.'

Pipa put her hands on Kelsey's cheeks. 'I member where we are. I find you again.'

She kissed the tip of Kelsey's nose, then giggled when Mark stood and swung her onto his hip. At the door, she waved to them and then they were gone.

Kelsey sat, counting her heartbeats as the urge to go after them swept through her. 'What really happened?'

'My house was broken into.' Brian slid a thick manila folder from the briefcase. 'It was meant to scare my sister and my three young nephews.'

She glanced at the door. How many times had she lived with that fear? Too many, but now she had a chance to stop it.

'They're okay?'

Brian tilted his head. 'They are, thanks.' He tapped a finger on the file. 'I'd like to ask you something, but we need to do this first.'

'You need me to identify Jaiyden.' Avoiding saying it hadn't made it any easier, so Kelsey lifted her chin and looked him in the eye. 'I'm ready to see her, to say goodbye.'

'We can do this with photos.' He put his hand on the folder. 'It sometimes makes it easier.'

Kelsey shook her head. 'No. I need to see her.'

He sat a moment, watching her, and then nodded. 'Okay. If you'll come with me, then.' He stood and led them from the room.

On numb legs, she followed, with Ethan a step behind her. If she stumbled, he'd help, and that gave her the courage to keep going, to walk into the tiny room with two lonely chairs and a curtained window. Cold, she hugged herself as Ethan stood beside her, hip to hip, and wound one arm around her waist.

'I know it's hard,' Brian said, 'but if you can remember any scars, birthmarks, tattoos, anything that can help identify her.'

When the curtain slid back, she made herself look. Not just glance, but really look at the woman she'd considered a sister, the woman who'd given life to Pipa, who'd given her own life to keep her baby safe. Jaiyden deserved to be looked at one last time with love and respect. To know she would be missed.

Kelsey let the guilt and anguish wash through her. Unable to stop the flood of emotions anyway, she used it to centre herself, to do what she needed to do, to look now, not as a friend, but as a witness.

The body—because that's all it was—lay covered from toes to chin on the metal table, the skin blue-tinged, the blond hair hacked away. She couldn't pick any of the features that were photographed in her mind. Couldn't pick any of Pipa from what was left of the bruised and smashed face.

'She has a scar inside her left elbow. One on top of her right foot.' She cleared her throat, determined to do this for Jaiyden without breaking down. 'And she has a star tattoo behind her left ear. It showed when she shaved the hair away.' She lifted a hand to touch her own hair. 'She'd broken her finger in a fight before I'd met her. A year or so before.'

A shudder ran through her body before she could stop it.

Ethan's arm around her waist tightened and he pressed a kiss to the top of her head. Taking the comfort he offered, she swallowed.

'She had stretch marks from carrying Pipa. And she lost a tooth, one of her eye teeth, that day, fighting off Spencer. I told her she'd suck at being a vampire.' The laugh she forced turned into a sob.

Silently, she said all the things she needed to and hoped Jaiyden forgave her for all the things she'd failed to give Pipa so far. She'd change that now and would show Pipa exactly what she could achieve if she wanted to.

Still, the grief she felt at saying the goodbye, that she'd been carrying around for four years, left a bruise on her heart. It grew as reality set in. Jaiyden had been murdered. She'd been beaten, tortured, mutilated. Pressing a hand to her mouth, Kelsey held on to the rage so the guilt didn't drown her.

'It's her, isn't it? He did this to her, and this is all that's left.'

Brian tapped the intercom button. 'Thank you.'

On the other side of the glass, the medical examiner nodded and slid the curtain closed.

Brian gestured to the seats in the room. 'Do you need a moment?'

'No.' Now that it was done, she needed to get out, to get away from the cold that had settled in her bones even though sweat made her shirt cling to her skin.

'Come on.' Ethan tugged her towards the door.

Brian held it open and led the way to the private room, glancing at her over his shoulder every few steps. If he expected her to faint or bolt, he'd be disappointed.

She kept pace with him, her hand in Ethan's an anchor to everything she had to fight for now.

'Will you let Mark know we're back, please?'

'Sure.' Ethan thumbed a text and his phone vibrated in his hand moments later. 'Pipa is negotiating their way back.'

'She said she would.' She smiled to ease his worried frown, then tipped her head to his shoulder for a few steps. 'I'm okay.'

'You don't look it.' He squeezed her hand. 'Expecting an outcome doesn't make it any easier.'

'No. Is there really ever closure?'

Ethan was no stranger to grief, to losing someone he loved. He'd experienced the worry and wait with his mother, and Kelsey's heart ached for him.

'Eventually you can think of them without being terrified of falling apart.'

She stopped in the hallway and faced him. 'I never knew what to do for you back then. I know I annoyed you, always hanging around and begging for lessons.'

'How do you think I know to put you with the filly when you look like you're going to lose it?' He smiled and traced a finger along her jaw. 'You helped pull me out of those bleak times, Kelsey. So I'll put you in with the filly as many times as you need it, and I'll be there to keep you from falling.'

She closed her eyes and rested her forehead against his chest. 'Just knowing you're here for me makes it easier.'

She fisted her hand in his shirt. 'But there's no one here for Jaiyden. How can I leave her here with strangers?'

'We'll figure it out.' He kissed the top of her head. 'Come on, or Pipa will beat us back to the room.'

Brian waited for them down the hallway. 'It's a stupid question, but I need to ask if you're okay.'

'I will be.' She rubbed her arms, the chill still heavy on her skin.

'If there's anything you need, anything I can do, let me know.' He led them into the room and waited for them to sit. 'Would you like some water?'

'I'm okay.' Not wanting to dodge around it, she lifted her chin. 'You haven't said, but it is, isn't it? It's Jaiyden.'

'I'm sorry.' He looked it, too.

Somehow, that made it worse. She wasn't the only one grieving. She hadn't been the only one wishing it wasn't Jaiyden, yet hoping it was.

'You've been waiting all this time.'

Brian gave a single nod, his gaze never leaving hers. 'I knew it was her as soon as she was found. I got the cold case last week, but I've been looking for you and Pipa for the past four years.'

'What happens now you know it's her and you've found us?'

'I make my case as strong as possible, no unanswered questions, no wiggle room.'

He wanted something else, then. 'What else is there?'

'DNA.'

She frowned at that and shook her head. 'You have her DNA.'

Then it clicked.

'You want Pipa's.' Kneejerk reaction had her shoving out of her chair. 'No. I don't want her being poked and prodded.'

'It's a simple mouth swab. And,' he held up his hands when she glared at him, 'I have three young nephews, so I can understand your reluctance. Believe me when I say I wouldn't ask if it weren't important.'

'And if I still say no?' She read the answer on his face before he said it.

'I can get a subpoena.' He sighed, ran a hand over his head. 'I'd rather not.'

'Where would it be done?'

'I can take you back to the station. There are family rooms that won't be scary for her, or you.'

Kelsey sat again. He only did his job, and he did it so that Spencer would have less chance of getting away, but it stabbed at her that Pipa would be brought so close to it all.

'It will prove beyond a doubt that it's Jaiyden?' She met his steady gaze again. 'And that Pipa is Jaiyden's and Spencer's.'

One eyebrow twitched. 'It will.'

She nodded. 'It's better if you just tell me the truth, Detective. I've lived my life dealing with manipulators and mind games, so I know when people are keeping things from me.' She put her hand in Ethan's and took a deep breath. 'So, what happens when you get Pipa's DNA and match her to both Jaiyden and Spencer?'

'I have a stronger case. One that leaves no wiggle room for Bristow to slip away.'

'And Jaiyden?' She cleared her throat. 'What happens to her now?'

'We'd like her released to us,' Ethan said. 'We'll take care of her.'

The burst of love streamed tears down Kelsey's cheeks and for a moment she let them fall. With Ethan's hand soothing up and down her back and Brian pressing tissues into her hand, she let some of the grief and panic of the last five years flow out.

'I'll get the paperwork started.' Brian scribbled something on his notepad. 'I'll get in touch with you when it's done.'

They sat in silence while she mopped tissues over her face and they all looked to the door when it opened and Pipa led Mark into the room. Mark took them all in, then held Kelsey's gaze.

'Mummy?' Pipa slipped her hand from Mark's and ran to her.

'I'm okay, Pip.' She scooped Pipa up onto her lap and leaned against Ethan's chest so that Pipa had both their comfort to draw on. 'It's going to be okay.'

Pipa cupped her hands against Kelsey's wet cheeks. 'The bad man?'

'No, sweet. I'm just tired.' She couldn't do it yet. Just couldn't form the words for Pipa.

'We all are.' Though Mark stood with hands in his pockets, one shoulder leaning against the doorjamb, he wasn't relaxed.

'I'd like to get back on the road if we're done here.'

'Just one more stop.' Brian stood, then looked down at Kelsey. 'Okay?'

She could say no, making an already nightmarish time ugly, or she could do what was right. 'Okay.'

CHAPTER TWENTY-NINE

It took longer than he'd have liked, but Brian had his warrant for a DNA sample. As he pulled into his parking space at the police complex, he hoped Kelsey would trust him enough to let him work with Pipa.

He'd made sure the three adults and Pipa were settled in one of the parents' rooms before he'd left to get his warrant, and Jewell had found some toys, paper and crayons for Pipa and some biscuits and coffee for the adults. They'd all thanked Jewell with smiles.

Only Pipa had thanked him with a smile.

Not that he could blame Kelsey. She'd faced a lot since the morning he'd first seen her, and more during the past four years raising Pipa on her own. According to her statement, she'd faced Bristow at least a half dozen times, and each time, she'd kept Pipa safe.

Pipa was a lucky kid, having such a ferocious protector. And now she also had the two men who'd come to support her and Kelsey. On paper, Mark Jones's involvement began and ended professionally, but anyone could see it went deeper than that. He'd said he'd known Kelsey all her life, and that showed in the easy way they were together. Ethan Ryder, on the other hand, had more invested in both Kelsey and Pipa. He had the look of a man intensely in love and was terrified of having it ripped away from him.

In the centre of it all, Pipa, so smart, so sure of the love around her, stood shielded but not cocooned. She knew about the bad man and that he was still a threat. She knew something else bad had happened, and he didn't envy Kelsey the heartache of one day telling Pipa the truth. Pipa knew all those things, but above it all, she knew that the adults around her would do their absolute best to protect her.

Taking the elevator to his floor, he detoured to grab what he needed, considered that he dealt with a child and not a crook, and grabbed extra gloves.

Back at the elevator, he sighed, relaxing muscles he hadn't realised were tense when Jewell looked over at him and smiled.

'I found some colouring pages.' She held up the stack. 'You can take them if you want.'

'Found, or searched for and printed?'

'Shh.' She elbowed him. 'You know we aren't supposed to print things like that.'

'I'll put in a good word for you if they haul you in.'

'They haul me in, I'm taking you with me.' She stepped into the elevator with him.

'I'm wondering if a life of crime wouldn't be a bad career move'—he quirked an eyebrow at her—'if you'll be my sidekick.'

'Maybe you should be mine.'

Because she tried to give him a moment, he laughed. 'Four brothers or not, I still think I can be more devious than you.'

She managed to look down her nose at him. 'Is that a challenge?'

He stared at her. 'It would definitely be interesting.'

The doors dinged open, and he had a job to do.

Jewell walked with him to the room and waited for him to open the door and step in first. He'd expected to see them all huddled together. Instead, Mark sat up one end of the table, playing on his phone. Kelsey and Ethan sat together, talking quietly, but Pipa sprawled on the floor on her stomach, happily drawing scribbles on the blank paper.

The adults looked up with various *are we done yet* expressions.

Pipa grinned, jumped up and ran to him, holding out one of the pictures.

'This is Max, and Snotty, and me, and Mum, and Ethan, and Muck, and this you,' she pointed to the last chunky squiggle that looked like an overweight octopus.

264

'That's fantastic.' He tucked the folder and kit that he carried under his arm, then hunkered down so she didn't have to nearly fall over backwards to look at him.

'I draw it for you.' She held it out.

'Wow.' He cleared his throat. 'Thanks.'

He took it, holding it out to study it. The boys often drew pictures of aliens, or cars, or dinosaurs, and he loved them and stuck them on the fridge. But he'd never had one drawn specifically for him, or of him, and it reached down and woke something he'd never thought he'd feel.

Catching himself wanting to glance at Jewell, he swallowed. 'I'll keep it at my desk.'

Her grin pulled an answering one from him. 'I have something I'd like to ask you, Pipa.'

He glanced at Kelsey as Jewell sat next to her. By her gestures, she explained to Kelsey the steps usually taken for a DNA swab. Pipa's case would be slightly different, done with more time and care. Even now, her smile faded as a frown scrunched her eyebrows.

No stalling then.

'I have this.' He pulled a lollipop from his pocket. 'It's a special lollipop, though, and I have to make sure you're okay to have it.'

'How?'

Yeah, she was smart. 'I have to test to see if I can give it to you.'

'How?' She eyed the lollipop, obviously weighing up what it was worth.

'First, I need this.' He reached into his pocket and deliberately let the other latex gloves spill out.

'I get them.' Pipa grabbed them and held them out.

'I just need this one.' He slipped a glove on his right hand. 'You can hold onto them.'

Taking the file and kit from under his arm, he sat them on the floor. Though it would be better to sit her at the table for the five minutes it would take to get the swab, Pipa was already comfortable where she was.

He opened the kit, Pipa watching closely. 'This,' he held up the swab, 'will tell me if the lollipop is right for you.'

'How?'

'Well, you put it in your mouth,' he opened his wide and kept talking, 'an ooub up an own, en e o-r ide.'

Pipa laughed. Brian glanced at Kelsey, taking her slight nod as encouragement before turning his attention back to Pipa.

'So, you got that?'

'No, silly.' She held her belly and laughed.

'Okay, I'll say it again. You show me, okay?'

'Okay.' She took the swab. It looked huge in her hand.

'You open your mouth wide, like you're cleaning your teeth.'

Pipa bared her teeth, then opened her mouth.

'Then you rub this bit,' he pointed to the end of the swab, 'up and down on the inside of your cheek.'

She did as he said and, he had to admit, did it better than most of the crooks he gave the same instructions to.

'Now the other side because we have to make sure. If I give you this,' he held up the lollipop, 'and it's not right for you, it'll taste really, really yucky.' He screwed up his nose and poked out his tongue.

Around the swab, Pipa giggled but kept rubbing.

'Okay.' He nodded to her and prepared the next part of the kit. 'Let's see how we went.'

He took the swab in his gloved hand when she offered it and let her watch him press it to the tabs and seal everything up.

'Done.' He pulled off the glove and shoved it in his pocket. 'How do you think you went?'

Her shrug was both innocent and hopeful.

He held the lollipop out to her. 'I'm proud to say you are exactly the person for this.'

Instead of grabbing it, she threw her arms around his neck. 'Thank you!'

Then she took it and skipped to where Kelsey still sat.

266

By the time Kelsey had given Pipa a quick cuddle and walked towards him, after sitting Pipa on Ethan's lap to tackle the lollipop wrapper, Brian had packed everything away and pushed to his feet.

Kelsey held out her hand. 'You made that easy for her. Thank you.'

He shook her hand. 'You made it easy, the way you've raised her. You've obviously given her the room to be courageous, to think for herself and be curious. And yet, she knows, doesn't even have to look, but knows you're right there if she needs you. It's a hell of a thing to see.'

'Thank you.' She swallowed. 'And thank you for trying to help Jaiyden back then, for not giving up.'

'I couldn't give up.' He shrugged and let her hand go. 'She reminded me of my sister, and I couldn't give up on either of them.' He was stepping close to a line, but he had to broach the subject. 'I think you and Haylee, my sister, have a lot in common.'

'Because they tried to scare her by breaking into your house?'

'Yeah, but it's more than that.' He checked his watch. 'I need to get things done, but I'd like it if you could think about catching up with her one day soon. I think you both might benefit from it.'

'I'll think about it.' She nodded, but doubt clouded her eyes. 'You'll let us know as much as you can about what happens next?'

'I will.' He took the time to say goodbye to everyone and got another hug from Pipa for his efforts.

Back at his desk, he sat for a moment and let everything sink in before he picked up the phone and began making calls to move the investigation to the next step. One that would bring him closer to getting Bristow a seat in an interview room.

CHAPTER THIRTY

The sun edged towards the western horizon as Mark negotiated the hills into White Wattle Creek. More than just time had passed for Kelsey, though. She'd left home that morning prepared to feel shattered and helpless against her grief but, although it would haunt her, seeing what Spencer had done to Jaiyden burned a new fire in her heart. He wouldn't get away with it. And he wouldn't get away with stilting her life anymore because she was taking it back.

'I want to start a rehabilitation centre for horses.'

Ethan and Mark glanced at each other.

'I figured you already had,' said Mark, meeting her gaze in the rear-view mirror, 'when you were thirteen and rescued that neglected pony.'

She frowned. 'It just needed some love and understanding.'

He tapped a finger against the steering wheel as he slowed for the main street. 'Don't all horses?'

'Yes. But I want to make it official. I want to start a business rehabilitating horses before finding them the right human.'

'So, like a holistic thing?' Ethan shifted in his seat to look at her. 'Kelsey's Holistic Horse Therapy.'

'I like that.' She smiled. 'And I know we'll need to talk about the logistics of it, and I'll still have to get a part-time job.'

'You've been thinking a lot on the drive home.' Mark turned onto the highway and sped up.

'I have, and I'm going to need your help, too.'

'Anything.'

His instant agreement cooled some of the fire threatening to burn through her conviction.

'I looked into enrolling Pipa in kindergarten and I need her birth certificate, which I've got, but I'll also need something to say I'm her legal guardian. And I figure having that evidence would help with child services, too, wouldn't it?'

'It would.' He nodded. 'So make sure you give me the name of the hospital and the midwife, so I can try and track it down.'

'I forgot you asked me the other night.' Most of it was a blur of exhaustion. 'And I will. Thank you.'

She wouldn't have anything but her love for Pipa when she faced child services in the next few days, but what else could she do? And what else could she give, other than what she already did?

'We'll work it out.' Ethan smiled, but his eyes stayed tired and worried.

She'd had a hand in putting that look there, so she'd have to find a way to ease it. She'd start tonight, by revising the initial rules she'd moved in with. She'd already broken the rule of not sleeping in his bed, and the implied rule of him not being a part of raising Pipa wasn't fair when he'd instinctively taken on the role and excelled at it.

By the time Mark pulled up in front of Ethan's house ten minutes later, she had a plan brewing, but it would have to wait until she got Pipa inside and in bed. She ignored her aching muscles and reached over to unclip Pipa's seatbelt.

'I've got her.' Mark slid his hands under Pipa's legs and back, lifting her to his shoulder. 'Want her straight in bed?'

'Yeah, thanks.' She pushed herself out of the car and smiled when Ethan slipped his arm around her waist. 'She's going to be cranky tomorrow.'

'I'm declaring tomorrow a day of rest, then.' He kissed the top of her head.

'The storm is closer, too.' She tipped her face to the sky and could almost smell the first drops splattering against the thirsty ground.

'Even more reason to have breakfast in bed, then lounge around for half the day.'

They followed Mark inside and in the lounge room, Kelsey tugged Ethan to a stop and wrapped her arms around him.

'I know it's not finished, yet, but I'm glad you were with me today.'

'No, it's not over.' He swayed with her. 'But whatever comes next, good or bad, we face it and deal with it together.'

'We do.' She reached up and kissed his chin. 'And that deal goes both ways.'

'It does.' He smiled, and this time it reached his eyes.

'Speaking of deals, I want to talk about ours later.'

'Really?' He quirked an eyebrow at her. 'Should I be worried?'

'No.' She dug fingers in his ribs. 'I just want to make sure Pipa is settled first.'

Mark walked in. 'She's tucked up with Max next to her and has asked if you'd say goodnight.' He nodded at Kelsey.

Untangling herself from Ethan, she hugged Mark. 'Thank you for today. You're already tired, but you were there for us.'

'No problem.' He patted her back. 'I've got to drop into the station and finish up some paperwork before I head home.'

'Do you have tomorrow off?'

'I do.' He cocked his head, a hint of a grin in his eyes. 'Going to invite me to lounge around? Or for breakfast in bed?'

'You can leave now.' Ethan walked over, clapped Mark on the back and pushed him towards the door. 'Have breakfast in your own bed.'

'Where's the fun in that?'

'I'm sure you'll be able to find it.' But he stopped at the door and pulled Mark into a one-armed hug. 'Thanks.'

'As before, no need.' He glanced over his shoulder at Kelsey. 'Get some sleep.'

'You too.' She waved and sighed when he stepped outside.

Ethan closed the door and leaned against it. 'Let's say goodnight to Pipa. Then I think we might as well fall into bed, too, so you can work out what this deal might be.'

Under the fatigue, mischief brightened his eyes, so Kelsey pretended to look at her watch. 'It's only eight thirty.'

'Well, it's bedtime somewhere in the world,' he hooked an arm around her shoulders, 'and I'm done for today.'

Kelsey was too, but she knew once they'd finished talking, the endless night would be filled with thoughts and worries.

'Come on,' he steered her up the hallway, 'if you can't sleep, we'll do something else.'

She smiled up at him. 'Considering you look like you're half-asleep on your feet, I don't think there's much else you'll be doing.'

'Oh ye of little faith.' He stopped at Pipa's door. 'My phone has buzzed five times in the last minute. I'll sort out whatever it is, you say goodnight to Pipa.'

Her heart gave a thump. Had they found Spencer? Had something else happened? Before the possibilities swamped her, she turned away and tiptoed into Pipa's room.

Almost asleep, Pipa held out a hand as Kelsey sat on the edge of the bed. Max lifted his head, huffed at her, then went back to sleep.

Kelsey leaned down and kissed Pipa's cheek. 'Goodnight, sweet. I love you.'

'Night.' Pipa yawned once, then slept.

Kelsey took a moment to smooth the sheet over Pipa's shoulder. She rose and turned to the door where Ethan stood frowning at his phone.

It took all her strength to walk to him instead of run. 'Brian?'

'No.' He shook his head. 'Morna.'

He held the phone out. 'I debated not showing you until tomorrow. But I don't want to lie to you, not even by omission. I don't want to hurt you, but showing you is going to hurt you anyway.'

'No, you're not hurting me by showing me. She is.' She read the first text message.

Kelsey, I've thought about what you said. It hurt me, and I realise I've hurt you.

271

'A bit too late.' But she kept reading.

Asking you to forgive me won't work when you don't know the whole story. Come and see me so that we can talk.

Ethan rubbed her back as she scrolled to the next message. 'What can she possibly say that would fix things?'

'Not much. I don't care about any excuses she has for the way she's treated me.'

People are talking now you're back, and I'd rather not be painted the villain in all of this. Let me explain what I feel so you can understand why I did what I did.

'That sounds more like it.' Huffing a laugh, Kelsey kept scrolling.

Are you punishing me now? Won't you even talk to me after I did my best for you for sixteen years?

Will you be this callous with your own daughter?

'She doesn't know you.' Ethan's hand kept soothing up and down her back. 'She sees everyone through the stain of her own deficiency.'

'That's one way of putting it.' Another text vibrated the phone in her hand. She frowned at it, her heart jolting.

I know you miss your father, and you were right, he did leave some things for you. I lied because I didn't want to lose anything of him. If you come and get them, we can talk, even if you still choose to walk away from me.

'I knew it!'

She looked up at Ethan and shook her head at his frown. 'I don't care what she has to say. I don't care about her or what she wants, but Ethan, she has the things he left for me. I have nothing of him.'

She didn't mean for the tears to spill out. Swiping them away, she clutched the phone to her chest. 'I have to get them.'

'We can go tomorrow.'

'She'll destroy them before tomorrow. You know she will. I don't know what she's drunk or taken to be nearly begging, but it won't last long. She'll get pissed off that I ignored her and hurt me the best way she knows how. She'll burn every last thing of his and will love telling me how she'd given me the chance to get them, but that I shunned her just to spite her.'

'I don't like the idea of you seeing her on your own.'

'She doesn't scare me. Nothing she can say or do will hurt me anymore because she means nothing to me. But my dad does, Ethan. I have nothing of Jaiyden's to give Pipa now, and it kills me. I have nothing of Dad's and it leaves a hole in my heart.'

He took a deep breath and closed his eyes. 'Mark will still be in town. I'll get him to meet you there. Take my ute. Take this,' he tapped the phone she still held to her chest, 'and you call me when you get there, okay?'

'I will. And I'll drive safe.' She kissed him.

Energised now, she hurried down the hallway and grabbed Ethan's keys from the bench. Typing a reply to Morna as she headed for the front door letting her know she was on her way, she shoved the phone in her pocket and ignored the return message. She wouldn't give her mother any more than that. Wouldn't say anything to her other than goodbye once she had her father's things.

CHAPTER THIRTY-ONE

Brian stood at the window, staring out at the brilliant pinks and oranges streaking the sky. Clouds, purpled and angry, gathered to the west, but the city wouldn't see any change of weather until the early hours of the morning.

Behind him, the TV murmured as it played a show the boys only half-watched as they swapped the clothes from the stormtroopers Jewell had borrowed from her brothers to the troll dolls he'd found in a second-hand shop.

Haylee came out of the bathroom, her hair damp, Rupert bundled in a towel in her arms. 'Are you going to stand there and brood long? You've got your own window to brood out of, you know. That one's mine.'

'Is that what you'll do tonight?' He watched her reflection in the glass as she dried Rupert, turning it into a game of peekaboo when he tried to roll away from the nappy.

'No. Or at least not for long.' She glanced at him as she pulled a singlet over Rupert's head. 'I've got three very good reasons not to.'

Brian nodded. He had four, still …

'I don't think the break-in was aimed at you.' He turned away from the lights of the city, the traffic still rushing to things, away from things, and faced his sister. 'I don't know if that makes a difference.'

Letting Rupert stand and bounce on her knee, Haylee frowned. 'How was it not aimed at me?'

'Someone pointed out that the best way to get to me, to shift my focus from the case, was to hit me in a way that terrified me.'

Denial came first with a fast shake of her head, but as his words, the truth of them sank in, she looked at each of her boys in turn.

She frowned. 'Is it awful to say it's a relief? It sounds more than awful.'

'It doesn't and isn't.'

Crossing to the bed, he sat on the edge and took the cocktail-dress-wearing stormtrooper Ashley handed him.

'I'd planned on gifting it to you. The house,' he added at her blank stare. 'The paperwork is all ready to go. I was just waiting for the right time.'

'And now?' She didn't move. Even Rupert stilled, his fist in his mouth as he stared at Brian.

'I guess I'm asking if it's what you want.'

His stormtrooper came under attack from a blue dinosaur three times its size. The battle was quick and brutal, the dinosaur taking a victory lap around the room with the stormtrooper clutched in its jaws, a victorious Ashley quietly cheering himself.

'I want them to have the space and security to be themselves,' said Brian, 'to have the freedom to play and run and be noisy, to know that home is theirs.'

'They do.' She watched her son. 'They've had that from the moment you opened your door.'

'But now? Can they, can you, go back there and feel truly safe and secure? Not just in planning and plotting what can be done, but really living there?'

'Better than I could anywhere else.' She sat Rupert between them on the bed. 'Besides, they've known where I was all along. They could have done it any time, if that's what they'd wanted.'

She met his gaze. 'It really wasn't aimed at me, was it?'

'No, it was me they wanted to scare.' He tickled Rupert's belly and got drooled on for his efforts. 'I still want to gift the house to you. If you decide to keep it, to live in it, I'll have security systems installed. If you decide to sell it, I'll help you find something else.'

'You would, wouldn't you? Either way, you'd stand with me, with us.' She rubbed a hand over her mouth as tears shimmered in her eyes. 'I don't know what to say.'

'You do.' He could say it for her, but it had to be her decision.

275

'I figured I'd do what I could to make myself useful until you either nudged me out again or found someone and wanted your space back. I never even bothered dreaming of a house. I have no credit history, no money, no job.' She sucked in a breath, her hand shaking as she rubbed her cheeks. 'I want to say yes, but how can I?'

'You start by giving yourself some credit.'

Pointing his finger at her before she opened her mouth to argue, he nodded. 'That's step one. Step two is to tell me, when you dream, what do you see yourself doing, what do you want to do with your life? Forget money,' he said, pre-empting her. 'You want to decorate people's homes with the adult version of tinsel and fairy lights, don't you? You want to turn discarded things into pieces of beauty and love.'

'I do.'

But she hesitated, and he cursed himself, Donny and even his parents for crushing an innocent girl's dreams.

'I tried once.' She gave a small smile, her gaze drifting to James. 'I rescued a pretty chest of drawers from the curb, scrubbed it down and scraped money together for some cheap paint. I had it all ready for when I brought him home.'

'And?'

'And, Donny found it and the paints and threw everything back on the curb. He made me watch as the garbage truck picked it up.'

One day he'd stop wishing Donny was alive just so he could make him pay. 'So, who's stopping you now?'

She frowned at him.

'The way I see it, you have a whole house to experiment with in turning one person's junk into another person's treasure.'

Her gaze on her sons, she shook her head and lifted a helpless shoulder. 'I don't know if I can do it.'

'Haylee.' He rubbed a fist against his forehead. 'You've survived the last six years while protecting, having and raising three boys. You keep everyone in line and happy. You keep everything ordered so I never have to wonder if

I have clean socks and jocks or enough food in the cupboards. You're a powerhouse and you're smart. So smart,' he said when she shook her head. 'I've seen what you've done with the bits and pieces you've brought home and transformed into something that fits the house. I want it to be yours. I want you to make it your dream. And I want you to make it your life, because I can see, under all the bullshit Donny has made you believe, that this is what you want, too.'

'What about you?'

'I'll be here for as long as you need me, but I'll be doing the same.' He smiled. 'I'm aiming for the life I want.'

'Good.' She rested her head on his shoulder. 'I like Jewell. Not just because she got us food and clothes and toys when I could barely think about what to do next—and I want to thank her for that—but mostly I like her because she brings out something in you I haven't seen since we were kids.'

'What's that?'

'Hope.' She lifted her head to look at him. 'Faith that what you're doing is right and good. It always has been, by the way. But you lost that confidence somewhere along the way. It's good to see you've found it again.'

'I think I'm falling for her.'

'I'm happy for you. For both of you.' Standing, she kissed his cheek. 'I'm going to get these boys to bed, then I'm going to stare out my window and dream a little bit.'

She picked up Ashley from where he'd fallen asleep on the floor and tucked him into the second double bed.

Brian picked up James and put him in the bed next to his brother. 'Sleep well, boys.'

He kissed both their foreheads, then straightened and turned to where Haylee stood by her window, humming as she rocked a nearly asleep Rupert. 'You'll sleep?'

'You made sure no one can get up here without a key card.' But her shrug wasn't quite steady.

'And I'm across the hall. Plus, there's an alert for Bristow and any of his goons that decide to surface.' He walked to her and smoothed a thumb over Rupert's cheek. 'It won't be long now until we find him.'

'Good.' She stood on tippy-toes and kissed his cheek. 'Now, go brood out your own window and fantasise about Jewell.'

'Haylee.' He clapped his hands over his ears, groaning and rolling his eyes at her laughter.

'Ha-ha, very funny.' He stood a moment. 'You know …'

'Yeah, I do. I've done some research now, too. I'm not a freak for not wanting anything sexual in a relationship. If I wanted to label myself, I'm asexual, but for now I just want to be a mum.'

'Okay, that's fair enough. Just know I'm here if you ever do want to talk about it.'

'I know.' She rested her head against his chest. 'I've always known you'd be there for me, but for a while there, I didn't think I deserved it.'

'Hales.' He hugged her, careful not to squash Rupert. 'You've always deserved so much more.'

'I think I'm ready to go out and get it now.' She tipped her head back to look at him. 'The boys will be apples under my tree, and I'm going to show them exactly where they come from.'

'I didn't think I could be any prouder of you, but I am.' He kissed her forehead. 'So, I hope you'll only brood for a bit while you watch the city lights and spend the rest of the time planning what's to come.'

'I don't think I want to brood anymore.' She walked him to the door. 'And I hope you don't want to for long, either.'

'I will, but just for a bit.' He held his thumb and forefinger an inch apart.

Haylee shook her head at him but smiled. 'Goodnight, Bri.'

'Goodnight, Hales.' In the hallway, he waited for her to snick the lock and slide the chain home.

He walked the length of the corridor before coming back to his own room. A mirror layout of Haylee's, it faced east and out over the CBD. With more lights and more traffic to watch, he stood at the window.

Haylee was right. The time for brooding had passed. It would only bog him in the past when it was time to live in the now and plan for the future. He'd done all he could on Jaiyden's case for now, so when they caught Bristow, and they would, he'd be able to close it and open another. Already he had several others on his plate, all at varying stages of the process, and they all deserved the same amount of time and effort. They all deserved everything he could give them.

His phone vibrated in his pocket. Glancing at his door, he pulled it out, then frowned at the private number.

'Brian Rowland speaking.'

'Rowly, Booker. The night crew have an oh-five that's associated with one Spencer Bristow that you've got flagged.'

'He's at the station?'

'Yeah, says he needs to be let go because he has a mission from God to collect the spawn from his boss and return it to its mother. He says he gets a Harley in return.'

'Shit! Wait.' He paced from the window to the bed and back again. 'I'm not lucky enough for him to have said where he was heading, am I?'

'You might have to buy a Lotto ticket.' Booker clicked his tongue. 'He had a map on the passenger seat with White Wattle Creek circled.'

'And he was going to his boss?'

'So he says.'

Stomach tight, lungs hot, he hung up, then dialled a number he'd committed to memory that afternoon.

'Mark speaking.'

He didn't bother with pleasantries. 'I think he's heading your way.'

Silence, then, 'Fuck.'

'Yeah, I thought you should know.'

'How far away? I dropped them all home about twenty minutes ago.'

'I don't know yet.' In the background, the coms radio crackled. 'You're at the station?'

'I'm just finishing my running sheet.'

'You've got someone on?'

'On call, not on.'

'I'll go through D24, then. You make sure Kelsey stays where she's safe.' He turned for his door. 'Let me know if anything happens.'

'Will do.' Mark hung up.

If this was another trick, another attempt to get him sidetracked, he wasn't taking the chance that Haylee and the boys could be a target again. So, until he knew more, Haylee would just have to share her window. And she'd just have to let him brood, too.

CHAPTER THIRTY-TWO

Kelsey rolled her eyes at the old Datsun sitting in front of her mother's garage. Other than the rust creeping up the sides and blending into the faded orange duco, it sported scratches and dents along the back bumper. Her mother's cars never lasted longer than twelve months before they died of terminal neglect and this one looked as if it were overdue for its last drive.

She stopped Ethan's ute behind the poor Datsun and sat a moment. She'd been right about the storm. Grey clouds covered half the sunset-streaked sky, inching even as she watched from the west to the east. Trees strained, caught in the strengthening wind. When she climbed from the vehicle, the summer-dry gum leaves chattering like tinsel, she lifted her face to the sky and felt the first hesitant drops of rain. It made her want to go home, to lie in bed with Ethan while the gathering storm raged outside. She wanted to be tucked up, safe and warm beside him while the sky split with light and the thunder drowned out everything and everyone but them.

The static-heavy air changed a moment before the first flash of lightning spiked the grey. As much as she'd come to appreciate storms, she didn't want to be out in one. So, hurrying, she headed for the back door because although she wasn't family anymore, she'd be damned if she would go to the front door and knock.

Thunder nearly drowned out the ring of Ethan's phone in her pocket as she rounded the corner of the house, and the spitting rain turned into a torrent the moment she scooted into the kitchen. Empty, the room held no warmth or welcome, though a box sat on the table. She could take her father's mementos and leave before Morna dished out more guilt and fury. So, ignoring the guilt she felt at coming in uninvited, she zeroed in on the box as she answered the still-ringing phone.

'Hello?'

'Kelsey? Where's Ethan?'

Kelsey frowned at the snap in Mark's voice. 'He's at home. Why?'

Morna stormed into the room and slapped a hand on the box. 'I thought I taught you how rude that was.'

'What the hell are you doing at your mother's?' Mark's voice clashed in her ear. 'Why the hell aren't you home where I left you?'

'I'm here because I came to get what's mine,' she said to Mark, hooking one arm around the heavy box and twisting away from her mother, managing to break Morna's weak grasp. 'And now I'm leaving.'

She turned for the door and froze. The phone dropped from her shaking hand to the top of the box.

Shock came first. He'd aged in the last six months, his skin pulled thin over wasted muscle and bone, his jittering eyes bloodshot and yellowed. It didn't stop the terror from blocking her throat as Spencer moved closer.

'Nice to see you again.' Rotten teeth bared, body trembling, he angled his head. 'You're not happy to see me? And I thought we had so much fun last time.'

The storm outside whipped the world into a frenzy of wind and rain, sliced with lightning and blanketed with thunder. It covered the moan that welled up from her belly and shook her chest. He'd kill her this time because he had nothing to lose. He'd beat and rape her, torture and murder her, just like he had Jaiyden. Then he'd find Pipa and Ethan, and he'd hurt them, too.

'No.' She shook her head. 'I won't let you do this anymore.'

'I'll do what I want, you know that.'

'Not this time.' Though her hands shook, she gripped the box to her chest. 'I'm leaving.'

'You'll give me the spawn.' He stepped in front of her. 'Tell me where it is.'

'She's safe from you.' Kelsey kept her gaze on Spencer even as bile coated her throat. 'You'll never get anywhere near her.'

'I wouldn't count on that.' He reached behind his back and pulled out a dull grey handgun.

Kelsey's heart stopped. It wasn't her past that flashed before her eyes but her future with Ethan and Pipa that would be stolen if she died right here and now.

'Sit,' he wheezed, his whole body jerking with erratic spasms. 'And don't bother trying to call anyone for help.' He pointed the gun at the phone in her hand.

She stared down at the darkened screen. Had Mark hung up? Had she?

Carefully, she slid the box onto the table and placed the phone face down on the box. She took a seat at the table, in the spot her father used to sit to tell her stories or help her with her homework.

Kelsey glanced at her mother.

'Dad would hate you for this.' Appealing to a softer side that didn't exist was futile, so she went for the truth. 'You loved him beyond measure, and he loved me. If you let him'—she nodded at Spencer—'do this, you might as well tell Dad that you hate him.'

'I'm doing nothing but reuniting a child with its father, because its mother is a selfish bitch.'

'Her mother is dead! Murdered by him.' She jabbed a shaking finger towards Spencer. 'He's a drug-dealing murderer. Do you think he's going to walk away after you've seen and heard everything he's about to do?'

Morna jutted her chin. 'He's a businessman. He has a balloon company.'

'How many businessmen carry a gun and are jittery from withdrawals?'

Her mother frowned and looked at Spencer a little more closely. 'I think we should all take a breath. Maybe we should wait until morning before we make any demands or decisions.'

'I don't give a fuck about what you think!' Spencer pointed the gun at Morna. 'Now sit the fuck down and shut your ugly mouth!'

Morna sat and clasped her shaking hands on the table. 'I didn't know what he was.'

'Yes, you did.' Kelsey eyed the door. 'You knew, you just chose to ignore it because it kept me away.'

'Shut up!' The gun stayed pointed at Morna, but Spencer glared at Kelsey. 'Shut the fuck up, both of you.'

Ignoring the ice settling in her stomach, Kelsey shrugged. 'You're going to kill us anyway'—she turned to her mother—'so I want to know the truth. Were you going to give me Dad's things?'

'I wouldn't have even let you look at them.' Pale yet still full of hate and scorn, Morna sniffed. 'You don't deserve anything of his.'

'At least I'll die with a clean conscience. And if I'm going to die, then I'm going to see what he left me and there's nothing you can do about it.'

She jumped to her feet, sending her chair crashing against the kitchen cupboards, and grabbed the box as Morna lunged from one side and Spencer the other.

Metal struck metal inside the box as she hefted it, its size contradicting its weight, and threw it at Spencer's head. He stood stunned for a moment, then slowly lifted his hand to the trickle of blood seeping from his hairline.

It wasn't a roar of pain that followed but a shocked whimpering growl that grew to a scream as he lifted the gun and aimed it at Kelsey.

Ears already ringing, she charged at him, her shoulder connecting with his ribs. Something cracked. Her bones or his, she wasn't sure. Pain shuddered through her neck and arm, but she followed through, taking him down, and they both hit the floor with a breath-stealing thud.

Forcing her lungs to empty before she sucked in more air, she grunted a cough as Spencer flipped them, his body holding hers to the floor.

Instinct made her buck and kick, try to roll to dislodge him. Twisting her wrists when he tried to grab them, she screamed, bit and scratched. Headbutted his nose when he leaned in.

'I'm gonna fucking kill you!' He sat to straddle her and cupped his hands over his face. 'I'll fucking kill all of you!'

She'd weakened him. It thrilled her, knowing she'd fought back and done some damage. Ethan's voice chanted the old self-defence lessons in her head.

Fight dirty.

Without mercy.

Go for the eyes, the balls, the throat.

A mantra she repeated as she jackknifed and punched his Adam's apple, following up with a slap to his ear that stopped his wheezy swearing mid-word. Still, he reached for her, his hands going for her neck.

'No!' She pushed him off. 'You won't hurt me ever again.'

She tackled him to his back and straddled him, had to grit her teeth against the bile in her throat as her fists pummelled his ribs, arms and face, again and again. Even as his movements slowed to defend his face and his spluttering cough dribbled blood from split lips, she kept hitting. If she stopped, he'd kill her. If she stopped, he'd kill Pipa.

When hands grabbed her, pulling her up and away from him, she struck out blindly. Connected with flesh.

'Stop now.'

Ethan's scent. His warmth. He wrapped his body around her, trapping her aching arms between them, holding her tighter as her breath ripped in and out of lungs filled with glass shards. Wind whipped around her and cold rain slapped against her back as Ethan pulled her outside. She fought the wave of shudders running through her body.

'It was all a lie.'

One hard shudder chattered her teeth.

'I know. We know.' His lips, warm and tender pressed against her brow. 'Mark heard everything.'

He nodded to the figure moving around inside the kitchen, then rested his forehead against hers. 'I've never been so glad of all the bruises we got teaching you to fight.'

'Me either.'

She tipped her face up to see the sky break open on another boom of lightning. 'I knew a storm was coming.'

'Yeah.' He tipped his head back, too. 'I'll remember this one forever, I think.'

285

'Me too.'

In the gap between the lightning, flashing red and blue lights filled the backyard.

'Mark didn't hang up.' Her words came in short bursts, even though her mind and her heart still raced. 'He came.' She looked at Ethan. 'You came.'

'He called me on the landline. I've never made it into town so fast.' His lips pressed to hers. 'I was terrified I'd be too late.'

'You weren't.' She'd been terrified, too. But she'd survived and he'd come.

As her breathing calmed, details returned. 'He had a gun. He was going to kill us, then go after Pipa.'

Not so steady now, her knees started to buckle. 'Where is Pipa?'

'Carol met us here. She's taken Pipa to play with Snow.'

One arm still anchoring her to him, Ethan caught her wrist and lifted her hand to study the swollen bloodied knuckles. 'You need these looked at.'

Frowning now, he ran gentle fingers over her face. 'He hurt you.'

'Not much.' But her whole body ached. 'I need to see Pipa.'

'I know, but you need to get cleaned up and cleared from here first.'

'She can go.' Mark joined them in the rain, his shirt and hair soaked. Serious, his gaze even, he nodded at Kelsey. 'Remind me to yell at you later.'

She shook her head. 'We all thought he was in Melbourne.'

She glanced back at the house, watching with detached fascination as paramedics strapped a groaning and cursing Spencer to a gurney.

'And now you've got him.' She met Mark's gaze again. 'And I'm the one that stopped him.'

'You did.' Mark reached out and pushed away the hair sticking to her cheek. 'And with everything you got him to say, plus everything Brian already has, he's got good grounds for an arrest.'

'So we're free? Pipa doesn't need to worry about the bad man anymore?'

'I'd still strongly suggest counselling. For all of you.' He gave Ethan a pointed look. 'But yeah, you no longer have to look over your shoulder.'

Only one thing niggled at her. 'Am I in trouble?'

'For defending yourself?' Mark shook his head and sighed. 'No, you aren't the one in trouble here.'

He lifted one of her hands and frowned at her knuckles. 'Maybe you should drop into the hospital on your way to Carol's.'

A wail cut through the storm.

They all turned towards the house where two officers held up a swooning Morna between them.

'You're wrong! I'm innocent in all of this.' When the officers ignored her, she tried to pull away. 'He said he was a loving father, a businessman.'

'You can tell us all about it when we get to the station,' one of them said, and kept walking her through the rain to the waiting police vehicle.

Feeling sad for the officers—and tired, so tired—Kelsey walked through the rain to where Morna stood, weeping in between fits of rage.

'Can I talk to her for a moment?'

Morna's tears stopped as she held out a hand to Kelsey. 'She's my daughter. She'll tell you I had nothing to do with it.'

'You had everything to do with it.' Kelsey stood just out of reach. 'You could have had a great life. And so much love,' she said, when Morna glared at her. 'All I wanted to do for so many years was love you and to have you love me.' She lifted a shoulder. 'All I feel now is sorry for you, because Dad cherished you and you punished him every time you turned away from me.'

'I don't need your pity,' Morna spat. 'You've always been selfish and self-centred. He died because you disappointed him. He died because he did everything for you, and you broke his heart.'

Had she really expected anything else?

'He died of an aneurysm, Mum. You know that. You've just never been able to come to terms with the fact that he left you, even if it was against his will.'

Her mother's face froze. 'Go to hell.'

'I'm not going anywhere. You are.' Kelsey lifted her chin and looked Morna in the eye. 'I'm not going anywhere because everything I love and want is here. I'm not going anywhere because this is where I belong. You're going where you belong, and I think I'll spend a lot less time thinking about you than you will me.'

Kelsey stepped back and nodded to the two officers. 'I'm done.'

Morna resorted to begging and crying as one officer opened the car door and the other bundled her into the vehicle.

Kelsey turned to Ethan and Mark. 'Can we go?'

Mark gave her shoulder a light squeeze. 'Someone will be at Carol's soon.'

'Not you?' She frowned, then shook her head. 'Of course, you're not on duty.'

'Not for another two days now.' He glanced back at the house. 'I've got some phone calls to make, though, so you go to Carol's, get dry and warm, and I'll come to see you when I can.'

'You'll call Brian?'

He nodded. 'He's the reason we got here so quickly. He'll want to know what's happened.' He grinned. 'And I want to be the one to tell him.'

He waved them off and headed back into the house.

Kelsey took Ethan's hand and they walked through the growing puddles to his ute.

She pointed at the old Datsun. 'It's his. He always drove shiny city cars. I didn't pick it as his.'

The sky above them broke open again, drenching Ethan with heavy drops that dripped off his chin, plastered his shirt to his torso and his jeans to his legs. Despite it all, he focused on Kelsey with an intensity that anchored her.

'Why would you?' He cupped a hand to her cheek. 'Like you said, we all thought he was in Melbourne.'

'I should have seen it.'

He shook his head, kissed her forehead, then pulled her close, his body shuddering against hers.

'You're cold,' she said, wrapping her arms around him and snuggling closer to trap the body heat between them.

'No,' he said, his voice hoarse. 'He hurt you.'

Kelsey cupped his cheek and kissed him. 'Not as much as I hurt him. And he won't get to ever again.' A spark lit inside her chest, settled. 'Neither of them will.'

Staring into his eyes, his arms and love surrounding her, she could speak the words burning inside her heart.

'I was terrified of losing my future with you, but in the end, that's why I won. I had everything to fight for.'

She hung onto him as her legs began to shake. 'I think I'm going to react now.'

'I think you have a right to.'

He opened the car door and eased her into the passenger seat. He didn't coddle her but squatted in the rain, watching her. When she leaned in and kissed him, she'd meant it to be a soft reassurance, but the spark that had settled in her chest now burst into flame and she had to show him what she'd fought for, why she'd been so determined to survive.

When he kissed her back with a wildness that warmed her, she smiled against his lips.

'I love you.'

***

'Pipa doesn't know anything.'

Ethan gripped the steering wheel as he negotiated the debris the storm threw across the road.

'She woke up when I got her out of bed, but I told her Snow was scared of the thunder and needed her. I lied to her, but there was no way I was telling her anything close to the truth.'

'You didn't lie.' Kelsey rested her hand on his thigh. 'You told her your truth because you love her.'

He breathed out the guilt. 'She's mine.' He glanced at Kelsey, needing to see her. 'Not just because she's yours, either.'

Leaning over, she rested her head on his shoulder. 'I know, and that's why I risked everything. Why I had to risk it all.'

It still twisted his gut, had a headlock on his lungs. He'd nearly had to face the rest of his life grieving for her. He'd panicked at how to tell Pipa, how he'd comfort her when she'd already lost too much.

They'd had to hold him back when they'd arrived. He'd come close to punching Mark for not letting him help her when they could all hear Bristow threatening her. Even now, with her hand warm on his thigh, her head perfect against his shoulder, that ice shard of panic still played with the reality that she'd walked away from the man who wanted to kill her.

He pulled up in front of Carol's house and sat staring at Kelsey's car in the driveway.

He rubbed unsteady hands over his face. 'I owe Carol. She met me out there and left her motorbike to bring Pipa back here in your car.'

'That's Carol.' Kelsey smiled at him, but it faltered. 'I want to say I'm sorry for scaring you. For making you think about what might happen if things went wrong.'

'You went through that watching Jaiyden walk away?' He tucked her wet hair behind her ear. 'I'm sorry.'

'You don't need to be. And I won't be either anymore.'

His heart swelled. 'I'm so proud of you. You faced your demon and not only defeated him but reduced him to a man. I'm in awe of you. And I love you, so much that I can't find the right words.'

'I think you found them.'

She unclipped their seatbelts, and when she pulled him to her, kissed him hot and hard, his heart leapt, found its rhythm and beat strong and hard. She hadn't needed him to fight her battles for her, but she wanted him, just as he wanted her.

Out of breath when she ended the kiss, he sat staring at her. 'I understand now, and I want you for everything that happens in life, too.'

Her smile started soft and then grew. 'I'm glad, because I really want you.'

Before he could let the adrenaline answer for him, Carol's front door opened, spilling light across the front yard.

Able to let Kelsey go now, Ethan took a deep breath as he stepped from the car into the fading storm. He met her on the lawn and took the hand she offered as they walked to Carol.

'Are you okay?'

Thrusting towels at them, Carol reached out and turned Kelsey's face. She frowned at the bruise on her cheek.

'I'm okay.' She patted Carol's hand. 'He looks a lot worse.'

'We'll see about that.' Eyes hard, Carol pulled them into the house and closed the door behind them. 'They wouldn't tell me anything and wouldn't let me stay.'

Ethan rubbed the towel over his head. 'We needed you to look after Pipa.'

'She hardly stirred once Snow curled up with her.' Carol followed Kelsey to the couch.

Gently, Kelsey put the towel down and dropped to her knees beside the sleeping puppy guarding her daughter.

'I love you.' She kissed Pipa's cheek, then rested her forehead against her sleeping daughter's shoulder.

Ethan cleared his throat as he crossed to her. 'We need to get out of these clothes or neither of us will be up to looking after her.'

With one last whisper to Pipa, Kelsey stood and reached out to Carol. 'You looked after Pipa for us and I don't think you understand exactly what that means to me.'

'I think I'm beginning to.' Carol eyed Kelsey's dripping clothes, then shrugged. 'What the hell.'

She pulled Kelsey into a hug and waved Ethan over to join them.

'Okay,' she said, giving a last squeeze, 'there are more towels in the bathroom. Give me your wet clothes and I'll put them in the dryer. Once you're both warm and dry you can fill me in on everything.'

Their wet clothes slapped against the tiled floor of the bathroom. Ethan ran the hot water until steam enveloped them. Lifting one hand, he touched the bruise Spencer had left on Kelsey's cheek.

'I could pull him apart just for this.'

'Can I tell you something?' She followed when he tugged her towards the shower.

They both barely fit and the tiles were freezing against his backside, but when Kelsey closed her eyes and moaned as the water ran over her, he didn't care about the tiles.

'You can tell me anything.'

Palms resting against his chest, she tipped her head back under the water, then met his gaze. 'I never thought I could actually do it until I was doing it. I never thought I'd have the courage or the strength to really fight back if I had the chance.'

'You think that makes what you've done less brave?'

He slicked the hair back from her face.

'You've always had that fire. You've always fought back.' He lifted her hands and gently ran his thumb over her swollen knuckles. 'Fighting doesn't always have to be physical.'

She frowned while that sank in. 'I guess not.'

Absently she picked up the soap, circling it on his chest. 'I guess when I was running, I was also learning how to be stronger, how to survive.'

'You've been doing that your whole life.'

He took the soap, turned her and simply wrapped his arms around her.

'Have I?' Her chest stilled a moment, then she blew out a breath. 'I guess I have.'

She turned in his arms and stared up at him. 'It's really happened, hasn't it? I really stopped him.'

Her words clicked, finally quietening the last of the storm inside him.

Cupping her face, he kissed her. 'It really did. You really did.'

And when her tears mixed with the water, he held her until the steam dripped from the ceiling and the water turned cold.

CHAPTER THIRTY-THREE

Brian parked in the Warrnambool Hospital car park. He'd taken the three-to-six-a.m. watch of Rupert and had then left the hotel just as the sun burst over the city, welcoming it into a new day. Now, four hours later, with the temperature already hitting the low thirties, he made his way to meet the man he'd wanted to see in the flesh for a long time. He'd have to wait to formally interview Bristow until he'd been released from hospital, but they could sit and chat a while, see what Bristow thought about the weather or anything else that came up.

Brian should be jazzed, jumping out of his skin, but he smiled calmly as he strolled along the corridor to Spencer Bristow's guarded room. Standing at the door, he gave the man lying in the hospital bed a once-over. The photos Brian added to Spencer's file last night had actually been kind to him. That, or the hospital lighting emphasised his red and purple bruises. They sat on his sallow skin like bad watercolour, his chest rising and falling to the beep of the machines hooked up to him. Though he lived and breathed, he knew his time as a free man had ended. Brian had him now and would make sure he was tried for everything he'd done.

Brian walked in and sat next to the bed. Reaching out, he tested the cuffs holding Bristow to the bed. His job dictated how he treated the public, victim or perpetrator, and he'd do his job straight down the line, no matter how he felt personally. With that firmly in mind, he shuffled the chair closer to the bed.

'I know you're awake.' He crossed an ankle over his knee. 'The doctor will be in shortly to verify you're up to talking.'

'Lies.' Bristow opened one eye, his other swollen shut.

'We can get into that once I've cautioned you.' And didn't that promising sentence prickle his skin.

Bristow shrank into the bed. 'I'm not under arrest.'

'Not yet, no.' He pulled a pen from his pocket and flipped open his notebook. 'But the caution is to protect you as much as me.'

When the doctor came in and gave the go-ahead, Brian started with the caution. 'Do you understand your rights?'

'Fuck you.'

He'd expected that. 'I'll ask again and keep asking until you tell me you either understand them, or you don't.'

'And if I don't?'

Spencer would probably stall for as long as he could, but Brian was used to waiting, and with this one, he would sit and wait for days if he had to.

'Then I explain them to you again until you do.'

'Fine, I understand. Now get on with it, then fuck off,' Bristow spat.

Brian bit back the retort that, yes, he would be the one walking out, not Bristow. Instead, he set the voice recorder on the bedside table and settled back in his chair. As he recited all the necessaries for the recorder, Bristow's eyes jittered.

'I didn't do it.'

It wasn't how he would have started the conversation, but Brian ran with it. 'Do what, exactly?'

'Kill that bitch.'

'Which bitch?'

'The one who spawned the devil.'

By sheer force of will, Brian kept his face neutral. 'You mean Jaiyden Anne Scott? The mother of Pipa Jade Scott?'

Bristow shrugged, then winced. 'Her and that Harley bitch got what they deserved.'

'And what was that?'

His grimace went sly. 'How should I know?'

'Yeah,' Brian clicked his tongue and shook his head, 'how would you know? You've been out of the game too long. No one would tell you anything.'

'I know fucking everything! I know the bitch stole from me and ruined everything. I know she paid for it. And I know the fucking Harley bitch isn't the innocent you all think she is.'

'Oh, please.' Brian rolled his eyes for form, even as his stomach revolted. 'If you're trying to tell me she had sex with you—'

'I fucked her, and she moaned like the whore she is, even though she fought me.' Bristow smiled. 'Never knew a virgin so old before.'

Time to take control while Bristow gloated.

'I've been going through some of the evidence again, and you know what I found?' He let Bristow sweat while he flipped through his notes. 'Ah, here it is. A fingerprint on the corner of the tarpaulin. Guess whose it matched.'

'Bullshit. I wiped it.'

And with that, Bristow buried himself.

Still, Brian sat, silently taking down every word that followed. As Bristow tried to backtrack and shift blame, he dug the hole of his own making so deep that he'd never be able to climb out again.

'Well, I'd say it's been nice chatting, but …' Brian clicked off the recorder and pocketed it. 'There's an armed guard at your door. As soon as you're discharged from here, you'll be arrested and taken to the police station to be formally interviewed.'

Brian had enough, more than enough to start the process for arresting and charging Bristow. He walked from the room as Bristow cursed and yanked against the restraints holding him to the bed.

Out in the hallway, he stopped near the uniform guarding the door. 'Make sure he has no unregistered guests. No phone calls. And I want to know when his lawyer comes.'

Outside, the sunshine after the storm was a welcome warmth.

All the way home, he ran through what came next. He had phone calls to make, but he looked forward to wrapping Bristow up in the hell of his own making.

By the time he got back to the hotel, he wanted a hot shower and a beer. First, though, he needed the innocence and love of three boys whose chaos gave his life meaning.

CHAPTER THIRTY-FOUR

One week later

Kelsey stood beside the grave up on the hill. Over the ridge to the north, sat White Wattle Creek, and if she squinted, she could just see the lookout. To the south, the bush and blue gum plantations stretching out before her, was home.

Hers, Ethan's and Pipa's.

The day after Kelsey beat Spencer, Ethan had taken Pipa shopping to pick out curtains, sheets and doona covers, making the spare room into one that was uniquely hers. They'd come back with more, of course, but all Kelsey had seen were their smiles.

Pipa had bloomed over the last week once she'd understood there was no more bad man, no reason to ever pack their few things and leave. Kelsey hadn't been able to find the words to tell her about Jaiyden yet, but Ethan had agreed that waiting a little longer wouldn't hurt.

'How are you going?' Ethan slipped his arm around her waist so they stood hip to hip at the edge of the freshly covered grave.

He'd made all the funeral arrangements. Everything had been simple yet elegant, just like Jaiyden would have chosen for herself. The detail on the headstone even matched the design of the bracelet Pipa had swapped for the pewter horse.

Now, it was time to say goodbye, but Kelsey felt as if the words she'd written weren't enough. Shoving the piece of paper in her pocket, she bent down and placed on the grave a bunch of flowers and weeds Pipa had picked that morning.

'I'll look after your baby. We'll raise her together, and she'll always know that you loved her.'

When Pipa understood the stories of the mother who had carried and given birth to her, Kelsey would bring her here. Until then, she and Ethan would give her what they could from the mother who'd died to protect her.

She stood, a second bunch of flowers cradled in her arm. Ethan hugged her to his side.

'She'll always know how much we love her.'

'Yes.' Kelsey tipped her face to his and took the soft kiss he gave her.

Together, they walked to her father's grave. Kelsey knelt next to the immaculately kept concrete slab and touched a finger to the wilting flowers sitting in a bright blue vase stuck near the headstone.

'She did love him. But she'd twisted it into something else. Something that would have shamed him.'

'And she missed out on the love you were desperate to give her for so long.'

Ethan squatted beside her, his shadow an umbrella against the sun.

'Others share the love they have. Did you know that Rita comes up here with her Blue Ladies volunteer group? They clean away the weeds from around the graves and leave flowers. She even leaves a cupcake for Dad to share with Mum.'

His gaze shifted across the hill to where Kelsey knew his parents' graves lay.

'Because their first date was sharing a cupcake at the old bakery.' Kelsey smiled and smoothed a hand up Ethan's arm. 'I don't know how many times they told that story.'

His gaze came back to hers. 'What will be our story?'

'I think that's the beauty of it, Ethan.' Head tipped to his shoulder, she breathed deeply. 'We have so many already, and now that I'm legally proven to be Pipa's guardian and child services are happy, we can keep writing our story.'

'I like that idea.' He kissed her forehead, then stood and held out his hand.

She took it, not because she needed to, but because she wanted to. He'd be there to help her with the huge and the small moments in her life, as she would be for him.

As they walked to his car, grey clouds slipped past the sun, dappling the hills with shadow.

He glanced at her as he opened her door. 'Another storm?'

'No.' Kissing him quick, she smiled. 'No more storms for now.'

***

Ethan jiggled the box in his pocket. He was sure that now was the right time, that balancing the good with the bad, the happy with the sad was a good idea. He'd had the ring since his mother had pressed it into his hand and told him to give it to the one who called to his heart, as his father had called to hers.

Kelsey was the one who called to Ethan's heart. Always had been. Still, his nerves skipped as he walked to the stables. But while Pipa spent the day at Carol's playing with Max and Snow, he'd take the opportunity to have Kelsey's undivided attention. He stopped at the round yard where she was working the filly.

Over the last week, she'd come out each day and spent time forging a connection with the pony. It had paid off, with the filly's confidence growing so much that she walked to Kelsey now for a scratch on the forehead. Kelsey had been working hard at night, too, planning and researching methods and protocols for Kelsey's Holistic Horse Therapy. It swelled his heart with pride and love every time her eyes brightened with passion and purpose, which happened so often now that she was nearly always smiling.

So, now was the time. Ethan wanted her and Pipa permanently with him, in his home, part of his life. And she'd been right. They wrote their own story now, and he wanted this to be what they told their kids every anniversary, what they told their grandkids.

Fisting the box, he climbed the round yard's fence and sat on the top rail.

'You're looking smug.' Kelsey glanced at him with that smile in her eyes. 'It looks sexy on you.'

'You look invincible, and it looks beautiful on you.'

She stopped working the pony. 'What are you up to?'

Below him, the pony stopped and sniffed his boot. 'I like watching you work.'

'No.' She shook her head and a frown clouded her eyes. 'You've been edgy all day. What's up?'

He tapped the wooden railing beside him. 'Sit with me for a bit?'

Giving the pony a pat on the way past, she climbed up beside him and sighed as she looked out over the paddocks.

'I always loved sitting up here, watching the horses doze under the big gum trees at sunset.' She lifted a hand to the riot of oranges and pinks that streaked the sky.

'I always loved sitting here watching you work.'

She smiled at him. 'Are you going to tell me what you're up to?'

'Maybe.' He kissed her. 'Maybe I just want to sit up here watching the sunset with you.'

Serious now, she turned to look at him. 'I know you, Ethan. What's going on? If it's about us accumulating a lot of stuff this past week, I'm sorry. Pipa's just so excited about not having to move again and that she can keep the things she gets. I never intended to take over your place.'

'I want you to take over. I want your things with mine. I want Pipa's room to be hers. And I want you to marry me.' He revealed the box and opened it to show her the ring.

'Oh.' She covered her mouth with both hands. 'Oh.'

'I waited this long because I thought you needed time. I was going to wait a few more days, and maybe I should have, but I want you to know exactly what I mean every time I say I'm yours and you're mine.'

Her hands dropped to her lap as she stared at him. 'I'd planned to give you until tomorrow and then I was going to drive you crazy in bed and ask you to marry me when you wouldn't have the sense to say no.'

He laughed. 'As much as I love your method, you wouldn't have to try to convince me to spend the rest of my life with you.'

'Good.' Nearly overbalancing them both, she threw her arms around his neck. 'And yes! Yes, you're mine and I'll be yours for the rest of our lives, whatever it brings us.'

She held out her left hand and wriggled her fingers.

All the knots in his stomach unravelled as he slipped the ring on her finger. Lifting her hand to his lips, he kissed her palm.

'You're the one who called to my heart, the one I'll cherish and keep for this life we write together.'

'I love you.' She settled her head on his shoulder. 'Pipa is going to have kittens when we tell her.'

'About that,' he said, playing with the finger that wore his ring, 'I have something else to ask you.'

CHAPTER THIRTY-FIVE

Kelsey crept down the hallway to the kitchen. In a few hours, the house would be filled with people, and it already held six extras. If she could have a quiet cup of tea before the festivities began, she might just get through the day without crying.

'Oh!'

Already in the kitchen, a cup on the bench before her, Haylee slapped a hand against her heart. 'I didn't know anyone else was up.'

'Sorry, I thought I was the only one up, too.'

Kelsey went to the fridge for the milk. As she still had those jolting moments, too, she gave Haylee time to recover before she crossed to the cupboard for another cup.

'Did you sleep okay?'

'We did, thanks. And thanks for squeezing us all in.'

'It's no problem.' She smiled past the awkwardness between them. 'I'm glad you could all come.'

Haylee filled the cups with boiling water. 'Brian put you in a spot, though.'

'No, not really.'

Kelsey added milk to her tea, then held the bottle up, adding milk to Haylee's cup when she nodded.

'He asked a while ago if I wanted to talk to you. At first, I didn't know how it would feel, talking to someone who'd been through what I'd experienced.'

Haylee stirred sugar into her tea. 'And now?'

'Now, I want to talk to you because I like you, because your three boys are whirlwinds of energy and love and have adopted Pipa as a sister, and because Brian is a man of integrity and compassion. He wouldn't suggest that we talk if he didn't think it would help.'

'All he wants to do is help.'

'Ethan is the same, and I love him for it. Because even though he might want to fix everything for Pipa and me, he knows we have to do some things ourselves.'

'Brian, too, with me and the boys. And he knows it goes both ways.'

'Yep.' Kelsey saluted Haylee with her cup. 'We have fantastic men in our lives.'

'We do.' Haylee's smile was slow but warm. 'You know he sees you all as family now.'

'I gathered that when you all arrived last night and he bear-hugged everyone, then asked Pipa where her beard had gone.'

'It's one of his favourite lines.'

Kelsey glanced through the kitchen door to the swag spread out on the lounge room floor. 'Are they used to that sort of sleeping arrangement?'

Haylee huffed a laugh. 'Brian sleeps anyhow, anywhere. Our dad was the same, and the boys take after him.' She lifted a shoulder. 'As for Jewell, she'd just say she grew up with four brothers.'

'I like Jewell. I think she and Brian are good together.'

'I do, too. She brings out something more in him. And he makes her laugh.'

Haylee sipped her drink and stared at the steaming liquid. 'I want to thank you, Kelsey.'

'For?'

'Breaking his nose, for one.' She wrinkled hers. 'And for making sure he didn't get away with everything.'

Kelsey nodded. 'I won't say it was a pleasure, because I would rather have not got that close to him.' The memory still made her shudder.

'I've been seeing a counsellor.'

'Me too.' Kelsey put her cup down. 'One thing I'm learning is to take back the power he stole, which includes being able to say his name without wanting to throw up.'

'Yeah.' Haylee took a deep breath. 'Thank you for breaking Spencer's nose and for helping to put the bastard away for raping me.'

'I'm glad I got to break Spencer's nose and helped to put the bastard away for raping us both. For everyone else he'd hurt, too.'

Haylee closed her eyes and tears squeezed out and ran down her cheeks. 'He won't be able to hurt anyone else now.'

'No, he won't.' Kelsey wiped her cheek on her shoulder. 'We'll make sure he doesn't.'

Haylee opened her eyes and her arms. 'I'm not usually a hugger unless it's for Brian or the boys, but he's right, you are family.'

Kelsey stepped into the embrace and held on. 'I have no blood relations in my life now. Everyone I call family are people I've chosen, and I'd be honoured to add you and your boys to that collection.'

'We'd be delighted.' Haylee gave one last squeeze before stepping back. 'You'll have to come and visit us in Melbourne next. I can show you a chest of drawers I've been working on that I think Pipa would love.'

'Brian said you were collecting things to start your own upcycling decoration business.' Kelsey smiled. 'I love old things. Finding a new purpose for them must be a thrill.'

'It is. I love it.' Haylee laughed. 'I really love it. And being my own boss means I can work around the boys.'

'That's always a bonus.' Kelsey lifted her mug and sipped. 'We're both doing what we love now, and those that tried to break us are living in a hell of their own making.'

'They are. And I want to say how much I love that you rescue horses and help them heal, like we're learning to heal. It restores my faith in humanity that people like you see what's broken and work to fix it.'

'I guess we both do that now.' Kelsey smiled. 'I think it's because we know what it is to be terrified that we often think we're too broken to be worthy of others' love.'

Haylee blinked a few times. 'That hits the nail on the head, doesn't it.'

'It took me a while to figure it out.' Kelsey sipped her tea and let the comfortable silence settle between them.

'Did I hear the kettle boil?' Brian stood at the door, his gaze on his sister.

'You know you did.' At home in the kitchen, Haylee made her brother a cup of tea. 'And I'm guessing you heard a lot more than that?'

'Only something about how fantastic I am.' He grinned.

Ethan strolled in and kissed Kelsey. 'Who's fantastic?'

Jewell joined them, smacking a kiss on Brian's cheek. 'I hope I'm included in that, though I'll happily give up my place on the fantastic scale for a cup of coffee.'

Kelsey's need for some quiet time disappeared as the kitchen filled with the joy of friendship and laughter. When Pipa and the boys joined them, everyone moved to the lounge room and shared stories that tied them together like the family they'd become. Kelsey cradled a warm glow in her soul.

A few hours later that glow grew into a brilliant flame as Carol slung an arm around Kelsey's shoulder.

'She's so happy,' she said, nodding at Pipa as she led her new pony around the yard, introducing the tiny gelding to everyone who'd come to celebrate Kelsey and Ethan's engagement.

At a trestle table, Brian sat talking to Rita as he held a wiggling Rupert, who leaned over and grabbed a handful of the pony's mane before stuffing it in his mouth. On the grass, Ashley and James wrestled with Snow while Haylee watched over them as she chatted to Jex and Jewell.

Kelsey's family had grown into something bigger and better than she'd ever dared dream. At its core, though, would always be Pipa and Ethan.

She wiped a finger under her eyes. 'I'm going to have to check her bed for that pony, I think.'

'Or the stable for Pipa.' Carol smiled, then bumped her hip to Kelsey's. 'But I meant she's happy here.' She swept a hand around the yard.

'Yeah, she is.'

'And so are you?'

'Yeah.' Kelsey's smile came easy. 'Very.'

'Yeah, yeah.' Carol waved her hand. 'Rub it in.'

'You'll find someone.' Kelsey returned the hip bump.

'I'm not looking. Not even going to look.'

'Carol.'

'Show me the rock again.' Carol grabbed Kelsey's hand and held the ring up to glint in the sunlight. 'Wow.'

'Yeah.'

Across the yard, Ethan stood talking to a steady stream of wellwishers, but his gaze met hers every few seconds. Holding it now, Ethan left the group, weaving his way through the crowd towards her, and pulled her into a kiss that left her breathless.

He stared down at her. 'I want everyone to know.'

'Okay.' She licked her lips and tasted him.

'Pipa?' He waved her over, handing the pony's lead rope to Carol, and hoisted her into his arms. He took Kelsey's hand, uniting them, and waited as the chatter died down.

'I'd like to thank everyone for coming and sharing our engagement with us.'

He paused as clapping, cheering and whistling erupted.

'I have one more present for Pipa, but I'd like everyone here to know as well.'

He let go of Kelsey's hand, reached into his pocket and pulled out a small silk satchel. Kelsey blinked away tears as he asked Pipa to hold out her hand, and tipping the satchel over her palm, he let the fine silver bracelet slide out.

'Oh.' Pipa stroked it. 'My baselet.' She held it out to Kelsey.

'Pipa, I gave your mum a ring and asked her to be my wife.' Ethan smoothed the hair from Pipa's cheeks. 'I want to give this back to you and ask if you'll be my daughter.'

Pipa flung her arms around Ethan's neck and kissed his cheek. 'I have a pony and a daddy now!'

She grinned and wriggled until Ethan set her on her feet.

Kelsey leaned against him. 'I think that's a yes.'

They watched as Mark hunkered down and clipped the bracelet around Pipa's wrist.

'To be put up there with the pony is more than I'd hoped.' But Ethan hooked an arm around Kelsey's waist, pulled her tight against him and rubbed his cheek against her hair.

'She loves you.' Kelsey tipped her head back and kissed him. 'Coming back here, I knew she would. I knew she'd fall for you and I wouldn't be able to leave.'

He smiled down at her. 'And now she has a pony as well, so you're stuck here forever, like it or not.'

Turning in his arms, she pressed her palms against his cheeks. 'Here forever is everything I've ever wanted.'

'Then forever is what I'll give you.'

He kissed her, even as their family made their way over to hug and congratulate them. Whatever came now, they'd face it, because no matter how the thunder crashed or the lightning spiked and blinded them, in the end, the sun would come out and wash everything in bright colour and the sweet scent of hope.

Because they could face anything together, Kelsey would never again be afraid of a storm.

About the Author

Vikki Holstein is the author of *Breaking Storm*, the first book in her romantic suspense series, *White Wattle Creek*. A full-time writer, between life's normal interruptions, she lives in country Victoria with her husband and tribe of animals.

Facebook: @vikkiholsteinwriter

Twitter: @VikkiHolstein

Website: vikkiholstein.wordpress.com